Damned to Live

Brian Hershey

Reader2writer Press
www.reader2writer.com

To request permissions, contact the publisher at hersheybm@reader2writer.com

Paperback: 9798218026370
Ebook: 9798218026387

Library of Congress Number: 2022944297

First paperback edition September of 2022.

Edited by Kayla Hardin
Cover art by Brendon Miller

Printed by Reader2writer Press in the USA.

Reader2writer Press
Cincinnati, Ohio

www.reader2writer.com

I would like to dedicate this book to all of my friends and family who have patiently waited for this exciting sequel.
- Brian Hershey

Preface

The misdeeds of others often go unnoticed by the world. They're covered up and lost within the folds of time. Occasionally, these evil acts come back to refresh nightmares of old. My account is one of evil and darkness that began long ago. We try to keep our fiendish natures hidden from the world; locked away in the deepest parts of ourselves. True darkness, however, cannot be contained. The violent, unhinged fury within blackens the soul and perverts the mind. Once a person has looked into darkness there is no turning back and they'll never be the same again.

There is a beast within us all.

Part I

Chapter #1

I hate them.

They have stolen so much from me; my friends, my family, my happiness. Savage and brutal, but werewolves are not dumb. I've hunted them. *We've* hunted them. I've known nothing else. Together we have killed many, but there are more. There are always more.

It was cold, very cold. The recent snowfall remained on the ground and covered the bare branches of the surrounding Larch trees. Most of the light had faded with the setting sun, but small rays of color still reflected off the thin clouds. A little over a kilometer east was the town of Glindenberg, Germany. My older brother, Garon, had moved us to this location for supplies but decided to stay after hearing of suspicious activity in the area.

This town was charming with its two-story Tudor buildings nestled within the snow-covered pastures and rolling mounds that lined the rural roads. It was quaint, touristy. Despite the lure of a warm bed at the Glindenberger Hof and a hot meal cooked in a real oven instead of our makeshift trailer ovens, we stayed on the outskirts. Garon felt that it was better this way. At best, people from these rural areas tolerated us. Most viewed us as vagabonds, not to be trusted.

We posed as upstanding biologists with the German branch of *Friends of the Earth* that were studying the migration patterns of wildlife. Fortunate for us, Glindenberg was not unaffected by the intensive agriculture, highways, and cities nearby that put a huge pressure on the ecosystems. This gave us some credibility, a reason to talk with the townsfolk, but more importantly it gave us the perfect cover to conduct our true purpose.

I tucked my blonde hair under my trapper hat and let the flaps hang freely against my cheeks. I didn't buckle the latch. It was too constricting, despite the cold. Beneath my boots, the snow squeaked with each step. Large pieces of ice bobbed in the River Elbe. I was wearing a coat, yet the wind carried a bitter frostiness and cut through it as though I was wearing nothing at all. It was too thin for this kind of weather. I didn't plan on being out long. Standing at the bank of the river, I could make out two silhouettes. It was getting hard to see.

"*Hallo Garon.*" He didn't respond. Instead, he just continued to talk with one of the camp guards, Ramond Metzger. "You hear me?"

"*Entschuldigen Sie mich Ramond.*" Garon held his index finger up to Ramond and looked down at me. "*Was hast du gesagt?*"

"I said, did you hear me calling you?"

"*Ja* Ada, but I thought that I told you to stay with Gerda? She does not do well in this cold. She is old. Besides, it is not safe for you here." He turned to face Ramond again, but I grabbed the sleeve of his heavy coat before he could continue.

"Gerda is fine. She's in the trailer with the heater on. I'm in no more danger than you two are."

"We have weapons that see in zee dark, you do not." Garon tapped the top of the scope mounted to his rifle. He was holding it across his body with the silencer attached barrel pointing upwards.

"Have you considered what I asked about going to London?"

"*Sie werden immer noch nicht über diesen Scheiß auf?*" Ramond said as he shook his head in disbelief and looked at Garon.

"*Ja*…I'm still *fucking* going on about that shit!" I shoved Ramond, but he didn't move much. Had it not been for his light brown hair, Ramond could have easily been mistaken for my brother given his strong stature and blue eyes. He was born in Germany and spoke it very well, however spent most of his life near Brussels. He didn't carry the accent Garon and I did, instead he often sounded English or even Dutch. "You know they are not going to last long unless we help them."

"Ada darling, they've lasted over two years. If something else was going to happen we would have certainly known about it by now." Ramond also held a large rifle with scope and silencer attachments. He slung it over his shoulder and crossed his arms over his chest. He continued to give me a skeptical glare from under his trapper hat.

"Do not call me darling. I am not a child." My brother stood nearby and watched as Ramond and I continued our unremitting banter. Both Ramond and Garon were twenty-six and often felt the need to coddle me with their words.

"Eighteen is hardly grown my dear, but all I'm trying to say is that the London has gone cold. We've not heard of any incidents, activity, or the like from London or anywhere in England. All the activity has been here, in Germany."

"There was a lot of exposure at the club and with the church incident. Hell, the damn thing went viral on the net with videos and blog postings. All with taglines of the *Beast of London* and *Werewolves DO Exist* or some other similar *Scheiße!*" I pulled my cell phone from my coat pocket and tapped the app that had my videos. "Look!" I held my cell phone in front of me for both of them to see the video. My gaze oscillated between the two of them.

"Turn off your phone!" Ramond blurted out. "Christ! Ada!"

"What?" I was utterly confused.

"Ada, the rules are to never use phones when we are in regions like this!"

"I do not understand. I'm only using an app already on the phone."

"We are supposed to be dark. It is does not matter that you have it on your phone…it only matters that it is on! The signal can be tracked. Turn it off!" Panic raced across Garon's face.

I quickly powered down my phone and slipped it back into my coat pocket. "There, it is off!" I said innocently holding up both hands.

Garon and Ramond looked at each other with worried expressions. Ramond sighed heavily. "You know Ada, you've shown us that video several times already. And I've already followed up with the contents of it along with several others of a similar nature. The club's representatives claimed it was a publicity stunt…supposedly to bring in more business. The name, *Club – Red*, red like blood. Besides, no moon. Now, I know you want to help, but –"

"You know damn well that wasn't a publicity stunt!" My stare fixated on Ramond. "Have you followed up with the club recently? Probably not…because it is closed. It closed shortly after the incident. What about the church? Did you follow up with that too? As usual they were trying to minimize the damage caused by one of their own, but they couldn't do it as well as they have in the past, something else must've happened. The enemy is just biding their time and they are not going to just attack randomly. We need go to –"

"Look – we sent word already! Twice!" Garon interrupted. His voice was stern and deep. I could tell he was still flustered from me having my cell phone on when I was supposed to be dark. "If they were truly involved with hunting these beasts, they would have responded to us. If we just go poking around now with a high-profile man, we are going to risk our secrecy again. We can't do that…we have already lost too many. We won't be able to get the cow off the ice this time if it goes badly."

I pursed my lips and held back the frustration building inside of me. Too many things *have* gone wrong in the past when we have tried to seek out other people affected by the darkness. Our group has survived by putting out markers for those individuals, clues for them to seek *us* out. This situation in London was different. "Osborne's daughter was killed by one. They may know things that we don't. You always said that those touched by this darkness are all touched differently. We need more people. And if you were so concerned about secrecy, then why did you stop here…out in the open. We are vulnerable. We are going to end up like Mom and Dad–"

"Enough Ada!" Garon paused and looked around. He sighed. "The full moon isn't due to rise for another three hours and if we are going to lure it onto this open bank, we still have a few preparations to make. There may be more than one." Garon looked at the river behind him. The wind continued to send chilling gusts. "This will give us a natural barrier. Parts of the river are frozen, but the ice is still too thin to cross. Since we have already placed the blood bait south of the town, it must come through here. If there is one or more in this area, we cannot go and leave them behind. The effect could be disastrous for the townsfolk nearby. Besides, the Hubers are already in position."

"I am not saying we go right now."

He held up his hand to quiet me. His voice softened and he stepped in closer to me. "The light's almost gone. You'd better head back to camp and ready Gerda to leave. After we are done here we will talk more about London. We are not going to go there for a while."

"But Garon –"

"It is final. Now please go help Gerda. We will not start the process until we know you both are at the safe house." Ever since dad and mom had died, Garon had overseen our group. He was a good leader but was always overly cautious of Gerda and me.

"I know how to fight Garon. I can help more." I wanted to help. We shared a hatred of these monsters.

"You are helping, just not out here. I can't take the risk of having Gerda be anywhere near these beasts. It is because of your skills that I need you to protect Gerda. Do you still have your radio?"

"*Ja.*" I tapped the left side of my hip where the radio was attached.

"*Gut.* Don't turn it on until you are ready to leave. Audrick and Alika have one too. Channel three." I turned from Garon and started to walk back towards the camp, defeated and frustrated. "Ada! Take this."

Garon reached under his coat and removed a gun with a silencer attached to the front end. "Keep it. We are not far from the camp and we will be gone before we need to use it. Besides, I am barely grown, remember. I am not sure I could manage that weapon," I said sarcastically and gave a last look to Ramond before Garon put the gun back into the holster under his coat.

"Tell everyone at the camp to cut the heat and lights. It is time to get those not involved to the safe house," Garon spoke out from behind me. I raised my hand in acknowledgement but didn't look back.

The wind whipped around me as I walked back to the camp. It whistled and howled through the surrounding trees. With each passing moment, it was getting colder. *I know how to shoot. Mom and Dad started training me at the same age as Garon. I still have Dad's HK USP 9MM pistol in the trailer,* I thought. *Why does he not want my help?*

In front of me the ground was dark. I wanted to use my cell phone for light, but after being scolded by Garon I held my arms tightly crossed over my chest to fend off the cold. I couldn't see the individual trees anymore. They were mere patches of shadow that broke the horizon and muted the soft glow of the trailer lights in our camp. The light was completely gone from the sky.

The snow continued to crunch and squeak under my boots. We had more people at one point and were part of a greater group that carried out separate hunts in areas that were supported by dark evidence. Several years prior, we had been cut off from the main group. The communication simply stopped one day, and no one came to the designated rendezvous points. Our strategy was not to seek out the other members absent from a group. Move on, never linger too long, leave no trace. Secrecy was our greatest strength and if our comrades had fallen, it was best to mourn their passing elsewhere, and pray for a reunion at some other place and time. It was hard to lose people, though. Tough to just move on as though they never existed. I had spent all of my life being involved with the hunt. On nights like this my duties were simple; protect Gerda and Marlie, the only two that were incapable of hunting. I have known no other life, but I had seen family members, friends, people that I had come to look up to simply disappear. No goodbyes, no funerals, just gone. It was something I could never get used to experiencing. It was also why I reluctantly obeyed Garon. The thought of being cut off from my only brother was dreadful.

Only a few of the trailers were still lit in the camp. No fires were burning, but I could still smell the kerosene heaters working in full force against the relentless cold.

BANG! BANG! BANG!

A slot opened in the door I had knocked on to reveal a pair of blue eyes looking out at me. "Olis! Garon wants us to go dark. Heaters, lights off," I said to the eyes behind the door.

The slot closed and moments later I heard the heater cut off and saw the lights from inside go out. One of the small windows opened, slowly. I could see the tip of a rifle poke out from within as I began walking towards the next trailer. All the rifles and handguns had silencers attached to them. Loud gunshots drew unwanted attention.

A year ago, Olis Klien's family was killed while we were on a hunt. Both of his sons and wife were taken from us. Torn to pieces. This was the same night my parents were killed. Olis *did* kill the monster that took our families, but he was left in a wheelchair after suffering a fracture in the first vertebra of his lumbar. I never knew how it happened and Olis hadn't spoken a word since. All I do know of the event was that the beast had caught the camp by surprise. Garon believed that we must have alerted the werewolf by something we had done, perhaps usage of cell phones. Silencers on all firearms were also required from that point forward. Dad's pistol in my trailer was the only one that didn't have one. I wasn't allowed to use it. *All he has to do is get a silencer and I'll be able to use it,* I thought as I walked away from Olis's trailer. *It is another way of keeping me out of the hunt.* Olis refused to ever go to the safe house after the night his family died despite his handicap. He took the charge of being one of the sharp shooters that stayed in the camp to prevent that from happening again.

Our group had been dwindled down to only twelve people, among a few trailers. Many had been killed, but several others had simply run-off. Kyland Drederick and his wife, Monika were the last to join our group from another group. Both Monika and Kyland were just over thirty, but never had any children. They were kind people, full of life, the ones that I wanted to be around. Always quick with a smile or a word of encouragement; I had great affection for both of them. Monika was drawn into this hellish lifestyle after the loss of her brother to one of these beasts. She met her husband in one of the groups that hunted down and destroyed the creature. They both came to us at a rendezvous point after being separated from their team. The location was agreed upon months in advance as our two factions were coordinating hunts. No one else from their team made it and as far as we knew the members of their group were gone.

BANG! BANG! BANG!

"Kyland! Monika! Heater and lights off!" I said. I didn't wait for them to come out. I kept walking, but I saw Kyland through the window hold up his hand in acknowledgement.

"Ada! Does Garon want me to get into position?" Kyland asked from inside the trailer.

"*Ja.*"

Kyland made his way out of the trailer towards the edge of the forest where he agreed to stay to overlook the clearing where both Ramond and Garon were stationed. Monika turned out the lights from the trailer and opened a window. I could see the tip of a rifle poke out. Monika was the other sharpshooter guarding the camp, mainly to offer her husband cover so that he didn't have to worry about anything sneaking up on him from behind.

We had tracked incidents across Germany. When the weather had taken a turn for the worse with snowfall, we stopped in Glindenberg for supplies. We figured the werewolf may have moved towards Magdeburg or may have continued east, but the man that ran the corner grocer warned us to be careful past borders of the town. *'Strange happenings'* he so boldly bolstered with the account of two Fallow Deer found dead, torn to pieces in the nearby forest. Of course we stayed to check it out. Foxes were the only canine species common to the area. Occasionally, a wolf would wander across the border from Poland or Prussia, but it would still have to travel hundreds of kilometers to reach Glindenberg. Even so, the broken antlers of the Fallow Deer, the necks that were torn out and the guts of the animals almost entirely consumed were the dark pieces of evidence to which we were drawn. It suggested an evil presence; not that of a lone wolf, incapable of that kind of damage, but something bigger, stronger, and much more fierce.

"Damn it's cold," I whispered. Most of the other trailers were dark. I stopped outside Gerda's trailer and looked towards the far end of the camp. One trailer still had lights on. It was the Vogal's trailer. They were the guards on the far side of the camp. Manny, Nadine, and their daughter Marlie had been with us from the start. Marlie was only five years old, dirty blonde hair and hazel-colored eyes; the perfect blend between her west European descendants of her mother who had light brown eyes with light brown hair and her east German father who had blue eyes with blonde hair. She was the only child in our group. Since our camp numbers were low, most of our group opted out of having children, claiming that it wasn't right to bring a child into this nightmare and that we had no means of protecting them, but Marlie was unexpected. *I'll check on Gerda first*, I thought.

I opened the door to the trailer and stepped inside. It was cool, but not cold. Gerda had already turned the heater off in the trailer. She was at the far end with only a small lamp lit beside her on a table. It was enough light to shine on an old book opened across her lap. The book was large and with several items tucked between the pages. Gerda didn't appear to be reading it. Her eyes were closed, and her weathered hands were fingering a rosary as her lips mumbled several prayers in German.

"*Oma?*" Gerda didn't stop her prayers, instead continued as though I wasn't even there. "*Oma* are you all right?"

Her lips stopped moving and she kissed the crucifix attached at the bottom of her rosary. Gerda sighed deeply and opened her eyes to look at me. One of her eyes was grey and her vision had faded from it years ago, but the other was a vibrant blue that cut through the dimness of the trailer. She smiled. Several of her teeth were missing, but her smile was still big and wide as she looked upon me. "*Ja, ich bin in Ordnung.*"

I smiled back and walked towards her. "*Gut.* We are going to leave soon. Are you ready to go?"

"*Ja.*" Gerda closed the book on her lap and placed it inside a burlap satchel along with a black pouch, some letters, and a small purse full of varying denominations of Euros. She wrapped the long string of rosary beads around her right hand until just the crucifix dangled below.

"It's cold *Oma.* That sweater is not going to be enough. Put this coat on." I helped her frail arms through the holes in the sleeves. Gerda was eighty years old and she looked it. Having been a street performer and an artisan dealer her whole life had taken a toll, but it was less of a burden than the worry brought on by the things we hunted. We didn't know how much longer she was going to be with us. The clock on the shelf read 6:50 p.m. *We have plenty of time to get to the safe house before the full moon rises,* I thought. I grabbed the keys to the truck that dangled on a hook. "I have to tell the Vogals to cut their lights and heater. I will be back with Marlie in a few moments to get you loaded into the truck."

I left Gerda's trailer and started walking towards the Vogal's trailer. The wind blew hard against me. Tree branches rubbed together and creaked in the darkened forest. Shivers ran down my body. My teeth chattered as I quickened my steps. I didn't want to be out in the cold any longer than necessary. Manny and Nadine's trailer was just past mine to the left on the edge of the camp. It bumped up against the tree line. Some snow had drifted along the edge of the forest. It was disturbed as though something had walked through it. I slowed my pace to a near stop. I could see through one of the windows. Inside the trailer, the lights were on, but no one was inside. "Manny? Nadine?" I whispered hoping they would hear me and come to the window. Nothing. "Marlie? Are you there?" Still, nothing.

I pulled out my two-way radio and clicked it on. "Audrick? Come in. Can you hear me? Alika? Do you read me?" I listened for their response. There was nothing but static. Both Audrick and Alika Huber were hulky, ex-military sharp shooters. They had been in position since before the sun had started to set, just south of the camp in case the werewolf tried to run towards the town. Their job was to intercept before it could get there. I was hoping the Vogals were with them or had at least made contact. Something wasn't right. "Come in Audrick. Are the Vogals near either of your positions?" Again, there was only static.

A door slammed to the right of me. I jumped. It slammed again. The door to my trailer was unlatched and blowing open and closed with each gust of wind. *I never leave my door unlatched,* I thought. The creaks from the trees that swayed and rubbed against each other echoed through the forest. My breaths were short, and my senses were very acute. The wind howled and bit my exposed cheeks. The beats of my heart muted all other sounds as I quietly made my way to the door. Inside my trailer all was dark. Things were wrong, very wrong. I felt a vague prickling on the nape of my neck. Something was waiting, watching. I could feel it. Just inside the door was a small cabinet where I kept Dad's gun, holstered, and fully loaded with silver rounds. I pulled it out and checked to see if there was one in the chamber. I held the gun with my right hand, the two-way radio in my left and walked slowly towards the back of my trailer.

Crouched in the corner with her arms wrapped around her knees was Marlie. She didn't have a coat, and despite her long sleeve shirt, pants, and boots, she shivered uncontrollably. "Marlie...are you ok? Where is your mum and dad?" She whimpered but said nothing. Her breathing was fast and heavy. "*Kommen Sie hier* Marlie." I gestured for her to come away from the corner. She stayed hunched down.

I pressed the button to the two-way radio again, "Garon, we got a problem–"

Before I could finish, the door to the trailer tore from its hinges and crushed inward as a huge beast came crashing through it!

YAAARRR! Its enormous, fur covered body ripped and thrashed as it continued to enter the small space. I dropped the radio, fell to the floor in front of Marlie and grabbed my gun with both hands. The werewolf's eyes were glowing red against the blackness. It snarled and paused for a moment to find its prey before it lunged forward with its mouth open and over-sized canine teeth ready to clamp down.

BOOM! BOOM! BOOM!

The bullets pierced the head of the beast, throwing the back of its skull against the wall of the trailer. Its momentum carried it to a stop on top of me. Blood poured from the beast. It was dead.

"Fuck! *Ficken*! Fuck!" I scrambled backwards and pushed with all the strength I could muster to free myself from under the beast. My hands shook and I could barely breathe. Everything was muffled. Deep thumps from inside my chest mixed with a ringing in my ears. Marlie covered her ears too. Frightful wails surged intermittently from her mouth and sounded as though they were at the far end of a distant tunnel. Tears streamed down her face. Forcing myself to my knees, I reached out for Marlie, and seized her by the arm. "Come on! We have to go!"

I pulled Marlie to her feet as I stood. The ringing in my ears was relentless. I opened and closed my mouth hoping to speed up the process. It seemed to work, my hearing began to return, but wasn't enough to stave off the splitting headache between my temples. I picked Marlie up into my arms and she clung to me as we stepped passed the werewolf that lay dead. My trapper hat lay next to it, yet I paid it no attention. Outside the wind kicked up and stung my ears.

OWOOOOAH!

I heard the howl of another werewolf amongst the trees, followed by a third. All around us the howls poured from the darkness. Too many to count. No moon could be seen in the sky. I ran towards Gerda's trailer holding Marlie in my arms the best I could, my gun in my right hand.

YAAARRR! From behind, red eyes from another silhouette of a werewolf were fixated on us as it charged forward. I dropped to the ground and Marlie tumbled from my arms as the beast leapt into the air. Its claws caught the back of my left shoulder as it overshot us and slid on a nearby patch of snow. Searing pain jetted down my arm. "GET DOWN!"

Marlie knelt and covered her head as the werewolf lunged at her.

BOOM! BOOM!

Its blood sprayed from its fur and coated the white snow with dark spots as it fell short of Marlie. I placed my foot on the beast's neck and fired again into its head at close range. *BOOM!*

Its glowing red eyes went dark as its blood turned the snow black.

I grabbed Marlie by the wrist and we ran. Blood dripped down my arm and trickled out of the bottom cuff of my sleeve onto her hand. We reached Gerda's trailer. I opened the door and forced Marlie inside. Another beast crashed head-first into the doorframe. My gun fell to the floor as I tried to hold the door shut. Gerda clutched Marlie close to her as she wailed in fear. Slashing ferociously, the werewolf ripped the door from its hinges. The brute started to lurch forward when blood from the beast covered the window to the right of the door. Its body shook violently as it crumpled to the ground in front of the trailer. Blood poured from a hole in its head. Garon appeared at the damaged doorway a moment later holding his rifle. He motioned for us to leave, "Hurry! Let's go!"

I grabbed my gun from the floor and motioned Gerda and Marlie to follow. Marlie ran out first and clung to Garon. Gerda grabbed for her burlap satchel. "Leave it! There is no time!" I shouted at Gerda.

"Grimoire!" She clutched the burlap satchel with both arms and moved as fast as her frail body would allow.

I followed Gerda out of the trailer and looked to my left. Standing a short distance away from the trailer was Ramond, with his gun pointed in our direction. "BEHIND YOU!"

Garon turned just in time to hold his rifle out in front of him to shield us as another werewolf collided with him. The beast rolled over Garon. The weight of the brute broke his gun in half. Righting itself the beast snarled and prepared to lunge. Instead, it yelped and howled in pain as Ramond fired several times into the beast. Garon pulled his pistol from his holster and fired three more times to finish it off. "Get in the truck!"

Marlie climbed into the truck, followed by Gerda. A scream erupted from inside Monika's trailer as a beast came barreling in on her. The whole trailer shook violently as blood coated the windows. Another werewolf leapt on top of Olis's trailer. Several bullet holes pierced the roof as Olis attempted to kill the beast from within. A separate monster crashed through the doorway. The last sound that Olis ever made was a scream of agony.

"Where is Kyland?" I shouted.

"Gone! Torn to pieces!" Garon replied. He turned to face Ramond who was trying to shoot the werewolf from atop Olis's trailer. "Leave him Ramond! Olis is dead! We have to go!"

I jumped into the driver's seat of the truck and turned the key to the ignition. Marlie screamed with her eyes closed as she clung to Gerda who had her arms wrapped around the small child and was clutching her rosary. Garon jumped onto the bed of the truck. "RAMOND! COME ON!" he shouted.

Ramond turned from the beast atop Olis's trailer and started to run towards the truck. It only took a few bounds for the werewolf to catch Ramond. It sunk its teeth into the top of his shoulder at the base of his neck. Ramond screamed as the monster dug its sharp claws from both paws into his chest. The brute shook its head from side to side and ripped upward as it pulled the torso of Ramond apart.

"DRIVE ADA, DRIVE!" Garon shouted from the back.

I pressed the gas pedal to the floor and felt the tires spin on the frozen ground. The truck slid from side-to-side before it gained its traction. The werewolf lunged from Ramond's dismembered body towards the truck. Garon fired three times from his pistol to no avail. Its weight crashed down upon the bed and caused the truck to fishtail as we drove along the back road leading out of the camp. Garon fired two shots into the belly of the beast. It howled in pain before it clamped its jaws down on the mid-section of Garon.

"AHHH!" Garon howled. *"Sie ficken!"*

I could see in the rearview mirror the werewolf thrashing its massive head with Garon in its jaws. Its eyes glowed bright red with powerful fury against the nighttime backdrop. I slammed on the brakes and the momentum of the beast slammed it head-first into the cab window. Gerda and Marlie both screamed as the glass shattered. Garon was free from its jaws. Seizing the moment, Garon shoved his gun to the side of the beast's head and fired two more times. The snarling stopped and the werewolf was dead.

Garon slumped along the opposite side of the truck bed. "Garon? You're hurt!"

"Drive...just drive," I heard him say through labored breaths.

I pressed down on the gas again and the oversized beast slid off the back of truck into the darkness among the trees. Garon lay in the bed of the truck motionless. Marlie cried and shook with fright. Gerda held her tight and continued to pray. I knew Garon was wounded, but I didn't know how bad.

"GARON! GARON!" I shouted hoping to hear something from him. I had started to go along the path to the safe house when I finally heard him.

"Drive Ada...not to zee safe house – it's too dangerous."

The truck was damaged and covered in blood. It was certain to draw attention if we got onto a major highway. We drove for about twenty minutes on a rural road leading away from Glindenberg before I heard the banging of Garon's hand against the back of the cab. "Stop." The word was muffled.

I drove another kilometer before I found a suitable place. Just off the road we were on was an old industrial park. It was getting late into the evening. The place looked abandoned as though it had been years since someone had used it for its original purpose. I cut the lights of the truck and drove to the back part of the complex. Between two of the structures was an alley where I parked to conceal the truck from prying eyes. Gerda and Marlie entered the warehouse first. Gerda still clung to the burlap satchel with one arm and held Marlie with her other. I reached into the glove box of the truck for a small flashlight before I followed. With Garon struggling to walk, he leaned over my right shoulder as I held the small flashlight between my teeth and my gun in my left hand.

Once inside, I leaned Garon against one of the metal walls and closed the garage door to the warehouse. It screeched shut.

Darkness filled the area, but I could still make out a silhouette of Garon from the muted light that came in from the windows. Several chains dangled from the hooks and posts all around. I pushed passed them as I made my way back to Garon. Kneeling, I laid the gun next to him. Both Gerda and Marlie were okay but horribly frightened as they clung to one another. The back of my coat was shredded. I fumbled with the zipper as my hands continued to shake. It wasn't easy but I managed to get it off. My left shoulder had three really deep lacerations and a fourth smaller one from what I could feel. They needed a bandage. I tore strips of fabric from my coat for makeshift bandages. Each gash continued to seep blood even after I wrapped it tight with the remains of my coat.

I handed Gerda the small flashlight. The light wasn't much, and the batteries were critically low, but it gave off enough light that I could see Garon.

"Ada…" Garon's voice was weak.

"Try not to talk."

"Ada, you have to do it," Garon said. Blood poured over his hand that clutched his stomach.

"Do what? What are you talking about?" I started to wrap the remaining bandages around his waist to cover the bite wound.

Garon placed his hand over mine to stop what I was doing. "You have to kill me."

"No! No, I cannot do that! We will find help –"

Garon coughed and blood came out of his mouth. "If I survive this, you know – you know vat I will become. I cannot live that way. I would rather be dead."

Tears welled up in my eyes. "It's my fault! If I would not have turned on my cell phone they would not have known where we were! They are all dead because of me!"

"No – stop. It – is God's will." He was struggling to breathe. "Not – your – fault."

"I cannot kill my own brother!"

"I – am already dead. My gun – is empty." He grabbed my gun that was lying next to him and placed it in my hand. With both of his hands, he pulled the barrel to his forehead. Garon's wound continued to bleed, heavily.

I let go of the gun and stood up from Garon. The gun fell to his lap, then back to the floor. I paced. "NO! Garon let us go to London. They may know something we do not! Please! I cannot do this!"

Tears flowed freely down my cheeks. "Go to London. Seek – them out. Be cautious. You are strong. Do what you have been taught. But – do not let me become one of those beasts."

Marlie crouched down and hugged her knees, not saying anything except for a few whimpers. Gerda walked over Garon. She removed the old book from her satchel and opened it. An envelope was stuffed into the binding. Inside was a minute crucifix. She knelt next to Garon and gently touched the crucifix to his forehead and slowly made the sign of the cross over him. *"Möge Gott mit dir sein."*

"Oma," Garon replied. "God *is* with me. He always has been."

Gerda laid the crucifix on his lap and touched his face with both hands before she kissed his forehead. *"Mein Vormund."* Gerda turned to me and nodded. It was time.

She stood sluggishly and took Marlie by the hand. They walked to a darkened corner of the warehouse and sat down next to a workstation. Gerda covered Marlie's ears and held her close to her body as she hummed a soft lullaby. Marlie wrapped her small arms around Gerda. The young girl let out a whimper.

Our beliefs prohibited us from taking our own lives. The ultimate damnation. I knew what I had to do. Garon was right. There was no way that I would be able to live with myself knowing that I let my brother turn into the very thing we were trying to destroy. And he was suffering. Tears continued to roll down my face. I placed my forehead against his.

"It is truth what *Oma* said. You *are* our guardian."

Garon looked into my eyes. A single tear fell to his cheek. "Do it. Ple – ease. Do it."

"God, have mercy on us and on those who are dying," I whispered. Garon handed me the gun from the floor next him.

He closed his eyes and I kissed his forehead the same as Gerda had. We both spoke, "May the demons of the devil perish to ashes."

I positioned my gun close to his temple and pulled the trigger. The shot echoed into the darkened gloom of the warehouse.

Chapter #2

Old is New
Robert Osborne
Friday, February 10, 2012
3:10 p.m.

"You know Grayson has been quite brilliant with his performance as of late. If he keeps this pace, he should have the remaining papers to become an active planner by spring." Ashland Simmons always looked to the brighter side of things. It was one of the traits I admired the most about him. His outward appearance teemed with prominence, always dressed properly to the occasion with neatly pressed suits like the grey one he wore. He hadn't bothered to remove his suit coat as I had done. Instead, he simply unbuttoned it to sit more comfortably. Crisp, clean, well-groomed even for afternoon tea. Yet, his demeanor was gentle. Caring, very compassionate and empathetic to the needs of others. Not quite what I would expect from someone as stately as he.

"You've trained him well Ashland." I sat across the small table from Ashland at the Café Rouge, holding my cup of Scottish black leaf tea. My suit coat was draped over the corner of my chair.

"He's *your* son. I merely helped him through the first couple of steps, that's all." Each Friday we would discuss the standings of the market and the upcoming week's projections over a cup of afternoon tea. The spots varied from time-to-time, yet this was a practice that we had always kept in our earlier financial planning days. I only nodded in response to his comment about Grayson as I brought the cup of tea to my lips. My hand shook as I placed the cup on the table. "Are you all right Robert? You seem displaced, even nervous."

I didn't respond right away. The nervous tremor in my left hand had started sometime in the days after the incident at St.

Teresa's Cathedral. My tea was warm, but bitter. The black leaf was left too long to infuse. It was a breakfast tea and naturally took on a bitter taste, yet it lacked the robust, malty flavor that I was hoping to get. There were no hints of cask oak and the smoky aftertaste that would warm my body from the pending rain and colder weather and sooth the tension from a long work week. In fact, it just made my tension worse. *Scotch would be better*, I thought. I drank the tea anyways. I didn't even bother to add milk. Most things lacked in flavor in recent days, adding milk certainly wasn't going to change it for me.

"It's nothing really. Just a few things that I need to get sorted," I lied to him. I knew that he saw the shakes in my hand, but Ashland knew nothing of what had happened over the past couple of years after Laryn's death. He, more or less, was happy that I had returned to the financial practice and was helping manage our older clients as well as the ever-growing number of new ones. I kept a lower profile than I had had as a member of Parliament. These meetings between us weren't the same anymore. What was once something that made the week easier to swallow was now a mere lump in my throat that was gagging.

"Does it pertain to the market? From what we've discussed…"

"No, it's not the market," I interrupted.

"Robert, we're friends. If something is vexing you then we should talk about it, I can help."

"Nothing ever good came from talking about one's feelings." My response was snappy. It had a touch of irritation. I wanted to talk about what I was feeling. I wanted to tell him everything that had happened with Laryn, at Cambridge, and at St. Teresa's Cathedral, the depressing months that followed, but I couldn't. *He would have me committed if I told him*, I thought. The café overlooked Hertford's Parliament Square. I turned away from his gaze to watch the people scurrying past the front windows. Most carried umbrellas and were dressed in coats to fend off the imminent rain.

"Come now Robert." Ashland sipped his own cup of Earl Grey. "I gave your son a compliment, but it seems to bear no weight. Most fathers would be overjoyed to hear that their sons are performing well, especially in a field that you and I both know is difficult, tricky and even elusive at times."

I *was* pleased that Grayson was doing well at the firm, but there was still guilt mixed with anger. It was I who was responsible for him being in London. Not by coaxing or encouragement, but by coercion. Fortunately, he was honorably discharged from the army. It was not his choice, it was mine. The events that happened thereafter left us at odds with each other. I didn't understand why he did *what* he did. *How he could betray me, his family, for a person that was helping the very thing we were trying to hunt down and destroy?* Nonetheless, he was still my eldest son and I needed him. It was my hope that he would come to his senses about Dr. Bishop.

"It's just… Codie. He's dropped out of another university. First it was the University of Cambridge…" Codie was easier to discuss than Grayson. I understood and actually encouraged him to stop attending Cambridge. My thought was that he would be better served at a university that didn't have such a close tie to the horrific events we all had to endure. He needed a distraction. "…then it was the University of London and now I've recently learned from Daphne that he didn't even enroll in the University of Hertfordshire."

"Perhaps he wants to enter into the service, like Grayson did. Have you talked to him about that?"

"No, I haven't. He's been living with Daphne and only comes to the manor to see Grayson, not me. I think that it has more to do with the loss of his sister, though." I knew it was about Laryn and the whole situation. Ashland's words were kind and his sincerity was genuine, but how could I tell him that Codie hadn't quite recovered from a *werewolf* attack? Deep hypertrophic scars stretched across his left shoulder into his chest. Codie spent most of his time lifting weights and learning about weapons from Grayson instead of attending university.

How could he understand that neither of my two sons regarded me well anymore? How could I tell him that my eldest son lost respect for me over the torture of Marcus Holland? How could I talk to him about the fact I had ex-Irish Republican Army mercenaries living at my manor, offering a constant reminder of the nightmare that I would never be able to wake from unless I knew the *monstrous thing* that killed Laryn lay rotting and stinking of decomposition? I paused and looked around the café.

Inside there weren't many patrons. The busy hours were later in the afternoon and into the early part of the evening. The few who were there sat at the tables against the wall and sipped coffee or wine. Most were enjoying the French inspired bistro that made Café Rouge, a popular chain. Modern splashes of red on the clock that hung by a wine shelf and on the lighting fixtures above the tables in the center of the space clashed with the dark wood paneled walls. Brass fixtures highlighted a few modern art pieces. No one significant, at best, maybe a local artist looking to break into the business or simply artwork that helped with the ambience. The place was chic, trendy, seeking to have an old world feel with a modern flare. *This place is trying to be something that it's not…much like me,* I thought.

"All people grieve differently. But you said it yourself Robert, he's coming to the manor to see Grayson. He may feel guilt over the effort you have given to provide him the opportunity to attend these universities, when in actuality he wants to pursue another type of career or service."

I glanced back at Ashland. "You're probably right." I was thankful for the opportunity to direct the conversation to more *believable* and common subjects. "Perhaps I'll talk with him if he comes to the manor this week."

"May I propose you schedule a time? Perhaps you need a holiday, a much-needed trip together. Don't wait on such things. And involve Grayson too. He may be able to ease your concerns if it happens to pertain to military service. I'll manage things at the office if it requires it."

Ashland's suggestions were insightful and observant, yet they were only based on what he knew. We had been financial partners several years prior, long before I held office in the House of Commons. His insights into matters both work related and personal, always seemed to be well informed. It was a trademark of a good financial planner. We were the same age and together with his insights and my drive for betterment, ambition, we built a hugely successful planning practice. It not only gave us wealth, but also financed my political campaign.

It was difficult to leave the position in the House of Commons I had worked so diligently to achieve, but it was necessary for the avenues I needed to pursue. Holding public office drew far too much attention. I knew that I wasn't going to be able to continue to serve in the House after the events surrounding St. Teresa's Cathedral. Hugh Bennett, my rival in the house, had seized the opportunity to exploit this event as a means to get me removed from office. Hugh even tried to have more legal penalties brought upon me. His goal was to derail my political party's polices but they still went through despite his efforts. Ultimately, it was my decision to leave, but his pressure certainly didn't make the transition back to the private business sector any easier.

More patrons were starting to come into the café. Some were seeking an early dining experience. Others sought a dry place to get a warm drink as they waited out the rain that had begun to fall. Fortunately, the café was only a few blocks from our firm. Walking in the light rain wasn't going to be pleasant, but at least my umbrella was going to keep me dry enough. I stood from our table and put on my overcoat.

"Are you ready to go back?" I asked.

Ashland stood and helped with my suit coat, followed by my overcoat, more as gesture rather than need. "No, I think I might grab a bit to eat first. I suspect that you'll retire for the day before I get back to the office. So, I shall see you Monday."

"Yes, give Alice my best."

"But of course." We shook hands before I turned and walked towards the exit.

Ashland liked to work late on Fridays. He claimed that overloading the last day of the week led to an easier start of the next week. I usually had enough energy after these afternoon tea excursions to check on any messages and maybe respond to a few e-mails before heading back to my manor.

Ashland had been happily married for twenty-six years and together with his wife, Alice, they had a daughter, Flora. She was a year older than Grayson and was a practicing barrister. Though Flora handled some of the firm's legal paperwork, she spent most of her time in court. His life was nice, quaint, and full of happiness. The balancing act that Ashland had always performed was something I had longed for but never really achieved with Daphne. I wanted to go home to my family to share in the warmth of my manor and bask in the glowing achievements of my children. I too wanted happiness. Bitterness and resentment eroded the foundations of my relationship with Daphne, until our marriage collapsed. I had clung to my children thereafter, only to have that too, torn from me. Emptiness had consumed me over the past two years. There was only one thing that I knew that could change this, but we had struck a dead end. All traces of the werewolf we had hunted were gone and maintaining the façade of normalcy was damn near impossible.

The menacing dark rain clouds carried a frigid wind and gusted misty rain. A fog had set in on the streetways and combined with the muted daylight made it difficult to see far down the road. I walked with my head hung low watching each step. There wasn't a day that had passed since St. Teresa's Cathedral that I hadn't thought about all of the events that transpired. *Where the hell did you go Dr. Bishop? You stole everything from me,* I thought. A sudden rush of panic spread over me.

I stopped walking just before the door to my office and dropped my umbrella. Images of the green eyes cutting through the darkness clouded my mind. Each breath was caught in my chest and my left hand shook with tremors. It was difficult to walk. I could hear my heartbeat, loud and riotous, drowning out the busyness around me. The breaths were hard, but I forced out several deep ones as I looked up through the fog. A silhouette of a petite woman standing across the street on the corner caught my attention. She wasn't trying to shield herself from the misty rain, nor was she preoccupied with anything else. She was facing me. I could tell that she was wearing a coat, but the hood was not drawn and that she had short hair which seemed to be matted to her head because of the rain. Filled with anxiety, but compelled by the mysteriousness of the woman, I moved onto the street and was nearly struck by a car.

The horn of a car shook me from my gaze as it slammed on the brakes to avoid hitting me. Startled, I held my hands up in an apology to the driver. Quickly, I strode across the street only to find that the woman was gone and with the thickness of the fog there was no telling where. My hand shook. I clenched it tight into a fist until the shaking stopped and my anxiety lowered. All that remained was a raw anger towards what I had lost and towards what constituted reality versus the nightmarish manifestations of things I desired the most.

Cautiously, I crossed the street to where I dropped my umbrella.

My anxiety subsided, but not totally. It never really left. I grabbed my umbrella from the walkway. It had closed when I dropped it. I didn't bother to open it again. Instead, I continued towards my office. Rain pelted my head soaking the shoulders and collar of my overcoat. All around me were people, but the woman was nowhere among them. *It had to be her. She had to be there,* I thought.

I opened the door to my office. Charlotte looked up from behind the welcome desk. "Are you all right, Sir? Did you get caught in a gust?" The concern was honest. Charlotte had been with our company for the past two years. She was good at managing the front desk, but more importantly she had little to no knowledge of what happened to Laryn and with the events that followed. I was sure that she probably had heard something but being at university during the events prompted little attention on her part to the social and political happenings of the House of Commons members.

"Uh – yes. I suppose I did. Were there any messages?" I asked to change the subject.

"Sir, do you need me to fetch you a towel?"

"No – no, I'm…I'm fine. Thank you." I hesitated and removed my overcoat. I wasn't fine. "Messages?" I asked again to redirect the topic back to business and nothing more.

"Uh, no Sir. There were a few calls, but Grayson managed them."

"Is he still here?"

"I believe he is still in the back office."

"Thank you." I didn't stay long enough for Charlotte to inquire any further about my un-stately appearance. Instead, I made my way towards the back office where Grayson conducted most of his duties. Grayson sat in his chair facing the far wall with the window reviewing over files. There was no artwork hung anywhere. Pictures of all of us filled portions of wall space, but it was obvious that Grayson simply used the office as a place to work and nothing more. The screensaver on his computer flashed pictures of Codie, Daphne, me but more painfully of Laryn. *I wish he would take those off his screensaver.* Each time I saw her smiling face during those captured moments of a happier past, sadness mixed with anger and poked again at my sanity.

Grayson turned in his chair to face me and lowered the file he was reviewing. His tie was loosened and hung haphazardly against his striped button-up shirt. Locks of his dark hair fell across his forehead and his face was expressionless. "What happened to you?"

"I saw her…Dr. Bishop…standing on the corner across the way. She was watching me."

Shaking his head, Grayson stood from his chair and arbitrarily tossed the file he was reading down onto his desk. "Nothing." His voice was low, but direct, cautious of his surroundings and who may be within earshot of our conversation. "You saw – nothing."

"You're wrong!" Frustration seeped out. I cared less than he did about who heard me. "This isn't the first time that I've seen glimpses of her. She's the same but different."

"Different how?" Grayson held up his arms to coax a response from me.

"Same petite frame, but not afraid, not shying away. Her hair was short, it was –"

"Did you get a look at her up close? Or was she gone by the time you reached her?" I knew what Grayson was doing. Having been a combat officer, he was trying to get me to see that it was a manifestation of my mind and nothing more. "Did you see her eyes? Were they glowing green like before?"

"Stop!"

"Or how about the time when you were convinced that Dr. Bishop was on a different street corner and you forced Henry to stop the car, blocking traffic for several minutes…only to discover no one was there…" Grayson continued, "…Perhaps when you and Codie were at the café –"

"That was an honest mistake!" I interjected.

"Mistake? You were convinced that Dr. Bishop was serving you tea! Neither you nor Codie are allowed back to the café after the scene you caused. He's still concerned about that day and it was several months ago."

"But this was different!"

"How…How was this any different from those scenarios?" Grayson asked.

"It just was…it felt different."

"It's just trauma." Grayson sighed. "It was traumatic for all of us, but I think it's time you spoke someone. A professional, someone respectable."

"Bloody hell! Talk to someone? You're quite serious?" My anxiety changed to annoyance. "Jesus, Grayson you know we can't talk to anyone. You forget that the world doesn't believe in what we know and any attempt to change that would end poorly for those who try... and I find your lightheartedness to this situation unnerving. This could mean it's starting again."

"I don't know." Grayson shrugged. "...however, I'm anything but *light*-hearted." Grayson clenched his jaw and shook his head as he turned from me. He made his way over to the window saying nothing further. Outside the rain continued to pelt the panes of glass with each gust of wind. It was pointless to argue. Grayson knew it too. I walked up behind him and noticed that he was rubbing his left arm as he stared out into the storm. Considering Ashland's advice, I seized the opportunity to not wait and speak with Grayson directly, on a level only he would understand. "We share the same pain. The hurt goes deeper than cuts and broken bones. It has scarred us into the very being that makes us."

"What would you have me do?"

"Let us hunt her again!"

"Then what?" Grayson turned to look at me again. "Killing Dr. Bishop won't stop the pain. It will only bring Inspector Lawrence back into our lives, asking questions. We can't cover up that kind of story again and we certainly can't tell him the truth. You said it yourself; the world doesn't believe in what we know and any attempt to change that would end poorly for those who try."

Grayson had a point. Even though enough time had elapsed from the investigation that had been conducted on Grayson and me to label it as a cold case, stirring things up again would certainly bring unwanted police involvement. "At least Laryn will be able to rest-in-peace." Our voices were calmer, more civil. "Dealing with police will be easier knowing that the werewolf that killed Laryn is dead. They'll forever be chasing the wind, never fully knowing the truth if we kill Dr. Bishop."

Grayson nodded as if to agree with what I said. "How do you propose we start? There are other beasts out there besides her. We do know that. Dr. Bishop was just the beginning."

"Let us start at the beginning then. The manor."

"For what? We were there already, after the church incident. She wasn't there then and she's not going to be there now."

"Maybe so...but there might be bits of this story untold that will point us in the right direction." Secrecy was my biggest concern. At no point did I want to give anyone any inclination that I was still involved with events of the past. Dr. Bishop's estate hadn't sat long enough to be turned over to the local authorities, yet as time passed the property would start to fall into ruin and would be labeled as abandoned drawing potential buyers or investors. If we didn't go back soon the likelihood that we would find anything useful would be reduced to practically nothing. Grayson was right though. The chances of her being there were slim, but we had no other choice. No other avenue to follow.

Whether the woman on the corner was real or a figment of my damaged conscious didn't matter. She was real enough, and I hated her. I had to find Dr. Bishop, otherwise the darkness was going to consume me. "I may die alone...but I'll have vengeance," I whispered through clenched teeth as I turned out of his office.

CHAPTER #3

A Book of the Past
Grayson Osborne
Sunday, February 12, 2012
12:45 a.m.

Night surrounded the manor. Its darkened windows revealed little of what was inside; like a black hole, a vacuum of light and life stamped against weathered stones that made up the outer walls. The ground was cold and wet. I could hear the earth squish under my boots as the rain continued to fall. Through the night vision scope, I could see no movement in or around the manor that suggested anything dangerous.

"See anything?" Dad asked.

"No, nothing yet." I touched the *Push-To-Talk* button and spoke into the in-line mic attached to my earpiece. "Snake. Do you see anything on your end?"

"No. It's the same as last time. The only things move'n out here are our bloody arses." Snake and Jinx were always a bit oppositional, but not being able to have any real action since the church incident left them in a constant state of hostility. They were certainly not shy about expressing their disapproval of any operation that we conducted. Their reasons for sticking around were centered on only one thing, money.

"Kap, what about you – see anything?" Over the two years, Kap and I had come to understand one another. He was the only one of the Irish lads that had actually seen the werewolf and never lost sight of the incredible violence of which it was capable of comitting.

"Nothing on my end. What are ya hope'n to find out here Grayson?" Kap asked.

"Hopefully nothing," I replied. "Alright, Jinx move towards the door. We'll cover your steps."

"Whatever your highness requests. Just don't let anything fuck'n bite me in the arse." I watched through the scope as Jinx cautiously made his way up the stone stairs towards the front entrance of the manor. His back was pressed against the exterior wall, a tactical AK 47 assault rifle with a collapsible stock and suppressor barrel clutched tightly to his chest. I watched closely for any movement other than him. Jinx peered down the barrel of the gun as he looked through the window to the right of the doorway. *"I don't see anything. Doesn't look like anyone's home."*

"All points ready to converge on the location as planned. Eyes on Jinx. Snake you're up."

"Copy."

Moments later I saw Snake approach from the wooded area to the right of the manor.

"Kap, you're next."

"I'm on it."

Kap moved from the pastoral stretch to the left of the manor and approached the front entrance where Jinx and Snake were already positioned.

"What is taking so long?"

"We have to take the necessary precautions," I replied to my father's impatience. I touched the PTT again on the in-line mic, "We're making our advance. Keep your eyes open for movement. We're approaching from the south drive leading up to the manor."

I stood from my kneeling position and re-hinged the stability leg on my Rangemaster rifle. Dad held his tactical AK 47 tight with the stock pressed into his shoulder. He faced me but the end of the barrel pointed towards the darkness behind us. The muffled sounds of the falling rain masked our steps as we moved down the main drive towards the manor. I kept my paces tight with the stock of my gun pressed firm to my shoulder with the barrel pointed towards the ground. My SIG Sauer P220 was holstered on my right hip. Like all the weapons we were using, the magazine was full of silver rounds. Kap had

had enough time to customize them to fit the rifling of each of the firearms we were using. Over the past two years I had learned a tremendous amount from him.

We took a few quick steps as we advanced, making sure to secure the ground we gained on the manor each time we stopped. We needed to do this quick and quiet. I looked through the scope of the Rangemaster. All three of the men were poised with their guns pointed outward from the manor. I lowered the rifle as we continued to move.

Pop, Pop, Pop, Pop, Pop!

Gunfire broke the monotonous drizzle of the failing rain. Shouts of profanity followed close behind. Our steps quickened with the second set of gun blasts.

Pop, Pop, Pop!

Dad and I both positioned ourselves along the main drive to provide a clear range of fire. "Who's shooting?" he asked.

Fast beats of my heart echoed in my ears. Each breath was short and controlled. I peered through the scope again to acquire a target. Through the lens I could see Jinx pointing his AK into the air, randomly squeezing off rounds.

I lowered my rifle and looked at my dad, "The bald tosser with his toy gun."

We both continued down the drive at a brisk jog until we came upon the turn-around space that led up to the stone stairs in front of the ornate wooden doors. Jinx was shouting profanities into the air to the amusement of Snake. Kap seemed equally as taken aback as we were.

"Bloody hell Jinx, what are you doing?" I asked.

"Haven't got to shoot this beaut in quite a while – Needed to have a go with it before the night's through."

"You fuck'n muppet!" Kap shouted at Jinx.

"I don't know what yer squawk'n about. There's no one here. The window we broke two years ago is still broke. The glass is still on the ground and the only thing that's changed is ivy has grown up the walls a bit more."

Pop, Pop, Pop!

Jinx fired into the air again. Snake continued to stand amused by Jinx's antics with his foot on one of the steps and his rifle's stock resting on his thigh with the barrel pointed up. He made no attempt to stop Jinx from carrying on with his charade. Unlike Kap, who displayed a shared disdain for Jinx that had been acquired after the night at the church when Rex had been killed and I was injured. As with my father and Codie, having come face-to-face with the werewolf had clearly left an impression on Kap. Jinx as well as Snake never got past the mythical idea of the beast. Both believed that werewolves existed but having never actually seen one in the flesh left them incapable of understanding the savage, beastly nature of the thing we were hunting.

"Enough!" I finally said to Jinx. I turned on my compact flashlight. The beam was small, but it was enough to cut through the darkness. I pointed it at Jinx. "You've pissed on our chips."

Knowing that I was irritated by the situation only fueled Jinx to continue his aggressions. "Well, I've got to shoot at something. It's not like you've been able to find us a suitable target, boyo."

"Jinx, you half-wit! I'm not paying you for this shit!" my father yelled at Jinx.

"Ya haven't paid me in a while. Besides there's no one around and we're surrounded by trees and roll'n foothills. Who or what do ya think will be coming for us out here?"

"Nothing – no one." I held my hand up to my father to stop his verbal advances and stood directly in front of Jinx. Rain reflected the glow from my flashlight and dripped down his face. His gaze was unflinching "You're right – no one is out here at this time of night and I want to keep it that way. Yet the door to the manor is locked and look –" I pointed to the door. Attached was a notice for estate auction to be set in April. "– someone's been here."

"You're not the full shilling you used to be boyo. I see it in ya." His taunts were direct and served a purpose. Jinx wanted to have another go at me to regain a foothold in the situation. No doubt to barter for more money. I was happy to give him another go, but not out here. I didn't want to engage the knobheaded git any more than I needed. Getting inside the manor quietly, without drawing extra attention was the mission. But Jinx was correct, I wasn't the same.

I turned my gaze to Kap. "See what you can do about getting us inside."

Kap gave me a quick nod and made his way through the broken window. Moments later one of the ornate doors creaked open and from the blackness Kap emerged to motion us inside.

"Keep your lights low and to a minimum. I don't want anything targeting us from a distance. Move in and sweep the lower floor for anything hiding about."

Once inside the manor, I made my sweep through the foyer and into the parlor off to the left of the entrance. It was the same as it was the last time we had been there, perhaps a bit more dust. None of the furniture had been moved. Two chairs still resided in front of a soot filled fireplace. Kap followed close behind. I motioned to him to set up in here to watch for movement outside. The parlor windows looked out over the turn-around space and the main drive. He turned his flashlight off and stood at an angle from the window so he could see out but made it difficult for anyone to see him on the inside.

I crossed the main foyer. Dad stood with his gun pointed upwards at the darkness that swallowed the spiraling grand staircase. Jinx and Snake seemed less interested in securing the lower floor. Both sat on the furniture in the formal living space that opened from the right of the foyer. Rain had been dripping through the broken window for a while as evidenced by the water streaks down the walls and damage to the hard wood flooring. Some of the ivy had started to grow through the open space and inch its way along the interior of the wall. A musty, mildew smell filled the air and a thick layer of dust covered most everything.

"Snake, I need your eyes out front," I said.

He gave me a two fingered salute, but still made his way over to the broken window and positioned himself to be able to shoot. Jinx did nothing except continue to sit and make sounds as though he was snoring peacefully. I wasn't going to ask for his help. He wasn't going to give it to me anyways. I could tolerate the mock snoring noise knowing full well that if there was a werewolf around, it would go after him first.

My father and I continued down the long corridor towards the library and various dens. At its end, the corridor broke to the left into a kitchen area. The air was more stagnant the further down the corridor and sat heavy as though it carried the laments of the past. A darkened archway led down to the lower level of the manor. We had been down there before, but it served no real purpose considering it was just a bunch of storage coveys with a built-in, oversized cage at the far end. Both dad and I entered the main den. Within the book-covered walls, an antique wooden desk still rested at the back of the room. The oil-painted portrait that had hung directly behind the desk was sitting on the floor exposing an opened safe that had been fixed into the wall. Whatever was in the safe was gone. My father shined his light along the shelves of the room, clearly interested in the many volumes of lore and literature that filled them.

"We should've spent more time in here," my father said. Annoyance bled from his words. "We might've been able to gain an edge on tracking Dr. Bishop."

I shined my light on the books he was seeing. Most were titles of mythology mixed with a few contemporary pieces all dealing with the origins of the werewolf or related topics of the occult. "It wouldn't have mattered. We were lucky to be able to track her the way we did the first go round." As stern as my father was, Laryn's death had deeply changed him, exposing his vulnerabilities. He was easily agitated by the mere mention of her name. I didn't want to provoke my father, but it happened often considering that our once respectable relationship had deteriorated down to a tolerance of one another's presence.

"What do you mean lucky?" he asked.

"She was hiding in plain sight. We only stumbled across her."

"Only stumbled across her?" The irritation was growing inside him. I could hear it in his voice and see it in his poised stature. He swept his light across the titles again. "Might I remind you that Dr. Bishop was the one who ripped your sister to pieces. We could've –"

"Reading these books may have helped, but we didn't have the luxury of time to study them," I interrupted. "Besides, what may have stood out to her as important may be meaningless to us. Mind you, there are thousands of volumes here and in the library one room down. She had over two hundred years to collect and examine these volumes. There's no telling the number of clues and puzzles she has been able to follow in that time period. We've had only two years."

I turned from my father. Now was not the time to continue our heated debate on what should've been done to pursue Laryn's killer. Books stretched from floor to ceiling on either side of the den. As I shined my light across the spines, topics stood out more so than the titles. Satanism, witchcraft, the occult, European geography, British history were among the many subjects. A stack of books also sat on the desktop. They were peculiar only from the standpoint that they weren't on the desk the last time we were there. Books on the British Monarchs, mostly. A title on witchcraft in England from the Middle Ages and one about curses rested next to one book in particular that lay open. I shined my light on the accessible pages. King Charles II's artistic representation was displayed on one page and a time-lined list of his monarchial decrees on the other. This wasn't the act of some random looters or vandals. Someone had been there, someone who had a specific interest in the history of our country. I rested my gun against the desk. Holding the light over the open book, I scanned the page with my finger to see if anything stood out. Most of the timeline entries pertained to Clarendon Code that came out of the Restoration Era, but I stopped on the line that designated King Charles II's proclamation that abolished the practice of being burned at the stake in 1676. *Why's that so familiar?* I thought.

"Did you find something?" my father asked. His voice was still firm, yet inquisitive, seeking to confirm that reviewing the books was the correct course of action.

"No, nothing more than bits of history about our past monarchial leadership," I lied to him. I didn't know what it was about the line on the page that was so familiar, but it was something from the recent past. I had read something related to this fact in Dr. Bishop's diary or Marcus Holland's journal, yet I wasn't about to divulge that I had secretly copied these materials and had been studying them. I had hoped to have had an answer to the riddle of why I was still alive before discussing anything with my father, or anyone for that matter, and I didn't want him hounding me to do more with the text than what I needed to do with it. Blind in his anger, my father would've considered it another act of betrayal. Not so much that I was reading and studying the writings, more so that I was doing it in secret for ulterior reasons. *Dr. Bishop should've killed me when she had the chance, but didn't,* I thought. This one detail tormented me and had kept me in a state of uncertainty. My father then, and in the days thereafter the church incident, never viewed the scenario as anything more than me being traumatized, in shock. His brooding anger kept him impulsive with reactionary reasoning in which he ultimately viewed me as a failure for not killing the beast that killed Laryn. He never accepted that there was more to what happened at the church than what he perceived happened; never really coming back to his rational way of thinking, so I didn't tell him about the pages. "It's nothing, just some random books."

"Who put them there? They weren't there the last time we were here." My father was keen to clue into the fact that someone in recent days had handled them. Having deported Marcus back to Australia, there was no way he would've been here, and it very well could've been Dr. Bishop. I was also aware that others may have been here too, following the same trail. The less our presence was known along this twisted path the better off we were going to be. Our chances of completing our own mission, whatever that had become over the past couple of years, were also higher.

"It could've been anyone," I said. "Judging by the notice on the door – appraisers, random people that know about the state of the manor who may be interested in its contents."

"Oh, come on. You don't actually believe that an appraiser or just some random person would specifically target this book to read in a dark manor in the middle of Essex, do you? No, I think not," my father answered his own question before I had a chance to do so. He closed the open book and tucked it inside one of his oversized pockets of his coat.

"What are you doing? The less people that know we were here –"

"And what of these? Witchcraft, curses…" he interrupted. "Three books won't matter all that much. Whoever was interested in them and what they were interested in is now of interest to me." He cradled the two other books under his left arm. From down the hallway, we could hear things crashing to the floor, followed by the wild hoots and clamor of Jinx who was now seeking attention in any fashion he could muster. "Besides, any hopes at secrecy have been lost with that ponce down the hall."

This was a point I couldn't argue with and the longer we allowed Jinx to act this way the more likely we were to run into an unwanted party. I still didn't like that my father had taken the books either. Both were evidence that we were here, which was something I desperately wanting to conceal. I sighed as I grabbed my gun and walked past my father towards the corridor. "Let's continue our sweep of the manor and get out of here."

My father said nothing more but didn't contest the notion of leaving. It was clear that he felt confident in having grabbed the books that the idea of coming out to the manor wasn't a total blunder.

It didn't take us long to make our way through the remaining parts of the ground level. Nothing more stood out as being out of place or even odd beyond the books in the den. The upper floor was much the same. Dust covered furniture, clothes still hung in the closet spaces, but nothing had moved since the last time we had been there. Nothing except the books. I too wanted to examine them further, but I couldn't discuss my purpose until I had read through the pages of Dr. Bishop's dairy and Marcus's journal again.

"Well, it's about fuck'n time you two ladies got done piss'n around upstairs," Jinx said as my father, and I walked down the grand spiral staircase that led into the foyer of the manor. He was leaning against the archway of the formal living area. Seeing that Jinx was not in compliance with anything that I had commanded, Snake had also taken it upon himself to abandon the outside watch in favor of complacency and sat in one of the nearby chairs with his gun resting across his lap.

"Goddamn it Jinx!" My father's voice was beyond irritation. "What in the hell is this? You're just lollygagging around when we needed you to be watching our backs?"

"Pay us more money and I'll be able to answer that for ya." Jinx moved from the archway towards my father. He stood facing Jinx directly, staring back. He shined his light on the books clutched tight under my father's arm. "Pay us more money and we'll go back to yer little game. Especially if we're going to come all the way out here fer books."

"More money –"

"This is not the time or place to discuss this!" I was equally as irritated as my father. Fortunately, the two of them had stopped their advances towards one another. Jinx turned from my father and continued to lean against the archway. Snake sat poised, unphased by the bickering back and forth between Jinx and my father. "Where's Kap?"

No one responded. I turned from the others and made my way into the parlor to find Kap still in position. His eyes were locked on the darkness outside. I moved closer and placed my hand on his shoulder. I felt him jump. "Shit!"

"Come on, we're leaving."

"I would swear there was something moving out there Grayson."

"Like what? What do you mean?"

"I don't know. Things, I guess. I see things in the dark. I try to fixate on them, but it is as though they're not there when I do. I see things – I can't trust my own senses anymore. It's the same every night. The darkness brings shadows and the shadows move."

I knew what he meant. I had felt it too, the shadows had eyes. They would appear to move without moving as though we had stepped into a world unbeknownst to us before Club Red and the church. Unbeknownst to the rest of the world who would only see it as insanity. I tapped his shoulder again. "Let's go."

No one in our party objected to leaving the manor and heading back to my father's estate. Despite being a quarter past three in the morning the spat between my father and Jinx continued. There was no holding back between either of them being in the security of my father's office. I sat at the far end and watched.

"You bloody ass!" My father stood face-to-face with Jinx in the center of the room. "Do you think that you can put us all at risk and then demand more pay? Piss off!"

"Might I remind ya, it's our weapons yer using. It's our man that's dead."

"And I have already given you his share per the terms of our agreement!" My father continued to yell. "I hired you so that you could kill the thing that tore my daughter to pieces! It's also the thing that killed your man!"

"Where is this beast, this so-called *werewolf*? Fer two years we watched ya fumble around and fuck up things. We're not going to just play *house* with ya fer the remainder of our days. Either ya pay us more or we go and let yer little secret out of the bag."

"You half-witted slimy piece of sh –"

"Enough." I got up from the seat and walked towards the center of the room where they were arguing. "Go. Take the money we gave you and leave. The world won't believe that a werewolf exists, especially if comes from you. Any attempt to slander my father's name will only be looked upon as opportunistic, so you're too late for that too."

"What in under fuck do ya think yer do'n. Ya better realize who yer talk'n to boyo."

"I'm fully aware of who I'm talking to, nothing more than Irish scrap."

Jinx shoved me with intense strength forcing me backwards. "Let's have a go then!" He quickly removed his coat, dropping it on the floor behind him. Jinx charged at me.

I pulled my Sig from its holster and pointed it directly at his face. He stopped and stared down the barrel. "Give me another reason! COME ON! GIVE IT TO ME!" I could feel my own anger boiling deep inside. I wanted to do it, I wanted to kill him. "I'll shoot you dead right here. The world won't miss you. You – are – nothing!"

Snake grabbed Jinx from behind and Kap stepped in front of the gun to stop the ensuing violence. I lowered it, but still held it tight. Jinx took a step backwards and shrugged Snake's arms from around him. "It's time to leave," Kap said looking over his shoulder at Jinx.

Jinx turned from Kap and grabbed his coat from the floor. "Come on. This place gives me the wild shits."

Both Snake and Jinx walked towards the doorway of the office. Snake stopped and looked at Kap. "Are ya coming?" he asked Kap.

"No…I'm staying."

Jinx walked in front of Snake. "Well, ain't this sweet. Ye fuck'n plonker. What, ye just go'n to stay around here and pet the puppies?"

"I have to see this one through," Kap responded.

"You fuck'n arse!" Snake said as he started to advance towards Kap.

Seeing the gun still in my hand, Jinx held up his hand against Snake's over-sized chest. "It's alright! Our day will come! And we'll remember ye not as a brother in arms but as a piece of shit beaten up in an English bucket." Jinx spit on the floor in front of Kap before walking out of the room.

Snake stayed behind a moment betrayal written in his eyes. "Are ya sure?"

"I have to know its dead."

Snake nodded, glanced at the floor as if considering Kap's last words. He looked at Kap one last time, nodded again before disappearing from the doorway.

A few moments past as I made sure that Jinx and Snake weren't coming back into the room in a fit of rage, guns blazing. I holstered my Sig and looked at Kap. "Why'd you stay?"

"The old biddies are hyped up off of money; neither of them realize there are more frightening things than being a piece of shit beaten up in an English bucket. They have never seen the beast; not like you and I have."

"You're not scared to continue going after these things?" I asked.

"Fuck yeah I am…I'm scared shitless. I haven't slept well in two years, constant nightmares – even when I'm awake I can still see it." Kap's breathing began to intensify as sweat formed across his brow. My father poured some whiskey into a glass and handed it to him. He nodded in thanks before shooting it down.

"I'm glad you decided to stay," my father stated as he took the now empty glass from Kap. His voice was still direct, although it was calmer now that Jinx wasn't in the room. "I can't pay you anymore money yet, but –"

"No." Kap shook head from side-to-side. "Its eyes – the teeth, the sheer thought of it. It's not about getting more money. Like I said to them, I have to know it's dead."

Chapter #4

12th of February 2012

I enter this text nearly a week after the attack on the camp. It came as a surprise. Their eyes were red, no other color. Very different from many of the other beasts we have encountered. There was more than one. They were not feeding. They killed just to kill and all of them had red eyes. No moon was seen in the sky, yet the werewolves were there as though it were. This confirms the suspicions we had about them. Somehow, they can harness their abilities and change into werewolves without the sway of the moon. Our only hope is that we discover something when we contact Robert Osborne in London.

Our suspicions started many years ago, but it wasn't until Hanover four months back when a man claimed that his livestock had been slaughtered in the night. This was evidence to support the claim. The full moon was not supposed to rise until the following week, yet the entrails were ripped from inside the animals and carcasses were left half eaten. Very characteristic of werewolves.

I stopped writing and grimaced with pain. My shoulder throbbed from the deep lacerations of the werewolf's claws. Gerda and Marlie sat across the aisle from me on the train to Brussels.

"Was ist falsch Ada?" Marlie had been watching me. Her question was innocent. Despite the horrors we had both witnessed she didn't understand the pain I felt as I made the new entry into the Grimoire. She was still learning English and only spoke it with brokenness.

"English! Use English. Nothing is wrong. I am fine," I scolded. I didn't answer her question, but after a moment I smiled warily to reassure Marlie that I was okay. "Remember the darkness can't put out your light…if the light comes from God." I could tell that she didn't believe me. Rightfully so, I wasn't fine, I was in terrible pain, and everything was wrong. We were surrounded by darkness. Red eyes of the werewolves cut through darkness every time I closed mine. Instead of asking anything else Marlie pulled her knees to her chest and nuzzled back into the fabric of her seat. Gerda just stared out the window, not looking at either Marlie or myself. I kept writing.

Local news stations and newspapers had a frenzy over it. Even though the wolf packs in Germany have only recently started to stabilize despite the over-populated areas, the papers still wrote it off as an unusual wolf attack which made national headlines. However, something very similar happened just north of Brunswick near the Ölpersee Lake a month later.

Residents nearby claimed their dogs had gone missing. It wasn't just one or two dogs, all the dogs in the region were gone. An unexplained missing person was reported in the news after the strange disappearance of the dogs only to be found later with his body dismembered and partially eaten. News reports classified the occurrences as the result of a deranged lunatic and only briefly mentioned the possibility of wolves.

Before arriving at Glindenberg, we learned of several small children that went missing just outside of Königslutter. They still haven't been found.

We should have been more prepared. I blame myself for the attack and that is why I have taken charge to translate the content within from German to English. It has become the way of the world and if our findings are to survive the way we have hoped, spanning the test of time, then this second copy must be in English. Among the deceased on 7th of February 2012
- Olis Klien -Confirmed
- Kyland and Monika Drederick - Confirmed
- Manny and Nadine Vogal - Not confirmed

– Audrick and Alika Huber – Not confirmed
– Ramond Metzger – Confirmed
– Garon Rothstein – Confirmed, Bitten, body was
burned...

The close memory of Garon's death and the loss of the others tormented me. A tear fell from my eye. I held Garon's body close to me throughout that night and into the daylight hours after he died. Not a single person came to the facility. It was truly abandoned. There wasn't much in the way of supplies, but we still managed to find some left over solvents to start a fire along with the scraps of paper and bits of wood lying around. We burned his body. *No way was I going to let the enemy have his skin,* I thought. Gerda hadn't said a word since, but merely nodded in agreement when I suggested going to London. Inside the Grimoire were several envelopes, one of which contained the login information to various bank accounts we had been using over the years. All it took was a Bankomat. Yet, I was cautious each time I used it. After the attack, I didn't want to draw any attention to the accounts should someone be monitoring them. There wasn't a lot of money in them, yet we had plenty enough Euros to get to London and buy some basics supplies such as bits of food, toiletries, a new coat for me and first aid necessities along with a few other odds and ends.

The gashes on my left shoulder continued to pulse with pain. We patched them the best we could and managed to clean the wound, but blood still seeped through the gauze pads and bandages. I kept my coat zipped up to hide the blood-stained sweater I was wearing. Movement in my arm was limited. Swelling caused portions of my arm to go numb and put pressure on nerves that made my fingertips tingle. The wound needed professional treatment and probably several sutures, but we couldn't risk going to a regular clinic or hospital. Furthermore, we weren't going to buy any international insurance policies to cover the cost of treatment. Our funds were limited, and it would lead to too much exposure. Gerda knew how to clean and suture wounds, which was going to have to be enough. *When we arrive at the safe house, we'll clean the wound again,* I thought. My hope was that the safe house that our group had established long ago was still useable, not compromised.

Most of our safe houses were nothing more than a room in a building within a remote part of a town. If they were not equipped with supplies, their locations were often near places to purchase supplies. They were safe because they were secret. I understood now why Gerda was so adamant about saving the book during the attack. The Grimoire listed the locations of all the safe houses that had been established and what could be expected upon arrival. The one that we were heading to in Brussels was nothing more than a self-storage facility. An access code was listed next to the detailed information about what was contained within and the hours of operation. Fortunately, we could access the storage unit twenty-four hours a day. It was set up for someone if they were traveling like we were and contained a couple weapons, medical supplies, a bed, and food. It was not meant for more than one or two people at a time.

Fortunately, no one was sitting in the seat to the right of me. It was odd given the time of the day and the popularity of the transit system. Nonetheless I took advantage of the time I had to compose the events that had happened. The train sped along the countryside of Germany at 320 kilometers per hour. It was comfortable, yet a little unnerving to be traveling as fast as we were. This was the first time I had been on an ICE train or any train for that matter. Most of the travel I had been accustomed to involved trailers and flatbed trucks. And in the eighteen years of my life, I had never been out of Germany. The padded seats were blue with overhead compartments to place luggage and carry-on items. Many of the passengers were napping, while others were reading books and newspapers.

We had caught the train at Berlin Hauptbahnhof. There was a brief stop in Koeln to switch trains before heading to Aachen for our last train change before entering Belgium. The entire trip was set to take just over eight hours and we weren't going to arrive in Brussels, Belgium until the early morning hours. This meant less people, less attention. *We need to rest for at least a day or so before moving on to London*, I thought. I paid no attention to the snow-covered landscapes as they passed by in a blur. Instead, I finished the entry in the Grimoire.

We need to link up with others that have been touched by the darkness. Gerda is old, frail and the last of our German speaking kin. Marlie is still too young, and I hope that one day she does not have to carry on this dreadful curse. I cannot do this alone.

-Ada Rothstein

I closed the book and tucked it back into the satchel. Inside the rucksack was the black pouch that Gerda stuffed in there before we were attacked along with a purse full of paper currency and some letters. Keeping it concealed within the satchel, I loosened the strings on the black pouch. Its contents were a dark powder with a tint of silver. *This isn't going to be enough*, I thought as I pulled the strings to tighten the opening and pushed it aside. Gerda's letters were opened and seemed to contain old photographs in addition to the handwritten letters. I made a mental note to look at them later when we had reached a safer place.

I pulled a piece of stationary from the sack of odds and ends that we had purchased. I wasn't about to walk right up to the home of Robert Osborne or even his place of employment. The safest way to communicate with him was through a letter. Though none of our other letters sparked any interest in what we were doing, this was truly our only hope. I placed the stationary on the seat tray in front of me and shook the pen I was using to start the flow of ink again.

Dear Robert Osborne,
I take an awful risk writing to you today as my brother once did. I know what killed your daughter...

CHAPTER #5

A Longshot
Grayson Osborne
Wednesday, February 15, 2012
5:30 a.m.

It was tough to see through the hazy darkness…candles flickered…shadows danced…distant howl…thumping of my heart echoed in my ears…the door was broken, splintered…the breeze from below kissed my face, neither warm nor cold…pool of blood…her torso lay still in the darkness…the howl was closer…A whisper…"It's coming for you Grayson."…snarling…the eyes of the dead open…a low growl…thumping of my heart…"Help me Grayson…Help me…" Green eyes in the darkness lunge with a snarl…

I sat straight up in bed. Sweat dripped down my face and I could still hear my heart pounding. I covered my eyes with my hand and breathed slowly, taking the air deep into my lungs to hold it for a few moments before releasing. Nearly every night I was haunted by dreams and was plagued with anxiety when I woke. Some nights it was Laryn lying there in the grass under the moonlight, dismembered, begging for help. Other nights it was Rex, taunting me. On really bad nights, I could hear them both. Eyes in the darkness remained the same and unnerved me more so than anything I had experienced in Afghanistan. I had seen my men shot, maimed, and blown to pieces. Nothing affected me the same as it did when I stared into the darkness and the terror within looked back. The death of Laryn and Rex, the beasts, and their eyes that cut through the darkness with sinister purpose, but most of all, the one with green eyes was the one I dreaded the most. The others were easier to understand. They were evil, easily identified and could be combatted. But not the green-eyed one. Relentless in her ferocity but controlled despite her wicked past and tormented being. *Why am I still alive? Why did I get to live?* I thought.

I hadn't gone into the office for the past two days. Dad mentioned that he had arranged for a few days off with Ashland Simmons. Books and papers littered my bed along with my tablet. I had fallen asleep searching for answers that had eluded me. Pushing them aside, I placed my feet on the cold wood floor. My room was dark, and the light had not yet begun to show in the sky. I switched on the lamp that sat on my bedside table. The holstered SIG Sauer P226, fully loaded with silver rounds, rested to the left of the lamp, ready to be drawn and used if necessary. Sweat continued to drip down my face. The perspiration soaked my shirt and chilled my body. I took it off and dropped it to the floor as I walked towards the lavatory attached to my room. A towel sat crumpled on the edge of the sink from the morning before when I had awakened the same. *Will this ever go away?*

I turned on the faucets and water poured over my hands. It was soothing. I splashed some on my face repeatedly and rubbed the nape of my neck. In the mirror looking back was a man that I didn't know anymore. He lacked confidence. Not so much in himself as a person but more so in the stability of his now fragile mind. I pressed my hands against the mirror frame and let my head dangle. Water still dripped from my face, but I paid it no attention. My eyes were closed again, and I continued to breathe deep, controlled breathes. I raised my head back up.

"Shit!" I stepped back with a start as my eyes glowed green against the dimness of the lavatory for a moment before returning to normal. Adrenaline rushed through my body and made me knees weak. I was no longer able to control my breathing. It was fast, acute, panicked. The vision of the beast passed. Leaning against the bathroom wall for steadiness, I rubbed my shoulder and down my arm where it was once cut and broken. Being startled by what I thought I saw in the mirror caused it to pulse with aches. *This is what Dad has been seeing too. It's all in our minds…all in our minds.*

I leaned forward again to splash more water onto my face. "Owe! Bollocks!" The water had gone from being lukewarm to scalding. I quickly turned it off and shook my hands before grabbing the crumpled towel. Though rumpled, the towel was cool and smelled refreshingly clean. I dried my hands and dabbed my face. I ran it over my hair and left it draped around my neck. My hands tingled from the scalding water. Gently, I rubbed them together alternating my palms over the backsides, then I paused and stared at them. *Burning… Burning…death by burning. Who though? When?*

I rushed over to my bed and sifted through the photocopied papers of Dr. Bishop's diary and then Marcus's journal notes. *Damn it! Where's that passage? Wait, it's not Marcus's journal*, I thought as I grabbed another stack of photocopies. "Where – are – you?" I whispered. "Come on, I know I saw you somewhere in these papers." I skimmed the pages, one after another, not concerned about keeping them in proper order. In fact, I simply let the papers fall to the ground alongside my bed.

"There it is! That's why the timeline in the book stood out!" In my hands was part of the account that took place after Dr. Bishop had been bitten by a werewolf and went into hiding.

As the legends have discerned, I shall be hunted such as those witches of old. The poor men and women accused of treachery, hanged, then dismembered and their bodies burnt. So many innocent people died. It has occurred to me that there have been and still are others like me.

Tormented and cursed, do they hide from the people of the world? Or are the damned, truly damned, only to come out during the moon's light to instill fear and suffering upon God's creatures? Yet how many were like me who met the fate they deserved? Is this my fate? Do I deserve to die or am I condemned to live with such an evil? For I am neither redeemed nor would I consider myself alive. My innocence and guiltlessness died along with my family only to be reborn as a demon, a true agent of evil. Though the days have long since passed that I shall be burned alive at the stake, but my neck would still be stretched at the gallows for what I have done. Should it come to pass that I am caught, there shall be no salvation for my soul. I must flee England to find the source of the legends and mythology, seek those that have knowledge of this curse...

Who are you searching for now? I thought. *Not Corbin. He's dead. Wait a second…he was ordered to die, but how?* I grabbed my tablet. Hurriedly, I tapped Corbin Paige's name into the search engine. Several results appeared of articles dated December of 2009 that recounted his death at the St. Teresa's Cathedral.

Titles such as *"London Club Owner Meets a Grisly End"* as well as silly links like *"Satan Returns to Church"* were among the many, but there was nothing about his ancestry. Nothing that was historic. *Come on, think! Who?* Several minutes past, then it hit me. *Corbin Paige was never sentenced to death, but the slave Kabona was.*

I adjusted my search and scrolled through several sillier postings until I came to the same small account that Codie had found two years prior. The short narrative gave a brief summary of the events that surrounded Kabona, but also had several related links to books and other research materials. One of which was a scanned PDF that I immediately recognized and followed. On the screen was the official statement ordering the death of the slave *Kabona* by way of burning to death at the stake, stamped 1753. "Gotcha!" I whispered. Unfortunately, the location of where he was held before his execution was too blurred to make out. One of the other related searches was the book titled, *British Monarchs* and was also one of the books taken from Dr. Bishop's estate. "My God. Dad was right. I need to look at that book."

I quickly dressed myself in one of my green army t-shirts, a pair of cargo pants and my boots. I had elected at that moment that I was going to spend the day focused on this. Anything else would pose too much of a distraction. *Dad certainly won't mind if I don't work, especially for this reason.* After strapping the holstered Sig around my waist, I made my way down to my father's study, carrying my tablet with me and Dr. Bishop's diary entry. The room was as dark as mine was upstairs. No fire burned forth against the chilliness as it usually did in the evenings. Each ember had turned to ash and lay cold atop the hearth. The books that he had taken from Dr. Bishop's estate now lay open on *his* desk. A Scotch glass sat empty on the edge of the writing space alongside a notepad with several bulleted inscriptions. I glanced over them. They made no sense, had no logical sequence, just ideas and showed that my father was just as lost in this ordeal as I was moments before my new epiphany. It didn't matter. I needed the book to verify what I thought I had found. His computer behind his desk had gone into sleep mode. I shook the mouse to wake it up. While it was loading, I laid my tablet and the diary entry atop the notepad and grabbed the book titled, *British Monarchs* that contained the timeline that interested me. As the computer woke back up, a soft glow filled the dim study. I sat in my father's chair and it let out a whooshing sound as I made myself comfortable. I typed:

Newgate Prison

Several *Wikipedia* search results came up along with other related topics. I wanted to find the prison registry. All prisoners were recorded into the registry at Newgate and any executions needed to also be registered with the church. It took several related searches before I finally found what looked like several scans of parchment that resembled both the Newgate and the church registries. Both lists were lengthy. Several minutes slipped by as I scanned the names looking for Kabona. It wasn't there. I turned to grab my father's notepad from under my tablet, but in doing so I bumped the empty Scotch glass. It tumbled from the top of the desk to the hard wood floor shattering.

"Damn it!" Before I could clean the glass, I paused for a moment taking in my surroundings. Footsteps could be heard in the open corridor just outside the room. Slowly, I pulled my Sig from the holster. The thumping of my heart drowned out the dull hum from the fan inside the computer.

"Who's there?" I whispered across the study.

"Oye…It's me mate." The silhouette of Kap emerged from the darkness and stood cautiously in the doorway. He too had his sidearm drawn and held it in both hands with the barrel pointing towards the floor. "What are ya doin' in here?"

I released my breath in a sigh as I re-holstered my gun. "Christ. Sorry…I bumped the Scotch glass…It broke…I guess I was a bit clumsy…not myself this morning."

"It's alright mate. Me too. I didn't mean to give ya a scare though. I just heard someone saunterin' about. When the glass broke…well, I thought I better check things out. Again, what are ya doin'?"

"Putting a puzzle together." I turned my tablet for Kap to see. He walked into the study as he re-holstered his gun too. I started to pick up the larger pieces of broken glass.

He stared at the screen for a few moments. "What am I looking at?"

"That's the official order of execution of *Kabona* the slave we have come to know as the late *Corban Paige*. Same one Codie found a while back. Unfortunately, the location of where he was being held was too skewed, so I was pulling up the registry for Newgate Prison to see if he was being held there and compared it to the church registry. No names match his on either registry. There's no record of him." I pointed to the computer screen behind me.

"Why are ya looking up stuff on his history? Didn't he get his head ripped off?"

"Yes, he did, but before his actual death, according to that document on my tablet he was ordered to die by way of burning at the stake in 1753."

"Why does that matter?"

I turned away from the computer and shoved some of the books that lay across the top of the desk. *British Monarchs* was closed but had a post-it note sticking out of the top that marked the page that it was opened to when we found in Dr. Bishop's den. No doubt from my father. "Look here." I pointed to the timeline. "This book was open to this page when we found it at the estate the other night. It says here that King Charles II abolished the practice of burning people at the stake in 1676. After some searching, I re-found the small account of Kabona and this official statement of execution we reviewed the night we went to the club. I didn't think much of it then. In fact, I wrote it off initially as a possible ancestor since Snake was able to track the lineage. After encountering Dr. Bishop at the club and then again at the church, I forgot entirely that *Corban Paige* may also have been the slave *Kabona*. General facts about everything, history included, simply disappeared from my mind in the wake of what we have experienced."

"So, yer say'n that he was ordered to be burned at the stake almost eighty years after the King's decree to abolish it and they still tried do it? Couldn't they have been executed themselves for going against the crown?"

"Yes!"

"Why would they do that? Ya know… risk being executed for one person."

"I don't know. But those set for execution would've appeared on a registry."

"He could've been held at one of the more rural prisons," Kap added.

"Very possible, but someone accused of his crimes and set to be executed would more than likely have been transferred to Newgate."

"Well…I don't know all that much about English history, given me Irish background. What I do know is that if he was a slave, they may not have written his name in the registry. They may have included him in an inventory list since slaves were property, but then why write an official order for execution?"

"It doesn't make sense." I thought for a moment before I continued. "Taking what we know, they could've been rural people, people that wouldn't have had access or even the ability to read the doctrines of the land. In their ignorance they may have been very afraid of Kabona for what they thought he did. They were labeling him as an agent of witchcraft. A more likely scenario, again given what we know, is that these people ordering his execution may have been hunting werewolves and knew he was going to change."

"If they knew he was gonna change, why didn't they kill him before the full moon?"

"Depends on who they were. My immediate guess would be to remain secret or something. If they had influence at Newgate Prison he certainly wouldn't have shown up on the registry, but they still had to follow the process of execution otherwise they might have been exposed. They probably thought the prison cell was going to hold him. Newgate, however, had a tremendous number of weak points. It had been expanded upon many times prior to Kabona being held there. He just found a weak point."

"Still a bit shaky, but I guess I follow…So now what?" Kap's question was honest and true.

"Unfortunately, we don't have Snake helping us find things in the databases like before, so we're going to have to try and track these things the best we can. I have a feeling that Dr. Bishop *was* at her manor and was also looking at this page. I believe she is also searching for those people. Here, read this." I handed Kap Dr. Bishop's diary entry. He took it and read the passage the best he could in the dim light. When he finished reading, Kap laid the entry down on the desk. "Dr. Bishop has been searching for answers too. My thought is that she wants to find the group of people who ordered the burning of Kabona. They may have answers to her curse. That's why all these books were on her desk at the manor. We find these people; we may find her."

"If they still exist." Kap couldn't be any more right. I nodded. The descendants of these people could've died off or been killed by werewolves a long time ago. "Something I don't understand though."

"What?"

"If these people hunt and kill werewolves, I can see how we could benefit from that, but I don't see why Dr. Bishop would want to find them. Wouldn't they just kill her on the spot?" Kap asked.

"I don't know. If it was her, then she must know something we don't. Equally as important is the notion of whether or not these people still exist. If they do, in what capacity?"

Kap thought for a moment as he paced around the room. He eventually made his way to one of the cushioned chairs in the study, seating himself down only to stare at the floor in front of him. I watched as he remained deep in thought. He finally looked back at me. "Do ya think these people know about us? Ya know…about the club and what happened at the church? There were enough people in there that night recording things on their phones. We've watched all kinds of videos online of that night. I mean the shit went viral for a while."

"Good question. But do you remember how things played out? The club classified it as a publicity stunt and then closed shortly after. And if you really think about it, how often do you trust the videos found online? Most people write them off as being doctored up in some way. Technology is too good for people to take these videos for face value," I added.

"That's true, but if these people were hunting werewolves, they certainly wouldn't dismiss something like that so lightly."

"I would think not, but why haven't we heard anything from them?"

"Maybe we have," he said as an obvious idea struck him.

"How so?"

"Consider this; How did we know that Dr. Bishop and Marcus Holland were communicating?"

"We beat him up after we caught him at Dr. Bishop's Estate." I wasn't sure where Kap was going with this, but I had come to trust in all his abilities. So, I let him continue.

"No, no, no. I mean, how did we know that he was helping her?"

"The letters!" we both said simultaneously.

"That's right," Kap reaffirmed. "If ya were going to communicate without being traced very easily in modern times, how would ya do it…ya would write a letter. Ya could drop it in any postal box without a return address. The only things that get mailed these days are greeting cards and bills. Working with the other blokes, we did similar things. In other words, if we wanted to stay *discrete*, we didn't send an e-mail or make a phone call. Too easy to track –"

"Shhh! Shhh!" I held my finger to my lips. We turned our attention to the doorway of the study. Footsteps again could be heard in the main corridor outside coming towards us. Both Kap and I had our hands readily positioned on our sidearms. The footsteps drew closer and into the study walked Henry, my father's executive assistant.

Henry raised his hand to his chest when he saw both Kap and I. "Sorry Sir. I didn't know you both were in here. I merely saw that the door open –"

"It's all right Henry." Kap and I released the handles of our sidearms. It appeared that all of us in the household were a little edgy. Henry turned from the doorway in order to maintain his polite mannerisms and not disturb our conversation any further. "Henry wait, you handle the post that comes to the manor, don't you?"

"Yes Sir." Henry paused and turned to face me again. "I do."

"This may sound strange, but have you noticed any handwritten letters in the past two years?"

"I've seen dozens of them Master Grayson. Were you referring to one in particular?"

"Any post without a return address?"

"Certainly. Why do you ask?"

I could see Kap glance at me from where he sat. A feeling of restlessness moved through me. "Do you know what was in these letters? I mean, did you get to read them?"

"Only a few Sir. Once I deemed them as personal correspondence between your father's colleagues and well-wishers pertaining to the tragedy that befell your sister, I simply left them for your father to peruse not wishing to pry."

"Does he still have the letters?" I asked. I stood from behind my father's desk and walked towards the center of the room.

"If he does, they're probably in the filing box with the unopened ones."

"Unopened?" Kap and I looked at each other, before I looked back at Henry.

"Uh yes...there were several letters your father never opened. I simply collected them and placed them into box for him to review later when he was feeling a bit more of a sound mind." Henry seemed cautious. I could tell that he was uncomfortable not being privy to the conversation that had occurred prior to his entry into the study. "Unfortunately, those letters are not here. I have the box stored at the financial office. You must understand Master Grayson, that your father was also getting these types of letters well after he had resigned from the House of Commons. Many were forwarded from his political office to the financial firm's office and never made it here to the residence. I do apologize if you were expecting something and it was lumped together with these other letters. I did not inquire about them with your father considering the heartache that he has been dealing with since the tragedy."

"No need to apologize Henry. You were simply being considerate," I reassured him. "I can certainly look through the box the next time I go into the office." I turned to face Kap who knew what I was thinking without me having to say it.

"Will there be anything else that you need Sir?"

I glanced over my shoulder at Henry. "No. Thank you Henry."

"Very well then. I shall set a pot to brew and lay a few things out on the table for breakfast. Both of which shall be ready by 6:30 a.m. sharp."

Henry nodded in my direction but gave no acknowledgment towards Kap. It was clear that Henry had never really warmed up to the idea of Irish Republican Army mercenaries living under the same roof as him. Even though most of the *barbarism* as Henry called it was caused and carried out by the two individuals that were no longer in the household, Kap was forever going to carry a lesser status in Henry's eyes.

More light poured through the window of my father's study. I walked over to it and looked out. The sky was relatively clear. Bits of light blue, mostly grey from the lack of daylight poked through the thin white clouds that appeared to be just above the tree line of my father's property. Yet, most of the landscape was brown, lifeless, and devoid of pending springtime colors.

"So, are we going to look through this box at the financial office?" Kap asked breaking the moments of silence that started after Henry had left. He stood next to me looking out the window.

"Yes," I replied facing him. "You know this is a long shot."

"Ya, but what else have we got?"

"Nothing…We have nothing."

Kap and I both left the study and headed for the breakfast area. My father was already in the eating space when we walked into the room. It was apparent that he too was preoccupied by his thoughts this morning as he sat at the table in a thinker's poise, holding his morning tea with an unopened newspaper in front of him. A couple of trays of bread, croissants and a few other pastries were next to a smaller plate of fruit in the middle of the white clothed table. As efficient as Henry was, he wasn't much for preparing a full English breakfast. Such tasks he considered beneath him. It mattered very little since none of us were too particular about what we ate. Most mornings I simply grabbed something on the way into the office or something quick such as what Henry had laid out for us from the cupboard. My father looked at me with an unsaid malice.

"Are you not going into the office today?" he asked.

"Yes, I am, but I'm not staying. I thought I might follow up on something."

He placed his cup of tea onto the table and steepled his fingers as he sat more upright in his chair. "Follow up on what?"

Kap was helping himself to the plate of pastries as he shifted his gaze back and forth between my father and I. "Henry mentioned that he had placed some letters addressed to you that had come from home as well as forwarded from the Commons after you had resigned from service. I would like to go through them."

"Those letters were merely well-wishers, people offering their condolences. Why do you want to look at them?"

"Have you opened and read all of them? Henry mentioned that many were unopened."

"Henry's right. I stopped reading them. Though they meant well, each one was like a sword to the heart. If a letter came into the office or was picked up here at home that looked like another person trying to make me feel *good* about what had happened, I felt it best that I just ignore them."

"I need to look at those letters. I have reason to believe that others may have experienced what we have and may have tried to contact us."

"Contact us? Who?"

"I don't know exactly. That's why I wanted to look at those letters. If anyone tried to contact us, they may've done so through a means that was less traceable."

"Are you sure about this?"

"No, I'm not. But we don't have anything else and from what I've read in Dr. Bishop's diary –" I tried to catch myself as I uttered these words, but they slipped out too fast.

"Stop! What diary? What are you talking about?" My father stood from the table and walked around to my side. I stood too. Kap leaned to the right as if he was expecting a physical altercation but said nothing to intervene. As my father and I came eye-to-eye with each other, his furrowed brow shadowed the resentment that filled his eyes. "Do you mean to tell me that you have something of Dr. Bishop's, and you have been keeping it from me?"

"Yes." I stood firm. My decision to keep it from him was nothing more or less than strategic. "I had copied her diary before giving it back to Marcus Holland."

"Goddamnit Grayson!" He slammed his hand down upon the table. Some of the undrunk tea spilled from his cup, staining the white tablecloth. "Is there *NO* end to your betrayal of me and this family? We could've learned so much more if you would've kept that book, but instead you gave it back to the very people who sought to destroy us! How could you do that to me?"

"I already said I had copied the whole thing. *HE* wasn't trying to harm us. The original book was better served in his hands." I wasn't backing down from my father.

"*Better* served – in *his* hands. How could you?"

"Yes...better served. You tortured him when his motivation was only to help. You have allowed your emotions to pervert your mind and have become just as bad as the beasts we're hunting!" My father took a step back from me as I stepped forward. "You have forced me to give up my command to hunt this thing and I did it with little complaint. I shot and killed two of the beasts that I had warned you might be there. I looked into the eyes of darkness and should have died, but here I stand. And I have worked tirelessly for two years reading and rereading those pages to *No* avail! NOTHING! If there was anything to report, I would have! According to her diary she was bitten! What else do you want to know? Perhaps that the years that followed only recount how she prayed, how she went to church to confess her sins every month before changing into that beast! She was hoping for redemption, but only found condemnation! If I wanted to betray you, I would've left you long ago to deal with this mess on your own! But again, here I stand, working for you still. So, you can shove that thought right up your ass!"

I turned away from my father. His fury provoked my already fragile state of mind and if we were to continue this line of communication, what little shred of the relationship we had would be swallowed by an enraged bitterness.

No one said anything for several moments. An uncomfortable silence set in on the room. Anger still burned in my father. It affected his thinking and poisoned everything around him whether he wanted to accept it or not. He was also not used to anyone talking to him in such a way. "Condemned or not, might I remind you that your sister is dead because of that maddened, uncontrollable beast."

"I know very well what Dr. Bishop did to Laryn. I think about it every day. Condemned, yes…maddened and uncontrollable are both things she is not, otherwise I *too,* would be dead!"

My father turned away from me and ran his hands through his hair in frustration. I could hear his heavy breathing. Codie happened to walk into the room providing my father and me a break from our bitter argument. My father seized the opportunity to redirect the conversation back towards his original inquiry. His voice was still low and gruff, "Why do you need to review my letters?"

"We found a clue that we want to follow up with," Kap interjected, also as an attempt to keep things more civil.

"I thought that you just said you had nothing." My father acknowledged Kap but turned to face me again.

"A clue, letters…what are you chaps talking about?" Codie asked as he reached for some bread.

"Morning Codie. We were reviewing some items that we had come across. Kap and I think we may have found something to follow," I said to Codie. I turned to face my father again. "Nothing stood out from her diary. It gave an account of how she became a werewolf and her travels thereafter. She was searching for anyone that could help her understand what she had become. It meant nothing to me, just a series of events, until we had found the books at her estate. You were right."

"You have Dr. Bishop's diary?" Codie was innocent with his question but had always fancied my father's notion of killing the beast and that anything of hers should be destroyed.

I gave Codie a commanding glance that suggested *not* to ask anything further. "Yes, I have a copy of her diary."

"How do the books from her estate relate to her diary?" my father asked.

"The book, *British Monarchs*, which was open had a timeline listed on that page that stated when certain execution practices in England were abolished. According to the account that Codie had found online about the slave Kabona, his official order of execution in 1753 by way of burning at the stake was almost eighty years after the practice had been abolished. Dr. Bishop's diary talks about the hangings and burnings of those accused of witchcraft. It also stated that she was seeking anyone who had knowledge of her curse. The only link we have to the book at her estate and her diary is Corbin Paige, also known as the slave, Kabona. Since he is dead and she was the one who helped destroy him, the only thing we can conclude is that she is seeking the descendants of those who had ordered the burning of Kabona."

"Just listen to yourself. You still think that she was helping you that night…and you say that I need to talk to someone." My father shook his head and paced around the table. Codie said nothing but continued to prudently listen to what was being argued. Kap followed suit, yet kept a closer eye on my father, his tight lipped, direct manner of speech and dominant posture. "I don't believe this. I don't *fucking* believe this shit. You realize that this could be her hunting someone else to kill. It could also be that this book on her desk was intended for another purpose entirely. It could be that it wasn't even her!"

"I *do* understand. There's clearly something we *all* don't know. But if these people do exist and have heard about our situation, they may have tried to contact us. As Kap pointed out to me earlier, if they wanted to stay secret, they weren't going to simply call us or send an e-mail. They would've left as little of a trace as possible. They probably would've sent a letter. There's no harm in checking."

This was a point that could *not* really be argued. Reviewing letters from the past posed a risk to no one.

"Fine, so be it." My father turned from us all and waving his hand in the air before walking out of the room. "You want to piss away your time, off you go."

"Can I tag along," Codie asked.

"Certainly." I sighed heavily. "Go get our coats and I'll see if Henry is available to drive to the office. We can't go on the tube with these strapped to us." I tapped the sidearm I had holstered.

Chapter #6

<pre>
Letters
Grayson Osborne
Wednesday, February 15, 2012
10:15 a.m.
</pre>

The skies remained pleasant as the three of us rode with Henry into the financial office. Given the middle of the work week there was a significant amount of traffic that swallowed a fair amount of time. Henry had informed us that the letters would be stored in two separate boxes in the back-storage closet and that they were marked with the labels that simply read:

Letters

No one said much of anything else, given the nature of the conversation over breakfast. Henry knew better than to pry. As outspoken and sarcastic as he was, Laryn's death had greatly affected him too. Once very strategic with political objectives and status, Henry's ambitions simply stopped when my father resigned from office. One could say that Henry had reached his political and career peak but didn't have the heart to abandon our family during these difficult times. Henry now took on a more somber, chastened approach to things, even the seemingly ludicrous pursuits of Dr. Bishop and anything that entertained the idea of a werewolf.

We stepped out of the car to air that was cold but dry. The sun shone brightly behind intermittent clouds that suggested nothing of rainfall. Behind the front desk at the office was Charlotte. The time was 10:15 a.m. but she was still scurrying about copying and readying things for the day. She was a little taken aback to see me come into the office later than normal, dressed how I was and accompanied by Codie and Kap, who typically stayed away.

"Good morning Charlotte." I kept my voice calm and polite. Also making sure not to expose my sidearm to her. "Any calls or any news?"

"Your father had called, Sir and…he stated that he won't be in until later this afternoon and mentioned that you'll only be here for the morning. Mr. Simmons inquired as to when you might be in and he is in his office. He's handled most of the phone calls over the past two days, so you might want to inquire with him about any particular clients that you may have been expecting to call."

"Thank you. We'll be in my office for the time that we are here. Please hold all calls for me please."

"Um, very well Sir." Our presence was suspicious, and Charlotte's reaction was genuine.

We found the filing boxes easily and brought them into my office closing the door behind us. Before I could say anything both Kap and Codie dumped the contents of the boxes onto the surface space of the cabinets along the wall and began sorting the letters into piles of ones that were already opened versus those that were unopened. I took the liberty of reading the opened ones first. Skimmed them mostly. If anything was of importance it would've stood out to me. Once finished, I merely placed them off to the side in a separate pile. Codie and Kap began opening and reviewing the other letters placing them in the same pile as the one I had started. Despite only having two boxes to go through, there were hundreds of letters. Some were sympathy cards whereas others were formally typed on official letterhead.

Most were from my father's colleagues and special contributors to his political party. All of them were well intended, deeply sympathetic to the horrific events that transpired with Laryn. It was moving to see how many people had expressed their condolences out of admiration and respect for my father, not for his political agendas. A twinge of guilt spread through me over the argument we had had this morning. I understood why he stopped reading these letters, but more importantly I understood the pain he felt and his conviction to see this evil banished. My father was ambitious, and these well-wishers gave credence to his character as a man, yet his ambitions weren't in the right place anymore. Several minutes slipped by as we meticulously searched through each letter. No one spoke. The sound of shuffling papers and the tearing of envelopes filled the room.

"Grayson, I think I found something. Tell me what ya make of this." Kap handed me a letter that was handwritten. The letter read:

19th of February, 2010

Dear Mr. Osborne,
It is with the deepest sympathies that we have learned about the loss of your daughter. Darkness surrounds us all. We take an awful risk reaching out to you. We would like to offer our support to your cause. Please respond to us by letter at the address listed below in order to keep the correspondence active.

P.O. Box 200150
04831 Eilenburg
Germany

"Bloody hell. Kap you were right." I looked at him awe stricken by the letter. "There's no signature at the bottom…was there a return address?"

"No. Just an international postal stamp that designates it was sent from Germany. More importantly, I found another one with the same handwriting, same kind of message, but a later date. Take a look."

12ᵗʰ of November, 2010

Dear Mr. Osborne,
*   It has been nearly a year and we have not been able to establish some correspondence with you. We are deeply sympathetic to the loss of your daughter. Darkness surrounds us all. We would like to offer our support to your cause. We take an awful risk reaching out to you. Please respond to us by letter at the address listed below in order to keep the correspondence active. If we do not hear from you by way of letter, this will be our last attempt to make contact.*

P.O. Box 200150
04831 Eilenburg
Germany

"Shit. I assume that this one didn't have a return address either?" I asked.

"No, it didn't," Kap responded.

"Do we have anymore unopened letters?"

"Yah, I got a whole stack of 'em over here." Codie held up a thick bundle of letters.

"Good. Let's try and match the handwriting from these letters to any unopened addresses. Even though this later letter states this would be their last attempt to contact us, they still may have sent another letter."

A knock on the door broke our conversation. "Grayson?"

"Damn it, Simmons," I whispered. Both Kap and Codie sifted through the unopened letters, each holding one of the unnamed letters to compare the handwriting to the addresses written on the outside of the envelopes.

"Got something!" Codie pulled an envelope from the stack and laid it down on the counter. The handwriting didn't match, but there was no return address and the international postal stamp showed it was mailed from Brussels, Belgium.

"Well done Codie!" He handed me the letter:

Dear Robert Osborne,

    I take an awful risk writing to you today as my brother once did. I know what killed your daughter. She was taken by the darkness. I too have lost so much to the darkness and seek now your help. My team has fallen into a dire situation, and you are the only one who can understand my plight. Come to the address listed below. There you will get further instructions. Please be careful, the darkness surrounds us all.

6 Hall Rd
London NW8 9PA
United Kingdom

-AR

"There's no date on this letter…what's the postmark date?" I asked Codie who was still holding the torn envelope.

"12th of February, 2012. Christ it was mailed this past Monday."

"All right, you two work on pulling up that address online. We need to know how far away it is, everything around it, so we can prepare. I'm going to go out and meet with Simmons. I'll be back in a moment."

Cautiously the door to my office opened and Ashland poked his head inside. "Grayson, I thought I heard your voice in the office." He glanced at Codie and Kap, then back at me. "Um, is there something wrong Grayson? Anything I can help with?"

"Uh, no...let us speak in the hall," I said as I guided him back. My attire was certainly not to his standards and the odd manner in which the letters were strewn across the countertop was cause for concern. I closed the door behind me and looked at Ashland. A troubled look spread across his face. "We can speak freely now."

"It's your father isn't it?" Ashland asked before I had a chance to explain.

"Uh, yes." I wasn't sure what he was getting at, but I was well trained in using bits of information that people gave me to cover my tracks and lead them down whatever believable path I felt they should go. "He has not been well."

Ashland sighed, "I know, I spoke with him on Friday over tea. He expressed concerns about Codie and the fact that he was not enrolled at university. Have the three of you talked about other pathways for Codie? Perhaps something more military oriented?"

"Yes, we actually had a good conversation this morning about our next steps." I chuckled to ease Ashland's worry, but more so by the ironic opportunity to not have to lie entirely. "I told Codie that he should tag along with me for a while in order to *learn* a few things."

"And the papers strewn across the counter? Anything I can help with?"

"Oh, that's for dear old dad. *Letters* to be precise. He was feeling a bit emotional this morning and was concerned that he may have missed a few letters that were mailed to the office. Well-wishers after the tragedy with Laryn. I said that I would search for the any letters that were unopened and make sure the proper correspondences were made."

"Ah, I see. Well, then I won't pry any further. I know how difficult it has been for your father as well as for you and Codie. Please, take as much time off as you need to get things sorted. I'll manage things here while you're on holiday."

"Thank you, Ashland. You're kind." We shook hands and nothing further was said. He merely turned from me and walked down the short corridor to his office. I took several deep controlled breaths in the hopes of lowering my heart rate. Reading the letters from these unknown people filled me with a terrible anxiety. Everything about them suggested caution and I wasn't about to rush off blindly into a scenario that could be potentially dangerous like the one in the club and especially the scenario at St. Teresa's.

Kap was on my computer and Codie stood behind him looking over his shoulder when I re-entered my office.

"Mate, yer not going to believe this."

"What?" I asked as I walked around my desk to view the screen.

"The address *AR* listed… is right here in London."

"Bollocks!" I sighed.

"What…I thought that would make ya happy." Kap was genuinely dumbfounded.

"No, it's that…we're going to need to move quickly on this one. We can't wait and we don't have a lot of time to prepare. Let's have a look at the address."

"What I've been able to pull up is this. It looks like a storage facility, Fort Box Storage, St John's Wood."

"Storage? As in Fort Box *Self*-Storage?"

"Appears so. Pretty nice area. Couple of tube lines nearby, lots of bus routes, mostly residential, flats and the like. Possibly a few corner markets maybe a café or two. We can approach from the south, but we'll both be exposed with this being the only entrance. They might have one in the back, but I won't be able to keeps eyes on you. Might be better if someone approaches head on from the south, while the others keep eyes from up top here." Kap pointed to a balcony that was above the facility. "If I'm watching from above, I'll lose ya as soon as you enter."

"I'm going with you two," Codie asserted.

"Are you sure." I glanced in his direction. "Remember you don't have to hunt these things."

"Yes, I do Grayson. The last time you said that you were nearly killed."

"All right with that, Kap?" He nodded in confidence. "It's settled then. The three of us will go. We're going to keep light though, looking glasses and sidearms only, .45s with silencers, concealed. I want the knock-down power, but I don't want to draw attention to us. You both know how London police are and there also may be *others* watching."

Chapter 7

Touched by Darkness
Grayson
Friday, February 17, 2012
8:00 a.m.

"Codie, are you in position?" I asked as I held the PTT on the in-line mic that I was wearing. Henry had dropped us off a few streets away from the storage facility. We rode in an unmarked cargo van that my father purchased a few months after the church incident. I figured that we would be able to put any logo we wanted on the outside of it if we needed to blend in with the populous. More importantly it gave us the freedom to carry weapons into an area without worrying about taking the tube or a bus.

"All set Grayson. I got eyes on you about fifty meters back in the thicket across the road. I can see all the way up to the entrance," Codie responded.

Though the day was clear and bright, there were several recesses behind the buildings that could lead to an ambush. I walked towards the south entrance of the storage facility. I was cautious.

"Kap, all set?"

"All set. I see ya approaching. I'm on the balcony to yer left along the rail."

"Do you have eyes on Codie?"

"Copy that, I see him."

The road leading up to the storage facility was wide but sloped into a narrow entrance. Both Kap and Codie could cover my position as I approached. Codie's main duty was to watch me all the way into the building then proceed to follow behind me, keeping a fair distance. In the event of an ambush, he would be my first responder. Once I was inside, Kap's duty was to cover Codie's approach. I was worried for Codie. Each time I had gotten close to the monsters, I was met with danger and tragedy, but I trusted Kap implicitly. His position gave him the advantage of having his back to the building so he wouldn't be ambushed from behind. We had to stay in close proximity of each other since we were using firearms that couldn't kill from a distance.

I was fortunate that the building had clear glass walls and doorway. I could see directly into the main service area. The cargo bay for loading larger storage items was open. Several small 2' x 2' storage units were visible. No patrons were inside. One individual wearing a blue company shirt sat behind the registration desk. A television was mounted behind the desk on the blue wall and was set on a news station. Another screen was mounted to the left of that one and showed nine smaller feeds from the various cameras that were mounted throughout the facility. Everything was clean and in its proper place. Nothing appeared out of order. The gentleman looked up from his workstation as I entered the building.

"I'm starting my approach," I heard Codie say through my earpiece.

"Copy Codie. All clear behind ya," Kap responded.

"Good day Sir. Is there something I can help you with?" The gentlemen smiled.

I returned the smile as best as I could. I felt more reassured that Codie wasn't far behind and could easily see inside and that Kap was also watching over him. "Yes, I hope so. I have a bit of an odd question." The man walked from behind the desk with his arms crossed in front of his waistline, maintaining his smile, and leaned forward with intent on listening. His hair was silvering, older but not too old. He was short with a pouchy stomach, possibly a manager. Didn't matter much. "Do you perhaps have a storage unit under the name, *Osborne?*"

"I can certainly check the name in the system, but I cannot give you access to any of the storage units without proper identification and written release from the unit renter granting you permission." I nodded in agreement and the gentleman returned to his workstation.

I glanced over my shoulder and noticed that Codie was leaning on the wall just outside of the entrance. He had one knee bent with his foot pressed against the wall, pretending to just enjoy the bright sunshine while he looked at his cell phone. I stood in front of the registration desk and turned my attention back to the gentleman helping me. "Anything?"

"Is the storage unit large or small?"

"I would suspect that it is small." I really didn't know. Whoever AR was stated that we could pick up information at this location and passing along information didn't require a large unit.

"Ah, there it is." The man smiled to himself. "Do you have identification?"

I took out my ID card and slid it across his desk. The man took a glance at it, registered the number on the card before he handed it back to me. "Do you need anything else from me?"

"No. There's a note in the system already that has granted you permission to access the unit. I'm just making another note of when the unit was accessed in order to communicate it to the renter. Just a moment Sir and I'll get the key for the unit."

I stood away from the desk and strolled around the service area. Codie looked in on me and he raised his hand to his ear. A moment later I heard his voice.

"So far everything is quiet. How's it look from up there Kap?"

"All is clear. Has Grayson made contact?" Kap asked. I gave Codie a nod that everything was ok.

"He's made contact. He's waiting."

"Mr. Osborne. I have your key here." I turned to face the gentleman that was helping me. In his hand was a white key with a number printed on it. "Your unit is number 017. The unit is just inside the cargo bay, on the bottom in the far corner."

"Thank you, Sir," I responded as I took the key from him.

"Is there anything else that I can help you with at the moment?"

"No, that'll be all." I glanced in Codie's direction again and motioned with my head where I was going. He interpreted it correctly as I heard his voice through the earpiece, *"Standby. Grayson is accessing the unit."*

"Copy that," Kap said.

"I'm giving you two minutes at the unit Grayson before I'm coming in." I nodded toward Codie again in acknowledgement. The unit was exactly where the man stated it would be. A small latch with a padlock was located along the right side.

A corridor continued on to the left which housed several larger storage units. No one was in the corridor or in the cargo bay with me. Cameras were mounted at either end of bay that recorded all activity of the units. I pressed the PTT. "Okay, I found the unit. No one is here but me."

I slid the key into the designated spot on the padlock. The lock popped open and I slid the metal latch to the left. I wasn't sure what I was going to find as I pulled open the 2' x 2' blue door. Slowly, I peered around the edge of the small door to find only a letter that was labeled:

Osborne

"I have the contents of the unit and I'm heading back out." I grabbed the envelope, closed, and relocked the door behind me.

"Copy that," Codie said.

Back in the service area, I handed the key to the service clerk and thanked him again. Before leaving I noticed the man behind the desk turned his attention to the news feed on the television. I paused, taking in the same report. The reporter was interviewing a stately woman outside of Club Red.

"Can you explain why the Met has issued a movement to condemn this abandoned building formerly known as the popular night spot, Club Red?"

"We have seen an increase in recent days of vandalism and several break-ins have been reported by some of the local business owners. In order to effectively service this district, we felt that issuing

this decree on this building and a few others in the area, might deter miscreants from using them as places to hide before and after the crimes have been committed. It's also our plan to have some much-needed upgrades to the camera system in the area."

"In other news…"

My thoughts raced as I stood awe-stricken by the news report. We hadn't been back to the club since Kap and I first entered in pursuit of Dr. Bishop. There was too much attention surrounding that club in the months that followed St. Teresa's Cathedral for us go anywhere near the building. I could feel my heart pounding and my nerves unraveling at the memory of what happened inside the club. I saw her change that night, change from innocence to savagery. I saw the furious monster she contained.

"Damn shame if you ask me." Snapped back to reality, I looked at the gentleman. "They should've put another business in there a long time ago. Something less rambunctious or they should've torn the building down. Vandalism and break-ins this close to this area does bad things."

"Yeah… I agree. Thank you again Sir. Try to have a good day."

"You too Sir. Thank you." I didn't acknowledge his response and continued to exit the building. A light breeze had kicked up into a heavier wind. The trees swayed and creaked as their branches rubbed together. *Something's not right*, I thought. Images of the green-eyed beast flashed into my mind, causing me to close my eyes for a moment as I walked. I could tell that Codie noticed something was wrong with me, but remained against the wall, waiting until I passed him before deciding to follow.

"We're coming up the road, Kap. Fall in behind us," I said.

"Follow'n behind. I've got eyes on ya both." Kap's words echoed as if bouncing off the walls of a tube tunnel. People appeared odd in front of me. They took notice of us and stared. I couldn't tell if they were reacting to how I was now behaving or if my mind was losing its grip on reality. *Can they see my*

nerves, my fear? Can they tell that I'm hiding something? I've been made! I shook my head a couple of times to rid the feeling. No good. A low snarling growl was getting closer. It was coming for me. Sweat dripped down the side of my face as I crossed Hall Road and moved away from the storage facility. Everything began to spin. The growl was closer as I stabilized myself against a wall along the walkway. The eyes of people glowed green against the now dim, overcast sky. They were coming closer.

"Grayson. Grayson. Are you all right?" Codie had caught up to me at the wall on Hall. Kap wasn't too far behind. I breathed heavy and wiped the sweat from my face. He had his hand on my shoulder. The sky was clear blue with thin, scattered white clouds. No one was looking at me except Codie. No green eyes and the breeze had returned to normal.

"Yah, I'll be fine." I continued to take slow, controlled deep breaths. Codie didn't believe me. I could see it in his crumpled brow and slightly agape mouth.

"Are you sure?" I swallowed and nodded closing my eyes one more time as I breathed deep. "Alright then...What did you get in the storage unit?"

"Not here," I told Codie. "Walk a bit further down Hall."

Codie didn't question anything. Instead, he crossed over Hamilton Terrace and sat down on a bench next to a bus stop about forty meters away. He pretended to be looking at his phone again. I motioned to Kap with a head nod to follow us. Kap and I had learned to be very cautious, and this situation warranted this behavior. We caught up to Codie.

I held up the envelope. My anxiety was subsiding, but not gone. "Odd. This was all I found." I tore it open. Inside the envelope was a map with three spots circled and three separate times listed across the top. All of the markings were done in distinct colors. "Just a map, no names...but look at these markings."

I lowered the map for both Codie and Kap to see. "What do you make of it?" Codie asked.

"I think they want us to go to one of these locations." Kap pointed to the three circles. "Look here at the times."

"You're right, that's why they're in different colors too." I looked at my watch. "It's 8:25 a.m. The first time listed here in yellow is 9:00 a.m."

Codie took the map from me and looked closely at it and then looked all around. He did this a couple of times. "Grayson this is a map of *this* area. Look here." He pointed. "We're standing here on Hall and it looks like the location circled in yellow is just around the corner and down Maida Vale Road. I think there may be a café there."

"All right, we go. We've gotta move fast too. Stay focused. Keep it staggered, but close. Always within visual. Kap you take the lead. They may know who I am and possibly Codie since the envelope was addressed to *Osborne*. However, there's a very good chance that they *don't* know you. So, if you're already at the location when we arrive, they won't even know your there. They'll be too concerned about Codie or I. Watch for anyone that stares too long at either of us or is looking very nervous. Like I said yesterday, we may have more of an audience than we think."

"I'm sold! Clock's tick'n mates. Let's move." Kap proceeded to walk further down Hall Road.

Codie waited a couple of minutes and then looked at me. "Sure you're all right?"

I merely nodded and motioned to Codie to follow Kap. "Off you go." I waited a few minutes and followed behind. I kept Codie in my line of sight at all times. The sunlight felt warm upon my face and helped to ease my tension but couldn't break the thought that we were in danger.

Two blocks down on Maida Vale Road a café overlooked the Regent Canal. The entire walk only burned about fifteen minutes. Kap was already at the café sitting at one of the outside tables with a to-go cup in front of him. I watched Codie walk a little past the café, stop and again pretended to be on his phone. He looked in both directions before walking across

Maida Vale Road. I stopped walking just before the café and stood next to the bus line stop. All of us were in position.

"See anyone Kap?" Codie asked still pretending to be talking on his phone.

"Negative."

"Stay where you are Codie. You're in a good spot to cover both of us and I can see you clearly." I released the PTT and watched Codie lean against the limestone wall of the Natwest building.

Several people walked past the café or rode bicycles along the walkway despite the coolness in the air. The red buses made it difficult to get a fix on any one person that was moving. Perchance this was the reason I was able to spot her. A young blonde woman had walked down Aberdeen Plaza towards the café but stopped and leaned against the backside of a telephone booth. She checked her watch once and continued to stand. While everyone else was walking about there she remained, not trying to go anywhere or buy anything, just oddly standing.

She hadn't noticed Codie or me, but was in fact staring in the direction of Kap. My watch read 9:02 a.m. and I pressed the button on my earpiece. "Kap, your twelve o'clock, Codie your ten o'clock…the blonde, she's been standing in that same spot for nearly five minutes and hasn't moved."

"I've got her. What do you want me to do?" Codie asked. Kap was smart enough not to respond since he noticed she was looking more in his direction.

"Nothing yet. Let's see what she does. She may be no one, but she may also be dangerous."

We all watched for another minute. The young woman made a slow sweeping motion with her head as if looking for someone or something. I tried to keep my gaze low, but she had picked up something odd about me. It may have been my nerves resurfacing or the fact that in my distraction of her presence a couple of buses had stopped and moved along without me climbing aboard. Her eyes met with mine from across the street, she locked on to me and before I could cover my presence, she took off running in the opposite direction.

"I've been made! She's running!" Kap quickly stood from his small table and ran close behind Codie who was chasing after this woman. I was only a few paces behind them. Codie followed by Kap turned right down Lyons Plaza Road chasing after the woman. I too was at a full sprint as I rounded the corner. Ahead of us by several meters was the young woman. She looked like an Olympic sprinter and was equally as fast. She had cleared two blocks before ducking through an open gate to the right into what appeared to be an industrial area just past a hand car wash business.

"Stop!" I said to Codie and Kap. Both were out of breath.

"Bloody hell she's fast. She went through there." Codie pointed to the open gate. Behind the gate was a wide space where several cars were parked, most of which looked in need of repair. The warehouse on the far end of the lot bore the sign *Paint & Bodywork Repairs*.

"My guess is that she's in there." Kap gestured to the warehouse. "This is a closed lot, a dead-end unless she went inside."

"Right. Kap see if there is another way out on the other side. Codie and I are going into the warehouse through that door." Three stories up, the fire escape door appeared to be unlocked and partially open. The other cargo doors were closed with oversized padlocks on them, except one. "Be careful. Don't draw your weapon unless you have to. We don't know who we're dealing with yet and we also don't know if anyone reported us chasing her. The last people we need involved are the authorities."

"Right, I'm on it." Kap hustled to the end of the block and turned right, around the corner of the fence.

"Come on," I said to Codie. "Draw your weapon once we're inside. Keep your eyes open and mind your backside."

Inside the only cargo bay door that was open, a man was working on a vehicle, but was too involved in buffing the paint off of a car to notice Codie and me. We shifted across the lot of damaged cars and up the fire escape. At the top, I motioned to Codie to stay quiet and to follow behind me as I gently nudged the door open. Inside there was a small hall that led to the right. In front of us was another door that was open, which led into a space that contained many boxes of car parts and equipment. By the sound of the grinding metal below us, most of the car repairs were being done on the first and second levels, leaving this third floor strictly for storage. With two fingers I directed Codie down the hall and drew my .45 ACP Sig P220. I made sure the suppressor was attached properly and that there was a round in the chamber. Codie did the same before maneuvering down the hall and through another door at the end.

The boxes of car parts and equipment formed a maze through the storage room. There were lots of places to duck and hide. Towards the center of the room, I could hear frantic whispers between the cutting and grinding of the body shop below us. I moved in that direction, cautious of what and who I might find.

"I'm coming up the same way as you and Codie. There's no way out of the space on the other side," Kap said into my earpiece.

This woman could easily double back on us, but she'll run into Kap. I thought. The whispers were no longer whispers. Instead, they sounded more like whimpers the closer I got. I crawled behind several large boxes and crates so that I could flank the position of the sound. Crouching along the floor, I judged that the whimpers were coming from the other side of the crates in front of me. With a quick motion, I stood and spun around the edge of the crates, pointing my gun in the direction of the whimpers. An elderly woman sat against the crates holding a young girl that I would wager was no older than five. I took a step closer, still holding my gun out in front. Fear was *not* present on the face of the elderly woman. She stared back at me with a piercing blue eye. The other was grey and I assumed was blind. The blonde woman was nowhere to be seen. I breathed out with a quick release of air. *She must've doubled back,* I thought again as I turned to retrace my steps. I stopped with the sound of a clicking mechanism and the barrel of a gun pointed at my face. It was held by the blonde woman.

"The gun. Drop it!" I held my hands in the air still holding my sidearm. "*Jetzt!*"

I didn't speak German, but I was familiar enough with it to understand that when she yelled '*Now*', she meant it.

"All right…I'm putting it down." Slowly I dropped to one knee in order to place the gun on the floor. I made a point to keep my hands in the air. Her eyes were fiery, fearless.

"Hold out your hand!" she said and pulled a small black pouch from her belt.

"Why?"

"DO IT!" she yelled. I slowly extended my hand but pulled it back before she could do anything. "I will not hesitate to shoot you dead!"

"Not before I kill you first." Codie had appeared behind the blonde. His gun was pointed directly at the back of her head. "You drop your gun."

The blonde lowered her weapon to floor as I started to stand. With a quick motion she dropped the black pouch and spun rotating her left arm over Codie's blocking his gun, which she followed swiftly with a stiff ridge-handed strike with her other arm to the side of his face. I charged at the blonde only to run directly into a back fist that split my lip wide open, causing me to stumble backwards. She swept Codie's legs forcing him to fall to his back with a crash. She twisted his right arm against his elbow joint and locked it in a way that pointed his own gun at his face. I regained my footing but stopped again as I saw how vulnerable Codie was. Her shin and knee were pressed hard against Codie's neck as she held his right arm twisted and tight.

"The pouch! Pick it up!" The black pouch was on the floor in front of her and Codie. I reached for it, careful not to upset her any further. The young girl continued to whimper in the elderly woman's arms. Blood trickled out of the left sleeve of the blonde's coat and dripped off the back of her hand as she struggled to hold Codie in place. "The powder…put your finger into it!"

"Why?" I asked a second time.

She pointed the gun just to the left of Codie's head and fired. The silencer made a distinct click as debris splintered from the floor. She pointed the gun back at Codie's head and twisted his arm even tighter. "DO IT!"

"Okay. I'm doing it." I stuck my finger into the black pouch. "Now what?"

"Place it to your tongue!" she responded.

"What?"

"I'm not going to ask again! Now do it or the next shot will be in his head!" I pulled my finger from the pouch. The tip of it was covered in a grayish black soot of some kind. Codie struggled under the pressure of her knee. I touched my darkened fingertip to my tongue. Immediately, I was met with an awful metallic taste which caused me to spit it out on the floor repeatedly. "DOES IT BURN?" she yelled at me. I continued to spit. "DOES IT BURN?"

"No…No it just tastes awful! What is this? Who are you?"

She ignored my questions. "Get on your knees!" she demanded.

"You better answer his questions first, lass." Kap was standing a few feet behind the blonde. His gun was drawn and pointed at her. He clicked the hammer of his gun. "A .45 mm at this range will blow your *fuck'n* head clean off and no one will hear me do it. Trust me, I don't mind shooting you in front of grandma and the little one, either. I have shot things much worse than you. Now stop threatening my mate and let the lad up."

The blonde released her hold on Codie's arm and stood. Blood continued to drip from her left hand. I grabbed my gun from the floor and wiped the blood from my mouth. Codie labored to his feet. A dark red lump had formed just above his left cheek bone where she hit him.

"Now who are you? And we're not going to ask *you* again." She remained silent despite the fury in my voice.

The young girl broke from the grasp of the elderly woman and ran to the blonde wrapping her arms around her waist. "Don't hurt her!" Tears rolled down the girl's face. "Don't hurt Ada!"

"Ada? What's your last name?"

She placed her hand on the back of the young girl's head to soothe her. Her eyes were filled with a ferocity that rivaled mine. "Rothstein," she finally said. "My name is Ada Rothstein."

I lowered my gun and so did Kap, but still gripped it tight with both hands. Codie looked at me then at Kap.

"You're 'AR', aren't you?" I asked.

A few moments passed and I could tell that she was calculating her next move. "*Ja.*"

"Are there any more of you?" Kap looked around the storage area, prepared if someone tried to attack us.

"No. Just us. We are all that's left. This young one is Marlie. That is Gerda." Ada pointed to the elderly woman who was still looking at us with cautionary eyes. "If you are going to kill us, then do it fast. We have suffered enough."

"There are days I have felt the same." I re-holstered my sidearm. "My name is Grayson Osborne. The younger fella who you seemed to have made friends with quickly, is Codie and the shy one back there is Kap." Kap gave me a two-fingered salute and a sarcastic nod. "We're not going to kill you. We got your letter and came looking. I'd hoped there would be more of you."

"I had hoped the same from you. My team was ambushed. That is why I had to do what I did, you know…with writing the letter to Robert and all." Her face almost turned to sadness, her blue eyes glassy and tearful. Underneath her strong exterior, was someone who had been touched by the darkness too. She was young and they were at a point of desperation. Dirty, tattered clothing, wounded, and scared.

"The pouch. What is it?" Codie asked. He was still rubbing his neck from where Ada had pushed her knee.

"It has silver nitrate in it. If you were a werewolf, one touch of it to your tongue would have burned you very bad."

I looked around the storage area. Small bags, food wrappers and bits of tattered clothes were placed off to the side. They had clearly been staying here, hiding. "We can't stay here. It looks like you've got a pretty good wound. It's going to need treatment. We can help."

"I will be fine. I just broke the stitches. No need for hospital, just a clean bandage," Ada said as she helped Gerda to her feet.

I nodded at Ada and turned towards Codie, "Call Henry. Tell him to pick us up. Make sure he doesn't tell dad we found them. I don't quite know how he's going to react."

CHAPTER 8

Red-Eyed Werewolf
Ada
Friday, February 17, 2012
6:00 p.m.

My wounds seeped and bled as the hot water rushed over them. It turned the water a light pink. I closed my eyes and let the soothing power of the shower wash away the days of dirt and sweat. We had arrived earlier in a district known as Hertford. We had never been to London or any of the regions of England. Gerda, Marlie and I had agreed to share quarters on the second floor of the manor that they had taken us to. It was a little cramped with three of us in one room, yet it was far better than sleeping in the warehouse, hiding from everyone and we felt safer together. It had a lavatory directly across the hall. Grayson had mentioned that this was our own private lavatory, so I had no problem with taking an extra-long shower. Steam filled the room. I breathed deep and slow. I could still see Garon's face, bright, free, a soldier, my brother, lost to the red-eyed beasts that took him. I hadn't cried since that night for Marlie's sake and Gerda's, but there was no stopping the tears now. They poured from my eyes and were washed away with the dirt, sweat, and blood. I placed my hands against the porcelain wall and hung my head. "No more tears. I will avenge you my brother. I will send the demons back to hell," I said as I turned off the water.

Drips of water fell from my chin as I pulled back the shower curtain. I grabbed a small beige hand towel and dabbed the wounds on my back. Blood soaked into the towel. From what I could see most of Gerda's stitches were still intact. I was fortunate that most of the wound had already healed to a point that the stitches only broke in a couple of spots. I held the towel against the wound for a few minutes to let the bleeding and seeping slow.

The men we had encountered were able to provide us with clean clothing, hot showers, and a meal. They promised us protection. A small window let in some of the fading light of the day. I wiped the steam from the glass and peered out into large English garden with rows of sculpted hedges and openness beyond. *This manor offers us no such protection. No barricades, easily accessible, exposed windows. We won't last long here, we're not safe,* I thought. *I need to talk with them about fortifying this place or leaving.*

I dried myself. The clothing consisted of a dark green colored pair of cargo pants that were a little too long and some female undergarments and a tan colored t-shirt, again that was a little too big. The clothing we were wearing reeked and had stains of blood. *I will make it work,* I thought as I pulled on the new attire. I walked across the hall into our room closing the door behind me. Gerda sat on a chair in the room praying over her rosary beads. A small lamp on an end-table was turned on offering a soft glow to an otherwise dim room. Marlie was asleep on the bed peaceful, quiet. *She's innocent; she doesn't deserve this kind of life.*

"Oma," I said pointing to Marlie. "*Schlafen?*"

Gerda stopped praying and looked up at me. "*Ja. Zwei Stunden.*"

Marlie hadn't slept for two hours straight in several days. I gently pulled an extra cover over her small frame. She wriggled a bit before giving back into her much-needed rest. A knock at the door startled me. Gerda too, by the look on her face. I quietly made my way to the door and cracked it just a little to see who it was.

"Hello, sorry to bother you, but I thought you could use these." Codie was standing outside the door holding another stack of clean clothing. "These were my sister's. I didn't know your size, so I grabbed several different items. It's fortunate that my father had held onto them, they have to be loads better than what my brother gave you."

"*Danke.*" I took the clothing.

"I also wanted to let you know that we have a pot of stew downstairs. Grayson and Kap would like to talk with you. When you're ready of course." Without saying anything else, he turned away from the door and walked back down the corridor. I closed the door and examined the clothing. A few pairs of dark denim trousers and several more feminine tops and undergarments. I removed the oversized tan t-shirt and tossed it aside. The cargo pants I was wearing were fine. I simply rolled the pant legs to an appropriate length. Gerda motioned for me to sit in front of her. "No," I said. "*Ich bin fein.*"

"*Nun! Und üben Sie Ihr Englisch*"

I knelt on the floor in front of Gerda. She had already prepared some clean pads and had a bottle of alcohol. Taking a clean pad in her hand, Gerda turned the disinfectant bottle sideways soaking the pad. She placed the pad over my wound.

"Owe! *Scheiße!*" The rubbing alcohol stung every part of the wound, then softened to a nagging burn.

"*Englisch!*" Gerda corrected. I took a deep breath and allowed her to continue cleaning the slash marks from the werewolf.

"Do we trust them, *Oma*?"

"*Ja. Wir haben keine Wahl.*"

"We always have a choice." Slowly and painfully, Gerda re-stitched the areas that needed it and placed fresh coverings over the spots that still seeped. There was also no sign of infection, though it was still painful, sore to the touch. Not debilitating like it was just after it had occurred. I could still fight, and I could certainly still shoot. The one advantage was that these men did have weapons, lots of weapons, all of which were loaded with silver. Whoever the Kap person was, he was very skilled at acquiring weapons and adapting them to rounds made of silver.

"*Danke*. I mean…Thank you." I put on one of the bras Codie had brought. It was a little big, but still offered support. Fortunately, he had also brought several tank tops that I could wear in layers. I put my boots back on and placed my father's gun in my back waistline. "I will bring you something to eat. Get some rest. I will go talk with them."

Gerda nodded but remained seated in her chair as I left the room closing the door behind me. The manor was warm, and the air was better for my wound than keeping it covered. I pulled back my damp hair and tied it off into a ponytail. The walls were a rich cream color and were littered with pictures. One in particular, Grayson and Codie I recognized, but I had not met the older gentleman in the picture or the girl, to whom I deduced was Codie's sister and whose clothing I was borrowing. She looked young, kind, and happy. It had been a long time since I had seen a picture that captured such gentleness amongst a caring family. *My life will never be like that*, I thought. I reached out for the picture and ran my hand over the glass, longing for something that was beyond my reach now. Friends, parents, and now my brother, just gone. Anger churned in the pit of my stomach. Hatred, deep rooted in loss, filled me as I breathed out slowly.

"She's gone you know." The voice startled me as I pulled my hand away from the picture and reached for the gun in my back waistline. "Whoa! Take it easy. Bloody hell, I didn't mean to frighten you. And I certainly don't want to fight with you again. My neck is still sore from earlier and I don't need another lump on my face."

Codie held his hands in the air as he stood a short distance from me. My heart was pounding. I let go of the handle to my father's gun keeping it in my waistline. It was tough to go through what we did and not feel edgy at the slightest sound. "Sorry." I looked at the portrait of the family again. "Her name was?"

Codie walked closer and looked at the family portrait with me. "Laryn. Her name was Laryn."

"Werewolf?"

He nodded, continuing to stare at her image. "Yes...and we've been hunting the beast ever since." There was pain in his words, a malice that matched my own. This was her, the light that was consumed by darkness and thrust them into a world filled with demons.

I looked at Codie. The side of his face was still swollen with black and blue marks that had formed just under his eye. "I am sorry for hitting your face."

"Don't be." Codie didn't look at me at first. Instead, he remained fixated on the picture of his sister. He reached out the same as I had done, touching the portrait of his sister before finally glancing at me. "I would've hit you just as hard if the roles were reversed."

With that he turned from me and walked towards the staircase. I said nothing more, but followed, cautiously behind, making sure to keep my distance until we were on the lower level. The staircase ended into a large foyer. To the right of the foyer was a room but the door was closed. Codie proceeded to walk down another corridor that opened into an eating space. Grayson and Kap both sat at one side of the table and stood as I entered the room.

"I trust that accommodations are suitable?" Grayson asked as he motioned with his hand for me sit at the table.

"*Ja*, thank you."

The eating area was attached to a large kitchen to which the man named Henry that picked us up from the warehouse could be heard laboring around for something. Atop the table was a large kettle with the stew that Codie had mentioned. Both Grayson and Kap had already eaten their fill by the looks of the empty bowls. Henry came from the kitchen holding two more bowls and the proper eating utensils. He said nothing as he placed them in front of Codie who was sitting at the head of the table. I eased myself into the chair, careful not to brush my wound against the back of the chair.

"How is your wound? Do you need any further medical attention?"

"No. It will be fine."

"Please eat something." Grayson grabbed one of the bowls and placed it in front of me. He then spooned some of the stew into the bowl. The aroma was spicy, rosemary and basil that blended well with the roasted beef, potatoes, and carrots. I ate it greedily. The food made my body feel warm and comfortable, something that I had lacked most of my life while hunting the same darkness as these men. After finishing two bowls of stew, Grayson leaned forward resting his elbows on the table. "Now, who are you and what happened to your group?"

"As I stated before my name is Ada Rothstein. I was part of a group of hunters whose sole purpose was to hunt down werewolves. On the 7th of February we were ambushed. Our entire group was killed except for the three of us."

"Was it one?"

"Many. Too many to count." Caution mixed with anxiety as I started to explain.

"How? Were ya out in the open?" Kap asked.

"*Ja.* We were just outside of the town of Glindenberg in Germany. We needed to stop for supplies and heard of dark activity in the area. We set up camp in an alcove of trees. The river gave some natural protection and we were trying to bait the werewolf into a trap."

"What kind of dark activity? What do you mean?" Grayson asked before I could continue.

"We figured the werewolf may have moved towards Magdeburg or may have continued east when we stopped for supplies, but the store owner talked about dead animals. Torn apart. Half-eaten." All three of the men listened intently as I recounted the horrors of that night. I told of our plan in detail. I talked about the how the group over the years had dwindled and for all we knew, Marlie, Gerda and I were the last. "Oddly, that night there was no moon. It had not yet risen."

"Yer say'n that there was no moon, they changed without it?" Kap asked. There was a concern in his voice, but something that also suggested new, but familiar information.

"*Ja.*"

Kap looked at Grayson and then back at me. "We saw something similar. Fuck'n beast changed inside the club. No moon. Next night at the church, three fuck'n werewolves and again, no – moon."

"This was something we suspected but had not seen until that night." I could feel the tension building inside my chest. My heart pounded. "Did the werewolves have red eyes?"

"No. None of them did," Grayson answered. My leg began to shake under the table. Nerves. I felt even less safe now, vulnerable with the confirmation that the werewolves had the ability to change without the moon.

"We should go. We should not stay here!" I stood from my chair. Continuing to urge them to follow.

"Why? I don't understand." Grayson looked back and forth between Codie and Kap who had equal looks of dismay.

"We don't have any time. We are in danger! Each day that passes they can attack us! They don't have to wait for the full moon!" I noticed that Grayson was looking over my shoulder at something.

Gerda was standing in the archway that led into the eating space. Her expression was calm and gentle. She was holding her satchel with both arms. The three men stared at her then back at me as she laboriously made her way around the table to where Grayson was sitting. Gerda laid the satchel onto the table and with both hands she placed them on either side of Grayson's face. "*Unsere Vormund.*" She leaned forward and kissed the top of his head.

"*Oma*, we don't have time for this. We have to go!" I urged her, but she sat at the table instead and proceeded to remove the Grimoire from the satchel along with the stack of letters.

"What did she say?" Grayson asked dumbfounded. "And did she just kiss my forehead?"

I was pacing back and forth, a little put out by her lack of urgency, but more so that she was looking to Grayson for leadership instead of me. "She said *Unsere Vormund*. It means *Our Watcher* or *Guardian*. It's her way of saying thank you."

"Right...Charmed." Grayson was very unsure about the situation as was his brother Codie and Kap. Grayson looked at me. "Why are you so nervous?"

"*Ihr Neukunden.*" I said to Gerda before I sat back down at the table next to her, no less nervous. "If they can change without the full moon, then we are not safe here. There are no fortifications, we are too exposed!"

"Nothing has ever happened here. Do you think they would risk exposure by attacking us here?" Grayson was still confused.

"*Ja* and the longer we wait –"

Gerda turned to me and tapped my arm gently. Her blue eye sparkled with kindness and sincerity rested on her weathered cheekbones. "*Es ist Zeit, dass wir alle gesprochen.*"

"What did she say?" Grayson asked again.

I shook my head and pursed my lips. "She says we all should talk."

"Does she understand English?" Codie chimed into the conversation.

"Mostly what is said. But she cannot speak it or write it well."

"*Übersetzen,*" Gerda said as she reached for the Grimoire.

"She is going to talk to all of you about the Grimoire and she wants me to translate." I rubbed my forehead with the back of my wrist and leaned forward resting my elbows on the table. Attempting to be patient, though I had little tolerance for idleness, my hands lay over one another as I rested my chin on them readying myself to translate what Gerda wanted to discuss.

All three of the men focused on Gerda as she began. "*Gott schafft Heiligen. Der Teufel schafft Dämonen.*"

"God creates saints. The devil creates demons." Gerda's voice was strained, tired sounding but she continued. So, I continued to translate for the three men. "Our tale of darkness dates back to the late 1500's. A man by the name of Peter Stumpp was given a magic girdle from the devil which allowed him to change into a werewolf."

"Hold on – Yer say'n that the *devil,* gave him a *magic* belt," Kap asked as he rolled his eyes in disbelief.

"Is it so hard to believe in the devil and demons, God for that matter, considering what you have seen?"

Kap said nothing more, but leaned back in his chair, pondering what I had asked. Gerda continued to speak, and I returned to translating. "The townsfolk of Bedburg were able to capture Peter Stumpp before he could inflict anymore harm on the village. He was later convicted of his crimes and use of witchcraft to change to the werewolf. During his execution, his skin was removed in ten places with hot pinchers, his limbs were broken, he was beheaded and his remains were burned. The evil had stopped in the region, but in 1593 similar things were happening on the Eastern side of Germany. There were reports of animals, livestock that were torn to pieces. Their entrails were pulled from their bodies. Worse were the reports that children were also attacked and killed, half-eaten. Our ancestors who dealt with Peter Stumpp traveled to what we know today as the Sachsen-Anhalt region of Germany to help."

The man named Henry entered the room with a pot of tea and several cups. He said nothing as he placed it onto the table but gave both Gerda and I a strange look before leaving. It was clear that he had been listening to the conversation and had formed his own opinions on the matter. He was gracious enough to keep his thoughts to himself. Grayson offered Gerda and me tea, but we both refused. Gerda continued talking as I continued her translation. "Educated by the church, our ancestors kept a written record of what happened to Peter Stumpp and sought to educate those in Sachsen-Anhalt region about how to rid the land of the beast. This terror came to its end when a young boy cried for help and the townsfolk came to his aid. The young boy pointed into the forest where the townsfolk, our ancestors included, found a uniquely cured hide as though it was stripped from the back of someone. A man by name of Johan Stich was later imprisoned for asking about a piece of hide he had lost. Stich was executed in the same manner as Peter Stumpp. Limbs were broken, skin burned from his body, but his tongue was cut out so that he could not scream for God's help and his stomach was cut open to free the souls of the children he had eaten. The priest, Father Amsel, who traveled with our ancestors grew angry with Johan and he banished his entire seed from the grace of God, condemning them to hell."

"Where was this town?" Grayson asked.

"I don't know. Somewhere north of Magdeburg. The town was later burned by marauders during the feuds over faith during the time period. Since most of the people of the time couldn't read or write, not many records existed. The ones that did were burnt." I reached for a cup and poured some tea before signaling Gerda to continue. "Set with child, the daughter of Johan pleaded with Father Amsel for forgiveness. He refused her and because of her persistence, he accused her of sympathizing with Johan and ordered her to be sentenced to death for consorting with a known witch. Those who were understanding of Johan's daughter, Lena, helped her to escape her fate. She wasn't safe. The evil continued with the rise of the full moon. Lena was found half eaten and her baby was removed from her stomach. Father Amsel was nowhere to be found, simply gone. The townsfolk immediately accused the husband of Lena, Manfrit, claiming he must've been bitten by Johan and they sentenced him to death by burning. No torture, just execution, despite his desperate pleas of innocence."

"The town and church had celebrated for there were no more attacks. No more violence for months. The church thought they had done God's work and banished the evil from the land. Months rolled by and turned into years with no reports of werewolves. Our ancestors had felt it safe to venture home to Bedburg and even to establish new homes in other regions in Germany and in Western Europe as to keep watch for any other evil that may arise. This was the start of our alliance. Each town we settled in we educated the churches and formed a group of watchers, *Wächter* or *Vormund*." I nodded in Grayson's direction, who simply nodded back. "And each group had one of these." Gerda held up the Grimoire.

"Are you Catholic or Lutheran?" Grayson asked.

"Neither. We are God's soldiers. Organized churches of the time fought too much and we could not educate them if they believed we were a part of another denomination."

"So how did it start again?" Codie asked.

"The year vas 1617, twenty years after the execution of Johan and Manfrit for witchcraft and the murderous acts they had committed as werewolves. A letter arrived in Duisburg with a report of darkness that had risen again and that urged the watchers to aid in killing the beast. Upon arrival in a village just outside of Magdeburg, the watchers discovered that a convent of nuns was torn apart. Some were half-eaten, while the rest were dismembered. No one in the convent survived. Blame was everywhere within the churches. But it was the first time the beast had been reported as having red eyes according to those who saw it fleeing the town. The townsfolk and the watchers burned the convent to the ground. It did little good. Rumors of the beast spread like the plague. More deaths, more werewolves, more of the red-eyed fiends, always around the full moon."

"It was only much later that we decided a piece of the hide from Johan Stich may have allowed evil to endure or something. Keeping with the other legends it only made sense. But we had no idea how. The only thing we could think of was that the torturous practices were equally as sinful, that maybe God was angry with us. By the 1700's, many of the groups we had established were starting to fall. Some were killed by the beasts, others simply gone along with their Grimoires."

Gerda held up the stack of letters. "These letters are all that remain of some of those groups. They contain the last known whereabouts of these groups."

"Did your group order the execution of a slave named *Kabona*?" Grayson asked.

Gerda nodded, "*Ja*. It wasn't uncommon to hear about a slave practicing the dark arts. It was part of how they justified enslaving the people they captured from Africa. We were, however obligated to explore anything that resembled a werewolf attack."

"Why did your group wait until the full moon if they knew Kabona was going to change?" Grayson shifted in his chair. "I mean he survived."

"*Ja*, he did survive." Gerda shook her head in disappointment. I finished my cup of tea before I continued translating. "Our group from Brussels, Belgium arrived late at Newgate. Kabona was already imprisoned. We wanted him to be burned and the first order was written as such, but the law of the land was that he was to be hanged and our request was rejected. By this time in history, we had already lost many of our groups and gone into secrecy. We could no longer be open about our intentions and most of the world by this time was starting to lose their beliefs in werewolves. We had to be secret with our influence, we submitted evidence and tried to petition, again we were rejected. Kabona was not to be listed on the registries, for if he were to be listed and found by the beasts before or after his death the consequences would be great. And they were. They did find out. We wanted the body after he was hanged to burn as we had done in the past to all others bitten by the darkness so his skin could not be reused, but the first order of his death by burning still remained, despite a re-issuing of a hanging order. This exposed our group. They were all killed before the full moon and Kabona was able to escape when he changed. Hearing of this terrible event, led us to suspect that the werewolves could change without the full moon." Gerda pointed to a page in the Grimoire.

"Why a wolf?" Codie asked no longer able to contain his silence. "I mean why do they turn into a were-*wolf* and not something else?"

"Der Teufel," Gerda responded.

"The devil, Codie." I looked at Codie who was completely drawn into the folklore, but still lacked an understanding of all of this darkness. Gerda was quiet as she looked at me. "The rival of the wolf has always been to humanity. The devil wanted to create life like God had done but couldn't do it *like* God. So, he mocks God with his attempts to create. The wolf hunts the weaker prey, keeping balance in nature. The devil taints God's perfect creations by seducing humankind with the need for power and offered the ferocity of the wolf. But it was a perversion of two creatures against their original purpose. The purpose of a werewolf is to unbalance nature and create fear. Demons feed on fear and there is nothing more fearful than these beasts. Remember Codie, God creates saints, the devil creates demons."

"Well, what can we do from here? We found ya two and the little one, but we've got nowhere else to go. We were hope'n ya be able to give some direction." Concern spread across Kap's face. It was clear that these men had dealt with the darkness, but we were in the same predicament that we had always run into and that was tracking down the beasts.

"I wish we could help more, but as you can see we have fallen on very hard times." Grayson and Codie both seemed stumped by the conversation. Codie leaned back in his chair and placed his hands behind his head. Grayson stared away from the table, pondering this thought with his elbows resting on the table and his fingers crossed. "Is there anyone else that knows about the werewolves that can help us?"

"No, afraid not, lass." Kap shook his head no.

Grayson leaned forward, uncrossing his fingers. "That's not entirely true, Kap."

"Wait Grayson yer not talk'n about Jinx and Snake, are ya? I would prefer that we kept them out –"

"No, no of course not. Piss on them," Grayson interrupted. "Initially I thought of Marcus Holland. No one has more scientific knowledge than he does, but he was deported back to Australia."

"Then who?" Kap asked.

"Inspector Lawrence."

"I don't know Grayson. Remember this chap plays by the rules, we don't. Can we trust him or do ya think he'll be try'n to get ya in a bealin' pile of shit?"

"This inspector, who is he?" I asked not privy to the events in question.

Grayson looked at me. "After we killed the werewolves at the church, he was the police inspector that was working the case. Pesky bastard, damn near uncovered the truth of what happened that night. He was relentless with his questioning, never really believing the story we concocted. However, he stopped pursuing us. The case may have gone dead on him. Nevertheless, he might've discovered something and if he did, he could be an ally in all of this."

"We still need to be cautious. Touting off about werewolves might get us thrown in the nut house or arrested." Kap shifted in his seat, seemingly uncomfortable with the idea of being arrested more so than the nut house. No doubt he wanted to avoid any entanglement with the English justice system for reasons that were still not yet known to me.

"Well, we haven't been arrested yet…and your right, we do need to be cautious, but I think he's worth talking to." Grayson looked away from Kap and towards the archway of the eating space.

"Who's worth talking to? What's going on in here?" A stately man dressed formally, but without a tie entered the dining area. His voice was calm, yet authoritative and inquisitive. He looked directly at Grayson, Codie and Kap, then swept his gaze down the table towards Gerda and me.

Something about him made my nerves jump; the way he stared into my eyes, aghast at the sight of me. I watched as his legs weakened, causing him to wobble a bit before stabilizing himself on the table. His eyes never left mine. "Laryn! It's you! It's really you! You're safe!"

The man rushed around the table making a beeline for me. I stood from my chair and pulled the gun from my back waistline. As he came closer, I pointed the gun directly into his face. "I will shoot you dead if you come any closer!"

Codie got in between both him and me. "Dad STOP! This isn't Laryn!"

"Don't be ridiculous, Codie! It's her!" The man was distinctly out of his mind, crazed and delusional over whom he thought I was. "Out of my way I want to hug my daughter!"

"Dad! Wait!" Grayson and Kap both grabbed the man, one on each arm and dragged him backwards.

"Get off of me!" The man struggled against both Grayson and Kap, slinging his arms about in a desperate attempt to free himself. Like a Red Deer tangled in a thicket of trees, the man thrashed furiously as he stumbled over his own feet and crashed to the hardwood. Tears poured from the man's eyes as Grayson and Kap both pressed him tight against the floor. "That's my daughter! What are you doing? LARYN! LARYN!"

Hearing the commotion, Henry had also entered the room and hurried over to Gerda who now stood with her back against the far wall, astonished by what was happening. Codie continued to back me away from the screaming man, not taking his eyes off him. I still held my gun with both hands, ready to kill him if I must.

Part 2

CHAPTER #9

Cold Case
Detective Chief Inspector James Lawrence
Saturday, February 18, 2012
6:20 p.m.

"Chief! Chief! We've got a body. They just brought it in. Bullet wound to the head and strange markings on the arms and legs," Lydia said. My office was dim except for the soft light that came from the brass lamp on my desk. The dreariness from outside blocked most of the daylight coming through the windows behind me. Her thin frame stood silhouetted at my door, eager, almost excited about the prospect of a new case.

"Alright, I'll be down in a bit." She turned and left as fast as she came. I watched as she walked past the windows that looked out over the rows of desks just beyond the wall. Lydia Cooper had only been a part of my group for the past couple of months. She was young and beautiful, but never let that interfere with her work. Today, like most days, her overly curly hair was pulled back into a ponytail. Lydia got a lot of shit from some of the uniformed lads. Little did she realize that pulling her hair back just enhanced her hazelnut skin and big brown eyes. She was too driven to notice the glances from the men, but she was a good constable and valuable to my team. Though still a sergeant, I had recruited her from uniformed duties and got her enrolled in the specialized training program to become a detective inspector in plain clothes like the rest of my team. She was tech savvy and blended in with younger crowds where I was a blemish amongst them, thinning silver hair, always in a suit and easily identifiable. My appearance suggested to those younger than I, avoid at all costs.

I closed the file I was looking at and shoved it into the top drawer of my desk. It was nothing special. Just a robbery gone bad and the suspect was still at large. Most of the time these suspects were apprehended by the uniformed constables. The need for an inspector was merely a waste of resources. Given the right amount of time, they usually solved themselves. The case, like the stack of other files that mounded across my desk, bored me.

After twenty-three years of being a part of *The Met,* cases that dealt with destructive cult and the occult practices in London had developed into a kind of specialty for my team. I had told Lydia to always keep an eye out for cases that fit this profile. Most of them resulted in a singular person with an untreated mental illness performing heinous acts of a sacrifice or self-harm. Often, they were ritualistic in nature and almost always involved some interpretive religious aspect. A few of the cases could be linked to groups such as the *Church of Satan* that started in the states, but had gained international attention, yet the others were copy-cat artists trying to carry on the customs of known dark practitioners. However, we hadn't received a case of that class since the incident at *Club Red* that ended with the owner being decapitated in front of the altar at *St. Teresa's Cathedral* at Cambridge in 2009.

My cell buzzed. It sat in front of my computer monitor to the right of hardline on my desk.

The message was from Lydia.

Inside my office was nothing fancy. Small, a bit cramped because of a bookshelf to my right, which was full of mostly manuals. Two metal chairs that sat in front of my desk. It wasn't a corner office, but I was happy that it was on the third floor, away from most of the station's commotion.

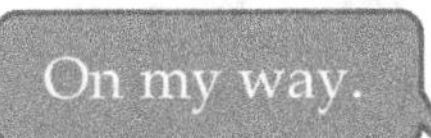

I stood from my desk after sending my response, switched off the goose neck lamp and slid my cell phone into my pants pocket. My overcoat and umbrella remained on the stand, by the door. I didn't need them. I was only going down to the morgue in the basement of the building.

Outside my office, things were buzzing as usual. Phones were ringing and chatter filled in the gaps. Many of the desks in the open area were empty. Some were occupied with inspectors like Richard Scott pecking away at their computers while others were busy with phone calls. Richard always fancied my team's work and had made several efforts to be a part of it. I could see him looking in my direction, though I tried not to make eye contact.

Several people sat in the hallway outside the front workspace. Most were more likely waiting to file a report, but some were there to inquire about reports already filed and cases that had not yet been resolved. I worked most Saturdays since the antics from Friday nights usually brought some interesting cases. Most of the drunken frolics from around the city were being processed on the first floor. This particular Saturday was filled with loads of paperwork that involved nothing more than the youth of England acting in stupid ways in an attempt to capture some existential aspect of their lives.

"Hey chief." Jasper Davis walked past me with a stack of files under his arm. He continued to walk backwards as he spoke. "I ran the reports you needed. Nothing came up as being linked to any of the religious groups you mentioned. As far as I could tell, they were just normal vandals with cans of spray paint. The graffiti in the abandoned club lacked the sophistication for which we were looking."

"Hmm. Well, it was worth a shot." I paused as I came to Sabastian Moore's desk. "Do you know when Sabastian will be back from the narcotics re-assignment?"

Jasper worked with Sabastian in the technology department. "No, I guess it's pretty secret stuff though." He was younger than Sabastian, but equally as skilled.

"I may be sending Lydia to you with a new case."

He simply held his free arm up into the air in acknowledgment as he continued to walk away from me. I looked down at Sabastian's desk. It was neatly arranged, with a photograph of him and one of his mates toasting drinks at the pub. He had been out of the office for several days and would often assist with cases involving a high level of surveillance. Sabastian was in his mid-thirties with hair starting to grey on the sides. He claims this is why he could never marry. Too much drama and not enough time to deal with it. Sabastian was the one that always helped me locate references for materials that suggested occultic practices and had been a part of my team since 2007. Narcotics often needed him to work on extracting files from seized computers or for tapping into online accounts of suspected dealers.

"Hey…James!" I tried to ignore Richard, but he made it devilishly hard to do so at times.

Richard made his way towards me from his desk. "Not now Richard. I've got to examine a body."

There were many *Specialist Casework Investigations Teams* at New Scotland Yard, but my *SCIT* team was the only one looking for things that had the essence of the occult. Wounds inflicted upon the body in a strange fashion, odd symbols such as the ones Jasper researched from Club Red and anything that would indicate a ritualistic sacrifice, or a stylized murder usually caught our attention. Richard was merely a troublesome insect, only interested in this work for the storytelling to the ladies at a pub bemused by these sorts of things yet mesmerized by the potential heroics associated with such cases. His employment at *The Met* was hazy at best. It was widely whispered that he manipulated his way through the training process and that someone higher up allowed it to occur. Richard delighted in bringing others down unjustly. He was no one I wanted to have handling delicate situations that often came about with our work.

"Why was my request to be a part of your team denied?" I simply turned from him and continued on my way. I didn't want to waste time explaining why he wasn't qualified. I preferred letting the appropriate channels govern his understanding. "I could help your team you know!"

His shrill whine cut-off as the elevator door closed in front of me. The ride down didn't take long. Inside the morgue was lit by several florescent overhead lights and the body in question lay atop a metal table, stripped naked. "Ok, what do we have?" I asked as I fully entered the room. Lydia handed me a pair of latex gloves. The coroner, Dr. Alastir Ledford, stood off to the side scribbling some notes onto a clipboard. He wasn't officially part of my team. Nonetheless he never refused a consultation and offered incredible insight into the cases we had.

"Male, unidentified, late twenties, maybe early thirties, shot once through the head. May indicate sacrificial execution," Lydia said.

"What was the estimated time of death?"

"Given the state of the wound to the head, and the deeper, open markings on the legs, I would estimate the time of death to be between 2:00 a.m. and 3:00 a.m." Dr. Ledford said as he looked up from his clipboard. "I won't know for sure until full pathology comes back. The bullet fragments in the skull haven't come back from ballistics either. I suspect that he was shot from a distance since I couldn't find any traces of gun powder residue."

"How long until we get the full report?" I asked, still examining the body.

"There isn't much to this one. I suspect we'll have the full report in less than twenty-four hours."

"Good. Where was he found?"

"On the bank of the Thames at Battersea Park. A couple going for their late morning walk found him," Lydia said.

I stopped and looked directly at her, "In the park?"

"Well, on the edge, just before the Albert Bridge."

The body had several scratches and what looked like bite marks. Some were deeper than others and more recent. Most resided on the legs of the individual, a few on the left arm. Nothing stood out as unusual. I stepped back from the body and took off my gloves. "Bollocks Lydia!" I sighed heavily.

"What?"

"I came all the way down here for this. I thought I told you to let me know when there was something worth investigating. Something that fit our profiles."

"Chief, the marks all over his body –"

"Mere cuts from jumping over wrought iron fences don't count as anything unusual. Battersea Park is littered with these fences. This guy probably jumped the wrong one too many times. I would guess this has happened more than once in recent days and he may have run into a fenced area that had a dog, judging by these marks." I pointed to the thinner lacerations around the ankles. "This guy might even be a criminal estimating by how old some of the scratch marks are. The owner probably left his dog out on purpose, as the dog was biting him, looking at these fresher marks, the owner shot him." I threw my gloves onto the metal table behind me. "Check the area for people with fenced-in yard space as well as ones with larger dogs. Also, see if anyone reported any suspicious activity recently in the area. I would wager the trace evidence will produce canine hair and saliva in addition to iron flakes from the fence."

"What about the *single* shot to the head?"

"*Lucky* shot to the head. Or unlucky depending on how you view it. I would guess that the owner didn't actually mean to do it, merely scared. The bullet hole is small. Look here," I removed a pen from my front pocket to use as a pointer. "Too big to be a .22, but certainly large enough to be a .380. The bullet entered here just above the right temple, with a small exit wound above the left ear. A .22 may not have left an exit wound from a distance. Most of the time a .380 will just piss someone off instead of delivering a fatal shot, unless it's a head shot. The owner was probably trying to shoot him in the ass. This suggests that this guy was probably looking over his shoulder when the owner shot in his direction; maybe as the dog was biting his leg. Panicked, the owner possibly tried to dump the body in the river but couldn't get it done given the amount of people that walk near the Albert Bridge. He should've just called us. There would've been no foul for defending one's property. Possibly a penalty for the firearm, but not murder." Lydia had been trying to make a good impression, but her posture was a bit dejected. Rightfully so, I was disappointed. I looked directly at her. "I brought you onto my team to work on the *occult* related cases. This is simply a routine shooting that doesn't require an abundance of our attention to solve."

Lydia opened her mouth to talk but stopped as if she had choked on her own tongue. She was no longer looking at me, but instead was glancing over my shoulder. I turned to face a middle-aged woman with salt and pepper hair pulled into a neat bun on the back of her head. Superintendent Iris Cornell pushed her glasses to her face. Usually her porcelain skin was soft and inviting, young looking, yet now it was tightened with cracks of disapproval. The navy suit coat that matched her pants was open and exposed a white blouse underneath. Her hands rested on her hips. "I truly hope that I did *not* hear one of my chief inspectors say that he was unwilling to follow through with a murder case."

"My apologies madam. I didn't know you were back from your trip."

"It doesn't matter even if I wasn't!"

Superintendent Cornell always made me nervous. It was her direct approach to things. "I – I was merely trying to educate Lydia on the proper distinction between a routine –"

"No murder case we take is routine, Inspector Lawrence. I would expect you of all people to know and understand that," she interrupted. "May I have a word with you in my office?"

I held back what I wanted to say. Superintendent Cornell was known for being by the book, never fully allowing my team to distinguish between the cases that fit the specialized profiles we were accustomed to handling versus random accidental shootings. "Certainly," I said. Alastir stood with Lydia off to the side of the table, "Thank you as usual doctor, for your assistance." He gave a short nod in response. "Lydia." She merely kept her gaze low as I followed the superintendent out of the examination room.

We said nothing as we walked down the corridor away from the morgue. Besides the tapping of her heels on the tile floor, the only other sound came from one of the florescent light fixtures that was buzzing and in need of maintenance. Most of the areas inside the station could be described as white and hateful, lacking in any kind of aesthetic quality. The occasional stripe of light green painted across some of the walls did very little to offer any calming effect, whether that was the true intention or not. It was simply a place to conduct work duties, nothing more. The ride in the elevator was also silent. Neither of us looked at each other. The doors opened to the third floor and we proceeded directly towards her office. She entered first as I followed.

"Sit," she commanded. I sat across from her mahogany desk in one of the fabric chairs. "Good God James, what are you doing? You are one of my more dedicated inspectors and I've known you for years, but lately you've been shucking your duties and for what?"

"I've not been shucking my duties. My team has been instructed to look for–"

"…For cases that fit the occult profiles," she interrupted again. "Yes, I heard you speaking to Lydia. Just because you have had experience with this kind of police work does *not* mean that you are above the normal duties of a *chief* inspector."

"Iris, you know that most of the cases that come through the office involve predictable, drunken fools that made bad decisions. The situation escalates and, *boom* we have a dead body. Rubbish if you ask me."

"We still have to deal with that rubbish!" Iris stood firm from behind her desk and put both her hands on the surface.

"I'm sorry to say that occult cases don't come around that often and when they do, you're given an opportunity to solve them."

"Huh! My team exists to push papers and nothing more."

"James, you don't even have a team anymore. Sabastian wasn't re-assigned; he requested to go into narcotics. Lydia is all you've got! Most people don't want to work with you anymore and when they do, they often come to me requesting a transfer to other units shortly after."

"Well maybe if you hadn't called us off the case we had, Sabastian wouldn't have left!"

"Oh for God's sake! You're not still going on about the incident at the club and the church in Cambridge? Get off it! I mean, bloody hell it's been over two years."

"We stopped right in the middle of our investigation! You knew there was more to the event than Robert Osborne and his son, Grayson, led on. It reeked of the occult, but you called us off it! I would've left the unit too had I not been in charge!"

"You were called off because the case went cold!" Iris slammed her fist against the top of her desk, catching me off guard and causing me to jump in my seat. "The direct evidence checked out with statements given from both Osbornes and there was nothing we could do with the circumstantial evidence when it came back tainted and cocked up!" She walked from behind her desk and stood over the chair I was sitting on. "I couldn't have my inspectors wasting time chasing ghosts! Besides, Cambridge was beyond our jurisdiction, and we were facing penalties if we continued. I allowed your investigation to go as far as it did because one of the victims was the owner of the night club which *was* part of our jurisdiction."

"What about the recordings from inside the club? We were never able to acquire them. What about all the videos that circulated there after? Viral, they went viral on the internet showing a person in an elaborate costume publicly harming other individuals!"

Iris put her hand over her face and shook her head before looking at me again. "We've been through this James. The club representatives claimed it was a publicity stunt that was poorly performed. The club closed right after that. Clearly, the stunt didn't work and in fact did more harm than good. Having had as much experience with this kind of work, you know that it was just religious fanatics who targeted the owner thereafter. It was unfortunate that it resulted in his death, but CASE – CLOSED!"

"There's more to it than that! How come we couldn't link these religious fanatics to any specific group? How come there were only three members from this group?"

"The third suspected member found in the crypt of the church was never confirmed as such. In fact, they still have him listed as one of the victims since he had a silver stake jammed into his chest. The fact that we couldn't link them to any known cults or religious groups is all the more reason why I took you off the case!"

"And the damage to the church?"

"What about it?"

"Doors weren't just broken they were torn from their hinges; they were splintered into hundreds of pieces! There was no evidence of explosive material and it was similar to the doors at the club, so what caused it?"

"James, I don't know! Some things we just can't explain. But the truth stays, I needed you off that case and back to the regular police work." She was getting irritated, but I didn't care.

"I was getting somewhere! I was close!" I stood up from the chair and started to walk towards the door.

"You were obsessed! Your team fell apart because you had them cantering about following smoke trails. Let's face it, you haven't been the same since Millie passed!" I stopped before I got to the door at the mention of my late wife's name and looked at Iris. She turned away and brought her hand to her forehead again as if to fend off the onset of a headache. Iris sighed heavily. "I'm sorry James. I shouldn't have said that."

I took a deep breath and let it out slowly. A few moments passed. "It's alright. I was out-of-line too." Iris was right. I hadn't been the same since Millie died. Her stroke was sudden and unrecoverable. The Club Red case came a month after her funeral and was a good distraction from the emotional pain. Not being able to solve it just added to the suffering.

Iris leaned against the front of her desk and looked up at me. Dark circles under her eyes shown more in the dimness of her office than under the florescent lights of the morgue. Perhaps it was just the play of shadows across her face, but the fatigue was apparent. Pursuing this line of argument was pointless. Though I was upset by the situation, I knew that I wasn't going to get anywhere by engaging in this battle of wits with her. Our conversation had gone awry and landed in a situation neither of us wanted. I needed to change the subject. "How was your trip?"

I could see her demeanor relax. She smirked and shook her head. "Exhausting. You know how family can be." Iris walked over to where I was standing and put her hands on my shoulders and looked directly into my eyes. "James – Go to the pub tonight, get pissed, stumble home and sleep for three days. Whatever you do don't come back here for a bit. It'll do you some good. I wish I could do the same but there's too much here that needs to be done."

My voice was softer knowing that we had crested the intensity of the conversation. "What am I supposed to do with Lydia?"

"Teach her. Teach her the right way to do things. I hope that one day she will be as good as you."

"No, I mean, I still have her looking for odd cases from last night."

"Well…I'll just have her finish processing the files on your desk. They seem to be overwhelming."

"How – I mean –"

"I stopped by your office before I came down to the morgue. I knew you would be down there. If not in your office, where else would you be on a Saturday?" She turned from me and walked behind her desk again. "And don't worry about Lydia, I'll tell her that you gave her the assignment with the notion that it'll do her some good. A learning experience. It's only a *partial* lie...Now, off ya go."

Iris opened a binder on her desk and started to work. No more goodbyes were necessary. I tapped twice on the doorframe with my hand before leaving. I walked towards my office to get my coat and umbrella.

Outside it was cold, foggy and the rain started to fall. Darkened clouds muted the already fading daylight. Broadway was busy as usual. Most people on the walkways weren't interested in the glass high-rise that towered over the street. Nor were they remotely concerned about the post office and small market across the way. They were running here and there trying to stay out of the rain or flag down a cabby. I opened my umbrella and walked down Broadway towards the St. James Park station. There was no sense in trying to get a cabby to avoid the rain. Most didn't stop in front of the police station. It was too busy with patrol cars and the like. There was no sense in waiting for a bus on Victoria Street. It was clearly the opposite direction and by the time I actually caught it I would be at the station if I just walked. *I bet the station is packed,* I thought.

I felt my cell phone buzz in my pocket. Rain poured over my umbrella and splashed up from the ground. My suit pants were getting wet. I pulled my phone from my pocket to check my message. It was from Lydia.

> Sorry Chief! I messed up! ☹

Her final text didn't warrant any reply. Even though I knew Lydia was hoping to get a confirmation about her newly imposed duty, I didn't care enough to give her one. Iris had obviously informed her of what she needed to do and that was sufficient for me.

I showed my credentials to the tube guard at his post as I readjusted my sidearm to a more comfortable position. I hated taking the tube at this time of the day. The station was full of people from all walks of life as I thought it would be. Despite the weather, many people were seeking the nightlife of London. Dressed in their suggestive clothing, they huddled against one another fending off the damp cold. *Bloody morons,* I thought. Theater posters littered the walls but could hardly be seen because of the amount of people walking about. It was noisy and smelled of a hangover from days ago. Fortunately for me it was only a thirty-minute ride before I got off the tube at the Liverpool Street station. Iris had suggested that I partake in the nightlife as well, but the weather was simply too dreary to get drunk and stumble back to my flat in the rain. It was not very appealing.

I was forced to stand for most of the trip. I didn't mind much and paid no attention to the conversations around me. My thoughts drifted to Millie. I tried not to, but it was impossible to avoid recounting the days of our lives together. We met when I was working a case similar to the one at the club. She was the owner of a small pastry shop that was due west of City University of London. Millie's shop was vandalized by some suspected cult members we were tracking. *She was scared, she needed my help.* Fortunately, the vandals turned out to be stoned college students, whereas the actual cult members were never apprehended. I continued to check in on her after the arrest. Millie never did get used to knowing that more menacing individuals were amongst the commoners she serviced. Our romance grew from there. Her shop eventually closed. Millie didn't like the idea of baking for other people anymore, other people excluding me. We had agreed after we married that we would be ok living on my salary as an inspector. Feeling my eyes well-up with tears at the thought of Millie not being at my flat when I got home forced me to think of other things.

The case involving Club Red and St. Teresa's Cathedral in Cambridge still baffled me. Just the mere mention of the case stirred my curiosity again. I had to know what happened. *What could've caused the damage to the metal doors of the club and the church? How come we were unable to obtain the videos from inside the club? They were part of our police investigation…all the paperwork was submitted and signed off on for us to obtain them. Who were those people involved? Who?*

By the time I had arrived at Liverpool Street station the rain had slowed to a drizzle. It was well after 6:00 p.m. and the remaining daylight was gone. My flat was on the fifth floor of a building four blocks away from the station. It was quite a bit calmer than near New Scotland Yard and busyness associated with the trendier parts of London. Shoreditch had more charm, more places to get tea or coffee or to even sample bits of wine while dining on fine cuisine. I hadn't been back to any of these places since Millie died. Dining alone wasn't very engaging. Still, given my age the atmosphere in Shoreditch fit me better.

Once inside my flat, I immediately removed my wet clothing and threw them on top of an already mounding pile of worn clothes. I put on a clean pair of lounge pants and a fresh t-shirt. A layer of dust covered the bookshelves and several of the picture frames. Stacks of papers filled various corners of the flat, but over-all the space was in fair order. I meandered into the kitchen and removed some bread from the pantry. Most of the knives were dirty in the sink, but I still managed to find one suitable for cutting the bread. I poured some gin into a glass with a few splashes of tonic. I swirled it and took a sip. No garnish was necessary. I bit into the bread as I walked towards my office space. The bread was dry and on the verge of going bad, but it was all that I felt like preparing. The gin burned the back of my throat, yet the warm feeling from the alcohol was euphoric.

I put the stale bread and the gin in a small space next to my computer and shook the mouse to wake it up. A picture of Millie and I sat adjacent to the monitor. As it was reloading, I pulled a box from a shelf in the small closet to the left of my desk. Inside were all the files pertaining to the Club Red case; all the interviews and statements from witnesses, all the reports, photographs, DVDs of the videos surrounding the event, copies of course, but everything.

I looked at the image of Millie and felt a twinge of sadness. Neither the gin nor the stale bread was going to be able to take it away. Since I was going to be off for the next couple of days, I figured that it couldn't hurt to revisit an old acquaintance. I needed the distraction again.

"Well, Professor Locard…let's put your exchange principle to the test." I took another sip of gin and one-by-one I removed the files from the box to start work again.

CHAPTER 10

New Suspicions
Detective Chief Inspector James Lawrence
Sunday, February 19, 2012
3:10 a.m.

I had finished drinking the glass of gin and tonic several hours prior. What little effect it had on me dissipated as I finished eating the stale loaf of bread. My eyes started to burn around 1:00 a.m. and had progressively gotten worse as I continued to comb through the case files and re-watched all the DVDs we made of the cell phone videos people had given to the police department. Several other videos had come from internet websites. They all showed the same thing, even the newer ones I had pulled from online. Flashing red lights, glass breaks, a touch of special effects with someone in an elaborate wolf costume, and people screaming. The sounds were always muffled and most of the videos cut off at that point because the crowd of people began to disperse. Oddly enough two security guards were reported as injured, Theodore Wells and Donovan Chambers, but neither were available for comment and no records were found of any medical treatment at the local hospitals. It supported the claim of this being a publicity stunt, but I was sure that the event at the club was linked to the event at the church more so than just religious fanatics being turned off by the exploits of the owner. *There must be something that I'm missing, some connection*, I thought.

I retraced my steps. I took the photos of those found dead at the church and held them up one-by-one each time I watched a new video to see if they appeared in any of the screen shots. No matches. I played them all the way through then replayed them and then played them again searching for anything that would stand out. Strange markings on the walls or people situated off to the side not part of the security personnel or dancing with the other patrons. I was looking for those that seemed suspicious, hiding something perhaps, but there was nothing, there was no one. *Perhaps Iris was right again, we were chasing ghosts.*

My internet search had led me to *www.obscuritiesdocupub.com*. Sabastian and I had used this site in the past as a reference when exploring aspects of the occult or religious fanaticism. Much of the content was documentary based, but occasionally the site owner would post *'societal obscurities'* that *'few have seen and that none would believe.'* It had been online for about four years. I entered my login information and started to download a video. I stood from the desk and walked back into the kitchen for a drink as the video was loading.

There was no need to turn on the overhead lights. The florescent lighting from under the cabinetry was plenty enough to see. Several dirty glasses sat neglected in the sink. I hadn't bothered to tend to them out of sheer laziness. It made more sense keeping the place tidy when Millie was still here. She never wanted a large estate or a grand manor of any kind, but a place that was clean, that helped people feel comfortable when visiting was all she valued. This was one of the many things I had adored about her. She was content with the simple things. *Why did you have to leave me*? I thought. I glanced at the bottle of gin but elected to clean one of the glasses from the sink for water.

The soap I poured into the glass foamed over the edge as the water rushed from the facet. As I swirled the foam around in the dirty glass, I looked over the open counter at the video I was downloading. This video was a newer post from this past January. The angle within the thumbnail was a bit different and the video's duration was two minutes longer than the others, but for the most part was pretty much the same. *"Beyond the Brink of Reality" by Duncan Sheehy* read the caption below the video. Though the site owner seemed to be a world traveler, the site was based out of the UK in Glasgow, Scotland.

Duncan's site had often captured bits and pieces of occult practices from around the states as well as parts of Europe.

The video automatically started as it finished downloading. I pressed the empty glass against the water lever on the refrigerator. I could hear a girl trying to take a drunken selfie but judging by the banter between her and the person she was with she managed to hit the record button instead. I wasn't expecting much more than a youthful, inebriated explanation of what was happening inside the club from whoever this person was. Instead, I heard something else, the sound of broken glass then a grisly howl, loud, menacing, clearer than the others. I dropped the glass I was filling. It fell to the floor, shattering against the tile. The howl was followed by the sound of gunfire. "Bloody hell, who's shooting and at what?"

Not concerned about the broken glass on the tile floor, I hurried back to the desk and hit replay. There had been several reports of gunshots inside the club that night. Unfortunately, no one was able to identify the shooter or shooters. We found bullet holes in the wood just below the serving area of a small bar and several more at the end of the hallway that led out to a back alley. The club representatives claimed that it was all part of the stunt. Since we didn't have access to the internal videos nothing could be proven. Ballistic tests reported traces of silver as the possible material of the bullets. No bullets were found, but this further suggested an occult practice and not so much a publicity stunt. Real bullets, silver or not, wouldn't have been used at all if it was a performance. Only the occult driven purists, not copy-cat wannabes, would take the time to construct bullets from solid silver instead of the standard copper-jacketed rounds. More importantly this video confirmed my lasting suspicion that there was more to the incident than we had previous discovered, and this new video was the closest thing I had to evidence.

It showed an angle from a girl standing near the stairwell that led onto the main dance floor. Amidst her pandering about she managed to spin several times in a circle before her date stopped her and began helping with the phone.

"Duncan, I can't get it to work."

"Yer daftie. You swiped it too far," Duncan responded.

"What the fuck…I did – I did what you told me."

"Here love, let's get you sorted a wee bit."

The young black man held the phone low by his waistline considering the view had changed to only include him and the flashing lights above. He was equally as drunk as his date and was having the same amount of trouble operating the phone. His finger pushed several times at the screen unable to stop the camera from recording. The sound of breaking glass caused him to abandon his attempts and turn the camera towards the dance floor.

"What the hell?"

I let my eyes fall upon the unimaginable. A young woman seemingly ripped from her clothing and morphed into an immense wolf-like creature. A hulky man lay flailing about at its feet, arm badly broken and dangling. The grisly howl followed. My breath had stopped, and I backed away from the computer awe-stricken. I nearly fell over my rolling chair. "What in God's name?" I asked to no one.

The young man continued to yell into the video, but it was muffled among the hundreds of other screaming people in the club. The creature had leapt upon the small serving bar and stared down at something behind it. Moments later two individuals emerged on the screen from the crowd with their guns drawn and firing at the beast. Dressed in black leather coats, the men had their backs turned towards the camera so there was no way to get a clear facial recognition from that angle. The beast they were shooting at was horrifying. I could hardly look at it, but it was impossible to turn away. It twisted to face the men and its glowing green eyes cut sharply through the flashing red lights and the shadows that filled the space. Spittle dripped from its canine teeth. The beast looked as though it was shot, yet powerful, strong it remained. With great agility and speed, it leapt from the men that were trying to kill it. Both the beast and the men disappeared down the back hallway before the video cut out.

I stood, motionless facing my computer. My breathing was fast and acute. And my heart beating wildly was the only sound amongst the silence of my flat. I wanted to replay the video, but I couldn't bring myself to do it right away. Fear had seized my feet and locked them in place. Inside I knew that pursuing this further down the rabbit hole would constitute more questions and would lead me along a path I wasn't certain I wanted to go. But how could I not, there were already too many unanswered questions that tormented me over the past couple of years. Too many things that called out, begged to my conscious mind to engage. *How is it that I had not seen this video before? Or anything like it?"* I thought.

Given the earliness of the morning, I didn't fully trust my senses. Yet, this was the most awake I had felt in a long time. Slowly, I repositioned my chair and sat in front of the computer. I rubbed my burning eyes. My hand shook as I reached for the mouse. With a quick click the video started again. I watched in horror as all the events transcended reality and the thought of this being a publicity stunt simply fell from the grand structure it had been placed upon as a reasonable explanation to what happened that night.

Was the thing on the screen real? Where did it come from? Why was it there? Who or what was it? These thoughts among others permeated my mind. A half-hour had past, and I lost count of how many times I replayed the video. At first, I just wanted to understand the video, to know it, to know what it was. Soon I started looking again. Looking for things that would tie this video back to rationale thought. I took the pictures of all those involved in the church incident and compared them to what was being shown in the video. Nothing. No one stood out as a direct match.

I had slowed the video down and clicked through the screen shots one at a time. That's when I saw her. A woman with a pale face, shoulder length hair, dressed in all black was sneaking through the crowd. She was clearly avoiding something or someone. I noticed her first as the video spun around in circles from the drunken debutant who was trying to take a selfie. I continued to click through the images in the video to see if I could catch a better image of her. She appeared again at a further distance, more towards the dance floor. This time her back was turned towards the camera and like the men in leather coats, I couldn't get any facial recognition. I let the video play again at full speed from this point being careful to follow her through the video. She was lost to me as the young man turned the video towards himself. Yet, she came back into view again as the commotion erupted. I stopped the video and began clicking frame by frame again. *She* was the one standing over the crumpled security guard. *She* was the one that people were running from. *She* was the one who turned into the beast.

"My God," I let slip.

I continued to click through the frames. I wanted to see if I could unravel the magic behind the effects, behind the mystery. Each frame showed a steady progression of her change. Nothing indicated special effects or even a costume. In all the occult cases I had worked, never before had I come across anything such as this. My eyes continued to burn, and I felt that they had betrayed me. *It must be some kind of illusion,* I thought. There wasn't. I felt my lips form the word I was thinking but couldn't believe. "Werewolf."

The moment I said it, my mind spun over something that was completely mythical and had no place beyond the world of cinema, but there it was in front of me without any rational explanation. None was needed for though it made no sense at all, it also made the most sense.

I reversed the video back to the original spot that I saw her. There was only a glimpse of her side profile. I made the video full view to capture a screen shot. After I saved it to a file on my desktop, I grabbed my cell phone.

A few minutes passed and there was no response from Lydia.

"Come on Lydia, answer the damn text!" I was impatient. I figured since she was still young that there could be a chance, she was awake, perhaps even still enjoying the nightlife of London. I was just about to send another text when my phone buzzed.

I could tell from the typos in her text that she wasn't fully awake. It didn't matter. I needed her help. On my computer, I attached the jpeg of the woman to an e-mail and sent it to Lydia.

I didn't want to wait for her response as to whether she got the e-mail. Knowing she was now awake, I just called.

"*Hello?*"

"It's me Lydia. Did the e-mail come through?" I asked.

"*You want me to check for it now?*"

"Yes, it's important."

"*Gimme a moment.*" I could hear covers rustling and some other muffled sounds before she came back onto the phone. "*Ok I'm heading to my computer.*"

She yawned twice into the phone. I was pacing around the room in front of my computer, just staring at the image I had sent her. "Did it come through?"

"Uh…hang on…still loading. Yes, it did. Who or what am I looking at?"

"I need you to identify this woman for me. I would do it myself, but Cornell told me to stay away from the station for a while, or at least until I can come back with a clear frame of mind."

"Ok, I'll check her out first thing on Monday."

"No Lydia, I need you to go to the station now."

"Oh, come on chief. It's Sunday and I've got the day off!" Her voice was raspy. Sleep was still very much present with her.

"Lydia this has to deal with Cl… an occult case from a while back. I need you to go to the station right now so that we can identify this woman." I didn't want to tell Lydia just yet why this was so important to me.

"Chief, you're not drunk, are you? Or are you just bloody mad? It's almost four in the morning!"

"Look I don't care what time it is. I need this done and I need this done immediately!"

"I was planning on using today to go by the Albert Bridge. Do you still want me to follow up with that shooting?"

"No, piss on it. Let the uniformed constables handle it. Pass it off to Richard or one of the boys that is always staring at you."

"What do you mean Richard and the boys that are always staring –"

"Lydia, I need you to do this for me," I interrupted.

"Alright, alright! I'll get on it, but you're buy'n drinks at the pub when this is all done."

"Deal."

We hung up with each other and I waited, watching the seconds tick off the clock that hung on the small wall space just before the kitchen. An hour had passed, and I hadn't heard from Lydia. I watched the video again and again. Each time I became more familiar with the intricate details of the people involved, especially the unknown woman. Everything from her hair to her clothing to the moment that she seemingly changed into a werewolf, I studied. I followed the beast screen by screen to the moment it was hit. I stopped the video then grabbed the main case file from the floor next to me. My eyes watered from fatigue. I could now confirm the eye-witness reports of gunshots in the club, but we found no blood. I looked up from the file and backed the video up. I clicked through it until the beast was hit with the first bullet. Blood could be seen as a silhouetted spray from the beast's left shoulder just before it turned to face the shooter. It was hit again in the leg. *Where did the blood go?* I thought. *Like the bullets, someone must've cleaned the blood before we arrived.*

It wasn't until just passed 6:00 a.m. that I heard back from Lydia.

> Found a match! But there's something odd about this chief.

I didn't respond to her text, I just called her again.
"Hello Chief."
"What did you get?"
"Well, the closest match in the system is a woman by the name of 'Dr. Cassandra Bishop.'"
"Good. Tell me about her."
"She was a professor of medieval folklore at Cambridge and –"
"What do you mean *was*?"
"Chief, it lists here that she died just over thirteen years ago."
"That's impossible. I just pulled this picture from a video that posted a little over a month ago and it's from an event that happened in 2009."
"Chief, that's what's listed here. However, I have another match."
"For the same picture?" I started pacing around my desk area again.

"Yes. A 'Dr. Mya Bishop' also came up. And get this…she's also a professor at Cambridge, same subject, and an author. She wrote the book, Demystifying an Old Myth: A Comparative Look at Lycanthropy."

"No way. This cannot be true." It was inconceivable that what I saw in the video was true, but it was also too coincidental that she had written a book about Lycanthropy. I stopped pacing, dumbfounded by what I was hearing.

"I don't understand Chief, what cannot be true?"

I didn't want to tell Lydia about the full contents of the video. There was a good chance she would deem me drunk or mad and no doubt fully expose what I was doing. I redirected the conversation back to the oddity of two profile matches. "Uh nothing, I mean this has to be a glitch or technical mistake. How can we have the same profile for two different people? Are they related?"

"They could be…or they could be the same person with different identities. I tried to pull other files in our database on Dr. Mya Bishop at Cambridge, but my access was denied. Chief, who is this person?"

"I don't know." I glanced at the computer screen again. "Why was your clearance denied? You should have full access being in the Inspector's training."

"I figured because I was only a trainee that that was the reason I was denied. All files associated with her are locked."

"Alright…Good work Lydia. Stay on the locked files. I want to know what they say."

"How?"

"Talk to Jasper in tech. He fancies our work and will probably help us. But keep it quiet and be careful…these files were locked for a reason. Also, see if you can bring a list of past employees of Club Red in 2009. If they were paying taxes, they should be in our system."

"Does this have something to do with why Club Red shut down? I remember the news reports."

"Yes, yes it does."

"Alright, I'm on it?"

"Let me know what you find *when* you find it."

"What are you going to do in the meantime?"

"I'm going to see what I can find at Cambridge."

We hung up with each other and I sat in front of my computer. I played the video one last time. The anxiety inside of me hadn't gotten any better; in fact, it had gotten worse. Each time I laid my eyes upon the beast, I was met with disbelief and confusion. *Traces of silver from the bullet holes...book on Lycanthropy by the same person who seemingly changed into a werewolf...but no sign of light from a full moon...how did she change?* I thought. I leaned back in my computer chair. *Whatever happened that night was not a publicity stunt...Lack of evidence and no other explanation to challenge the notion has kept it perpetually locked as such.* I turned the computer monitor off, grabbed the picture of Millie and made my way towards the bedroom of my flat. Bits of daylight were starting to poke through the windows. I pulled the curtains to block it out entirely. Fatigue had completely set in on me. I wasn't going to be able to go to Cambridge until tomorrow and I planned on sleeping most of Sunday away. I stared at Millie's picture as I lay down. Having spent so much time in front the computer, it was difficult to release the images from inside my head, but I needed to try. We had just celebrated our 18th anniversary together in the picture. She had her hair cut for the occasion and colored to cover the gray. It was beautiful, dark, and matched the youthful expression she always seemed to possess. Her smile was bright, full of life as she wrapped her arms around my torso, and I held her close with one of my arms. I let the picture fall flat upon my chest and I held it tight. Even as I lay on my bed, exhausted, clutching the picture of Millie and me trying to block out some of the terrors I witnessed, visions of the horrible monster danced across the ceiling and tormented my sensible beliefs. *Was this actually real?* was the repeating thought that dominated until sleep finally overtook me.

Chapter #11

Familiar Pain
Robert
Monday, February 20, 2012
8:00 a.m.

My study was dark and cold. I hadn't burned a fire in several days. There was no comfort in this room or anywhere in the manor. Worse yet, I was embarrassed, to say the least. At the sight of the young girl named Ada wearing Laryn's clothing, her blues eyes like Laryn's, her youthful appearance just like Laryn, proved to be too much and threw me immediately into a complete breakdown. *My child, my poor child. That beast stole you from me,* I raged inside as I placed my hand over my forehead and leaned back in my desk chair. All of Sunday, I avoided Ada and spent most of my time in my study area being debriefed by Grayson and Kap. We discussed how they found Ada, Gerda, and Marlie as well as their group, *the watchers.* They informed me that there may be more people from their group that were cut off from the main group, but there was no way of knowing for sure and it was too dangerous to go looking for them. A tightly bound knot of remorse sat in my stomach over not opening the mail, over not reading the letters that were sent to me from their group. *We could've helped them. They may not have died.*

Grayson and Kap had also explained that Inspector Lawrence, the little prick, may be a person that could help us in hunting down Dr. Bishop. Lawrence, relentless in his pursuit of the truth, nearly uncovered everything behind the bullshit story we fed him. He had cornered Grayson and me several times at the office to continue his line of questioning about the events that occurred at Club Red and the church. There was an unspoken assumption in his mind that we were involved with both events, not just the church. He was right but had fortunately stopped his search before this fact was apparent. Yet, his inquiries about the dark events didn't come without a price. The sheer publicity of what had happened was enough to throw my world into a tizzy. Lawrence's constant involvement gave fodder to Hugh Bennett to insist upon my resignation, in which he claimed, "...*that a gentleman of the House should not be involved with matters of questionable legality."*

I didn't trust Lawrence at all, and I was pleased that we had agreed to wait to speak with him about his inquiries. There was no need to stir the police involvement about things that *we* didn't fully grasp yet. Grayson said that this would give Ada a little more time to heal and all of them a little more, much needed rest. As greatly as I didn't want to work with the asshole, Grayson was right. Inspector Lawrence had resources and insight that may prove helpful. If he did know about the werewolves, then he would be even more useful and may even consider hunting the damn things.

At that moment, Ada was more of a concern than Lawrence. I knew what I had to do to make amends with her. The three of them knew more about what we were hunting then any of us and we needed them here instead of being frightened off by my out-of-control antics. I got up from my desk and paced around the room.

Though the house had been completely restored over the years and nearly everything had been replaced since I had settled there, it still wasn't without its creaks and subtle noises that echoed strangely throughout. Someone had walked into the kitchen area and was rummaging through the ice box. The sound carried through the quiet corridor and was strange enough to prompt me to investigate who and what was causing the noise. Several quick bangs were followed promptly with a light, metallic scratching noise that was repetitive and odd. Hoping it was either Codie or Grayson, even Kap, I quietly strolled down the corridor through the eating space and into the kitchen.

Sitting across from the ice box on a stool at the kitchen island was Ada. She was filing what appeared to be a small metallic object over a plate she was using as a basin to catch the debris. "Good morning," I said knowing full well this was probably going to startle her.

Ada jumped and reached again for the gun that she seemed to always keep on her. "What do you want?"

"To beg your pardon for my behavior on Saturday evening." My voice was flat with the apology. "I allowed my emotions to get the better of me and what I did was simply not very becoming of a gentleman. I *am* truly sorry for frightening you. You're a guest in my home and should be treated differently, with more respect." I crossed my arms behind me so as to not appear threatening in any way to her.

Ada released her grip on the gun she was carrying. "*Danke*," she whispered.

"I'm sorry, what did you say?"

"*Danke*…Thank you. But I do not know you and I do not trust you." Ada's voice was serious, icy as she continued to file the metal object.

"I understand." I watched for a moment. What Ada was doing was certainly something I had never seen someone do before. "Might I ask, what are you doing?"

"I'm filing these batteries." She stood, walked over to the freezer, and grabbed a couple more button batteries from inside before turning to face me and shutting the door. "Button batteries have a zinc and silver interior. Freezing them weakens the seal and the clamps so I can get more of the core out."

Ada grabbed the hammer that was lying on the counter next to the plate and a metal file. She held the circular battery between her thumb and forefinger as she struck the edge with the hammer. Two swipes and the battery cover came loose. Ada pried open the battery's shell and tapped it on the counter to get the core out. "What are you going to do with that?"

"Use it to make this." She showed me a small black pouch. Inside was a greyish black powder. "It's not harmful enough to kill a werewolf. At best the silver content is forty percent but thrown into the face of the beast will burn its mouth and maybe even blind it. The particles are too small to pull out without damaging the eye. Even if they turn back into humans, the silver dust will still be in their eyes. Codie brought me these tools and the batteries."

"I don't mind. Help yourself to whatever you need." Ada nodded and continued filing the interior of the button battery. I watched for another minute, marveled by her ingenuity. "Have you ever used this on a werewolf?"

"Not personally, but members of our group have. I was taught as a child how to make it. It was always my contribution to the group. The way I could help. I always thought of it as a game, especially when I was little. Other children made art and crafts, I made silver dust."

She dumped the contents from the plate into the black pouch and began hammering another battery. I didn't want to disturb her any further. I said what I needed to say to her and as far as I was concerned this situation was resolved.

"Let us know if you need anything further." I turned to walk away from her.

"Mr. Osborne." The heaviness in her voice stopped me at the archway of the kitchen. I looked back at Ada. "I'm sorry about your daughter. I too have lost my family to the darkness. They took my parents and thirteen days ago they took my brother. It is an impossible feeling to get over."

Fury burned in her eyes, a channeled rage, a ruthless focus. I knew that feeling very well. I knew her pain. It was something that gets buried deep within, only to surface when provoked by an obstacle. By the look in her eyes, we understood one another. Nothing more needed to be said about what had happened on Saturday. Our shared single-mindedness drove what needed to be done from this point on. Ada didn't have to trust me yet to be part of our group.

Footsteps in the corridor caused me to turn from Ada. Grayson nodded in my direction as he walked into the eating space and stood next to me in the archway of the kitchen. "Everything alright?" he asked glancing at both Ada and me. I nodded yes without saying anything. He turned to Ada. "How's your wounds?"

"I will live. They have healed a little bit. I keep them clean…I will be fine."

He turned to face me again. "Are you up for a drive?"

"Where to?"

"Club Red." Grayson was dressed and ready to leave. "Kap and Codie are in the lower level. Kap is showing Codie how to use the MP-5s –"

"MP-5s? Where the hell did he get those from?" I asked.

Grayson shrugged. "You know Kap, he doesn't say much about his sources." Grayson looked at Ada. "Anyways, you're welcome to join them. We have three modified tactical .40 caliber HK's, knock down power and speed. It may be to your advantage to get familiar with them. He figured that we were going to need concealment at some point, especially if we're going into the city. Each gun has a set of two interchangeable thirty round magazines that he's filling with silver rounds."

"Where are you two going?" Ada asked casually.

"Henry is going to take us into London so we can look at the abandoned building that was once Club Red. We never got a chance to go back to the club after the church. It's now condemned and is under the supervision of *The Met* due to vandalism and break-ins. If we're going to eventually involve Inspector Lawrence from New Scotland Yard, then I want to see how we might need his help."

"I'm going with the both of you." Ada stood from her seat in the kitchen. "Let me get something warm to put on."

I certainly wasn't going to stop her from coming. Grayson also didn't seem to mind. "Please help yourself to any of the coats in the hall closet. Several of them are leather and very warm. I recommend the sheepskin, the bomber jacket."

Grayson looked at me for assurance. He knew as well as I did that the coat was Laryn's. It was her favorite to wear when she rode Rupert in the colder weather. The poor horse had to be put down after the attack. It was fortunate that she wasn't wearing the coat the night of her attack and I had kept it as a reminder of them both and how they were taken, taken by the darkness, as Ada put it; just as her family was taken. Knowing the pain Ada was experiencing inside, I felt the coat was symbolic, symbolic of vengeance.

Ada pulled the coat from the hall closet and slipped it on. Wearing Laryn's dark trousers with her own boots, Ada looked more like Laryn now with the coat on than she did when I first saw her on Saturday.

"Are you sure you don't want to stay and learn from Kap how to use the weapons?" Grayson asked Ada.

"I already know how to use the submachine gun."

Grayson asked no further questions. The seriousness in Ada's voice commanded respect. Henry pulled up in the van out front for us. The wind blew hard as I zipped my own coat. Overhead the sky was grey. Rain spat at us, but nothing more. Dismal was the only way to describe the day. Our moods were directly connected to it, cold and unyielding.

A nervous tremor ran down my arm and shook my left hand. *It's just because we're going to the club, nothing more*, I rationalized as I flexed my hand to help subdue the shakiness. The tremors were growing in frequency. Suppressed emotions, stress even anxiety could have been the cause, but like most things we all were experiencing, it had to remain secret. The trip into the city seemed longer than it actually was. We left the manor at 8:32 a.m. and we arrived at the Soho district at 9:10 a.m. Taking into consideration the Monday traffic and the loads of people that had started their work weeks, nearly forty minutes wasn't too hateful. More importantly, the tremor in my hand had stopped, for the moment.

The Soho district was more of a night spot. Given the earliness of the day, most of the businesses were closed. Though the abandoned club was in plain sight, we had parked a fair distance away from it. Fortunately, we were very unassuming and blended in with the delivery trucks and passersby. People meandered about, mostly tourists. Some shop owners were coordinating their deliveries and the like. Grayson leaned out from the front passenger side window of the van with a camera. I stared absent mindedly out the front window wrestling with thoughts of the future. Henry remained poised in the driver's seat and Ada shifted anxiously beside me as she repositioned herself to also see out the front window.

From Greek Street, I could see the club's front entrance was boarded up. Vandals had spray painted various insignias over the boards and on the walls of the nook leading up to the door. The boards appeared to have been rotted, yet undisturbed for a long period of time. A thin alleyway stretched behind the building, just as Grayson had said. The opening into the building from the alley wasn't visible from our position. Grayson continued to snap his pictures.

"What are you hoping for Grayson?"

He stopped for a moment and glanced back at me. "I don't know. When I heard the building was condemned, curiosity got to me. I wanted to see if it was closed because of the vandals or if there was another reason, perhaps because of the werewolves. I thought with any luck that we might be able to see something from the outside, some clue or lead, but I fear that if anything they'll be on the inside, not in plain sight out here."

Grayson mumbled something to Henry, but his words seemed indistinguishable, muffled. My left hand started to shake again. Even as I flexed it repeatedly, the tremor would not stop. I could feel the deep drumming of my heart against my chest. Something was not right. I sat back and took a deep breath. It was no good. The feeling only got worse. I tried to conceal the shaking from Ada, except she was too keen *not* to notice. She could tell I was out of sorts.

"We have to go," Ada said still watching me. Before I could rationalize to her that I was all right, she turned to the front. "Grayson, it's not safe here. We go, now!"

Grayson turned from the front seat, "What do you mean?"

"Something draws near, I feel it."

Grayson glanced around to survey the other parked vans and cars along the road in search of anything that stood out as odd. Henry had remained quiet as an uneasy expression spread across his face. He nervously tapped his fingers on the steering wheel. Grayson looked back at Ada. "You might be right. I feel it too."

Grayson's words echoed in my ears as my gaze locked onto an individual that was standing sheepishly alongside a delivery van a good way down the street. It was a woman with a petite stature and shorter looking hair, the same as I had seen outside of my office a week and half prior. "There! She's there!" I blurted out and pointed to the woman. Visions of the green eyes at night flashed into my mind and assaulted the very confines of my sanity.

Anger coursed through me, and I reached for the sliding door. "No!" Ada said as she grabbed my arm. "We are not prepared for this!"

"She's right! Henry, get us out of here!" Grayson said.

"NO! What are you doing?" I blurted out as Ada continued to grip my arm.

"If that is her, we've got no weapons and we certainly can't assume she's alone!"

Henry started to pull away from the curb. I looked back towards the woman, and she was gone, as if she knew I was coming for her. The anger inside turned to rage as I forcefully freed my arm from Ada and ran my hands through my hair. "GODDAMN IT!" I yelled. I slammed my fist against the side of the van door repeatedly like a caged animal desperate to be free to hunt its prey. "DAMN YOU! DAMN YOU!"

Chapter 12

Cambridge
Detective Chief Inspector James Lawrence
Monday, February 20, 2012
9:35 a.m.

My Sunday consisted of getting up to use the lavatory only twice before crawling back into my bed and sleeping away the day. The picture of Millie and me had fallen to the floor at some point while I slept, but thankfully the frame wasn't damaged. Monday's breakfast was no more than a couple of scrambled eggs and a few bits of bacon I had in the icebox. I had eaten the remaining bread on Saturday night and there was no time to go to the market to get the ingredients for a full English breakfast. I sipped some tea as I adjusted my clothing in the full-length mirror. There was no need for me to be dressed in a suit for this venture north. Outside was still cold and dismal. Thankfully the forecast suggested somewhat drier than the weekend. A pair of grey trousers with casual shoes, a dark blue sweater over top of a white button-up shirt would be sufficient. I wanted to look sophisticated, yet not stand out any more than a faculty member would. Looking like a police inspector on a college campus that was beyond my jurisdiction was the last thing I wanted. *If Iris knew that I was investigating this case again after placing me on holiday, it would certainly result in a suspension,* I thought.

Sleeping through Sunday had done very little to rid my mind of the horrible images. I combed my hair as I replayed the video repeatedly in my mind. I didn't understand it. *Was this real? Where were the injured security guards? Why was there no blood from that thing when we arrived at the club? Why didn't we get access to the videos inside the club? Who was Dr. Mya Bishop?*

These among other questions remained unanswered. They were as much of a torment as the dreadful images of the beast.

Parts of this suggested that it *was* just a stunt, something to draw in patrons, however there was no denying the realism of the video. The broken glass, the screaming, the howl, the shots fired, and this mysterious woman that appeared to be locked away from the outside world. I needed to know who she was. I needed to know why she was at the club. I needed to know if it was just an act. *Was she really that monster? If not, why was she there?* My wool sapper jacket was tan and contrasted relatively well with my blue sweater. I placed my phone and a small notepad with a pen in the pocket on the inside of my coat and my badge with my police identification in the other pocket. I put on my wristwatch. *I can't imagine a professor at Cambridge wanting to be a part of or would even fancy a place like Club Red.*

The Old Street station is where I caught the tube. Cambridge was just under 30 minutes on the northern line. Inside the station, it was busy but not like it was on Saturday. Tourists from all walks of life mixed with businessmen and women dressed in suits, carrying umbrellas, small tote bags, and briefcases. It was more pleasant to ride the train at this hour of the day. Most of the hordes of people had already passed through with the morning rush and wouldn't return until the early evening.

Outside, the weather in Cambridge was comparable to that of Shoreditch. Thick, grey clouds disrupted blue skies. I hadn't bothered with my own umbrella. Despite the clouds, rain was not in the forecast until later in the afternoon and I had planned to be comfortably at my flat when it started. I caught the bus that led to the campus. It cost £2, but it was better than walking to the Arts and Humanities building on Mill Lane from the station.

College age students populated Trumpington Street in front of Emmanuel United Reformed Church. It looked like a café rather than a church. White tables in front, inviting, suggestive of a welcoming place to have tea, but it was simply the place where the bus had stopped. Mill Lane was the narrow street a little way up on the left. It was lined with old world structures, some of which stretched back nearly eight hundred years.

I stopped just before the entrance to the Arts and Humanities building. Though not raining, puddles still collected along the base of the building walls. The wind blew hard enough to ripple the standing water. I reached for the door handle. Something inside me stayed my hand. With each chilling gust a ripple was carried across the puddle. *Am I just the ripple effect of some other event? Part of some scheme that exists in the past?* I thought. *You can stop now, go back home. This could end here and now for you.*

There was no way I could stop. No way could I abandon this. I noticed my hand shook slightly as I positioned it on the handle. I knew that breaking the threshold of the building was a pathway unlit, darkened to the outside world. *For Millie. She made you who you are. She needs you to do this again.* I pulled the door open and walked through.

Inside the grey brick building the lighting was soft and inviting. Most of the offices that stretched down the hall were lit, and the lighting rolled out gently from within the rooms. The flooring was marbled and had been polished recently. Portraits of deans were proportionally placed along the walls. A young man with scruffy hair sat quietly behind a wooden welcome desk, pecking away at a computer. Thick sweater with the college logo printed on the front, denim trousers, typical for a student.

"Excuse me." The young man stopped typing and looked up with a polite, inquisitive expression. "I was hoping to be able to speak with a Dr. Bishop, a Dr. Mya Bishop to be specific. Do you know where I might be able to find her? Or if she has scheduled office hours that I might be able to attend?"

The young man smiled again, "One moment sir. Let me check the registry." I looked around as the student commenced his search. A few other students walked about the hallway. The ceiling was high, but any echo was muffled by all the extra people strolling in and out of the offices. "I'm sorry sir. It looks like she is no longer employed here."

"Are you sure? I recently performed a search and it specifically said that she was employed here at the university, in this building." This was curious. Our database at the station had her listed here for employment. Yet, all other files at the station were locked. Dr. Bishop was becoming more and more mysterious. I wasn't about to tell the college kid I was an inspector; it would draw far too much attention. "Thank you, for checking." I was about to turn and walk away from him when I stopped to ask, "Who is the current dean?"

The student pointed to one of the portraits along the far wall, "Dean William Garris."

"Would he by chance be available?"

"One more moment, let me check." I could hear him typing away as I walked over to the portrait of Dean Garris. From the painting, his mannerisms looked distinguished, polished yet kind. "Sir, it says here that his office hours aren't for another 40 minutes at 11:15 a.m. Would you like me to leave him a message?"

"No, I think I'll wait on him."

"Uh – o-kay." Clearly, he wasn't expecting my answer. His helpful expression turned more cautious. His eyes suggested mistrust, uncertainty. "Well, if you would like to have a seat over there, I'm sure it would be a bit more comfortable."

"Cheers." I nodded my head and made my way over to a row of padded chairs that he pointed to which sat beneath the portraits along the wall. He looked back at me only once while I waited. Time ticked away as I took in all the sights and sounds. The area was stuffy, not bad though. It took on the smell and feel of a library that housed many volumes of old books. Occasionally, the atmosphere was broken by someone walking past me or leaving one of the offices to run some errand. A hint of Earl Grey steamed from the office across from where I was sitting. *Perhaps I should stop at the Emmanuel United Reformed Church to see if they have a brew.* My thoughts were disrupted as the entrance door swung open and a stately man entered dressed in dark trousers, a white button up shirt and a grey sport coat. The man held an overcoat in his left arm. I knew from the portrait that this man was Dean William Garris, more so by the reaction of the student behind the desk as he arrived. He stood from behind the desk to greet the gentleman and pointed in my direction as he spoke. The regal man eyed me from a distance before tapping the student worker on the shoulder and making his way towards me.

"Good morning, Sir. I understand that you were looking to speak with me about a matter?"

I looked at my watch. It read 11:12 a.m. "Yes, but I didn't expect you so early."

Dean Garris looked at his watch too, "Three minutes is hardly early, but punctuality is something I value."

"Right." I tried to make light of the situation, but I couldn't. His tone was direct. The stern expression implored me to get on with it. "I was wondering if you might be able to assist me with something. Well – someone actually. I'm trying to find Dr. Mya Bishop. I understand she was employed in your department."

His forehead creased as his silvering eyebrows turned inward and his breath was caught behind his teeth. This name clearly resonated with him. "Allow us to speak in my office," he finally said sternly.

I followed the man to the first office on the right. Across the hall appeared to be a small conference room. He shut the ornate door, hung his over coat on a rack to the right and made his way to his desk chair. Bookshelves were built into the wall behind him. Volumes of lore I had never seen or heard of overlooked the office space. Dean Garris sat in his chair with his sport coat unbuttoned. His grave expression hadn't changed. "Who are you?"

I sat in one of the fabric chairs across from his desk not waiting for his invitation to do so and crossed my legs allowing my hands to rest in my lap. He meant business, but I wanted to give him only little bits of information at a time. I wanted to see how he handled me inquiring about this mysterious woman. The less he knew about me from the start, the better. "I'm an interested party."

"Interested or not, I'm not at liberty to discuss anything that pertains to current or past employees. It's a matter of confidentiality. Now, who the hell are you?"

My tone now matched his. "As I said, I'm an interested party. I am seeking the counsel of Dr. Mya Bishop. It pertains to an event that she may have been involved with in 2009."

Dean Garris stood from behind his desk and slammed his hand flat against the desktop. "Damn it! Don't play with me good sir. I have stated my stipulations on the matter and if you cannot abide as such, then I am going to have to ask you to leave!"

Whatever brief thought I had of limiting the information I gave fluttered away with his outburst. He was smart and there was no avoiding it. I had to tell him who I was and why I was there if I was going to get anything out of him at all. Though his reaction was very curious. "Dean Garris I believe we got off to a poor start. My name is Chief Detective Inspector James Lawrence of the London Metropolitan Police Department." I showed him my identification papers. "I have reason to believe that Dr. Bishop was involved with an event that is linked to a case I've been working for some time now. If she is not available perhaps, I would be able to speak with a Dr. Cassandra Bishop."

"Dr. Cassandra Bishop died thirteen years ago." Dean Garris sat back down in his chair. His countenance didn't change, and his breathing was heavy. Anger teamed at his lips. He remained poised enough to keep it at bay and lowered his voice to a more civil level. "Dr. Mya Bishop – is her daughter."

"Is she here? The desk clerk out front said that –"

"No, she's not. Not anymore," he interrupted. "London Metropolitan Police Department – aren't you a bit beyond your jurisdiction?"

I removed the small notepad and the pen from within my coat pocket and made note of his last comment, completely ignoring his question. "When was the last time you had contact with Dr. Bishop?"

"I don't take too kindly to being ignored, Sir. If I were to proffer a phone call to your superiors, would they even know that you're here? And what repercussions might come of it?" Dean Garris reached for the phone on his desk.

I sighed deeply. No doubt he would still place the call to the station to see if I was sent to his office or if I was operating on my own accord, even if I disclosed more information about why I was there. Be that as it may, I needed to try to win his favor again. "There will be no need for that. Just over two years ago I came into a case that was odd in nature. A club in the Soho district of London known as *Club Red* had a very unusual event where there was a shooting, and several people were injured. Initially the disturbance was labeled a publicity stunt that had gone poorly. A little over a day later the club owner showed up brutally murdered in a church not far from here."

Dean Garris removed his hand from the phone and sat back into his chair. The information I was giving appeased him. "What does this have to do with Dr. Bishop?"

"I believe she was at the club the night of the disturbance." I didn't want to tell him that I had a picture of her from inside the club and that she was more involved than what I had already divulged. I especially didn't want to tell him *how* Dr. Bishop was involved and what she seemingly turned into. "There was lots of evidence that suggested an occult or religious following was responsible for the murder of the club owner. Considering that she teaches or taught as you so keenly put it, Medieval Folklore and Mythology, has published works on the darker side of this – this *mode* of thought, she's bound to have come across this kind of stuff in her studies. If she was at the club, she would be the foremost authority on the findings I have come across."

His demeanor had changed. Dean Garris continued to sit back in his chair. He overlapped his hands and held them close to his chin as if in deep thought. Several moments of uncomfortable silence had passed before he spoke. "When in 2009 did this event at the club happen?"

"It was in the first part of December," I responded relieved that the conversation had taken on a different, more civil direction.

"The last time I saw Dr. Bishop was a few days before beggar's night in October. After that she cancelled all her remaining lectures for the semester and took a medical leave of absence. I haven't seen her since."

"Do you remember the last conversation you had with her?"

"Most of it. The Arts and Humanities department was holding a 'Common Talk' and I wanted Dr. Bishop to participate. It would've been very fitting for her to speak on Halloween, given that her book and lectures had been on Lycanthropy. Purely academic of course, myths, legends, perspectives from different cultures, you know the sort." Dean Garris rubbed his forehead with one of his hands. I didn't say anything. I feverishly continued to scribble these bits of information into my notepad. It was again too coincidental not to write them down, knowing what I knew. "Mildred, my wife, and I were also hoping to have her over for dinner after the talk."

Their relationship was more than just that of colleagues. I could sense a longing for something, perhaps sadness over the loss of this relationship that I knew nothing about. "I'm assuming that she didn't give the talk. Do you remember why she cancelled?"

"She claimed that she had another appointment that she couldn't miss and that we should reschedule dinner. Dr. Bishop could be a recluse, too involved with her work at times. When you mentioned she was at a club, I was hopeful that she was getting out of her home, being more involved with people.

Since you say it was in December, it's just heart-breaking really."

"Why's that?"

Dean Garris hesitated. He didn't want to discuss this at all. There was dread in his voice now. "I fear that she was being pursued. Perhaps she was involved with things of an unbecoming nature." I gave Dean Garris an inquisitive look. My posture and expression all suggested to *go on speaking*. His anger had turned to sadness. "You are not the only one that has come seeking her or her counsel. Father Preston Mathew, a priest at St. Teresa's Cathedral, came looking for her too. He was equally as concerned about her as I was. We had agreed to stay in contact if either of us had any discourse with Dr. Bishop." I was astounded by the information I was getting from Dean Garris, and I fanatically wrote it down. "Don't bother trying to locate Father Mathew. He stopped by to see me once, a year after Dr. Bishop had disappeared to inform me that he was going back to Rome. He seemed very troubled over it."

"I don't understand. You think this priest was pursuing her? Perhaps for an ill manner?"

"No not at all. He was genuine, a true priest."

"Who then?"

"Robert Osborne."

"Robert Osborne? As in the former House of Commons, Robert Osborne?"

"Yes."

"What did he want with her?"

"The same as you, her expertise. Knowledge of her subject matter. He wasn't alone. His two sons were with him and two brutish lads that I couldn't help but dislike by just their appearance." My hand couldn't move fast enough to keep up with the information Dean Garris was giving me. What I was hearing spoke more into the validity of the video I had seen and the suspicions I had had about the Osbornes. *How could I have missed so many connections to the club and the church? Perhaps these details were meant for me to miss*, I thought. "I knew those men were trouble from the start. They promised to donate to the Arts and Humanities Department, but never did. Worse yet, it wasn't but a day later that the incident in the library occurred and I believe them to be the cause of it."

"Incident? What incident?"

"I don't like this conversation and I've told you enough." Dean Garris sighed and stood from behind his desk to regain his stately demeanor. He re-buttoned his sport coat and made his way towards the door. "However, I feel inclined to believe that you'll seek out the answers on your own, possibly causing a stir. With that said, your question may be better suited for Dr. Reynolds. His duties reside in the rare books section of the university library. It wouldn't be fair to relay the information second hand when he was the one who actually saw the events unfolding and then reported them to me. Now if you will allow me to pass. Dredging up painful parts of history was not what I intended to do with my office hours." Irritation had returned to his voice.

"Thank you very much for your time." I extended my hand for a gentleman's goodbye, but Dean Garris simply walked past me into the hallway and waited for me to leave. He locked his office door behind me. "Andrew, if anyone needs to speak with me, please inform them that I shall return in fifteen minutes."

"Yes sir," the boy behind the desk affirmed. Without saying another word, Dean Garris proceeded down the marbled hallway and disappeared around the far corner.

I looked at the student still working behind the welcome desk. "Andrew, is it?" He didn't respond, instead he just stared at me. I could tell that he was sharing in the distaste Dean Garris had towards me now. "Can you direct me to the university library? I need to meet with Dr. Reynolds."

He simply nodded and handed me a brochure that had a map of the university on the inside fold. Andrew pointed to a spot on the map. "We're here, the library is here. Dr. Reynolds should be there unless he stepped out to get a bite to eat."

"Thanks." Andrew said nothing more and watched me closely until I left through the front door.

Outside the weather hadn't changed much. A few more clouds filled in above as the wind continued to blow in gusts. According to the map the library wasn't far, maybe a full kilometer or so. *There's no point in taking the bus, by the time it comes around I'll be nearly there,* I thought. I needed time to sort out some of the new information before I spoke with Dr. Reynolds anyways. I made sure my coat was buttoned all the way up as walked down the road headed towards the library. *What appointment couldn't you miss, Dr. Bishop? Where did you go? What were you doing? Why were you at the club? And I knew it Mr. Osborne, you did have more of role in this than you led on, but what? Young Grayson, how did you get involved?*

Several students walked along the streets around me. Most carried messenger bags and all were dressed comfortably against the cold wind in their Barbour coats. The River Cam was empty. No one seemed brave enough to be out on the river punting on a day such as this. I continued my steady walk until I came to Queen's Road. According to the map the private access lane that led to the library was a little way up. I could see the center tower reaching towards the heavens over the shrubs that lined the street. The handsome structure stood silhouetted against the clouds. As I approached the library, its wings appeared to open before me. Reflections of the sky were caught in the columns of windows. Parts of the standing water had dried, leaving nothing much more than an outline of a wet spot upon the ground. This wasn't going to last long. I could feel the approaching rain. The air had grown dense since I started my walk, and I felt a twinge of regret for having not brought my umbrella. *This was unexpected, but important. I must talk with Dr. Reynolds,* I thought.

I looked at my watch. The time was just before noon. I walked through the tan brick archway into the grand foyer. To the left was a reader's service desk where two young ladies sat behind computers. I unbuttoned my coat as I approached their workstation.

"Excuse me. I'm trying to find a Dr. Reynolds. Do you know where he might be?" My cell phone buzzed inside my pocket. I ignored it.

"Is he expecting you?" one of the young ladies asked.

"No, he is not, but I do need to speak with him about an urgent matter." I held out my police identification papers. The young lady seemed surprised and a bit nervous.

"One moment sir. Let me see if he is in."

She proceeded to type at her computer. My phone buzzed again inside my pocket. I pulled it out and the screen read:

IRIS
CALLING…

I pressed the answer button. "Hello Iris."

"Please tell me that you are not at Cambridge University!" Her voice was laced with anger and venom.

"No of course not. I'm at the library." I had to lie to her.

"Can you explain to me why I received a phone call from a Dean William Garris?"

I knew that Dean Garris was going to make a call to the station but didn't know how much he had actually told her about our conversation. I needed time. If I could find the right answers and show cause for me being at Cambridge, Iris would have no other choice but to allow me to proceed. "I don't know. Are you sure that he didn't get me mixed up with someone else?"

"Bloody hell James, I put you on holiday to get some rest and watch the telly– but I certainly didn't intend for you to dig up bones from the past."

The girl from behind the counter looked at me. I could tell that she wanted to speak but was being polite. "Hold on – Hold on a second Iris."

"James! James!" I covered the mouthpiece of the phone and held it low so that Iris couldn't hear the conversation.

"Dr. Reynolds is in his office. Go down this hallway and make a left onto the North Wing corridor. His office is also on the left a bit down the way. Just look for his name plate."

"Thank you my dear." I held the phone close to my face again. "Gotta go Iris. Ready to checkout and don't want to be rude."

"James! James! Don't you hang –" Her words cut off as I pressed the end button. I turned my phone off so that she couldn't call back.

Etched woodworking covered the sides of some shelves, while others were more modernized. There was warmth about the place that was comforting. Perhaps it was in this solitude, the quietness of literary exploration that spoke so eloquently to the situation and not the ornate fixtures. I walked past students lost in stacks of books upon their tables. Collections of older books filled the rows of shelves and had an earthy scent, with a sort of musk to them. Gods and generals fought silent wars. There was no answer that could not be found in this place if one was simply willing to look. I was willing, but I was also desperate. Desperate to know the truth, to solve the puzzle.

I approached the office door of Dr. Reynolds. He stood from a padded rolling chair. A small wooden desk faced the right side of the wall. Opposite was a full, built-in bookshelf. The blue carpeting clashed heavily with the rich mahogany molding that lined the floors. He was dressed in dark trousers and a brown sweater over a white formal shirt. The collar poked above the sweater and contrasted starkly against his deep ebony skin. "Inspector Lawrence I presume."

We shook hands. "Yeah – but how did you know my –"

"Dean Garris had phoned to notify me that you might be stopping by for a visit. So, when the desk clerk informed me an inspector was here to see me, I presumed it was you."

His accent was heavy, South African, but no brokenness. Flawless in his manner of speech. He may not have had the same title as Dean Garris, but he was no less in stature and confidence. Since he already knew who I was, it was pointless to play quid-pro-quo with the man. I was better served to be considerate, yet direct with my questions. "I was hoping that you could help me with a case I've been working. The case involves Dr. –"

"Dr. Mya Bishop," he interrupted a second time. He wasn't being rude, but he clearly wanted to cut through the civilities and get straight to the point. "Dean Garris informed me of the details."

"What happened here at the library?" I took out my notepad and made ready for his response. I sat in the only other chair that was in his office. Dr. Reynolds sat back down in his own chair. Direct he was, not at all as standoffish as Dean Garris though. It was clear that he didn't want to discuss the matter, nonetheless he was more welcoming of the conversation by his posture alone. He crossed his legs and let his hands overlap as they rested in his thighs.

"It was Saturday, 5th of December 2009." I scribbled the date onto the notepad. My heart quickened at the mention of this date. The publicity stunt at the club immediately came to mind. *The two events happened on the same day. They're linked, but how?* I thought. I continued to listen. "I greeted her as I normally did, and we exchanged pleasantries. Then I inquired as to how I could assist her. Every time she had come into the rare books section of the library, I knew it was for more than just common talk. Dr. Bishop always had a purpose. She was always seeking out specifics that had to do with her research that weren't kept in general circulation."

"Do you remember what she was looking for?"

"Certainly. She needed help finding writings on the Catholic Church, writings or pamphlets that dealt with curses. Curses that may have been issued by holy men or priests in the time period of 15th through the 17th century."

"Did you find anything?"

"Yes. Not exactly what she was asking for, but categorically related." I continued to write as he spoke. *"Modern Thought and Faith* by Father Bentini was the first title I found. A secondary search had produced artwork, a pamphlet more closely to what she was seeking. The names mentioned in both were the same, Johan Stich."

"Is there any reason that you remember this so clearly? Memories aren't really rational thoughts. I would think that with the popularity of the library and your role here as…" I glanced at his name tag. "…curator, you would have examined hundreds, even thousands of books and helped countless people."

"We tend to remember the things we want to forget and forget the things we need to remember." I stopped writing and looked at him. Seriousness washed over him, and concern escaped his mouth. He leaned forward in his chair as if to keep secret the words he was about to utter. "I kept those materials out of circulation to the general public as well as from the faculty. I wanted to know why those materials were worth shooting someone over."

"Shooting? How? Who?"

"It was but thirty or forty minutes after I located the materials for Dr. Bishop that they showed up, looking for her."

"Who?"

"The name on the registry was Robert Osborne. He had entered the library with several other men to whom I didn't know but were later divulged as personal security. They tried to shoot Dr. Bishop." His lips trembled as he spoke. A deep-seated anxiety, even fear was apparent. "They later laid claim to the notion that it was a matter of personal security, and they were acting *justly* with their chosen actions." *The shooters in the club. Who else could it have been?* Dr. Reynolds stopped talking. I finished writing a bit of information and looked at him again. His words were stifled, heavy in his mouth as if he had no faith in or resolve with their meaning. "What I saw next was burned into my thoughts nearly every day thereafter."

"What?"

"As Dr. Bishop was fleeing these men, she ran straight at the electronically sealed door. The door was ripped from its mounts as if they were made of paper instead of reinforced steel."

"How?"

"I don't know." Dr. Reynolds shook his head in disbelief.

"I mean someone cannot just crash through a door such as this."

Dr. Reynolds said nothing at first. He rubbed his forehead collecting himself for a moment before speaking again. "When the doors were installed to help with climate control, I tested them myself, pushing hard against the doors when they were sealed. I couldn't get them to budge. Like I said, I don't know how she did it, and that has bothered me every day since."

This was difficult to hear, but not as surprising after seeing the video. The idea of Dr. Bishop being something other than a troubled human, involved with things beyond her own understanding or control, was still preposterous. I wasn't convinced that this was anything other than an occult practice. *She must've used some sort of theatrics, some form of deception, illusion, or special effects, something.* I thought. I doubted everything I was hearing and seeing. *There has to be a logical explanation for the events here at the library, for what I saw on the video of the club and for the murders at St. Teresa's Cathedral.* I was certain that the Osbornes were involved in all three, but more dubious was the role that Dr. Mya Bishop played and how she was enmeshed in this web of duplicity. *Doors. Here, at the club, was she at the church too?*

"May I examine the materials she was observing that day?" I asked.

Dr. Reynolds leaned back in his chair, steepling his hands and holding them close to his mouth. He looked over his fingertips at me. "Inspector, I knew the day would come when someone would inquire about the materials. I'm willing to discuss the matter with you despite Dean Garris's advisement, but I'm hesitant to allow anything further unless you have the proper documentation that suggests as such. Please don't take this as being obstinate."

"I understand." I was already pushing the boundaries of this situation and I had crossed the line with Dean Garris and most undoubtedly with Iris. I didn't want to do the same with Dr. Reynolds. He had been very informative and rather pleasant to talk with. I stood to shake his hand again. "Thank you. You've been most helpful."

"Good luck inspector. Please, do keep me informed. I did care for Dr. Bishop."

I simply nodded as I turned from him. *Why were the Osbornes trying to kill you Dr. Bishop? What answers were you searching for here? Dean Garris mentioned they were only trying to solicit your knowledge. Your knowledge on your subject…your subject of lycanthropy. No, no it's just not possible. I cannot believe it.*

These thoughts repeated in my mind as I walked back down the North Wing Hall. I turned my phone on again. I had two messages. *No doubt from Iris. She's going to be quite put out by me.* Sure enough the first message was from Iris, which stated that I had better have a good explanation for what I was doing. The second, more mercurial, was from Lydia.

"Chief. I ran into a few snags. But still managed to get a few bits of information. Call when you get a chance."

I deleted Iris's message. Dealing with her would have to wait. I immediately called Lydia.

"Chief" I heard her say.

"What did you come up with?"

"Nothing on the files. We couldn't get past the cyber locks. It kept requesting an administrative password."

"Bloody hell, curious, was it Iris that locked them?"

"I thought that she might have, so I had Jasper trace the cyber steps in an attempt to locate the IP address. It wasn't Iris. It was Sabastian that locked the files."

"Sabastian? What? Why would *he* lock any files?"

"I don't know chief, but the files appeared last active in January 2010."

"How do you know?"

"That's when his IP address for his computer was last tied to the files."

"This doesn't make any sense." I made a mental note to inquire about this later. "Did you find anything else?"

"I found the list of employees that worked in the club just before it closed."

"Security…names. I need you to see if any of the security personnel were treated at a hospital – anywhere in London or nearby, specifically Theodore Wells and Donovan Chambers."

"Chief, that could take a while. What do you hope to find? Most of those files are confidential."

"I just need to know if any were treated for broken arms or even facial lacerations on the night of December 5th, 2009. Also, I need you to pull up Robert and Grayson Osborne. I want to know about events surrounding both of them in December of 2009 and the months leading up."

"Okay, I'll do it, but you've got to tell me what this is all about. I could be more help if I knew the background of the case or at least what has changed in last couple of days."

"You're right and I will. Get the information I requested, and I'll explain everything. I'll call you later."

I didn't say goodbye. Instead, I simply ended the call and walked back to the service desk. The young girl looked up at me from behind the counter. "Is there something else I can help you with Sir?"

"Yes. I was wondering if you could locate *Demystifying an Old Myth: A Comparative Look at Lycanthropy* by Dr. Mya Bishop."

"Let me see if it is in." She took a moment to type the title into the computer. "No, I'm sorry. It looks like all the copies are in circulation. Would you like me to place a hold on it for you when it is returned?"

"No that's all right. I'll get it somewhere else." I wasn't surprised by this. Everything surrounding Dr. Bishop was a mystery.

The girl said nothing to me and proceeded to help the next person. I walked past those still in the lobby of the library paying them no attention. Outside the darkened clouds rolled overhead. I re-buttoned my coat. Wind carried the imminent arrival of rain. A storm was brewing, and it was apparent that I was going to be caught in the middle of it.

Chapter 13

A New Understanding
Chief Inspector Detective James Lawrence
Tuesday, February 21, 2012
9:30 a.m.

"Goddammit James! Are you mad?" Iris fumed at both Lydia and I as we sat in front of the desk in her office. She stood behind it staring down at us with nothing but anger. "I had hoped that you would get some rest. Come back clear headed! Not break jurisdiction exposing this department to legal ramifications, re-open a closed case and waste the man-hours of good inspectors chasing dead-ends!"

"But Ma'am, we weren't…"

"Not a word from you!" Iris interrupted Lydia. "It took special approval to get you into the inspector's training program, my approval! Don't think that I won't remove you from this program and have you thrown back into uniform working traffic duty at a kiddy daycare center!"

Lydia crossed her arms and stared at the floor saying nothing further. "Lydia was only following my directives. The blame resides with me." I tried to redirect her onslaught of fury towards me.

"Then perhaps both of you should be reduced to traffic duty! I expected more from you Chief - Inspector - Lawrence. I asked you to train her not corrupt her."

"She has not been corrupted. Iris you're being unreasonable –"

"Superintendent Cornell if you may *Sir*! And I'm not being unreasonable. You deliberately disobeyed me and drew other officers into your antics. You have left me with no other choice. Lay your credentials on my desk as well as your pieces. Both of you are hereby suspended from duty for two weeks with no pay while I decide what further consequences that need to be upheld. That'll be all!"

Lydia got up first, laid her credentials and sidearm on the desk before storming out of the office. I stood shortly after and did the same. "There's more to this case than what we had known before, Superintendent. I will get you the proof of that _"

"No, you won't because I don't care, James. If you had good evidence, it would be dismissed by any barrister before it even got to court. You broke pro-to-col! Protocol exists for a reason." Iris leaned over her desk a bit more. Her eyes were sharp and the muscles in her jaw flexed as she spoke through gritted teeth. "I'm very disappointed in you. Now get out of my office."

I said nothing further. Instead, I turned and walked out. Half -way back to my own office, Richard Scott called out to me, "Chief, Chief!"

"Piss off Richard!" I was in no mood to deal with his desperate plea for attention.

"I just saw Lydia, she's fuming. What happened?" Care for her welfare, I assumed was at the bottom of his list. I took his advance to be more opportunistic, lobbying to be a part of the work I was doing.

I ignored his question but turned to face him. "Where did she go? I need to speak with her."

"I don't know. She just stormed past me. I would wager that she was headed for the exit."

He pointed towards the main hall, and I didn't wait for him to say anything else. Instead, I moved past him in an attempt to catch up with Lydia. Chatter and the echo of ringing phones filled the busy main hall. I looked over the banister, but Lydia was nowhere to be seen. I hustled down the steps taking them two at a time. It was tough to see around the people walking to and fro or being brought into the station in cuffs. The first floor was even busier than the floor I worked on, but I caught a glimpse of Lydia as she walked through the glass doors that led onto Broadway.

"LYDIA!" She didn't respond to my call. I hustled past the hordes of people and pushed open the glass door. "LYDIA!"

She continued to walk away from Scotland Yard, unphased by my attempts to call after her. I quickened my pace to a light jog, knowing full well that she was heading towards the stop on Victoria Street to catch a bus. Fortunately, the red bus was still a ways down the street and Lydia was forced to wait, giving me a moment to speak with her.

"There's not much to be said, Chief. I'm going get pissed at the pub and I don't want you around." She didn't look at me. Lydia stared past me at the approaching bus.

"Lydia, give me a second to talk with you. Iris is just mad. I've known her a long time and if we give her the right evidence then she'll be much more forgiving of the situation. Nothing further is going to happen."

"All due respect Chief, she is your boss and by in turn she is my boss. I have worked too hard to become an inspector only to be placed back on traffic duty and for what? You haven't even told me why we're doing what we're doing."

"Lydia, I can explain. Just listen-"

"No! You listen! You wake me in the middle of the night, have me go into the station to look up photos of people that are dead, or secret, or something…I've gone against protocol seeking out information you say is linked to the Club Red case and this Dr. Mya Bishop person, but you don't elaborate, you don't tell me why I'm searching for the information, but it's too late now. I don't want to know."

"Lydia –"

"No, Chief! I don't want to know. I like my job and I want to do my job properly." She reached into the pocket of her pants to collect the fare for the bus. "I don't get it. Why have you kept me in the dark? Why haven't you told me who this Dr. Bishop person is and why you went to Cambridge in the first place? Why –"

"Lydia –" The brakes of the red bus squealed as it came to stop in front of us. Several people stepped off as a few people started to make their way on. "Let me explain…" I finally blurted out. "She's a werewolf!"

"Who? A what?" Lydia stopped rummaging around in her pocket and looked up at me.

"A werewolf…Dr. Bishop is a werewolf."

"You're taking a piss."

"Ma'am are you getting on the bus or not?" the bus driver asked. Lydia looked at him and then back at me.

"No…I'll catch the next one." Her words were reluctant as she stepped down from the entrance. The glass door closed, and the bus proceeded further down Victoria Street. Lydia looked directly at me, bewildered by the seriousness of my last comment. She sighed, "You've got some serious explaining to do. Otherwise, I'm going to deem you fucking mad."

"I know." I paused and looked around. A small café was just a few blocks down the street. I finally looked at Lydia who continued to stare back with pursed lips and a furrowed brow. "Come on…let's get some tea."

Outside, clouds covered the sky and hardly any sunlight came through the window that Lydia and I sat beside. Patrons came in and out of the café. It was small, with a few tables against the rear wall. Conversations from those around us were muted, reduced to a dull hum, nothing more than white noise in the background. Lydia's tea remained untouched for nearly an hour. Her arms were folded across her Higgs leather coat, and she said nothing more than a few words of acknowledgement. Her facial expression remained static but was overflowing with a level of disbelief that mixed with confusion as I recounted everything I had learned about Dr. Bishop.

"Stop, stop…let me get this straight…you're saying that all the stuff that happened at Club Red, the church in Cambridge –"

"St. Teresa's Cathedral," I corrected.

"Whatever…and the stuff at the University Library at Cambridge, are all tied to and possibly the result of this professor, Dr. Bishop, who you claim to be a *werewolf*?"

"As hard as it is for me to believe, I don't have any other explanation."

"This is lunacy! And it's going to land us both in the nut house. How do you expect me to believe all this?"

"Like I said, I'm not sure I fully believe this. I still think there has to be a rational explanation, perhaps theatrics of some sort. What I do know is the more I uncover, the further from the truth I feel. It's as though some darker force is at work here."

"Darker - force?" Skeptical, Lydia shook her head from side-to-side as she reached for her tea. She brought it to her lips and sipped it slowly as though it was still hot but placed it aside in disgust at the realization of its cold bitterness. "This is madness."

I leaned back in my chair, sighed, and looked around the café for something to distract me from the fact that Lydia was right. Just saying it aloud to another person *was* madness, crazy, even ridiculous. I had no solid proof; nothing that swayed my thinking one way versus the other on the matter, only hunches, not anything tangible. Even the video from *obscuritiesdocupub.com* was easy to rationalize as doctored up or having been pushed through some video editing software. Yet, there was a realness to it and the other facts surrounding this mysterious person. I glanced back at Lydia. "Were you able to find anything out about Robert Osborne or the security personnel from the club?"

"Yes and no."

I leaned forward placing my elbows onto the wooden table, pleased the conversation had drifted back to something more concrete, more towards reality. "What did you find?"

"I couldn't find anything about the security personnel. Per the criteria you set, no one, no security, were treated at the hospital. No broken arms or facial lacerations. The strange part about it is that there were no current places of residency, no next of kin listed for either Theodore Wells or Donovan Chambers. Nothing we could follow up on if we wanted to. It's as if they simply vanished after working that night."

"Strange indeed. Were there any last known addresses?"

"No, the only address was for the club."

I crossed my arms and shifted in my seat. "What about Robert and his family?"

"His daughter, Laryn, was killed on the 27th of November 2009. Reports have classified it as an animal attack." She stopped and shook her head again in disbelief. "This madness...Chief, the report stated the body was dismembered."

"How? I mean…what kind of animal?"

"The forensics report left the animal type as unclassified. It suggested large, carnivorous species given the bite radius and the amount of damage to the body."

"Anything that could dismember a body doesn't exist anymore in England. Bears, a pack of wolves, have been hunted to the point of extinction."

"I know."

"I mean one might encounter a fox or a lone grey wolf, but neither are capable of dismemberment. Are you sure it didn't say anything else?"

"A few bits of fur were collected, but again it was left as unclassified, no specific match."

"Do you still have the file?" I was desperate to comb the file for any other details that Lydia's inexperience may have overlooked.

"No. It's in my desk back at the station. Like *I* said, this is going to land us in the nut house." I understood her implication now. It was evident she too was grappling with a few unknown questions and the fact that I mentioned werewolves only exasperated her inability to think critically. "This means we're stuck, doesn't it?"

"Not exactly."

"What do you mean? If we can't go back to the station –

"We don't need to go back there," I interrupted. "Iris said we were suspended, but that doesn't mean we can't travel to Glasgow, Scotland."

"Glasgow! What for? I can't go to Scotland!"

"You have the capability of buying a train ticket, right?" I asked as sarcastically as I could muster. "Then you can go to Scotland."

"Again, what for?"

"The image I sent you of Dr. Bishop came from a video posted on a website that I've used in the past to research obscure happenings. The site owner, Duncan Sheehy, lives in Glasgow, Scotland."

"Why can't we just talk to Robert Osborne or his son, Grayson?" Lydia was uneasy. I could hear it in her voice as she shifted in the hard chair.

"We don't have any sufficient evidence, nothing that would warrant us talking to them."

"That's not true. What you found at Cambridge is plenty enough for questioning. How can you say we have nothing?" Lydia wanted a resolution to this mystery too. I drug her into this muddled situation and frustration permeated her essence. I owed her more than this.

"Consider what we would be asking. As you already stated, this is lunacy, madness and if we approach a high-profile man such as Robert Osborne to confront him about werewolves without any solid proof of such things, our careers *will* be over. I'm afraid that his resources probably surpass ours."

"So, you're telling me that going to Glasgow, Scotland to search for the owner of a website that posted a suspicious video of a supposed werewolf is better? Chief! Do you know how crazy that sounds? Not only are we going to be out of jurisdiction, but we'll also be out of the country!" Lydia sat straight up in her seat dropping her arms to her sides.

"Shhh!" I waved my hand at Lydia to quiet her voice. Some of the other patrons had stopped their conversations to observe the commotion she was causing. They stared at us for a few seconds before resuming their talks. "I know it's crazy, but he's the only connection we have and the only option we have if we want to continue this investigation."

"*If* we find him. After that, then what?"

"I just want to talk to him. I mean come on he was there that night. He saw first-hand what Dr. Bishop supposedly turned into. He might be able to explain what really happened, if it was just a publicity stunt or some kind of theatrics."

"And what happens if we don't find him? And we don't have sufficient evidence to support our actions? What then with Superintendent Cornell?"

"Then we just accept our two-week suspension and any other consequences she may issue to us." I didn't like telling Lydia this and she didn't like hearing it, but it was true. If we didn't produce anything concrete, then we were stuck and there wasn't anything that we could do about it.

Lydia turned her gaze away from me, crossed hers arms again and stared out the window. Several moments of uncomfortable silence slipped passed before she looked at me again. "Why do you care about this case?"

Her tone was soft, almost consoling as if she was searching for a deeper meaning behind just the facts. I hesitated before I answered. "These cases are the ones that shape us as inspectors."

"That can't be the only reason. I mean, we –"

"I owe it to someone," I interrupted.

"Who?"

I didn't want to get into the reasons behind why I wanted to solve this case. I didn't want Lydia to know that I thought the innocent and pure of heart were at stake, but if she was to be involved with this case and I needed her to be, then I could see no other option. I had to tell her. I had to tell her that people like my late wife, Millie, may be in danger or suffering at the hands of the wicked. Yet, the unknown in this case and the question that beckoned to be answered was who were the innocent?

~ 169 ~

Chapter #14

We had caught our train at the King's Cross Station at 10:00 a.m. and traveled up the East Coast of England through Peterborough stopping only for a bit in York before continuing to the Newcastle station. Lydia didn't say much the entire four and a half hours we spent on the train. She sat across the aisle from me and simply stared out of the window at the landscapes that passed by us…rolling pastoral land with a mixture of green and brown. It all looked the same to me. Occasionally the scenery would be broken by a cluster of leafless trees or a small ravine that had been carved into the landscape by a river. It wasn't until we crossed over into Scotland that the scenery took on something of interest. Beautiful foothills, some topped with a dusting of snow, others simply brown but distinctive. The occasional farmhouse lined with split-rail fencing or a quaint town nestled into the hillside, all alluded to a majestic history, and charming allure. Even the ruined castles that were built as outposts of war had adopted this new purpose and stood weathered, but grandiose against the folds of time. The world was full of untold stories.

Our route was longer than traveling up the Western Coast by about two hours, but Virgin lines didn't have a train departing London on that route until 4:00 p.m. I couldn't wait that long and taking another train service meant that I wouldn't get to use the trusted *Bag Magic* service offered by Virgin lines. Most of our things were packed into my small suitcase, including two of my personal handguns locked in a small case. Though privately owned, I ran an awful risk bringing them into Scotland and didn't mind paying the £10.00 for the service and the discretion to have it delivered directly to the hotel. *I hope I don't have to use my guns*, I thought. *The last thing we need is to explain to the local authorities why we have guns, or worse why we're even here.*

I occupied most of my time by organizing the photos I had on my phone. I had created several albums, one of which was labeled *Cases Pics* which contained all the photos we had of Dr. Bishop as well as the Osbornes, both professional in addition to the more peculiar ones at the club. I was fortunate that no one had purchased a ticket for the seat next to mine. It gave me a place to drape my leather coat and stretch out my legs. I had hoped that Lydia would take the opportunity to sit next to me so that we may form a strategy. Still upset with me over this whole ordeal, not once did she look in my direction. Lydia was significantly less interested in this trip. *I have put her in a tough spot,* I thought. We had planned to stay at least one night in Glasgow looking for Duncan, yet I was still plagued with the question of how we were going to find him once we arrived at Glasgow Central station. As most of the passengers around us got off the train at Edinburgh, the seat next to Lydia became vacant and I placed my phone inside the interior pocket of my coat seizing the opportunity to move next to her in order to speak about Duncan.

"The way I see it is this, once we check into the Rennie Mackintosh Station Hotel, we can start making inquiries about Duncan and his website."

She unfolded her arms and turned to face me. "Wait, wait…You mean to tell me that *that* is your big plan? Start making inquiries? Please tell me you at least know who we're going talk to about Duncan."

I hesitated before I answered. "No, I don't, but his site is popular enough that someone is bound to know him."

"Bloody hell, Chief!" She shook her head and placed one hand over her forehead. "Just because his site is popular doesn't mean anything. He could be some nerdy kid that's living in his mum's basement playing video games all day.

Why don't you just call someone at the station and get them to run a check on his name and background?"

"I would've done that already if I *could* have. We're suspended, remember." My tone was sarcastic. I was slightly irritated by her obvious demeanor, but she had every right to be put out by me. I had dragged her damn near kicking and screaming into this lunacy. "I would normally get Sabastian to do this kind of stuff, but –"

"– You don't trust him anymore now that you know he locked the files at station on Dr. Bishop." Lydia interrupted. "I'm right. I know I am."

I lowered my gruff voice to a solemn whisper, "I don't know. As I stated before, the closer I get to the truth the further away I feel. My gut is telling me that there's more to those files than what we know and that being cautious is probably our best choice of action."

"Is there any other person you can call? I'm not going to walk around the city asking people if they know Duncan Sheehy."

"You're right. Simply asking around is idiotic."

"What about Jasper Davis? He helped us when you had me looking for the security guards' medical records and was able to find the information on Robert Osborne and his family."

"No, we can't use him either. He's a good kid and I like him, but he works closely on things with Iris. That's probably how *we* both got busted for all this instead of *just* me."

"There has to be someone?" Lydia's voice had grown taut. Again, her feelings were justified. "How about Richard Scott? He's always asking about what we're working on."

"Oh God no! Not Richard. That knobheaded git will get us in trouble or worse, killed. There's no way I'm going to ask for his help."

I could feel the train slowing to a stop just before a voice came on the loudspeaker inside the train announcing our arrival at Glasgow Central Station.

"Look, if we don't get someone back at the station to help us find Duncan then I simply going to board another train when it stops and head home!"

"Lydia, please no! I can't."

The train glided to a stop and the voice on the speaker system continued to announce where the train would stop next along with a few other pointless broadcasts. Lydia crossed her arms undaunted from her decree. "So that's your decision then?" I didn't answer right away. I was buying time to come up with a better solution, yet Lydia thought otherwise as she stood from her seat and pushed passed me. "Fine. Off you go."

Lydia joined several other people walking down the aisle in order to exit the train. I stood, grabbed my leather coat, and walked after her. "Lydia! Wait a moment!"

She continued to exit the train and made her way towards the nearest ticket queue ignoring my call. I pushed past the crowd of people that had flooded onto the platform, scattering in all directions. Opportunely there were a few people in the queue ahead of Lydia. I needed her. As stubborn as she was being, I needed her help. Finding Duncan would be impossible without her and any attempt at doing so would be futile. "Okay, Lydia. Have it your way. I'll call Richard as soon as we check into the hotel."

Her stern gaze was unnerving. No words were necessary to explain the frustrations she had towards me. "This is your last chance. If you're taking a piss this time, we're through! No words, no anything, just done!"

Her voice had become increasingly sharp, almost strident. I simply nodded, "I understand."

Lydia said nothing more but turned away from the ticket queue. A sense of relief washed over me as I sighed releasing the breath that was choked up. I was happy that she wasn't leaving, but the thought of bringing Richard Scott into this ordeal was certainly unappealing.

It only took ten minutes or so to walk to Rennie Mackintosh Station Hotel. The hotel was attached to Glasgow Central.

Inside the lobby space was tight. The blue wall behind the check-in desk stood out symbolically against the cream trim and white panels. I felt as though we were moving into darker territory, something that was more than unknown, but dangerous. I could feel it.

There was a bar attached to a small dining space just down the corridor from the lobby. No doubt it would be better than the fast-food restaurants situated in the same building as the hotel. I didn't plan on staying long enough to get more than one or two meals. We had work to do, and I was anxious to get on with it.

Once in our room, I tossed my leather coat upon the far bed to the left of a small television. Favorably, there were two beds. I turned to emphasize this point to Lydia and found her standing in the doorway of the room, staring at me. Her face was stern, steadfast. "Call him," she said.

"Huh?"

"Don't be daft or I'm walking away. Call him, call him now." Lydia extended her hand that held a cell phone.

I walked towards her and took the phone. "This isn't going to bode well for either of us. You know this, right?"

She said nothing but urged me to proceed with a nod. I dialed the number for New Scotland Yard and waited for the automated system to connect.

"SCIT 221275…Family Liaison." Again, I waited while the system ran its check on my credentials and connected me to the Family Liaison Advisory Team that Richard worked under. Lydia continued to stare. She crossed her arms and leaned against the wall. I waited for nearly a minute listening to a recording of pertinent information for various problems a person may have when trying to contact the authorities.

A monotone voice finally broke the repetitive recording, *"Family Liaison. How may I direct your call?"*

"Sergeant Richard Scott." I was hoping that Richard wasn't going to be available. That he was away from his desk for some routine duty and that some other solution would present itself in a manner that would no longer require his assistance.

As luck would have it, the deafening silence on the line was broken by the grating sound of Richard's voice, *"This is Sergeant Richard Scott."*

"Richard. This is James Lawrence."

"Yes…I mean…is this the Inspector James Lawrence who was recently suspended for misconduct?"

"Yes - Richard. Both Lydia and I need your help. Are you still looking to help my team?" I laid the phone on the nearby desk and put him on speaker phone so Lydia could also hear what he was saying.

"Huh, why should I help you? I mean, wasn't it you who denied me access to your team? And also told me to piss off?"

Richard's smug implications were an irritant. "I told you this was a bad idea," I whispered to Lydia before looking back at the phone on the desk. "Look, Richard, are you going to help us or not? I really don't have time to play this game with you."

"Tell me why I shouldn't tell Superintendent Cornell right this very instant that you are trying to solicit my help when you're supposed to be on forced leave?"

"What do you want Richard?"

"You know what I fancy."

"To be a part of my team? Consider it done upon my return." Everything inside of me cringed at the thought of working with Richard, but he was right. He could alert Iris to what we were doing and that would surely mean the end of both Lydia's and my careers.

"And if you don't return? I certainly haven't heard that you were going to be able to return."

"There's a lot you haven't heard Richard. Again, are you going to help us or not?"

"Fine. Done and done. I'm now officially part of your team. What do you need me to do?"

"I need you to look up someone for us in the database at work. His name is Duncan Sheehy, and he runs a website known as *obscuritiesdocupub.com*. We need to talk to him and need his current as well as all last known addresses. Be quick about this and keep quiet, I don't want the superintendent finding out what we're doing."

"Al-right. This may take a moment to find. Is there a number I can call you back on?"

"Lydia's cell phone number." I hung up before he could respond with some self-satisfied comment about joining the case. My hope was that I could back out of our arrangement when this was all said and done. More importantly, my hope was that he wasn't walking directly into Iris's office to expose what we were doing to gain more of a foothold over the cases handled by my *SCIT*.

I sat on the edge of my bed and looked at Lydia. She continued to stand against the wall by the doorway with her arms crossed staring down at the floor. We waited, neither of us speaking. The room was a dull tan color with nothing on the walls except two mounted light fixtures above each bed. The silence in the room was deafening. *That little twit is probably squealing to Iris right now*, I thought. *I knew I shouldn't have used Richard.* I glanced back at Lydia just long enough to catch her gaze before she let her eyes fall back to the red mosaic printed carpet. *She knows I'm right too. She knows that both our careers are over and it's going to be because of Richard Scott.*

Several minutes slipped by and the digital clock that sat on the nightstand read 3:40 p.m. I leaned back on the bed and crossed my arms over my face. *Why did Sabastian lock those files? What are in those files that are so important?* My thoughts broke and I sat straight up on the edge of the bed at the sound of a knock on the door. Lydia had jumped too, but then looked through the peep hole. "Who is it?" she asked.

"Luggage service madam. I have a bag here for a James Lawrence." I rose from the bed and made my way over to the door. Lydia backed away and sat on the edge of her own bed. As I opened the door a uniformed hotel staff member stood before me with my overnight bag in his hands. I took the bag from him. "If I could just get you to sign here sir stating that you did in fact receive your luggage."

"Certainly." I scribbled my name onto his form and tipped the gentleman some of my pocket money before closing the door.

I walked past Lydia and placed my bag onto my bed. As I started to unzip the bag, I stopped to turn my attention to the ringtone on Lydia's cell. She gingerly grabbed the phone from the desk and returned to the edge of her bed across from me. The caller ID read:

No Caller ID...

My heart pounded in my chest. The look on Lydia's face suggested the same. I pressed the button to accept the call and turned the phone back onto speaker for Lydia to hear. "Hello?"

"Hello mum? It's Richard."

Both Lydia and I breathed a sigh of relief. "Bollocks Richard! Why the hell were you blocking your number?"

"Now mum, don't take that tone with me. I'm using my cell and maybe I don't want you to have this number. Did I give you a bit of a fright mum? Good. Consider us even for telling me to piss off."

Lydia shot me a smug, *I- told- you- so* look as she pursued her lips. Playing along with what he was saying I purposely hesitated before saying, "Uh...I think you have the wrong number, *sir*."

"Oh, shut up mum! The person you're looking for resides at Westmuir Street, Parkhead, Glasgow, apartment G31."

He was an ass, but he was proving to be very useful. In all seriousness, if someone is to trace this call between us, he now had an alibi by saying that he was trying to surprise his mum with a well-wishing phone call and didn't want to let her know it was him; but carelessly dialed the wrong number.

Lydia wrote the address onto a small notepad she pulled from the nightstand between the beds. Continuing to play along with his antics I made my voice a bit more stern, "Sir, I do believe you have the wrong number."

"Oh, silly me, I was trying to call my mum. Good day to you fine Sir." Richard hung up without saying another word. Lydia grabbed the phone and immediately punched in the address on her phone's GPS.

"Well, it looks like he's twenty minutes away if we are driving. We could take the train but I'm sure we can catch a cabby that'll drop us right in front of his flat." Confidence filled her voice over the course of action we were currently pursuing, more so than an hour earlier.

I turned back to my luggage bag and pulled from it the small case and two holsters. Inside the case were two Glock 17 semi-automatic pistols. "Here…take this." I handed Lydia one of the holsters and a sidearm.

She looked at it with ambiguity. "Do you really think we're going to need these?"

"I don't know…but I would like to be prepared in case we do." I finished strapping on the holster and positioned the Glock securely.

"Come on this is Scotland. The crime rate isn't high enough for us to carry guns even if we were a part of their police force. Besides, if he sees these guns he's just going to run."

"I hear what you're saying, and I understand that in London it's different, we're part of a special crimes unit that is allowed to carry firearms. But we don't fully know what we are dealing with here and if we run into something unpleasant my goal is to be prepared for it."

Lydia shook her head from side-to-side a couple of times before grabbing the weapon. Both concealment holsters were designed to be worn under our coats. Lydia removed her leather coat and slipped her arms through the shoulder loops of the holster and secured it just as I had done. She put her coat back on and zipped it. The sidearm was completely concealed. "This could get us into a lot of trouble."

I zipped my coat too. "I know. This goes without saying, but we're going to exercise caution and restraint. I'm not going to expose my weapon unless you or I are in great peril."

"Let's hope it doesn't come to that."

Lydia followed me out the hotel room and back to the main lobby to exit the building. Union Street was buzzing with people. Not like London, but nonetheless it was active and busy. People waited patiently for the bus whereas others were simply walking in and out of the local shops and bakeries before continuing down either side of the street. Outside the air was cold. Dampness from recent rainfall hung heavy from the lack of breeze. Overhead, grey clouds blocked the sunlight. Any hope of seeing the light blue sky that made the buildings look more luminous, was gone. The dull greyish-tan bricks of the buildings appeared even more dreary without the bright light. Several black van cabbies were parked in a line outside of the hotel and the train station.

I opened the door to a cabby and the driver immediately asked, "Where to Madam, Sir?"

"Can you take us to this address?" Lydia asked in return as she handed him the original slip of paper she had scribbled the address onto.

"Certainly."

Within moments were heading south on Union Street before turning left onto Clyde Street that ran parallel to the River Clyde. The water looked dark and cold. The entire trip was just under twenty minutes, but dreadfully boring. Nothing stood out as exciting. Most of the architecture was the same with only a few varying colors. The dreariness of the day made them look worse. Lydia said nothing but appeared to be more actively engaged in this pursuit. When we came to a stop on Westmuir Street, I handed the taxi £10.00 to cover the fare and provided him with a tip before exiting the cabby.

"Thank you, Sir. Do you need me to stay?" he asked.

"No. That won't be necessary." I waved my hand and watched for a moment as the taxi drove away.

There were significantly less people walking along the sidewalk. Looking up at the tan and reddish buildings in front of us, we noticed that there were several satellite dishes mounted to the brick. "Someone is in the building," Lydia stated as she continued to look up.

She was right the satellite dishes were mounted too high to be associated with Hair and Beauty Shop, the Pizza –Kabob – Burger eatery, or the Polish Specialty Store & Café located on the street. "Let's go around back to see if we can see a walkway or stairs to those flats."

Lydia nodded in agreement and followed me around the building down a side alleyway to the back. Sure enough there was a set of stone steps with wrought iron railing that ascended to the back of the flats. We both walked up the first set of stairs. Lydia stopped and pointed, "Look."

A small well-kept courtyard could be seen and sat adjacent to a primary school. Laughter of some young children could be heard as they skipped and played along the walkways. Others toddled along hand-in-hand with adults. It appeared that the school had let out a little earlier, but some students were just now being picked up by their parents or guardians. I turned to Lydia, "What was flat number?"

"G31. What does he look like again?"

"African decent, young, maybe your age," I replied.

"Sorta like that?" Lydia gestured with her head towards a young man who had exited the school and was walking across the street towards the courtyard and the flats talking on his cell phone. He carried a brown, leather courier bag over his shoulder and was very unassuming, yet still had a serious manner about him that made me cautious. "I'm going to stay down here to see if he comes up the stairs," Lydia stated as she pointed towards a small alcove beneath the stairs.

"Right. I'll go to the flat." I walked up another flight of stairs and the flat was just to the left. I knocked on the door but there was no response. A couple moments past and I heard a voice I recognized, but it wasn't Lydia.

"Yes, but I think I need –" The young man stopped what he was saying into the phone when he saw me. Our eyes met for a moment before he dropped the phone and turned to run. "Shit!"

"Wait! Duncan!" I grabbed his phone and started down the stairs after him, calling his name. "DUNCAN!"

I cleared the first sets of stairs going down but stopped before continuing when I heard a thud and sound of leather bag falling to the ground, followed immediately by some commotion.

"Stop - struggling!" It was Lydia. Her voice was clearly strained. I hurried my pace down the remaining flight of stairs. I started to unzip my coat to reach for my gun when I saw Duncan lying on his stomach, struggling to crawl away from Lydia who was desperately holding onto to his legs.

"Stop! Both of you!" Lydia released his legs and Duncan scurried to his bottom and backpedaled until his back rested against the concrete pillar. "Duncan! We're not going to hurt you. We just want to ask you a few questions."

"How – How do ya know my name?" His breathing was heavy, and it was obvious he was scared.

I looked at Lydia who was also out of breath from tackling and struggling to hold onto to Duncan. "Nice work." She nodded but said nothing as she placed her hands on her hips and continued to take deep breaths. She was ready to chase Duncan down should he try to run again. I turned my focus back to Duncan. "We are police inspectors and all we want to do is to talk about a video you posted on your website. I'm Inspector Lawrence and this is Inspector Cooper."

"Police! For What? I know the videos don't quite fit the school curriculum, but it's perfectly legal and I have a license and I was told to post –"

"I know your business is perfectly legal," I interrupted. His demeanor appeared calmer, but he was still on edge. "We want to discuss the content of one particular video. It's relevant to a case we're working. Is there some place we can talk in private? Perhaps the café around the front?"

I extended my hand to help him to his feet. Lydia kept a close watch in case he tried to bolt again. He stared hard at me and oscillated between my hand and eyes, not trusting anything. Rightfully so, had I been in the same situation, I would've hesitated too. Still breathing quite heavy as he slowly grasped my hand and struggled to his feet. I handed him back his cell phone. Duncan took it and looked it over. It appeared that the casing had taken the brunt of the fall, but his call had ended. He blew some dust from the screen. "So, I've done nothing wrong?"

"No, not that we know of," I replied.

"It's about the video in the club, isn't it?"

"Yes."

"Just to be clear, yer not here to hurt me, right?" he asked as he straightened his blue sport coat and brushed off some of the dirt from the walkway off his trousers.

"No, why would we?" Lydia interjected.

"Good, Thank God." Duncan grabbed his courier bag as he stated, "The café will be better place for us to talk."

"Why did you try to run?" Lydia probed. I glanced at her then back to Duncan. "Who would be trying to hurt you?"

Duncan met her gaze and then mine as he rubbed the nape of his neck. He looked over his own shoulder again. "I don't know. I'll tell ya inside the café. Not out here and certainly not in my flat."

Inside the Polish café, the smell of freshly baked bread and rolls permeated the small space and blended with the rich aroma of coffee and various other hot beverages. Other decadent dessert items such as raspberry filled cakes and scones could be seen behind a glass encasement. Patrons came into the café to pick up cooked as well as raw meats, no doubt for their evening meals. All the food tugged at my stomach and reminded me that I hadn't eaten since the morning. I promised myself that I would buy something from the hotel or even the dining car of the train if we decided to leave tonight after we had completed our talk with Duncan. Those that stayed in the café did so to enjoy a warm drink in a social atmosphere before retiring for the day. No one paid any attention to the three of us. Despite this, Duncan insisted on sitting at a small table to the left of the entrance. Both Lydia and I sat across from him. He had his back to the far wall of the café so he could see out of the glass windows at the front and nervously sipped a specialty drink.

"Okay, so what do you want with me and what do you want to know?"

"Why were you trying to run?" Lydia blurted out.

I held my hand up to Lydia to stop her verbal onslaught. It was clear that she was still a little hyped up from tackling Duncan. "We are inspectors from London. As I already mentioned we are here to talk to you about the video you posted to your website titled, *Beyond the Brink of Reality*. It is relevant to a case we are working on." As gruff as my voice was, I was trying to keep it low and calm. I could see that Duncan's hand was shaking from nerves. "Can you explain to us what happened that night in the club?"

"Aren't ya a bit beyond yer jurisdiction?"

"Yes, that's why we only want to talk to you."

"Alright then…It's exactly how I described in the title of the video, *beyond* - the brink of reality. I've never seen anything like it."

"What were you doing there?" Lydia's impatience was getting the best of her.

"Same thing everyone our age was doing sweetheart, getting pissed and having a good time. I didn't mean to run across that fuck'n thing!" The sound of breaking glass caused Duncan to jump and turned his attention to behind the checkout counter where one of the employees of the café had dropped a plate. He breathed heavy several times then greedily drank his beverage. "Couple mates and I decided to go to

London on holiday. We had run into a couple of ladies that fancied us at the French House Pub. They said that they were going to a club nearby. We didn't think anything of it, other than a good time. All of us stumbled down the street to this club."

"Club Red, right?" I asked urging him to continue.

"Yeah, that's the one. We waited in the queue for over an hour before we got in. All was well. I was dancing, having fun, so was the lass that was with me. She wanted to take a selfie of us. Nothing fancy. But she started recording, instead. This was only for a bit of fun. That's when I heard this God-awful screaming. The music shut off and we turned to see one of the big blokes wriggling around on the floor like little child, with his fuck'n arm broken and dangling." Duncan gestures with his own arm to illustrate his point. "What could do such a thing to someone that big and strong? Then I saw it."

Duncan paused as if he had tapped back into something dreadful. His breathing intensified and grew rapid.

"What did you see Duncan? What did you see?"

"I don't fuck'n know, but the goddamn thing looked like a werewolf!" Sweat started to form across his brow. Lydia had scrawled a few items onto a note pad but had stopped as the story developed into something unusual. She stared at Duncan, said nothing, clearly enthralled by what he was saying.

"Did you notice anything theatrical? Anything that looked like stage props or stage 'magic'?"

"No. Nothing. I saw a small woman change into a terrible thing. If it was just a prop or as you said, stage 'magic' then it was the most convincing illusion I've ever seen and one I hope I never experience again."

I unzipped my coat and took out my cell phone. I tapped on the photos app and scrolled through until I saw a picture of Dr. Bishop. "Was this the woman who changed?" I asked as I turned the phone so Duncan could see.

"Too fuck'n right it is!" I scrolled through the pictures of Dr. Bishop in the club then stopped at her University of

Cambridge profile picture. "I don't want to look at her any further. It's her eyes. Those green eyes cut through the darkness that night and have burned into my memory. They haunt my dreams and I think about them daily."

"There was shooting in the club." Lydia turned her attention back to her notepad and wrote a few more items. Sweat was now dripping down the side of Duncan's face and his hand was shaking worse than before. I wanted to direct the conversation towards something other than the beast. I tapped the photo of Grayson Osborne. It was his military profile picture. "Could you tell me if this man, Grayson Osborne, was the one doing the shooting?"

"I don't know. It was dark."

"Can you look at the picture again? We have reason to believe he was there."

"Sure mate. He looks a little familiar. If you say he was there, then he was. I had forgotten I was even recording until much later because I was so frightened of what I was seeing. Like I told you, I don't really know."

I laid my phone on the table and sat back in my chair. Lydia finished writing and looked up from the notepad. "Why were you running and why did you think we were going to hurt you?"

Duncan looked around the café again and then back at Lydia. "After that night, I was a mess. I couldn't sleep and when I did, I had nightmares. I teach children you know, the site is just a side business, you know for extra pocket money, but I found that I couldn't do my job well anymore. I took sick days and ended up seeing a therapist. I told her everything that had happened. She diagnosed me with generalized anxiety disorder and prescribed me some medicine. She told me it was probably a manifestation of the alcohol and that I shouldn't be worried. But I didn't get any better. I would see the eyes of the beast everywhere I went. Scrolling through the photos on my phone, I found the video. I watched it a hundred times, trying desperately to understand it. I even showed it to my therapist who said something similar to you Sir." Duncan pointed at me. I leaned forward again and rested my arms on the small wooden table. "She said it must've been something created from the theater and these things didn't exist. She again stated it was a manifestation of the alcohol. She then encouraged me to post it on my website and let others post comments explaining what really happened. So, I did it. I posted it. Several other people that were there that night ended up finding it online and expressed similar problems, nightmares, anxiety, same as me. No one could explain it. Then shortly after the comments were posted, it started."

"What started?" I asked.

"Paranoia according to me therapist. I feel as though people are follow'n me. I walk down the street and the anxiety will hit me and I can't identify the source. It overwhelms me. People will look at me from within crowds. I'll make eye contact with them, but as soon as I am distracted or break my gaze, they're gone. They'll disappear in a crowd of people like a puff of smoke in a strong wind. That's why I ran from ya. I thought ya were part of the ones who are following me."

"Did you keep in touch with the ladies you met that night?"

"No, no I didn't. As soon as the shooting started I lost her in the crowd." I grabbed my phone from the table and pulled back the lapel of my coat to place it inside the interior pocket when Duncan pointed to the holster with the Glock 17 under my coat. "What's that?" Duncan asked exasperated.

"We're inspectors. We're allowed to have registered firearms." I was trying to calm him down and prevent him from throwing a fit.

"Ya said ya only wanted to talk. Show me yer credentials."

Duncan's eyes were wide with fright and his breathing was acute. I was also a little unnerved because Iris had taken both Lydia's and my credentials. "We don't have them with us at the moment. But I can assure you we are telling you the truth."

"Yer talkin pish! Ya are with them!" Duncan backpedaled to his feet from the small table and with a violent thrust he flipped the table upside-down. The contents of his specialty drink splashed down the front of Lydia. She stood to her feet in disgust and started after Duncan who had already ran from inside the café out onto Westmuir Street. I too stood but I knew chasing Duncan was pointless. Instead, I threw out a half-hearted apology to the café employees and the few patrons that were disturbed by Duncan's outburst as I grabbed several napkins from the nearby countertop before following Lydia.

I caught up to her about a half a kilometer down the street. She had her hands on her hips and was breathing hard again. Light brown liquid from Duncan's drink was still dripping from the front of her leather coat. Lydia continued to look around for signs of Duncan. He was nowhere to be seen. "Here take this." I handed Lydia the handful of napkins.

She snatched them from my hand forcefully as she turned to wipe the drink from her face and coat. "Well, that was bloody brilliant! I goddamn told you bringing the guns was a bad idea!"

Lydia was right and it was unfortunate that this situation erupted the way that it did, but I wasn't going to chance entering an area to look for someone we didn't know without being properly prepared. "Come on. Let's go back to the hotel."

"What about Duncan?" Lydia held her arms out to either side, dumbfounded with wide eyes and an open mouth.

"Forget about him. We know where he lives if we need to find him again."

"What? We came all this way only to talk for ten minutes, have a table dumped on our heads, my coat is going to be stained, and you say forget about him when he runs off." I smirked as Lydia continued to stare at me. "I don't find this funny." Lydia turned away from me shaking her head again, hands still on her hips. Several quiet moments passed before she held both arms in the air and shouted, "This has been a complete waste of time!"

"Not exactly," I responded. "Duncan did offer more support that Grayson Osborne was at the club. He did confirm that the woman who changed into a werewolf was Dr. Bishop and he also stated that there were no theatrics involved when she changed. He seemed pretty convinced of that."

Lydia looked over her left shoulder at me again. "So, what does that mean?"

"It means that there was more to that club then we previously found. You heard Duncan say it himself, best illusion he's ever seen."

"I don't think he said it quite like that, but I see your point."

"I was thinking this whole time that the *people* at the club may have performed some trick, but the thought never occurred to me that the club itself was set up to perform the illusion. There were mirrors everywhere in the club. Magicians can make just about anything disappear, why couldn't they perform an illusion of transformation?" I paused for a moment to flag down a cabby that was driving down Westmuir. The cabby came to a stop in front of us and I opened the door for Lydia. "I just want to know what are on the files of Dr. Bishop that Sabastian locked. But since we can't get at those files –"

"We're going to inspect the club," Lydia added as she ducked into the cabby.

"Eventually, but I think it's time to talk to Grayson Osborne again."

"Hopefully not tonight."

I could see the concern on her face from the thought of riding four and a half hours or so back to London and then going into an abandoned club. I slid into the cabby with her and shut the door. "No, of course not."

CHAPTER 15

Target Practice
Grayson
Thursday, February 23, 2012
12:00 p.m.

Click, Click, Click

The silencer on Codie's Glock muffled each report as three rounds pierced a paper target mounted to a stack of sandbags twenty-five meters down a row of hedges. All three bullets struck within the kill zone of the thoracic region.

"Brilliant. Now two in the head," I instructed Codie. The day was overcast, and a chilling breeze kicked up and stung my cheeks. Codie was undeterred as he took aim again. His focus remained a picture of fortitude.

Click, Click

Two more muffled rounds found their marks dead center of the head portion of the target.

"Well done. You've gotten much better. Go change the target."

"Right." Codie trotted towards the paper target.

With all the adjustments that Kap has made to the HK's, he and I needed to set up the sandbags to test if the weapons were working properly. Secrecy has always been a concern, so the only logical place to establish a concealed shooting range was in my father's garden along the hedges. What used to be a point of pride and prestige for my father as he entertained bureaucrats and other business leaders at the manor, now looked ragged and unkempt. I couldn't help but notice the similarities of my father to his garden. A ragged, unkempt heap of poisonous emotions was he, no longer the point of pride and prestige to his constituents. Nonetheless, the overgrowth proved useful for weapon tests and target practice.

"What next?" Codie asked. His words snapped me out of a daydream state. I never imagined that I would be training Codie in tactical procedures, and I too was a bit ragged.

"Um yeah…how many rounds do you have left?"

Codie slid the magazine out of the Glock. "Five."

"Okay…I want you draw up on the target and run towards it. Fire at the target on the run…empty the magazine, slide the magazine out, let it fall to the ground. Reload, and attempt to get three more rounds off before reaching the target. Got it?"

"Got it!"

"Alright then, off you go." I stood back and watched as Codie readied himself. He took a deep breath and started running with his handgun pointed towards the target.

Click, Click, Click, Click, Click

I could see the bullets hitting the target, but I couldn't tell the accuracy. I wanted to make sure that he was able to master this technique given that the beasts we faced were *not* stationary targets and that it was highly likely that he would have to reload on the run.

Not once did Codie slacken his pace. He pressed the release lever on the side of his gun and with one quick motion the empty magazine fell to the ground as he reached for another one clipped to his belt. It wasn't more than a second or two before he had the other magazine jammed in place.

Click, Click

Two more rounds hit the target before Codie stopped running. He quickly holstered his sidearm and stood in front of the target. He didn't turn to look at me but instead hung his head forward and rested his hands upon his waistline.

"I'm sorry Grayson," he finally said.

I walked over to Codie, "Sorry…sorry for what?"

"I know you said three shots after I reloaded, but I was only able to squeeze off two."

"How's your shoulder?" I asked. Even though Codie had gone through an extensive amount of therapy and had added fifteen pounds of muscle from weight training, the nerve damage in his shoulder from the claws of the beast, still caused him problems now and then.

"My shoulder's fine…I just wasn't quick enough," he finally stated.

"Codie, look at your target." He raised his head up to see what I was pointing out. "All of the rounds you squeezed off were kill shots. Look, five in the body and two in the head again. Do you know what that means?"

"No, what?"

"It means you're still alive! If this were a real scenario, whatever you were shooting at didn't have chance." Codie mildly smirked as his confidence seemed to return. "You've come very far in the last couple of years. Now empty your firearm and call it quits."

Codie slid the magazine from its cavity and discharged the round from the chamber. "What's going to come of all this?" he asked.

"You become an even better shot then you are now."

"No…I mean of all of this hunting…" Codie paused before he continued, "…will life go back to normal?"

His question was one that I played out several times in my head and implored numerous outcomes and scenarios, but I still didn't have a good answer for him. "I don't know…I don't know Codie. My concern right now is getting through all of this and once we survive this, then we'll put the pieces back together."

"Dad hasn't been same since Laryn died." Codie and I have never really discussed how Dad had and still was spiraling out of control, yet his probing statement warranted a response.

"None of us have been the same since her death." It was a safe reply. Codie hadn't opened up to anyone about that night. Laryn was dead, but sometimes even I forget that Codie was a victim too, he was just lucky enough to survive. I hoped my answer would spur more conversation from him.

"I know that, but Dad especially." Codie paused before he continued. "Dad is losing his fucking mind. I mean look at the way he has been acting towards you, or the way he responded when he saw Ada for the first time, and the other day when you all went to Club Red on…on –"

"Greek Street."

"Yeah whatever…the point being, he was pissed when you guys returned. He was pissed at you, Ada, even Henry!"

"I know…come on, let's go inside." We both walked towards the manor from the garden. I wanted this opportunity to talk with Codie, so our pace was slow. "Look, Dad is filled with rage and there isn't much that is going to change that except for killing Dr. Bishop. At least in his eyes. However, the deeper we get into this the more I come to realize a larger part of this story is greatly unknown to us. So, whatever happens to me, dad, Ada or whoever, you have to keep your mind intact. Meaning, always think, problem solve…don't let your emotions run wild or you'll end up like Dad."

"Can we trust her?"

"Who? Ada?"

"Yeah, and Gerda for that matter."

"Ada is young and full of anger, but yes, I believe we have to. All the more reason for you to keep your wits about ya."

"Wits…I feel like I'm at my wits end…if I had any to begin with." Codie shook his head and stared at the ground.

"What do you mean *if you had any to begin with*?" I asked.

"I've let everyone down," Codie started.

"Codie you haven't…" Codie looked up and held up his hand to interrupt.

"I have…I wasn't able to help Laryn when she died…fear has been my constant companion…so much so that I couldn't concentrate on school. I mean, how many universities have I dropped out of now? I even got my ass handed to me by a girl. Let's face it Grayson, I have been and probably will continue to be useless to this family."

I paused. Codie hadn't ever opened up like this. In fact, he had gone to great lengths to keep it concealed from everyone after Laryn's death and was probably why he had been spending so much time with Kap. "Rubbish…"

"What?"

"Rubbish…what you said about being useless…it's rubbish. Ada's tough…she could probably take me down too. Fuck the universities, that shit can come later…and Codie, none of us could've helped Laryn that night, but we all came face-to-face with something that the rest of the world doesn't believe exists. It left a terrible scar on you…both physically…" I pointed to the area of his shoulder and chest where the claws had dug in leaving behind a nasty scar, then to his head. "…and mentally, yet your resolve has remained intact."

"So what? What does that even mean?" Codie asked.

"It means everything…it means you have the fortitude of a good soldier…you're resilient."

"Even with fear?" he asked.

"Yes…fear doesn't ever leave us, even with the strongest fortitude. Learn to use it, though. It's our warning mechanism in our brains to be cautious, but it sharpens our senses. And I need you to remain sharp, especially with Dad losing his shit." Codie seemed to respond to this with a reassured nod. "There's no telling what the darkness has in store for any of us," I finally said as we continued to walk toward the manor.

Chapter 16

Forbidden Pathways
Chief Inspector Detective James Lawrence
Thursday, February 23, 2012
12:30 p.m.

"I'll be sure to forward the message to him and stress that it is urgent, Sir. Is there anything else that I can do for you?" Charlotte, Osborne's receptionist, asked.

"No. Thank you." I leaned back in a wooden chair that sat across from Lydia. She had her hands poised around a glass of ice water with her elbows resting on the matching wooden table. There she sat, calm and seemingly un-phased by the other patrons in the café, watching me, waiting for me to explain our next move. I was pleased that she didn't just leave me to brood alone. "Damn. We should probably just go to their manor."

"Chief you're going to have to get off it. Like you said if we approach him again, we better have hard evidence to bring him in and more importantly *not* be on suspension. Otherwise, we'll lose our jobs and probably, seeing how pissed off the superintendent was at both of us, bring about more consequences." She looked out of the glass wall at the people walking past. "I mean…what are we doing here anyways? Is this café just going to be our new place to meet before we go out on wild chases that dead-end us?" Despite her direct questions, her tone was calm, not at all plummy, yet still irritated. It suggested that she had accepted this was an odd case. She was very observant though, I was running out of avenues for this case and if something didn't manifest soon, I would have no choice but to let it remain as a cold case.

"It's not even about arresting him anymore. It's simply about knowing the truth…and we're not dead-ended." I was still gruff, aggressive. In fact, I was livid. Grayson was at the club, I knew it, Lydia knew it, but there was nothing we could do about it. "And no, this café just happens to be close to the station. I talked to Richard this morning and asked if he would let me know *if* and *when* Sabastian comes back into the station. As it turns out he was there yesterday, late in the afternoon. So, I'm having Richard keep an eye out for when he comes into the office today."

"When were you planning on telling me this?" Lydia had a genuine sense of disappointment in her voice. "What are you going to do?"

"I just told you. All I want to do is talk with him. I want to know why he locked the files and see if he had anything to do with what happened at the club."

Lydia took a deep breath and released it fast. "Just talk with him. Like everyone else we 'just' talk to?" Her sarcasm returned. "And we're just going to sit here and wait. What if he doesn't come in today because he's back on assignment?"

"We'll give him a little more time, that's all."

"Why don't you just call him and ask him to meet here or wherever? You both were on the same team for quite a while, and I would assume you have his phone number."

"I do and I would call him, but –"

"You don't trust him…I know. This is really pissing me off."

"It's not just that. If he did lock the files and I call him asking for a meeting outside of the station, he'll suspect something and have time to prepare an answer. If I catch him by surprise, we may get an honest reaction."

"You want to see if he's lying?"

"Yes."

"I've got *one* problem with this…we're – still – suspended! We can't just walk back into the station and corner the poor bastard."

I nodded and looked away from her. We sat not really saying much of anything for quite a while. I watched Lydia's expression change from an active listener to someone who was put out by being left out of the loop. Lydia crossed her arms, leaned back in chair, and watched the people outside. She had nowhere else to go. Our suspension was in effect for another week and half. Inside the café more people came in looking for seating. Several individuals eyeballed Lydia and I for our lack of conversation and the occupancy of the table. Other conversations around us were background noise, indistinct and irrelevant. An hour slipped past before my cell phone buzzed with a message.

> Sabastian just walked in.

"Who's that?" I looked at Lydia for a brief moment but didn't answer before I sent my reply.

> Coming up.

"You're right, *we* can't go into the station…but *I* can." Swiftly I stood from my chair and walked out of the café.

"Chief wait, wait! What are you doing? Bollocks!"

The café was just a block away from the station. "Go back Lydia, you've got a bright future as an inspector, and I have already gotten you into enough trouble as it is."

She grabbed me by the arm forcing me to stop. "You're taken' a piss!"

"Lydia, I mean it. Go!"

"Shut up and listen!" No longer was her tone calm, or even low. She was clearly angry. "I lobbied to be part of the candidates that you were going to recruit for your team. I worked my ass off to get noticed, not because I wanted to be an inspector, but because being an inspector was the *only* way that I would get to do this kind of work. Now if you feel strong enough to put your career on the line, drag me to Scotland while illegally carrying firearms only to do something this ridiculously fucking stupid, then fuck it…we'll see it through to end! But to shove me aside as the only team member you've got right now in a self-sacrificing gesture…well, if I needed that I would buy a fucking dog! Now let's go get fired to-geth-er!"

At a loss for words, I watched Lydia walk ahead and through the New Scotland Yard doors. I had to admit as poised and controlled as she was at the café; this was a side of Lydia I hadn't fully seen but admired. I quickened my pace to catch up with her. We said nothing further to each other as we rode up the elevator. As the doors opened to our floor, Lydia walked out first and strode across the open space in front of the elevator and past a few of the desks in Sabastian's direction.

"Sabastian! Can I talk to you for a moment?" Direct and authoritative, Lydia walked right up to him. Her furrowed brow betrayed the calm exterior she usually kept.

"Uh yeah…why do you look so pissed?" Sabastian asked.

"Because James and I are at a sticking point in our case, and you seemed to be involved."

"What the hell are you talking about?" Sabastian stood from his chair. He towered over Lydia. His hulking muscles made her look tiny, but she wasn't backing down. Sabastian looked in my direction as I approached. "James you better call off your new kitten. What's she talking about?"

"Tell us what you know about a woman named Dr. Mya Bishop." My tone was more controlled than Lydia. I stared directly into Sabastian's eyes. He was clearly put out by how this exchange started but having worked several cases together, he knew where this line of interrogation was headed.

"James what is this? I don't know what you're talking about!"

"Just tell us what you know about her, Sabastian," Lydia said more under control.

"I would lass, if I knew what he was talking about."

"Sabastian, we know. We know that you locked the files on a woman named Dr. Mya Bishop back in January of 2010.

You're one of the few people that have the ability to lock and unlock digital files administratively. With Jasper's help we were able to trace it back to your computer. Now why did you do that?"

Several other officers, Richard Scott included, had stopped what they were doing in order to watch what was happening. Phones continued to ring as most of the officers focused on us.

"You're joking, right? I don't know who this Dr. Bishop person is. Never in my life have I heard the name until just now."

"You're lying!" Lydia asserted with her voice flaring back to frustration.

"Lying? Well, aren't you bloody charming." Sabastian looked back in my direction. "James, we've worked together a long time, why are you treating me like this?"

"We have reason to believe that you may have been more involved with the events at Club Red and possibly the events that took place at St. Teresa's Cathedral. Are you involved with any occult activity?" I asked.

"I think too many of these cases have got you wacked out!" He crossed his arms. "To be honest, this is why I left your team. Too much of this speculative shit! Now you've turned it on me."

A stinging irritation washed over me upon hearing the real reason he left my team. "Sabastian, just tell us why you did it!"

"I'm not going to listen to this any further. Piss off you tosser! And take your new kitten with you. Her claws are barely sharp." Sabastian walked away from his desk mumbling indistinctly.

I was surprised that Iris didn't come out of her office to address the commotion. Perhaps lucky was a better way to describe it. She may not have been present at the time of the debacle. Lydia stared at me for a moment before shaking her head and pursing her lips in irritation.

"Damn it!" she said as she kicked over the small trash can by Sabastian's desk. Most of the other officers immediately went back to work once they realized that the distraction was over.

"Wooo weee! You really baked your balls with this one!" Richard Scott made his way over to us. "I thought it odd that you were being so secretive about Sabastian, but I had no idea this was going to happen. I don't think either of you are going to be coming back after that display."

His shrill, grading voice had a smugness to it that goaded me, as though he was proud of his himself for something. Though he had come through for us when we were in Scotland, Richard was proving himself nothing more than an opportunistic vulture that waited for others' vulnerabilities to be exposed before taking his share.

Lydia stepped in front of Richard. Breathy, "What next Chief?"

"How do you feel about going to the club tonight?" I asked as we started to walk away from Richard.

"Why not? We're probably getting fired. Adding jail time will make it all the sweeter," Lydia said with as much vinegar and sarcasm she could muster.

"Hold on!" Richard pushed passed and stopped in front of us holding his arms out to either side. "Aren't you forgetting something? I'm part of this team now and it sounds like you're discussing *our* case without me."

"We can discuss the case after the weekend. There's too much to get you caught up on. Besides…I don't want to take away from your *other* duties." Low and gritty, my voice insinuated deviance as I leaned forward into Richard's personal space.

Taking a step back, he didn't even bat an eye. "Well, seeing how it is that you both don't have anything else to do for the rest of the day and *wow*…look at that! My schedule just got cleared. You've got plenty of time to get me caught up before we *hit* the clubs tonight."

"As you pointed out, we're probably not coming back. We don't have to include you on anything." I wanted him gone and was hoping this was going to be the end of it. I turned from Richard as Lydia and I made our way to the elevator. She pressed the button to open the doors.

"No, you don't. But I can certainly include Iris." Lydia walked into the elevator, but I stopped and held the door open while I venomously looked over my shoulder at Richard walking towards us. "I'm sure she would be delighted to hear about what you're doing tonight and may even show up with a welcoming party of other officers. If you don't want that to happen, I suggest you recant your statement about excluding me."

There was no way around it, no way of shaking him from this. Irritating and relentless, Richard was determined to get what he wanted. His reward for helping us in Scotland was leverage. Richard walked into the elevator. "Have it your way," I said as I too entered the elevator and let the doors shut.

I insisted that we discuss the matter at my flat in Shoreditch. It was the only bit of control that I had left over Richard. We sat in my living space and reviewed the case files of Club Red and St. Teresa's Cathedral with Richard. I went into great detail about Robert and Grayson Osborne and how they may be involved with the occult. I disclosed how Lydia and I had traveled to Scotland to find Duncan Sheehy and showed him the video of Dr. Bishop changing into a supposed werewolf. We discussed for several hours the different possibilities, the ways in which the club as well as Dr. Bishop could've pulled off such a display of theatrics.

The video wasn't any easier for me to watch. It bore the same level of mystery and caused the same level of anxiety as the first time that I had viewed it. What I had forgotten was that this was the first time that Lydia had seen the video in full. Both Lydia and Richard were not only taken aback by it, but also disturbed by what they couldn't fully explain. As manipulative as Richard was, all his cunning and twisting of the situation had given him little understanding of what we were trying to accomplish. It wasn't until he saw the video that he fully understood the rationale of going to the club to search for clues; something that would lead us to comprehend how the video magic was performed.

"So why did you feel the need to confront Sabastian the way you did? It certainly was quite a show," Richard asked. His voice was more inquisitive now and carried manipulation.

"While trying to pull up the files on Dr. Bishop, we discovered that anything outside of her work profile was locked and we were able to trace the IP address of the computer used to lock the files to Sabastian's desktop. If he truly did lock the files, it wasn't going to be something that he was readily going to admit. So, we decided to surprise him to determine if he was lying," Lydia explained.

"Clearly he wasn't lying," Richard added.

"I agree," I said. I didn't like agreeing with Richard. It only gave him more credence, but there was no denying it. Sabastian was telling the truth. "We came at him a little aggressively, but I think his reaction was genuine. If he didn't lock the files then the question is, who did and why not use their own credentials?"

"What exactly do you hope to find at the club?" Richard asked. He sat on my couch writing notes onto his own notepad. His sarcasm had been replaced by a level of seriousness which made him more tolerable. "You said that there was probably some theatrics involved, perhaps some illusions or stage magic, but you didn't specify anything."

"I don't exactly know. I want to examine the flooring, anything that might open down that something could've been planted in or came up from. There may also be a device that portrayed the image or something."

"Are you talking about a hologram? Come on James. That stuff only exists in science fiction stories."

"Richard, I'm not talking about that. I'm making reference to things that magicians use to create the illusions, some device that may be set with mirrors as a way of redirecting an onlooker's eye away from what created the illusion, projectors certainly *do* exist."

"Why would the club do this Chief?" Lydia's question was equally as unknown as how the illusion was created. "People go to a club to dance, to get pissed and have fun. The club didn't need any more publicity."

"Publicity or not, let's look at what we know about the occult. The different sects that exist operate under one banner, *fear*. And they go to great lengths to instill that fear into their followers. They sacrifice non-followers in grisly fashions, there's almost always a ritual and with the ritual, comes theatrics. If we understand the theatrics then we can understand the ritual better and come closer to making a positive ID on a particular group."

"I don't know James. Rituals, theatrics, instilling fear into their followers; sounds a lot like church to me." Richard again was right.

"Most of the occult is a mockery of the modern church. But to the followers of an occult group, the type of stuff we viewed on the video *is* their church. They believe in it and often will do whatever it takes to protect it. This is what makes them so dangerous. And I'm not referring to the Wiccans, naturalists, or herbalists of any kind. Though often lumped together with satanic practices by the church, they are generally peaceful, accepting, and tolerant. I'm referring to the groups that have a direct hatred for anything the modern church stands for. Groups that are atheistic, agnostic, and even deistic foundationally but go to extreme lengths to act and profess self-interest and egotism. Often criminally or to indulge secret desires and fetishes."

Richard put his notepad onto the small table in front of the couch. He leaned back, held his own wrist, and placed the back of his hand against his forehead. The challenge of this kind of work was taking a toll on his wits. Whether he would ever admit it or not, it was far more involved and encompassed darker things more so than he was accustomed to dealing with.

He sighed and said nothing further about the occult to Lydia or me. Several moments of uncomfortable silence drifted by before Richard sat forward on the couch. "So, what do we need to do for tonight?"

I shifted in my chair to glance at the clock. It was approaching 8:00 p.m. in the evening. Leaning forward, I looked at Richard and then back at Lydia who sat across the small table in another chair. "We need to wait."

"Wait?" I thought you said –"

"Wait until much later in the evening," I interrupted Richard. "This is a Thursday night in London. The Soho district may be packed. We have to wait until most of the establishments are closing down for the night or until the patrons of the places staying open later are fully pissed and won't care what we're doing inside an abandoned building."

"Well, you know the tubes don't run all night. We may get caught waiting several hours for a train in early a.m. Not something I want to have happen considering what we just discussed about the occult." I sensed more apprehension in Lydia than Richard. "How are we going to get in without people noticing?"

"There's an alleyway along the right side of the club, if I remember correctly. A set of metal doors that lead into the club were heavily damaged. My hope is that no one took the time to fix them after the club closed and we'll be able to enter through those doors. If they did fix them, I would rather break-in through the dark alley rather than in front of the building. I rose from my chair and walked over to the table by the front door and grabbed the LED flashlight from the drawer. I did the same in the kitchen before moving to the dining table in the space next to the living area. On the table were the Glock 17 firearms that we took to Scotland. I hadn't unpacked them from the trip. I brought the case back into the living room and laid it on the small coffee table, open so the contents could be seen. I handed Lydia a flashlight. "We're also going to take the necessary precautions again."

Lydia took the flashlight. "This is risky Chief. *Again*. How are we going to get those guns onto the tube? We turned in our credentials to the superintendent when we were suspended and there's no special luggage service like before. We have to show credentials to the guards every time we ride. You know that."

"Not to worry, sweetheart." Richard looked at Lydia. She gave a disapproving glance back for the comment. "I can carry the firearms until we get to our location. I'm more worried about what damaged the door. Oh, and I have my own flashlight, by-the-way. Thanks for the offer you *didn't* make."

Richard looked back at me. I said nothing in response to his comments. I simply gestured as though I didn't know, because I didn't know what damaged the doors and I certainly didn't care if he had a flashlight or not. I glanced back and forth between the two of them. "It's settled then. We'll wait until around 11:00 p.m. to catch the train to the Soho district. If it so happens that we have to wait a long time for a train home, we'll just call a cabby. It'll be more expensive, but at least we won't get stuck."

The hours ticked by on the clock seemingly slower than normal. We all continued to sit in the living space not saying much to each other. Lydia would glance at me for a moment but then get lost again in her thoughts. She got up only once to check the times of the train that traveled to Soho before returning to the chair. The exact departure time of the train we were going to take was 11:15 p.m.

Richard proceeded to alternate back in forth between his notepad and phone before being content to simply stare at the floor as he too was in deep contemplation of the events that were going to happen. As soft as the cushions were on the chairs and the couch, we all seemed uncomfortable, even nervous. Perhaps it was because of the legalities. None of us would be able to explain breaking into a space that was clearly forbidden to go. Maybe it was the unknowns, the things we couldn't explain collectively or conceivably, it was the one thought that haunted me from the start and had continued to grow in an ugly, troubling comportment of people that suggested this very well may be real. All I knew was that the closer the clock got to 11:15 p.m. the more anxious I became. Beats of my heart echoed inside me as visions of the video replayed in my head blended with the uneasiness of everyone that I interrogated. *Everyone I questioned was either nervous or standoffish, why?* I thought. *What did they know or see that I have not?*

My thoughts were broken by Lydia announcing it was time to go if we wanted to catch the train. I must've been in a daze because Richard was already standing and working to strap on the two concealment holsters for the two Glock 17s. We walked out of my flat and down onto the street. The night air was cool, but not overly cold. A few scattered clouds made for a nicer evening, clearer than normal. *No moon…If the legends are true and these things are real, at least we don't have a chance of running into one…but she changed inside the club…how?* I felt silly over this thought. Nevertheless, this case had more unknowns and dark things than any of the cases in the years that I had been an inspector.

"Let me talk to the gentleman at the police box," I said as we entered the Liverpool Street station. "I know him, and he'll let us through."

"With all due respect James, whoever you think you know may not be working. Allow me to take the lead on this one." Richard took great pride in saying this. It was almost a jab, a joust from his newly acquired position on my team; a step towards overthrowing the old lion in order to lay claim to the pride.

In the guard station was a younger looking gentleman that I did not recognize. I had so transfixed on what we were going to do that I had let slip my mind that this was not my normal traveling time and those that worked the night shift were typically the younger constables that had not yet earned their seniority.

"Excuse me young sir," Richard announced as he walked up to the guard station. The station was busy with people entering and exiting. "I'm inspector Richard Scott and these are two of my associates. I work on a special cases investigative team, and I'm licensed and issued the privilege of carrying firearms. The two behind me do not have any firearms on them whereas I do."

A twinge of irritation poked at my pride as Richard said this. Yet, he looked the part still dressed in more formal attire whereas Lydia and I were dressed down in trousers, casual tops, and leather coats. Richard flashed his credentials allowing the officer a quick glance and nothing more. It was clear that the officer wanted to take a harder look at the credentials but was getting a bit overwhelmed by the amount of people that were coming through the station gates without being watched. We hadn't transferred over Richard's credentials and they still said *Family Liaison Unit*. He placed them back into his coat pocket as he revealed the firearms he was carrying.

"Sir, I just have to check your associates' identifications." The constable was desperately trying to slow the process down, but the horde of people that were behind and around us made it difficult. *This isn't going to work*, I thought.

"If you may constable, our case is a little time sensitive, and we really need to get moving." Richard had been planning this whole time to take advantage of the crowd in order to get through the line without any delay or being denied.

"Very well, you're clear," he said to Richard. He glanced at our ID cards and motioned to us with his hand. "You two, lift up your coats."

Both Lydia and I did as he asked. The officer said nothing further to us. Instead, he waved us on with the rest of the bystanders and handed us back our ID cards.

"Bloody hell, that was easy," I said aloud as we road down the escalator.

We boarded the train and Richard sat next to me. Without looking directly at me stated, "I know you think of me as a manipulative bastard, which I am." He turned his head to face me and let out a toothy grin. "But you have to admit that it's proving very useful for your cause."

Richard remained smug the entire train ride. Fortunately, the trip only took us about twenty minutes to get to the Soho district. When we arrived, the time was 11:35 p.m. and just as I had suspected most of the restaurants were closing up while the pubs and night clubs were all busy with drunken patrons who paid very little attention to three additional people walking up the street.

From Greek Street, the club was dark. No light came from within, and the building was in stark contrast to the other active establishments that stood around it. No one except the three of us seemingly noticed the building. The front entrance remained boarded up. We intended to keep it that way. The thin alleyway stretched into darkness behind the building, just as I had remembered. One at a time we moved into the shadowy space. Richard handed me my firearm and unstrapped the holster from beneath his coat for me to put on. He did the same for Lydia.

"This way," I said assuming control of my team again. The three of us cautiously marched down the alley until we came to the metal doors, or what was left of them. Both doors were horribly bent as if something large had pushed through them from the inside out. One lay on the ground, barely attached to a mangled, rusted hinge while the other was securely attached at the top hinge. The bottom hinge had been torn from its mount.

"When you said they were damaged I figured that they were just rusted with a broken latch. You didn't say they were nearly torn from the frame," I could hear the fear in Lydia's voice. We clicked on our flashlights. I examined the doors for any kind of gimmickry. Nothing, at least nothing that was noticeable in the dark. Lydia squatted next to me. "Are you sure about this Chief?"

"The good thing is we don't have to *break* into anything." Richard added. "You both can stay out here, but I didn't come all this way to stop at the door." Richard maneuvered passed both Lydia and me holding his own firearm and flashlight out in front.

"Come on," I said as I stood and followed Richard into the club. I heard Lydia check to see if there was a round in the chamber of her Glock. I did the same.

Past the metal doors was a short corridor with two swing doors that opened into men's and women's lavatories on the right. The walls were covered with spray paint. Some of it was just lettered graffiti whereas images of skulls and demonic symbols filled the remaining parts. I snapped a few pictures of them with my cell but continued around the corner to the left. We followed the corridor until it opened into a vast space. A musty smell filled the dense air, and everything was completely dark except our flashlights. I moved around the main bar area trying to recreate the angle of the video in order to know where to look for any kind of mechanisms. Lydia and Richard walked away from the corridor off to the right. I swept my light around behind me and shined it up the stairwell. A booth was visible from the foot of the stairs as was another archway that I deduced led out to the main entrance. Broken glass littered the floor, mostly from beer and liquor bottles that once resided behind the main bar. It crunched under my feet. I could hear the sounds of people enthusiastically hollering from outside the club as they took in the nightlife of London. I turned to face Lydia and Richard. *This is it! This is the angle,* I thought.

"Lydia. Richard," I called out in a loud whisper. Both of them stopped in front of the small bar area as I started to piece together the video. "Stand to the right of the bar for a moment. This is the angle of the video. Look around on the ground or along walls for anything that stands out as mechanical, something that appears *not* part of the normal structure."

Richard examined the small bar area and Lydia shined her light all around the surrounding walls. I moved to the far wall and looked up with my light to see if there were any projectors but only saw mounts for broken lights. Nothing stood out as odd.

"Chief, there's a couple more rooms back here and a staircase going up. VIP lounge maybe."

The area was dark that Lydia was pointing into. Above her I could see an office space. I remembered that it had glass windows that overlooked the entire inside of the club. The glass had been broken out and shards lay across the main dance floor. I walked to the spot where I thought Dr. Bishop made her mysterious change. Richard continued to examine the small bar area, having seemingly found the bullet holes I felt possibly came from Grayson's gun. "Lydia, you and Richard inspect the rooms back there and tell me what you find."

I watched for a moment as Lydia's flashlight disappeared into the obscurity of the room. I knelt down on the spot I was standing and pushed the broken shards of glass out of the way hoping to reveal something, anything that was different, perhaps a trap door, but there was nothing.

"James. Have you seen this? There are some serious pressure cracks in the wood over here."

I looked up at Richard. He was still by the small bar instead of helping Lydia. "Richard, go help Lydia."

"Oh…right." Concern and a sort of disbelief accompanied his words as he backed away from the small bar and walked towards the back rooms. The sound of a heavy stone door closing with thud stopped him before he got to the archway where Lydia had entered.

"What was that?" I asked. Richard looked in my direction.

"I don't know. Lydia!" Richard called out. No one replied. "Lydia. Lydia is that you back there?" Richard held his Glock out in front of him in his right hand with his left holding his flashlight crossed underneath. I stood and held my Glock in the same manner as we both converged on the dark room. Richard shined his light into the blackness, making a sweeping motion. "Lydia! Is that you? James there's something –"

I continued to walk towards him as his words trailed off and his light came to rest upon something. "What it is?"

Before he could answer there was a deep snarl and his whole body was thrust backwards into mine knocking me to the floor. Richard's flashlight fell from his hand and spun along the floor. Shards of glass crunched underneath me and imbedded into the forearms and elbows of my leather coat. I held onto to both my flashlight and gun. Several gunshots rang out and mixed with screams of pain. I pointed my gun and light towards the screams to find my target. An immense black furred beast was snarling and thrashing at Richard's midsection. He was desperately trying to shoot into the torso of the brute, but it had little effect.

I took aim and squeezed off two rounds.

Pop, Pop!

My bullets struck the creature but had no effect either. I quickly pushed myself to a standing position and took aim again.

Pop, Pop!

Again, the bullets had no effect on the beast. It was as if they simply passed straight through. It continued to rip and thrash at Richard's midsection, and he wailed in agony. "HELP ME! HELP ME!"

I knew what I was seeing. The nightmare was real. The werewolf sunk its strong clawed hands into Richard's chest and shoulders. It lunged forward grabbing Richard by the face with its jaws. His screams of pain were muted as his entire face fit within the monster's mouth. It bit down, twisted, and thrashed a bit more before yanking upwards removing Richard's face from the rest of his skull. I felt his blood coat the front of my shirt and the base of my neck and chin. Blood continued to squirt from the fatal wound, silhouetted against the glowing beam from Richard's flashlight. The werewolf held its head high, stood on its hind legs and chewed greedily as

Richard's body twitched on the floor. With a vicious snarl it took one more swipe at Richard's head and neck ensuring he was dead.

I fired again.

Pop, Pop!

Its head snapped towards me from the sound of the gun and growled. Blood dripped from the werewolf's mouth and its red eyes cut through the darkness better than any flashlight. I turned to run for the stairs behind me as I heard it snarl deeper and more malevolent than before. I peered over my left shoulder only to see the beast lower itself and leap in my direction. It bounded twice before it swiped at me catching my leather coat and raking its claws over the muscles in my back. It crashed shoulder first into the main bar in the center of the old dance floor.

I tumbled to the foot of the stairwell, but my momentum caused me to land on one knee. Blood was dripping from my back but the searing pain that it ushered wasn't enough to keep me on the floor. I could hear the fiend crunching the shards of glass as it attempted to right itself. Adrenaline surged me forward, up the stairs and into a darkened hallway leading towards the main entrance. Looking down from the top of the stairs, the werewolf stood on all fours, shook itself once and bounded up the stairs after me. I could see rays of light through the rotted boards on the front entrance and I sprinted towards it. Wood splintered and cracked behind me as the momentum carried the werewolf into the wall atop of the stairs. I lowered my right shoulder and barreled into the rotted boards. They broke as though they were made of Styrofoam, and I toppled onto to the walkway of Greek Street.

I rolled to my back despite the pain and fired the remaining shots in the magazine into the dark corridor.

Pop, Pop, Pop, Pop!

A few of the broken, rotted boards swung from rusted nails that were able to withstand the force of my crash. The rest were littered on the sidewalk around me. Red eyes peered out from the dark. The werewolf had stopped. My hands shook as we locked gazes. It was unaffected by any of my shots. I heard it growl and then let out a hell-howl. Shivers ran the length of my body while tears streamed down my face out of fear and pain. I blinked twice and the werewolf was gone. Back into the shadows of the nightclub. My body shook with deep tremors. Blood pooled beneath me from my wounds. People from across the street knelt around me to help. Their conversations were indistinct, fragmented. One urged a couple to call for an ambulance, while others were trying to assess my condition. I closed my eyes as their voices faded from reality and my vision spun into the blackness of the nighttime sky.

PART 3

Chapter #17

The week moved slowly for us. Kap spent most of his time preparing the sidearms we had and double checking MP5's. He and Codie reviewed the mechanical workings of each gun repeatedly, to the point of redundancy. Ada spent her time with Gerda and Marlie, only to commune during mealtimes. Collectively, we all reviewed the photographs that Grayson took of the club, but nothing stood out as anything more than an abandoned building with rotted boards covering the entranceway and amateur graffiti sprayed on its walls. The building was merely a blemish on an otherwise thriving social district. Grayson was probably right, if any clues were to be found they were more than likely on the inside of the building rather than anything we could see from a few simple pictures. However, entering the building was a challenge in and of itself. Grayson continued to insist on employing the idea of Inspector Lawrence as a means of legally entering the building. Yet, if he didn't agree to it, then our search would once again come to a close.

I tried to distract myself with work by combing over client profiles and logging onto the office's e-mail and financial planning programs, but the tremors in my hand proved to be a greater distraction and a constant reminder of the darkness. A reminder of the woman that I was convinced was more than just a stress reaction. All of us in the car felt her presence. It was as if the light of the world was muted by a dark cloud that threatened rain, an eminent storm that would surely consume us all. At best I found myself sitting in my office chair staring at the computer screen with little ambition to work as my mind neurotically chased fleeting thoughts about our next steps. *I will have my vengeance*, I thought.

Henry knocked on the door and leaned into my study. "Sir, I just wanted to inform you that Grayson and the others have come down to breakfast."

"Henry," I said before he could leave.

"Yes Sir?"

"Why did you stay?" This question was genuine. After Laryn's death and my resignation from the House, Henry could've latched onto any other candidate or member of the House and continued a very promising career in politics, but he continued to stay.

Henry fully entered my office and sat on the leather sofa and rested his elbows on his knees. He looked down at first, then empathetically at me. "At first, I wasn't sure why. I thought you were completely delusional, bloody mental for bringing the barbaric men into your home. Your conversations were madness. They appeared not to be grounded in any rational reasoning. Selfishly, I thought that this was a phase and that Laryn's death would've have gained us sympathy in the eyes of our constituents and that when you came to your senses, we would be able to regain the foothold we had lost." Henry shook his head and looked at the floor. "Policies, political advancements, status…for what?" He looked up again. "I have grown more fond of your family than our political gains. Guilt ravaged my mind for even thinking such horrid thoughts and the more involved you became with chasing this Dr. Bishop, the more I started to believe werewolves and the darker sides of things were real. So, I resolved to be whatever help I could, even if that meant keeping things in order around your home."

"I'm glad you stayed Henry. Whether I ever said this or not, you've been one of the stable figures in our lives since Laryn's death and someone we've truly come to trust implicitly. Thank you."

Henry merely nodded in appreciation before standing. "Don't forget breakfast."

"Henry, one more thing. Can you call into the office to see if there is anything that Ashland may need or if there is anything I need to do?"

"Oh, nearly forgot. There was a message this morning from Charlotte. Apparently, she had phoned yesterday afternoon stating that Grayson had two urgent messages from an Inspector Lawrence."

"What?" I stood from my chair. "What did she say?"

"Just that he was trying to reach Grayson and that the matter was urgent. Shall I call her now at home for clarification?"

"Uh, no…no Henry I'll handle it. I need to talk with Grayson first. Thank you." I followed Henry out of the office and to the breakfast nook where Grayson, Kap and Ada sat somber; eating the pastries that Henry had placed on the table. I looked at Grayson. "He called you!"

"What? Who?" Grayson asked.

"Inspector Lawrence. Twice. Yesterday. Charlotte left a message on the machine stating that it was urgent. What are you playing at? Have you been talking with him this whole time? Keeping more secrets? Is that why you wanted to employ his services with getting into the club?" After everything that Grayson had done in secret, it wasn't beyond him to have kept this from me too. My trust in him had all but diminished.

"Stop! No, of course not. I don't understand, why would he call and leave a message for me?"

"I was hoping you would tell me that."

"Well, I can't. I don't know."

"So, in other words this is strictly coincidental?"

"Yes, but it does give credence to my original thought. He may have uncovered something about werewolves."

"I don't know, sounds hokey to me," Kap stated. "I mean, come on the bastard damn near uncovered everything we did. This might be a ploy of some kind. A trap."

"No, if he had something to put us in jail over, he would've showed up at the manor with armed constables to arrest all of us."

"We should go talk to him," Ada added. "It is truth what Grayson says. He would not leave an urgent message. He could help us, no?"

"Yes, he could." Grayson stood from the table.

"This could land us all in jail. We could lose everything if you're wrong. Grayson, I need your assurance!" I stated.

"I have none to give, but we don't have anything else."

Codie walked into the breakfast nook. "What are you guys talking about?"

"Inspector Lawrence. He left me two urgent messages yesterday at the office," Grayson said.

"Is that a good or bad thing?"

"We don't know," I said. "But we are going to go talk with him to find out."

"Well, I am not much for a social setting, especially when it involves the authorities," Kap interjected. "I'm going to stay behind to keep an eye on things."

"Right…Ada, you need to come with us. You know more about these beasts than any of us." Grayson had way too much confidence in Ada, but I agreed that she needed to come with us.

"*Oma*, Marlie… they be safe here, yes?"

"I'll stay behind too," Codie spoke up. "I'm feeling very comfortable with the MP5's, but it couldn't hurt to go through it one more time with Kap."

"*Danke*," Ada said to Codie.

Kap nodded at Codie. They had a mutual respect for each other. Though not at university, Codie had matured much like that of a soldier that had finished camp in preparation for war. I had *both* Grayson and Kap to thank for that.

"It's settled then. The three of us will go into the city." Grayson turned to Ada. "We still can't carry weapons, are you going to be okay with that?"

"*Ja*, I am more worried about him." Ada pointed to me.

There was no escaping the fact that she had seen my handshake, but also, she witnessed firsthand a second emotional breakdown. Her trust in me still had not been established. "I'll be fine, but I do want you to bring that powder you were making. That's the only thing that we'll be able to carry with us."

Ada simply nodded.

Ada was reluctant to leave her gun at the manor, but she did it anyways. Henry let us off in front of New Scotland Yard. We were fortunate that the silver powder didn't set off the metal detectors as we walked through.

"Excuse me," I said as I approached the front counter in the lobby of New Scotland Yard. The officer looked up from his work. "We are here looking for a gentleman by the name of Inspector James Lawrence. Can you direct us where to find him?"

"His office is on the third floor, Specialist Casework Investigations Team. Homicide Department." The clerk pointed to the elevators to our left.

"Thank you, Sir." He didn't respond. We didn't care. Instead, we made our way to the elevators. After a short ride up, the door opened to a small lobby space and another desk. Several other desks were located behind it with inspectors and constables walking all around. The uniformed constable at the desk looked at us. "Is there something I can help you with Sir?"

"Uh, yes." I walked over to the counter. Grayson and Ada followed. "We are here looking for Inspector James Lawrence."

"Chief Inspector James Lawrence," Grayson chimed in.

"One moment Sir. May I ask what this pertains to?" The uniformed constable also had a cautious expression.

"We are here to discuss evidence that relates to a case that he has been working on for some time now. I'm sure that he'll be happy to make time for us."

"Your name Sir."

"Robert – Osborne."

Ada looked the most uneasy. Her head was on a constant swivel, as if scanning the room for anything that might look out of place. Rightfully so. We weren't here to discuss simple matters. The content of our discussion was lunacy to minds of those not affected by the evil.

A moment later a large, burly fella approached from one of the back offices. He stood tall, six feet or more if I would wager. Hulky, bulging muscles that would've made Jinx look like a school-aged child. "My name is Inspector Sabastian Moore. Why are you looking for James?"

He growled as he spoke. Deep and gruff, the man sounded angry. He was an intimidating force. I made a mental note to choose my words carefully. "My name is Robert Osborne."

"I know who you are Mr. Osborne. You can stop with the pleasantries."

"Very well." I wasn't sure how he knew me, but it was a fair guess that he may have worked with the inspector at some point on our case. I couldn't trust this man. "We need to speak with Inspector Lawrence about evidence that pertains to a case that he's been working on for some time."

"Are you going to answer my question or are you going to continue to stall all day? If it is the latter of the two, then I suggest you piss off. I have work that needs to be done."

This man was clearly not playing games and he was growing more agitated by the minute.

"He's not here, is he?" Grayson asked. He had been listening to our exchange. "Based upon your insistence of information Inspector Moore, I suspect that James may be on assignment or even in trouble. Clearly you are trying to ascertain if the information we bear will be relevant to a case you may be working on with him or if the information could cause him harm."

The inspector looked hard at Grayson, studying him, but didn't challenge what he was saying. "Truth be told..." Inspector Moore finally stated. "He's not here. But if you would like to make a statement, I'll be sure that it gets into the system as well as into any relevant case file."

He started to walk away from us, but Grayson chimed back in. "You know as well as I do that information pertaining to the cases that he handles is sensitive material and may endanger others. Filing a report simply will *not* do."

I admired Grayson's cunning, as well as his gumption. Inspector Moore looked around the room before re-approaching the front desk. He lowered his voice. "What are you gett'n at?"

Grayson didn't back down, instead leaned in closer to the man. "What I'm getting at is that Chief – Inspector James – Lawrence called twice, insisting upon us delivering a statement directly to him. Now we are only going to give the statement to him."

"You're not taking a piss, are you? I mean, he didn't set you up to do this did he?"

"No, of course not. I'd rather *not* talk to the man at all."

The hefty man took in a deep breath and sighed heavily. Again, he glanced around the room. "Look, I know that he's been put out by your case for some time. But the poor bastard's gone daffy. He came in here yesterday with his new kitten and together they accused me of locking some files. They were convinced I was involved with some occult activity. I have to say that it really pissed me off. I thought about it though…he's been through a lot in the past couple of years, losing his wife and all." Inspector's Moore's face softened. I could hear the concern in his voice. "I don't know what he's been working on and I'm not at liberty to say even if I did, but what I do know is that he only deals with the heavy shit. It's probably taken a toll on him. If you want to tell him your statement in person, you're going to have to see him at University Hospital. He suffered a pretty bad injury last night and he's recovering there."

"What kind of injury did he get?" Ada was insightful to ask, but it wasn't out of concern for the inspector's well-being. Grayson and I both knew what she was implying.

"Again, I'm not at liberty to say. And I told you more than I should have already. Stubborn, bullheaded, but James is still a good person. I'm not out to tarnish his reputation, no matter how angry I am with him."

"Thank you for your time, inspector," I said as we all turned back towards the elevator. The look on Inspector Moore's face remained one of trepidation and unease. He continued to stare in our direction even as the elevator doors closed.

"Do you think that he's been bitten Ada?" I asked.

"Possibly. I won't know for sure 'til we talk with him."

Grayson dialed Henry on his cell to have him pick us up outside. The drive to University Hospital wasn't far from NSY, yet traffic for a Friday had begun to pick up and the business of the day had certainly taken hold.

The hospital was grand in structure. Modern, with windows interspersed amongst the white center tower and various wings that extended along multiple curvatures of the street. Henry dropped us off at the main entrance on A400. Inside the revolving doors was the front information desk. To the left of us was the accident and emergency wing. Several intake medical assistants sat behind computer monitors.

"Good morning. We are here to visit a friend of ours by the name of James Lawrence and we were wondering if you could direct us to what room in which he is being treated," I said to the older lady working at the desk.

She smiled. "One moment sir." As she typed into her computer the three of us stood at the yellow information desk observing our surroundings. The lobby area was busy with people coming and going. Doctors and nurses walked about discussing patients or some hospital policy they didn't deem fit for the medical procedures they needed to perform. Their voices echoed in the open space. A few people waited in the black, leather seating and were unconcerned about our presence. Ada seemed nervous, edgy, and generally uncomfortable. Grayson was more composed than usual. "Mr. Lawrence is being treated in the Critical Care Unit located on the third floor. You'll take these elevators up and you'll need to check in at the nurses' station. Only two of you will be able to visit with Mr. Lawrence at a time, that is, if the doctors are not performing their rounds."

"Thank you," I said as we headed to the elevators.

The nurses' station was busy with medical personnel. Most were coming and going pushing trollies with laptops computers on top with an assortment of medical supplies strategically placed below for patient care. *Damn. Maybe there's some way we all can speak with him,* I thought.

"Can I help you?" One of the nurses asked from behind the counter.

"Maybe. We're here to see a friend of ours by the name of James Lawrence. What room is he in?"

The nurse continued to look at her screen. The time was approaching 10:30 a.m. and the longer we stayed here the more likely we were going to draw unwanted attention. "He is in room 3812. It's just down the hall a bit on the left. Check in with the constable to verify your identity and state your purpose."

"Constable? What do you mean?" I asked the nurse.

"I'm not at liberty to disclose that information. The constable will determine whether or not you are allowed to enter his room."

I nodded to the nurse and walked down the left corridor with Ada and Grayson following close behind. Poised about three quarters the way down was a uniformed constable. He was standing at attention until he noticed we were approaching.

"May I please see your identification?" The constable held up his left hand to signal us to stop. I handed him my identification card and Grayson did the same. Ada stepped back to disengage from the request. "Ma'am I'm going to have to see your identification too."

"She's shy," Grayson said. "We didn't realize that we were going to require our ID cards and the poor girl forgot hers back at the manor."

"Then I'm afraid that I can't allow her to enter the room." The constable looked from Grayson to Ada then back again.

"Is there any way around that?" I asked thinking that I might be able to bribe the officer.

"I'm afraid not. I have strict orders."

"Why is he being guarded anyway? We heard that he was involved in an accident, not anything criminal." Grayson started to probe for an opening, with the means to solicit information from the officer without being confrontational. I glanced over the shoulder of the constable and saw James through the long observation window. He was lying flat on his back with his head facing the far wall of his room. His arms appeared to be secured to the bed rails.

"The gentleman is being brought up on charges. He'll remain here until he is fit enough to be transferred to a holding cell."

"What charges?" Grayson continued to probe.

"I can't tell you Sir. I'm going to have ask that you to state your purpose."

Ada grabbed Grayson's arm and pulled him away from the constable. I continued to talk with the constable so he wouldn't be focused on her. "We're friends of his from a few years back. We helped advise him on a case that he was working on. Are we going to be able to see him or not?"

"You sir and the other gentleman may enter the room for five minutes. No friends or family members are allowed to stay longer than that."

"That'll be fine." Grayson stated, rejoining the conversation. "We only want to wish him well and then we'll be on our way."

The constable allowed both Grayson and I to enter while Ada stayed just outside the room. We walked slowly around to the right side of James's bed. His face was scrapped in several places. A few bruises that looked fresh started from his forehead and stretched down to his right cheek bone. Mindless ramble poured from his mouth. Both of his arms were secured to either side of the bedrails. Each breath he took was fast, acute, brought on by a deep-seated anxiety. James was nothing like the harassing, assertive pain-in-the-ass he was when he was investigating the shootings at the club and deaths at the church. Frail, damaged, but most importantly he looked sacred. Upon seeing both Grayson and I his eyes grew large with panic and began struggling against his restraints as his words grew more frantic and nonsensical.

"How did you find me? Stay away! Stay – away!"

"Inspector Moore told us you were here." I hoped that he would be sound enough of mind to be able to piece together that we had come to the station to find him.

"The files…locked! Locard's principle…they couldn't have just disappeared. Don't you get it! She's gone…they're both gone. It's my fault… my fault. Gone, gone but Locard was right…there's an exchaaaaaange…there has to be an exchange. The back room was dark!"

Grayson leaned down close to his bedside. "Who's gone? What are you saying?"

"Gone, gone, just gone. Eyes red…surprised us. It's real. It's real!"

"*What* is real?" I asked cautiously, but I had a good guess of what he was referring to. No man would be acting with such psychosis and babbling rubbish unless he saw it.

"Those eyes. Those eyes were real. Dead, dead. Can't be real. Dead though. He's dead." James twisted in his bed and pulled against his restraints.

"Who's dead? Who are you talking about?" Grayson asked. The constable from outside the door looked into the room. "Shhh. Who's gone?" Grayson lowered his voice in an attempt to calm James down. He drew closer to him.

Perspiration had formed across James's brow and dripped down his face as he struggled. "Gone, they're just gone. His face gone...dead...it tore him apart." Tears rolled from James's eyes and blended with the beads of sweat.

Grayson pulled a black pouch from his coat pocket. *Ada must've given it to him while I was talking with the constable, I* thought. He stuck his finger inside the pouch. Grayson withdrew it and held it low. The black powder coated his fingertip. "James, this is a matter of life and death. I need you to open your mouth."

His eyes were wide, breathing still fast and heavy. "Why?" he whispered quickly and with firm resolution.

"We're not here to harm you." Grayson spoke soft. "You saw a werewolf, didn't you?"

James nodded vigorously. "Yes...yes...it – tore – him – to – pieces. It's reeee-al!" His hands were shaking as he was quickly losing himself to fear and anxiety.

"Touch this to your lips. Taste it." Grayson held out his finger. James shook his head no at first. Grayson gestured with his darkened fingertip. "Life and death."

James leaned forward and Grayson quickly swabbed the inside of his lip. Immediately, James spat. "What are you doing to me? What have you done?"

"Does it burn?" Grayson asked. "Does - it – burn?"

"No – NO! What are you doing to me?" His voice grew louder. "You're in league with Sabastian. The files. He locked them! You're with him! He's one of them!"

The constable entered the room, accompanied by two nurses. "Gentlemen, you have to leave!" Both Grayson and I stood with our hands in the air as if we had done nothing to provoke James. Grayson had carefully placed the black pouch back into his pocket without the constable noticing.

The nurses rushed to the aid of James as he thrashed against his restraints. "They're werewolves! All of them! Beasts of darkness!" James continued to yell and wriggle to no avail.

We moved into the hallway and walked towards the nurses' station, hoping not to draw any more attention and exit quickly. Ada joined us. "Did you give it to him?" she asked.

"Yes. He spat it out the same as I did when you gave it to me, but I didn't have time to ask if he was bitten."

"We have to know for sure." Ada stopped in the middle of the hall and turned back towards the room.

Before she could do anything further, Grayson grabbed her by the arm. "Stop. There's *nothing* we can do now."

"Mr. Osborne," a firm voice cut through the busy floor. Grayson and I both turned to look towards the nurses' station. A woman had called out to us and was walking around the edge of the counter in our direction. Despite the bits of gray in her hair, she was youthful in appearance and carried herself with a stern maturity. Dressed in a full-length black suit and the fact that she knew who we were, suggested that she was in law enforcement and held a particularly high rank. "Mr. Osborne. You are certainly the last person I expected to see here."

"I'm sorry. I don't believe we've met." I looked at the woman and tried to get a read on her, but remained calm, light as to conceal my purpose.

"Allow me to apologize, not just for my direct comments, but on behalf of the entire department. My name is Superintendent Iris Cornell." She extended her hand in a considerate gesture of greeting. I shook it with confidence, but also with vigilance. "It has come to my attention that Inspector Lawrence may have been giving you and your family a bit of trouble, by not following protocol."

"Yes." My voice was low and cautious, the same as I always had done when working in Parliament. It was a mannerism that I often incorporated when negotiating with members from opposite political parties or when handling objections from would-be supporters and groups that had the influence that I was hoping to acquire. My nerves were jumping again. I turned the conversation directly towards the notion of Inspector Lawrence breaking protocol to conceal our purpose. "He unfortunately has harassed us by means of phones at our place of employment to continue a pointless interrogation with the statements we had provided over two years ago. We had come down here hoping to put an end to this rubbish once and for all. Unfortunately, we seemed to just agitate him."

Ada and Grayson stood off to the side but stayed watchful. Superintendent Cornell sighed. "Inspector Moore had notified me that you were stopping by the hospital, was this *the statement* that you could give only to James? A decree to stop bothering you? Why didn't you just phone into the station and file a complaint?"

I felt my face starting to flush. I was caught in a lie, and I needed a way out. "Perhaps it's in my nature."

"I don't follow," she said.

"I learned long ago while I held my seat in the House, that sometimes you have to take the challenges people bring to your doorstep head-on. I can't say it is the most becoming of my qualities, but it has brought about a certain level of resolve in the past."

"Walk with me." She gestured again with her hand towards Inspector Lawrence's room. Never once did she address or even look at Ada or Grayson. "James has been a part of the Special Cases Investigative Team for a long time. It's hard work as you would guess. There are a lot of unknowns and unfortunately a lot of very bad things that happen to innocent people." We stopped walking in front of his room. One nurse remained in the room. James was now asleep.

The constable looked at the Superintendent. "I do believe they gave him a sedative Ma'am."

"Thank you for keeping me informed. Take a short break while I talk to Mr. Osborne." The constable nodded and made his way towards a vending area at the end of the hall. Both the Superintendent and I looked in on James. Grayson and Ada continued to remain back, but still within earshot of our conversation. "James was a good man but has been through a lot."

"So I've heard. Loss of his wife?" I kept my question simple yet related to what I had spoken with Inspector Moore about.

"Correct. It hasn't been that long. Couple of years. James took it very hard. But James has also been involved with this line of casework for over twenty years. A person can only do and see the darker side of humanity for so long before it starts to pervert the mind. This is why we have to follow such a strict protocol. It is not just so that we also abide by the law, but it is for our protection. Occult groups often become vengeful and seek retribution in dangerous and often violent ways. Doing things by the book establishes a sense of duty that most people, even the occult types, tend to respect. This doesn't mean that my inspectors aren't attacked or even killed in the line of duty, but the protocol we follow draws a line between us and them. When my inspectors start to break protocol, then they are apt to start seeking vengeance for loss of colleagues or like with James, they become obsessed with cold cases. Cases that have seen their end but are resurrected by a belief that they are linked to a larger more insidious plot to unravel humanity as we know it. Often these inspectors slip into a brooding depression, thinking humanity has no redeeming qualities. Or they go mad because they never acquire enough evidence to bring up charges against someone, someone like you. They often blur the lines between fiction and reality. They act out like those whom they seek to arrest."

I looked at the Superintendent. "Now, I don't follow."

"James was training a Sergeant by the name of Lydia Cooper, who has recently gone missing along with another inspector, Richard Scott. We suspect that James in his obsessed delusional state, may have killed them both." I simply stared at the Superintendent. My eyes suggested to *go on*. She looked at me once before continuing. "James was seen crashing through the boarded-up entrance of the abandoned building that once held Club Red. He crashed through from the inside out and then proceeded to discharge his personal firearm into the building. He had sustained several slash marks across his back but was also covered with blood not of his own. Until the tests come back, we suspect that the blood may be either Lydia Cooper's or Richard Scott's. But we have no bodies in the club, and no other bits of blood to compare it to."

"No bodies in the club…then what was he shooting at?" Grayson asked.

Superintendent Cornell looked at Grayson, "That remains a mystery. Like I said, he is delusional. It could've been nothing more than a mental image. Without any bodies in the club, one can only speculate that he was having a hallucination."

"You said slash marks. What kind of slash marks?" Ada chimed into the conversation. She and Grayson were not shy about the fact that they were listening to everything we were discussing.

"Just slash marks. After reading the full report, I learned that James was brought to the A & E with several glass shards imbedded into his leather coat at the elbows and around the wounds. I suspect that he may have crashed through a pane of glass or something while he was struggling with someone, possible Lydia or Richard, but maybe someone else."

"Inspector Lawrence just accused us of being tied into the occult…Is this the result of his delusional state?" Grayson asked to distract the Superintendent from Ada's question. I could see it on Grayson's face. He didn't want to have to explain to the Superintendent why we were asking about the lacerations on James's back. Accepting that it was from shards of glass rather than teeth or claws was a much safer route.

"Yes. He also accused Inspector Moore of tampering with evidence and being involved with the occult too. James had been teetering on the line of sanity for some time, but with the accusation of Sabastian's involvement in the occult I do feel is where James stepped over the sanity line and crossed into his delusional state. And it's not uncommon for people to manifest strange hallucinations in accordance with their belief. James believed that there was a conspiracy, a cover-up, something more to the case than what there really was. I'm not surprised to hear you say that he thinks you all were participating in the *occult*. It's his metaphorical manifestation of people living double lives and a definite sign that these cases in combination with the loss of his wife, the only stable factor he had in life, caused him to lose control." The Superintendent turned to look at James through the observation window.

"Could it be that this *someone else* you speak of could've done this to him and possibly the other two?" Grayson continued to probe.

"Maybe. It's been my experience though, that when a colleague is killed in the line of duty in front of other officers, depression, PTSD, adjustment disorders, drinking problems are more common than full on psychosis like he's experiencing. This psychosis leads me to believe that he either saw some horrible occult practice that has caused him to snap, or the more likely of the two, that he had already snapped, and this is just the manifestation of the mind losing control. But like I said, I've got no bodies, no blood and an inspector that can't communicate in sequential thoughts. It's sad really."

"What's to come of him?" Grayson asked.

"Treatment, like any other person suffering from psychosis, while we continue our investigation. My hope is we'll be able to find something or that he'll be able to come out of this delusional state to tell us what really happened. Even if there is not enough evidence to support his charges, if he doesn't come out of this state he may never get out of a mental hospital."

Ada continued to shift on her toes. She was uneasy, as was I. All of what was being explained to us sounded good, but bad at the same time. Having seen the beasts first-hand, we knew there was truth to what James was saying. The red eyes, the surprise, the ruthlessness, the darkness that followed, we had all experienced it. Sensing the conversation was about over, I turned to the Superintendent and redirected it back towards my original statement on why we were there in the first place. "Thank you for informing us of the situation. This certainly explains a lot, but I trust now that this has been cleared up, and we won't have any more problems from your department? And we can lay-to-rest the tragedies that befell the innocent a couple years back?"

"Certainly, Mr. Osborne. We shall have no further communication with you unless you come to us."

We shook hands again before Ada, Grayson, and I turned from the Superintendent and headed for the elevators. All of us breathed a sigh of relief as the doors closed and the elevator headed towards the first floor. Grayson dialed Henry again for him to pick us up in front of the main entrance.

"I don't like this situation," Ada said breaking the silence that held back the thoughts the three of us had.

"I don't either. He may or may not have been insane, knowing what we know, but they are certainly making him think he is."

"I heard him yell about files and some *Locard principle* or whatever. What was he talking about?"

We made our way out of the hospital and stood on the walkway waiting for Henry. Grayson was scrolling through his phone as he spoke. "I have no idea about the files but look here." He showed his phone to Ada. "*The Locard Exchange Principle*, by Professor Edmund Locard. It suggests that whenever a person or thing comes in contact with another person or thing, there is an exchange between the two. Blood, salvia, other bodily fluids, bits of clothing perhaps, metal fragments from a bullet, DNA…you get the point. These are all things homicide inspectors look for on dead bodies. I think he may have been saying that there had to be an exchange between the victims and the werewolf he encountered."

"What are you getting at Grayson?" I asked.

"He was shouting that they were torn to pieces. That they were just gone…into the darkness. If that's so, then there would be evidence of that. Evidence that we may be able to follow 'into the darkness'." Grayson looked at Ada then back at me. "What I'm getting at is that I think it's time to go back to the club. All of us. Tonight."

CHAPTER 18

Doorway to Darkness
Grayson
Saturday, February 25, 2012
12:30 a.m.

We spent the day in preparation for going into the abandoned club. Black clothing, LED flashlights, small pry bars, small packs to carry bottles of lighter fluid that Ada had insisted on us having, sidearms with extra magazines, and most important the HK MP5s with two 30 round exchangeable magazines each, all filled with silver rounds. The sniper rifles we were using at Dr. Bishop's estate were too big, clunky, and would draw even the drunkest of on-lookers towards what we were doing. Kap was right. We needed concealment, especially after Jinx and Snake had taken with them most of the other submachine guns and AK's.

No doubt there would be police monitoring the club, making sure that no one else entered that could possibly get hurt after Thursday's incident with Inspector Lawrence. We had to wait until dark but also the early morning hours. Less people out meant less monitoring of the club. Kap and I both new where we could park and had decided to execute the same way we had the first time we went to the club, only this time we planned on entering from the alleyway. Our cargo van we were taking could pose as any commercial van that was making nightly deliveries in the area, giving us the freedom to park in spots not frequently used by patrons of the businesses. A stealthy approach was our aim, so we needed to avoid being on Greek Street. However, we had learned the small alleyway twisted and turned through the tight buildings before exiting out onto Charing Cross Road a couple blocks away from the club. Most the alleyways between the buildings were inaccessible, made-up to look like one long continuous structure. A glass doorway constructed to look like part of the black façade of the building was our entry point.

Much of the day was also spent learning the tactics that we were going to use and our approach to the club. We all convened in my father's study to review the plans.

"Are we all clear on how we're going to approach the club?" I asked. No one responded beyond a head nod. "Once inside, I expect it to be dark and unpredictable. Kap, Codie –" They both looked directly at me. "Both of you will be a team inside, should we need to split up. Sidearms and HKs, got it?"

"Got it," Codie asserted. Kap looked at Codie and nodded in agreement.

"Ada, my father, and I are the second team. My father and I will carry the sidearms. Ada a sidearm and the third HK."

"What about Gerda and Marlie? I no leave them here alone."

Ada was right. If we did leave them here alone, they would be exposed, vulnerable. Gerda was too old and Marlie was too young. There was no one that we could trust to care for them in our absence. Henry, though reliable, was not accustomed to using a firearm should the need arise, but more importantly had stayed along the fringe the entire time we had aimed to hunt these monsters. Never did I hear him state for or against our actions and I scarcely believed that he had even accepted the fact that we were hunting werewolves, despite having spoken openly about such things in front of him. Henry took a more secure approach by remaining my father's administrative assistant and political analyst, taking on more butlery duties after his resignation, but a soldier he was not.

"I'll stay back," Codie stated with a solemn voice as he switched his glances back and forth between Ada and me. "I'll stay back again and watch over everything here. Just leave me with one of the HKs."

Codie had always sought my approval since Laryn's death,. Yet, a touch of fear held him back. I could see it. However, whenever Ada came around, his fear lifted a bit. I could see that he wanted to face the beasts again, and maybe by protecting Gerda and Marlie for Ada, he could make up for his belief that he didn't protect Laryn that night. Plus, whether he would ever admit it or not, I truly believe Codie fancied Ada or at least didn't want to add her to the people he felt he let down.

"Right then. Off you go." Codie nodded towards Ada, who softened her face for a moment in appreciation, and then he exited the study to fetch his weapons. "Kap, with Codie staying behind, you and my father are now team one. Ada and I will be team two. We'll stay in contact over the radio –"

"No," Ada said.

"No? Why not?" Kap asked.

"The night my brother died; I used my cell phone…we were supposed to be dark. They may have tracked us. They have grown smart. We not take chance."

I thought for a moment. "Then we ghost it. Forget the teams and we don't split up. Travel silent, no noise, no communication." I looked at Kap. "I've got an idea. In my army pack I've got several glow sticks. A box or two."

"I'm on it." Kap also left the study.

"Why? All they do is glow. If I know what you're thinking, wouldn't the LED flashlights work better?" My father was correct that we were going to communicate through light signals rather than sound, but that wasn't what I had in mind.

"LED flashlights are bright and draw too much attention. We can use them in a concealed space, the flashlights could be too revealing if we use them outright. If I remember the club correctly there were several hallways and other rooms. We'll use the glow sticks to establish a base light for hand signals. Also, we can use them as a bread trail, if we do discover a pathway or basement, we'll need to know how to get back out, especially if we get separated. It's risky and not as good as a two-way radio, but if what Ada says is true, then the radios would give us away before we even entered the building, and the flashlights will give our individual positions away."

Concern swept across my father's face. Ada said nothing more, nor did my father. We readied ourselves to leave.

The ride into the city was silent. A level of nervousness filled the van leaving no room for idle chat. Missions in Afghanistan were similar, especially the seek-and-destroy target operations. My comrades would say nothing as we ghosted into a region. We would meet at our rendezvous and go dark until we reached our target. Everyone knew their roles ahead of time and pushed to do their jobs. For king and country, none of us were toy soldiers then, just as none of us in the van were.

We were different. We were *watchers* that faced darkness unknown, bound together by a greater threat that wrenched at our sanity and tugged at our very souls. It was an evil undefined by the conventions of political ambitions or economic gain a country may undergo. It was loosely stitched to religious explanation, and it superseded even the soundest of scientific research. This evil was not simple, but complex with many levels that were knotted together and produced suffering oddly unique in its manifestations.

Some touched by this evil sought vengeance, though it could be said that it was not theirs to seek. Others sought understanding and peace of mind, though no answers could be acquired, and the very pursuit of such resolutions left the seeker empty. I stood for nobility as I always had and I didn't doubt my conviction or the thought of pulling the trigger should it come to be that I encounter her, the one that seemingly, yet unintentionally drug us all into this uncanny dance of death.

The eye of the beast, as I had come to call the moon, hung barely open in the dark sky just above the city skyline. A slit, a sleepy eye, obscured by the grey clouds that passed over it. I knew that it mattered very little to these beasts whether it was barely open or fully wide and bright for the world to see. Change, for them, apparently could happen at any time and was not contingent upon the moon's full glory two weeks from now.

A strange quiet spilled into the streets of London. People still littered the walkways and carried on about their business. The silence was emanating from us. We walked in a world between happiness and hatred, between light and dark; cursed in our own way that we may not be able to partake in the pleasantries of others, yet damned to live on with the darkness at our doorstep.

Before exiting the van, we secured our firearms and backpacks, making sure that all the items we needed were accounted for, flashlights, glow sticks, pry bars, extra magazines, and bottles of lighter fluid. Being dressed in all black was cause for concern in the eyes of others. We didn't delay in making our way to the alley access point, relying entirely on the thought that most people still out at this hour of the night were party goers and would care very little about four individuals dressed in black. Once we were covered by the shadows of the alleyway, Ada and Kap tactfully removed their HKs from concealment and made sure that each of the modifications were still intact. Both Ada and Kap unfolded the collapsible stocks, securing them tightly to their shoulders. We proceeded through the alleyway as it snaked between buildings under the cover of darkness using only hand signals to communicate, no lights. It wasn't long before we had covered a couple of blocks and found ourselves standing in front of the side entrance.

The mangled metal doors had yellow police tape stretched across the threshold. We wasted no time pondering whether or not to enter and pushed on into the blackness. Kap secured the hallway and made a point to check the men's and women's lavatories to our right. I paused at the corner of the hallway.

"Glow stick," I whispered to Kap. He pulled one from the back of my pack, cracked it with both hands and shook it vigorously until a neon green glow filled the corner space illuminating the hallway behind us and in front of us. It was musty, un-kept and deathly silent. Graffiti covered the walls, accentuating the abandonment of the building. "Drop a glow stick every so often."

Kap said nothing but nodded. He and Ada took point as my father and I cautiously covered the rear. The club opened into a large space just as I had remembered. I clicked on my LED flashlight and began scanning the ground for anything that stood out. My father did the same, while Ada and Kap continued to provide us with cover. Both of them clicked on the lights attached to their weapons. I pulled another glow stick from my pack, cracked it, and shook it until it too began to glow. I rolled it out into the center of the open space to provide us with more visibility. Both my father and I turned off our LED lights. The club appeared empty, deserted. However, this was not cause for us to let our guards down. *Inspector Lawrence, I bet he assumed this place was abandoned too,* I thought.

My father also cracked a glow stick and dropped it further away from the other one by the main bar area of the club. A green neon glow spread throughout the dark club. It was easy to see shards of glass that glittered amongst the glow. *Shards of glass embedded into his leather coat. Nothing looks big enough to cut through a leather coat to inflict injury.* The small bar area where we encountered and shot at Dr. Bishop was now visible as well as a dark room to the right of it. I signaled to Ada and Kap to throw two glow sticks into the room so we could see what was there. Both my father and I held our sidearms ready as Ada and Kap tossed the glow sticks into the room and readied themselves for anything they might encounter. Empty, but now fully visible. It resembled a lounge space, with broken, overturned furniture scattered here and there. Another small bar could be seen at the far end of the wide room along with stairs that led up to the office space which overlooked the dance floor. A closed door could be seen on the opposite wall.

I drew my other sidearm. Ada positioned herself in the middle of the room and aimed her HK at the door. My father stood to the left side of Ada, covering her rear but also ready for anything that might be behind the door. I took one side of the door while Kap reached for the doorknob. It was locked. Kap removed his pack and withdrew one of the small pry bars. He jammed it in between the edge of the door and the strike plate of the wall. "On three," Kap whispered. I nodded. "One…two…three!"

Kap yanked hard against the pry bar. Wood cracked and split as the locking mechanism failed to stay intact. The door swung open as all of us aimed our weapons inside. It was nothing more than a broom closet that had a few old mops and buckets.

"This doesn't make any sense." Kap kept his voice quiet and lowered his weapon. I cracked another glow stick, shook it, and dropped it into the broom closet. "Why would this door be locked? I would think the police would've unlocked this door during their investigation."

"I don't know. Look around though, remember we're looking for any sign of a struggle or *exchange*. Like James was insisting upon."

Ada remained poised, ready to fire at anything unnatural. My father turned his flashlight back on and scanned the ground, but still held his sidearm in his left hand. Several minutes past as we scoured the area for anything that stood out, anything that could give a clue to what might have happened here on Thursday night. Despite the disarray of the club, nothing gave the impression of being disturbed. Flashlight back in hand, I shined it up the stairwell to the space. Cautiously, I ascended into the office. All the glass had been broken out of the windows that overlooked the dance floor. A desk sat in the center of the room. Its drawers hung open or dislodged from their tracks. Nothing remained. *I bet you saw us coming that night*, I thought. *You saw her too, didn't you? This is where you overlooked the club, but for what Corbin? Why? What are we missing?*

"Look here!" My father knelt down close to the floor. A strange eagerness filled my insides as I hurried down the staircase to where he was. Kap remained ready to shoot just like Ada.

"What did you find?" I asked.

My father pointed to the floor. "The dust. It's disturbed here, but not over there."

He was right. The floor was covered in dust, yet there was a disturbed patch as though someone had drug something over the floor. I followed it back out to the open space to find its origin. Sure enough, amongst the broken glass were clean spots where the dust had not yet settled. "Someone has cleaned this area, but also drug away something, perhaps a body or two. They placed the glass back over the area to make it look like nothing happened."

We followed the path all the way to the broom closet. *James was right, someone or something had been there.*

"I don't get it though, the Superintendent told us there was a police investigation and they couldn't turn up any bodies or blood, but they had to have noticed this." My father swept his flashlight back and forth as he spoke. "I mean come on, if I was able to spot this then surely, they were able to as well."

"I agree. Unless there was no investigation, only a report."

"Are you thinking the Superintendent covered this up?"

"Maybe Inspector Moore. Remember James accused us of being in league with him and spoke about him locking files at the police station. Someone of Ms. Cornell's rank wouldn't be directly involved in the investigations, but Inspector Moore would have." I walked back over to the broom closet. "James may have had good reason to believe he was involved and I think James was on this same path before he encountered the werewolf…and means this door may have been locked for a good reason."

"Ya think'n there's more to this closet, Murphy's door?"

"Something like that Kap." I entered the small space and began tapping the floor. Nothing. The sound changed as I came to the back wall of the closet. "Bloody hell. It's hollow behind this wall."

The back wall was seamless, but the shelves stopped a solid meter and half away from the wall. The dead space in the closet was filled with empty mop basins. Quickly we shoved them out of the way and began manipulating the wall the best we could. Kap and I pushed hard against one corner of the wall until it shifted a few inches. "Grayson, yer right! A bit more and we might be able to squeeze thru."

My father pulled on the edge of the wall that was dislodged as Kap and I continued to push. Sound of stone sliding across the floor echoed around us. The wall had shifted enough that we were able to get through. Kap cracked another glow stick and threw it into the open space and quickly aimed his weapon.

No one was there, but it did open into a courtyard between four buildings; concealed and secret to the public. All four of us entered the newly found space. Just above the building I could see the sliver of the moon. In the center of the courtyard was a large circular glass structure that was inlayed into the ground. I walked to the edge of it and peered below. Blackness was all I could see.

"Bastards." Anger was apparent in my father's voice. He was seething at the deception these monsters had created.

"Ah *fuck me*! There's another set of stairs." Kap pointed across the courtyard at a stone archway with stairs that descended into a subterranean catacomb below. I looked at the glass structure once more and immediately deduced that the two were connected. "I don't know about this one Grayson. We've got no idea what awaits at the bottom. With a structure like this there's bound to be more than one."

"This club is a bloody outpost. The office space that overlooks the dance floor; it wasn't something chic or trendy. It was built to see who could came in and out, people like us."

"What do you mean people like us?' my father asked.

"Hunters, watchers. People seeking to destroy or expose them. Perfect really. It hides them. And with thousands of party goers coming in and out of the club, it would slow any form of attack and then they could spin the events any way they wanted. Just as they did when Kap and I encountered Dr. Bishop here."

"I've heard enough." Casting aside our moment of trepidation, Ada walked across the courtyard and stopped at the stone entrance. "Come on. This is what we are here for, no? Our fate awaits us." She cracked a glow stick and dropped it at the opening.

I looked back and forth between Kap and my father, before I sighed. "Right. Ada take point." I looked at my father. "No flashlights, glow sticks only."

"Why? It's a concealed space?" he asked.

"If we're using our flashlights, then we're not using both our sidearms."

"So be it." My father turned off his flashlight and withdrew his second sidearm.

"Kap cover our rear."

He stood in front of me, holding the HK in both hands. "We are brothers in arms. I will follow yer lead." We went dark as we descended into the bowels of the buildings.

A hideous smell permeated the stairwell as we spiraled downward. Ada was the first to reach the bottom and immediately cracked a glow stick and tossed it into the middle of the stone room. She remained alert with her weapon pointed towards a solitary corridor on the opposite side. With both guns drawn, my father positioned himself along the wall to the left. I was to the right and Kap remained a few steps up from the landing making sure nothing was following us. The acrid air was dense from the mildew covered walls and the remains of a recent fire that was burned in the oversized fireplace along the right wall. I moved towards the fireplace. It was over two meters tall and twice that wide. I could easily stand in the hearth without my head touching the stone. Inspecting the back portion of the fireplace, I noticed moist ashes at my feet, and the smell of burnt flesh. The fireplace was being used as an incinerator and I could only *speculate* as to what I was standing on.

The corridor in front of us stretched into another open space. We tossed two more glow sticks ahead of us. The ceiling was much higher than the corridor from which we had just come. Several stone chairs were carved into the walls, all facing the center. In the center of the ceiling was a green glow that poured down. *The glow stick from the courtyard. This must be the glass structure I was looking at,* I thought. Through the glass I could see the Waxing Crescent-moon in the sky. *This is where they change. Secret from society with the freedom to roam in the dark corridors.*

Several corridors broke off from this main room and extended in different directions. I turned to the others. I motioned with my hand that we would follow the corridor directly in front of us. "Remember every fifteen meters or so drop another glow stick," I whispered.

Silently we explored the corridor, no words just hand gestures in the dim glow. It appeared to be just as abandoned as the club. Endless dark except for the green from behind us. The glow sticks had begun to look like glowing dots the further down the corridor we got. It dead ended into a T-junction. "We could be lost down in these catacombs for hours, even days unless we split up. But I'm not willing to take that risk," I whispered to the others.

We were almost out of the green glow sticks. The corridor continued on in either direction, but to travel without any more light was too dangerous. "Whatever was here, decided not to stick around. Now that we know it's here, we can plan –"

"Shh!" Ada brought her finger to her lips interrupting my father. "Look."

Ada pointed back down the corridor we had just walked. It appeared dimmer, less of the green glow. I stood staring for a moment as one-by-one the green dots went dark.

"The sticks are goin out?" Kap whispered continuing to look down the corridor.

"Those sticks can't just go out. They last twenty-four hours. Something is blocking the light… we're not alone."

"Well, that's enough to give ya the wild shits." Kap took a knee and steadied himself with his HK pointed down the corridor.

"Fire two shots down the corridor," I said.

Pop, Pop!

The glow sticks stopped going dark. Ada also pointed her gun down the corridor. A light breeze caught my right cheek and I realized that they not only knew our position, but they were coming for us from the other corridors.

"How many glow sticks do we have left?"

"Three," my father responded.

I took them from my father cracked all three and tossed two down the left corridor and one down the right corridor. The corridors glowed green and gave a short but clear firing lane. From the depths of the dark erupted a howl that made the hairs on the nape of my neck stand up.

OWOOOOAH!

It was immediately followed by several more that echoed in the darkness. The howls overlapped with each other and made it impossible to pin-point the exact direction from which they were coming.

"Ada, right corridor!" Ada moved into position with one knee down and her barrel pointed into the shadows. "Dad, stand and cover me!" I knelt down with both sidearms drawn. My father stood adjacent to me standing with both of his weapons drawn pointing down the right corridor. Snarling blended with the howls and scratching of claws against the stone walls, but no werewolves were visible. "Short, controlled bursts! After the first wave we move!"

"Here they come!" Kap squeezed off three rounds.

Pop, Pop, Pop!

A beast down the corridor in front of us yelped before retreating. Red eyes cut into the darkness down the left corridor and was shrouded by a black silhouette against the green glow. Both my father and I fired.

Pop, Pop…Pop, Pop!

The beast yelped and fell to the ground in front of us. Ada opened fire into the corridor to the right.

Pop, Pop, Pop! Again, a beast yelped. *Pop, Pop, Pop!*

Sounds in the deep intensified and howls continued to erupt amongst the shadows. "Kap! Covering fire, then move forward!"

Pop, Pop…Pop, Pop!

"Clear! Move!" Kap yelled. Ada continued to fire down her corridor in short bursts. Yelps mixed with snarls and howls, but there was no way to confirm their deaths in the dark.

"Ada fall back!" I yelled.

Kap continued to provide covering fire along with my father. Ada began to fall back as she reached into her pack and pulled the small bottle of lighter fluid. She proceeded to spray the ground and walls as she back pedaled. Another set of red eyes pierced the darkness. Ada fired against the stone ground and walls sending a flurry of sparks from the silver rounds into the air igniting the lighter fluid. A flame burst forth catching the beast on fire. It howled in pain as it stood on its hind legs. Fire erupted along the walls and the ground where Ada had sprayed the fluid. It cast a shadowy glow down the corridor to the T-junction revealing several more sets of red eyes and the hulking bodies they belonged to.

"RUN!" I yelled. I fired into the crowd of beasts and watched as the fiery monster fell to the floor dead becoming fully engulfed with flame. Ada fired into the crowd before tossing the bottle into the burning tunnel. We both turned to run. Flames exploded behind us.

The flame burst only slowed the beasts temporarily. Kap and my father continued to fire in front of us providing cover for us to escape. There were too many of the beasts and we were ill equipped to handle such a horde. Ada and I stepped over the body of a beast that Kap killed.

"Stop!" Ada yelled. "Give me your bottle of lighter fluid!"

"There's no time!"

"I need it!" Trusting Ada, I turned my backpack towards her so she could retrieve it. She pulled the cap and dumped it onto the body. "Come on!"

We ran a few more steps and she started firing against the stone again throwing sparks onto the body. It was enough to ignite the body, but Ada's gun jammed. She turned to run as she repeatedly pulled the bolt mechanism to unjam the gun.

YAAARRR! A brute emerged from the fire and bounded down the green glowing corridor silhouetted against a fiery backdrop. I took aim. Everything seemed to slow as the walls of the corridor strangely resembled the walls of St. Teresa's Cathedral with flickering candles that cascaded down along either side of the sanctuary. The eyes of the beast rolled over from red to green. My heart pounded and echoed in my ears causing the snarls of the fiend to be muted and distant. Breath held tight in my chest. It drew closer. I felt my arms fall and my sidearms lower. The werewolf grabbed me, and I held up my right arm as we tumbled over one another. The brute sunk its teeth around my elbow, piercing my bicep and upper forearm. Searing pain caused the walls to flash back to fiery stone. Its immense head thrashed back and forth with its eyes held tightly closed. I forcefully jammed my arm to the back of its mouth to stabilize the beast's thrashing. The werewolf opened its eyes which were no longer green but back to a fearsome red. I jammed my sidearm into the belly of the beast and fired twice.

Pop, Pop!

The shots appeared to have little effect as the beast clenched its teeth down even harder forcing me to drop the gun to pry the jaws from my arm. I pushed hard, upward against the snout of the monster. Without warning the beast released its grip upon my arm, stood on its hind legs clutching and pawing at its face that was smoking. The beast fell backwards snarling and scratching at its right eye. Two more beasts emerged around the wounded werewolf as Ada stood over me holding her sidearm and an empty black pouch. She had thrown the greyish-black powder containing the silver nitrate into the face of the werewolf. "Come on get to your feet!"

Boom, Boom, Boom!

The sound of her 9mm was deafening without the silencer. She continued to fire at the new werewolves, causing them to yelp, but unable to kill. I forced myself to stand with my good arm, holding my wounded one close to my body. Kap and my father appeared by her side providing covering fire down the flaming green corridor while Ada assisted me.

My arm burned and pulsed with pain. Blood poured from the wound and dripped onto my pants and the stone floor. All of us entered the open space below the glass structure. We could still hear the snarls and howls down the corridor from whence we came. Other sounds of evil emanated from the unexplored tunnels. We wasted no time in the open space and made our way towards the short corridor that led into the incineration room. Several monsters materialized from the gloom. Kap stopped at the entrance to the short tunnel. "Ada! Shoot the glass!"

Ada helped my father drape my good arm over his shoulder. She then fired at the werewolves that were advancing on us with her sidearm before giving her HK one hard bang on the bolt to unjam it. She turned it towards the glass above them and emptied the remaining rounds of the magazine. Kap did the same. The bullets pierced the thick glass causing many spider cracks that gave way to several large shards that fell to the stone floor like swords.

Two of the brutes yelped while the others viciously roared as they leapt away from the falling glass. All of us passed the large fireplace and hit the stairwell at a run following the trail of green glow sticks we had left behind. In the courtyard, I glanced through the broken glass into the glowing abyss below. One beast stood on its hind legs and stared up from the depths. It had only one glowing red eye and let out a menacing roar that was followed by a sinister growl. It was my attacker, seemingly undaunted by the two shots I gave it. Malevolent, formidable evil that was wicked to the core and unlike anything I had come across before. Dizziness began to overtake me as both Kap, and my father aided me while Ada covered our escape from the club.

CHAPTER #19

The entire trip back to the manor, Grayson wriggled and writhed in anguish. Sweat poured from his brow and his body shook. Ada and I forcefully tied a tourniquet around Grayson's upper arm to stop the bleeding. Kap drove the van. I could see several deep puncture wounds and lacerations from the bite. Fear raced through my body and flashes of the night Laryn was killed intermixed with the present moment. He was in more pain than I had ever seen a person endure.

"Kap! We need to go to hospital! Now!"

"No! It's too dangerous. Gerda will be able to help him!" Ada continued to apply pressure on Grayson's wounds.

"My son is dying!" I fumed. Darkness had taken hold of Grayson as his breathing intensified in between grunts of pain.

"The hospital will do him no good! But it will draw attention to us." As much as it pained me to admit, Ada was right. There was no way we would be able to go to the hospital. They would ask too many questions and may even involve the authorities. Considering the club was marked as a crime scene and all individuals of the general public were strictly prohibited, we had no good reason to be there in the eyes of the authorities. Being placed in the nut house like Inspector Lawrence or detained was something none of us could afford.

"Where to Robert?" Kap asked.

I hesitated, looking at Ada again. "To the manor. Take us back to the manor Kap."

Ada placed a fresh cloth around Grayson's arm. They weren't proper bandages; but these simple cloths were what we had in the van and had to work with until we were able to get Grayson back to the manor. He lay on the floor of the van, shaking; eyes closed tight, and he said nothing. My nervous tremor also returned as my hand shook uncontrollably.

Grayson was barely able to walk into the manor. Delirium had caused his eyes to flutter and roll back into his head. Kap and I both assisted him into my study, while Ada made sure nothing was trying to follow us through the back door.

"Get him onto the couch!" We laid Grayson's shaking body onto the couch. Ada stood at the doorway. "Go and get Gerda. Tell her what happened and to bring any supplies she feels may help!"

Ada said nothing but turned from the study doorway and made her way up the stairs towards her quarters. It wasn't long before we saw the frail lady descending the steps with Ada's assistance, followed closely by Codie, who still had his weapon in hand. Gerda carried her satchel.

"What the hell happened?" Concern filled Codie's voice. "Where is he? Is he going to be all right?"

"I don't know Codie. He was bitten," Kap answered before I had the chance. "Go get a pail of warm water and some fresh towels or bandages or something."

Codie immediately followed Kap's instructions, while both Gerda and I moved to Grayson's side. Together we removed the make-shift bandages around his elbow. The tourniquet kept the bleeding to a minimum, but blood still seeped and dripped from Grayson's arm. The teeth of the werewolf nearly shredded his arm. Bits and pieces of flesh and muscle dangled from thin threads of tissue.

"*Alkohol,*" Gerda mumbled to Ada. Ada removed the rubbing alcohol from Gerda's satchel. She continued to examine the gouges, seemingly undeterred by the damage to Grayson's arm. Codie also returned to the study carrying a pail of warm water and several towels of varying sizes. Gerda motioned for Codie to place the pail of water on the floor next to her along with the towels and bandages. She removed the lower fragments of Grayson's sleeve. Holding his arm up with her right hand, Gerda reached for a clean towel, dipped it into the basin of water and began cleaning the wound. Parts of the injured tissue grew bright crimson with each dab of the clean cloth. The powder that Ada had thrown in the face of the werewolf remained on parts of Grayson's arm and was causing an obvious amount of burning pain. Gerda unscrewed the cap to the bottle of rubbing alcohol and poured some onto a clean towel. Without hesitation, she wiped down the wound with the alcohol-soaked cloth.

"AHHHH! SHIT, FUCK!" Grayson screamed as he desperately pulled at his arm to free it from the sting that Gerda was causing. Both Kap and I had to hold him in place while she continued to clean the sooty powder from the lacerations and clean the exposed tissue below. Blood dripped to the floor. Ada stood at the doorway, while Codie paced back and forth seemingly out of place in the situation.

Soon Grayson's wound looked clean, but still bled. "What are you going to do?" I asked Gerda as she continued to hold dry clean towels over the bleeding areas. She didn't respond. Instead, she looked up at Ada. I too looked at Ada. "Why isn't she answering me?"

"She doesn't know."

"What do you mean she doesn't know?" I asked through gritted teeth. "I thought you said she would be able to help him. So far all she has done is clean the wound! Something that I could easily do, and a hospital could've done better!"

"She doesn't know what's going to happen to him. She'll stitch him the best that she can, but the wound will heal on its own and at an alarming rate. The full moon is close." Ada remained at the doorway still clutching her gun.

Her words struck me like an anvil falling from the sky. The reality set in that this wasn't just a normal bite from a dog or even some wild animal that might require a series of rabies shots. This was a werewolf and this bite, under Ada's implication, meant that Grayson was going to succumb to the darkness. Panic raced through my body. My hands shook as I ran them through my hair and stood up straight from where Grayson lay.

"No. No you have to help him! You said that she could help him!"

"He doesn't have much time." Ada's words were calm but carried a menacing message. Direct and deeply centered on other implications that I couldn't bear the thought of let alone an utterance of such notions. Grayson and I had some deep unresolved conflicts, but he was my son. I couldn't let things end between us in such a manner, I couldn't let things end.

"Marc –" Grayson tried to talk but stopped as his breaths remained short, acute. His eyes opened and closed slowly.

"What was that you said?" I asked moving closer to him.

"Come on mate, say it again," Kap urged.

"Marcus –" Grayson let out a grunt of pain. "Marcus Holland."

The name conjured as much hatred as the beasts we sought to destroy. "Grayson no. You cannot ask me to do that."

Grayson shook his head. "No – other – way."

"Grayson you don't know what you're asking of me. We'll find another way. We cannot go to him."

"Who is this Marcus person?" Ada took a few steps further into the study. Gerda continued to apply pressure to Grayson's wound observing, listening intently to the exchange.

"He was the bloke that was working with Dr. Bishop, the werewolf that drew us into the hunt. He's an animal researcher from Australia." Kap was as apprehensive as I was but remained calmer considering that he had not actively participated in the torture of Marcus at Dr. Bishop's estate.

"I've heard Grayson talk about him a great deal. He's the one whose notes we've looked over for clues. The one with the charts and data and shit." Grayson nodded yes at Codie's reference. "He's bound to know something. Where is he?"

"Australia. I had him exiled for his involvement with your sister's death!" I looked directly at Codie. "Don't seem so eager to talk with this man! Remember he was aiding the very thing that killed your sister!"

"Trying to save her, if I remember correctly," Kap added. "He was studying her. Codie's right, he's bound to know something."

"It was HIS idea to have the werewolf run free that night! HIS idea to study her that led to Laryn's death! I'd just as soon see myself in hell first before I go begging for the help of such a reckless, dim-witted piece of shit such as Marcus Holland!"

Boom, Boom, Boom!

All of us in the room flinched. I raised my hands to protect my head as I squatted closer to the floor. Codie and Kap were similar in their reactions but turned towards the doorway of the study with their weapons pointed at Ada. Three bullet holes could be seen in the ceiling. She had her sidearm pointed at Grayson. "PUT YOUR GUNS ON THE FLOOR!" Her voice was loud and angry.

"Calm down Ada," Codie said softly as he started to lower his HK. Kap kept his pointed at Ada.

"What are ya doin' lass?" Kap asked still poised with his weapon.

"I said put – your – guns – on – the – floor! Or I will shoot him dead!" Ada remained with her sidearm pointed at Grayson who was seemingly well aware of what was transcending. A look of surprise filled his eyes.

"Ya don't want to do that, lass. You'll be dead the moment ya do. I don't want to do it, but I will kill you."

"I can die knowing that one less werewolf will be in this world. I shot my brother through the head after his bite and burnt his body! I have no reservations about shooting him. Now put down your gun!"

"For God's sake, Kap! Lower your damn gun! That's my son!" I yelled.

Kap began to lower his weapon but remained engaged with Ada. "What do ya want, lass?"

"If what you say it true, this Marcus person has studied the beast, then we go to see him, or I'll shoot Grayson."

"Listen to her," Grayson whispered through pain and anguish. Kap lowered his weapon all the way but refused to place it on the floor as Codie had done. Gerda remained silent, but steadfast in her expression knowing full well that Grayson would turn on the next full moon, which was on the eighth of March, just over two weeks away. I was tortured in the days after Laryn's death. Losing Grayson would be too much. I couldn't bear it. Yet, this wasn't a burden neither Gerda nor Ada bore, but with the fast-approaching full moon I was going to lose Grayson regardless if it came from a bullet or the dreadful glow of sinister moonlight. I had no choice but to seek out the person I tortured and banished from England. Turning from the situation, I ambled over to my desk and with one swipe of my arm threw all the contents atop the flat surface to the floor of the study. I stared upward with clenched fists held into the air above my head.

"WHY ARE YOU DOING THIS TO ME? You took my daughter and now you threaten to take my son! Demons walk the earth and you do nothing! NOTHING!" I grabbed the edge of my desk and in a fury I lifted it with an intense, forceful thrust causing the entire desk to plunge over to its side with a crash. Staring at the wrecked desk, I placed my hands upon my hips, breathing hard and long, I allowed the thoughts of the moment to play over in my mind. After a few moments I turned to Ada, who still had her gun pointed at Grayson, but remained resolute with her furrowed brow in the ultimatum she had posed. The rest of the present company stared at me. "So be it."

CHAPTER #20

Australia
Ada
Monday, February 27, 2012
7:30 a.m.

The rest of the weekend was set with preparation for us to go to Australia. Plane tickets and arrangements were made by Henry. Robert informed his business partner, Ashland, that he was going to take a much-needed trip. Codie spent most of his time tending to Grayson, who was having violent fits of nightmares and night terrors. He would wake from a sound sleep in full sweats, labored breathing, often panting with delusions of a demonic nature. I kept watch from outside of his bedroom door in the event that a change occurred, and we had no other choice but to put him down. Grayson's healing was abnormal as predicted. This was always something that was told to me or that I read about in the Grimoire. However, seeing it firsthand was astonishing, yet unnerving. Grayson had regained the use of his hand and elbow. The lacerations that were once open, gory, and debilitating appeared as though they had been treated professionally and were several weeks older than just a couple of days. Codie was the first to accept what I did as a means to spur action, rather than be crippled by petty grudges and prideful declarations. He accepted that I wanted these beasts dead just as much as anyone and that threatening his brother's life was in a way an act of mercy. Mercy from the dreadful thing that Grayson would become and the harm that he could possibly inflict upon others. No human could truly bear the burden of such guilt without becoming twisted and warped.

Kap checked in with Grayson on occasion and even made a point to converse with me. Less than Codie, but still enough to show concern and try to smooth over the near deadly exchange we almost had. It was obvious that he and Grayson were close, but Kap still saw me as a valuable member of the team. Making Kap an enemy was not something I wanted to do. I viewed him as of sound mind, a soldier against the darkness, but caught off guard by my ultimatum just as much as everyone else. Most of his time was being consumed by replacing the silver rounds we used in the MP5s with fresh ones. All the magazines were nearly filled now, but he had run low on silver and couldn't complete the task. No matter, he was able to fill the sidearm magazines completely, which were the only weapons we were going to take to Australia.

Gerda and Marlie stayed within our quarters, not choosing to venture forth unless they needed to use the lavatory or if it was time for another meal. I stood staring at the portrait on the wall a bit down from our room. I noticed it the first day I arrived. A smile spread wide across Robert's face. *Don't trust him*, I thought. I glanced at the girl in the picture Laryn. Dark hair, bright blue eyes and like her father, smiling, frozen in an expression of happiness. *His emotions are wild. The grief he feels over her death has clouded everything he does. He won't trust me now either since I threatened Grayson. I had to though, Grayson knew it too. If this Marcus person has knowledge of these beasts, then we must seek him out.*

Robert stayed clear of me completely, confining himself to his study, speaking directly with only Henry and Kap. I could feel the tension between us as we had the unfortunate timing of passing each other in the hallway. Stern looks. Furrowed brows. Menacing thoughts untold but expressed through body language. Knowing that I was watching to see if there was a change in Grayson and that Codie had taken on the duties of being the main caregiver, Robert simply avoided our area entirely. Not coming to check on Grayson's healing and relying completely on Codie for such reports. I understood why, though and was okay with not having as many encounters. His rash thinking combined with my sheer presence might provoke more of his unwanted behavior and he may be inclined to lash out in ways that would be more detrimental to our objective than simply having a flashback of his late daughter. There was no avoiding him in the long term. He was in fact planning to go to Australia and I would be forced to interact with him. *Mind yourself Ada, he's unpredictable,* I thought.

The door to Grayson's room opened. Both Codie and Grayson emerged from within. I reached for my gun at the sight of Grayson.

He held up his hand. "No need for that," he said as he motioned for me to look at his wounded arm. The lacerations were nearly healed over. He continued to move his wounded arm about. "You were right. I'm healing fast. I don't know how fully, but I can use it as well now as I could before the bite."

I released the handle of my gun. "You know I had to –"

"I know," he responded before I could finish. "I would've done the same thing if I were in your shoes. And if we fail to gain any more insight from Marcus and I change, I expect you to finish the job. Promise me you will."

I nodded. We had a soldier's understanding of each other. As much as I didn't want to shoot him, I would if I had to and like he said, if the roles were reversed, I would expect him to do the same to me.

"Well let's just hope that it doesn't come to that. From what we know of Marcus, he studied Dr. Bishop pretty extensively and may have answers for us." Codie couldn't hide his concern, but also had a grave understanding of the situation that implored him to stay objective to what the future reality may entail.

"Are you going to be able to travel," I asked looking now at Grayson.

"I think so. Yesterday, I would've said no, but given the rate of my healing I might be able to without a hiccup. Nights are still terrible. Horrible visions, nightmares. It's as though I'm forced to look into the pits of hell and the things that dwell there look back. But I don't feel quite as delusional as I did in the first twenty-four hours. Fevered yes, but more under control. I suspect that has something to do with the closeness of the full moon."

Grayson did appear to be more under control, yet I wasn't letting my guard down for an instant. He was now very dangerous whether he or anyone else wanted to accept that. The three of us walked down the staircase. I trailed behind them both as Codie led Grayson and walked into the main foyer area. From his study both Kap and Robert emerged.

"How are ya feeling mate?" Kap asked Grayson.

"Better, I guess. At least I can function. More importantly, have a look here." Grayson held up his wounded arm to show how fast the wound was healing.

"Bloody hell." Robert examined Grayson's arm. "Does it still hurt?"

"Not as much as you might think after seeing it the first night." Grayson looked at his father. "I don't have much time. I can feel the darkness moving within me."

"Right then. Our flight leaves in a couple of hours. Henry has agreed to drop us off at the airport. We've also located where Marcus Holland currently lives in Australia. He still works for the same company he once did but does more data analysis according to the company's website. Nonetheless, we were able to find a local address in Sydney where he stays and locating him shouldn't be too difficult. Are you sure this is the only path we can take?"

"Yes." Grayson's voice was solemn, low, and weary. "With Inspector Lawrence in the psyche ward of the hospital, he certainly can't help and we don't know of anyone else who has actually studied these things like Marcus has."

"I'm not staying behind this time. I'm going with you," Codie asserted breaking the fervent dialogue. Having tended to Grayson over the past couple of days, reaffirmed his resolve to continue to look after Grayson as we traveled.

"Someone will have to stay behind to watch over Gerda and Marlie again." Robert looked back and forth initially between Kap and Codie, but his eyes came to rest upon me. No doubt he wanted to continue his avoidance of me, but he also didn't want me around Grayson.

Before he could directly suggest that I stay behind, Kap spoke up. "I'll stay back this time." He looked at Codie. "We are brothers in arms, but he is yer blood. Go. I'll stay behind and watch over the little one and Gerda. I still need to scrounge up more silver fer extra rounds anyways. Not to worry though, I'll keep them locked up away from the little one." Kap looked at me and gestured with his head to prompt my agreement.

Robert was obviously put out by this, however, could say nothing further as both Codie and Grayson seconded the notion. "Very well. Double check and ready our supplies," Robert addressed the three men. "Off you go."

The three men exited the foyer. I turned to climb the staircase again to say my goodbyes to Gerda and Marlie and inform them of what was decided as Robert stopped me. "Ada."

I stopped and looked back at Robert. Anger again filled his eyes and wrinkled his brow. "If you ever point a gun at my son again, I'll turn your head around one hundred and eighty degrees, then drop your body off the highest building in London. Do you understand me?"

"No. Should things take a turn for the worse, rest assured I shall fire upon him instead of your ceiling. But you *should* take comfort in knowing he will be in the presence of God."

Robert moved closer to me. "Don't give me that *he'll be in a better place* shit! With all the stuff that has happened my faith in God has grown thin. I'm not sure I even believe he exists anymore."

"With all the stuff that has happened, how could you *not* believe? If the demons exist, then so does God." With those words, I turned from him and continued up the stairs towards our quarters. Robert did not follow and did not respond.

Upstairs was quiet. Floorboards creaked as did the door to our quarters when I nudged it open. Gerda sat in her chair again with her rosary in hand and eyes closed tight in prayer.

Marlie sat up straight with her knees pulled into her chest, clutching a small pillow. A look of concern spread across her face. Worry. Fear of things that she didn't understand. "You go soon?" she whimpered from behind the pillow.

"*Ja.*"

"I go with you Ada." Her eyes told a story of pain. Gerda and I were the only stable, familiar parts of her world. The thought of me leaving and possibly not returning was apparent and caused her eyes to well up with tears.

I sat next to her and wrapped my arm around her. "No child. You must stay here with *Oma*. And continue to practice your English, which you are becoming *so* good at, yes?" I smiled at her, but she did not return the gesture. Instead, she reached for some of the stationery that we had purchased a while back.

"You have this." She handed me a folded piece of stationery. I unfolded it. It read:

DARKNESS CAN'T PUT OUT

YOUR LIGHT

IF THE LIGHT COMES FROM

GOD.

Her note tugged at my heart as I pulled her closer to me and squeezed. Marlie reciprocated. I pulled back a little and looked directly into her eyes. "If the darkness comes, you hide, and I'll find you."

She nodded. Tears rolled down her face. It was clear that she didn't want me to go. I looked away from her towards Gerda. She had stopped her prayer and had been watching our exchange. I released Marlie, tucked her note into one of the pockets on my cargo pants and walked over to Gerda. I knelt down and held both of her hands in mine. "*Oma*, I must go soon. Kap is a strong soldier. He will –"

Gerda pulled back from my hands and gestured with her finger up to silence me. She placed both hands on either side of my face. Drawing me closer to her, she pressed her lips to my forehead. She then wrapped the rosary beads and crucifix around my wrist, so the metallic cross lay against the palm of my hand. Gently, she closed my hand around it. *"Gott sei mit dir."*

I held the rosary close to my chest, closing my eyes tight. Her heavy words were the same spoken to Garon. I opened my eyes and looked at her frail face. "God *is* with me, *Oma*." I stood in front of Gerda and Marlie. "I love you both."

With that, I exited our quarters with my bag of personal belongings in hand, ready to leave. My duty was to protect them. It always had been, and I intended to continue protecting them until their death or mine. Unraveling the crucifix from my wrist, I draped it over my head and let the cross dangle around my neck. A strange eeriness swept over me as I strolled down the corridor, away from our room. A longing, a lament for things that had not happened, but feared could happen. I feared my death and what that would mean for Gerda and Marlie. Vulnerable. Alone. *Kap is a strong soldier. He'll protect them,* I reaffirmed.

Nothing was said the entire car ride to the Heathrow Airport. Our weapons were securely sealed in protective cases, with locks. The four of us appeared to the rest of the world as normal. Grayson was still having a few visible effects from his bite. Sweat would form upon his brow from his fever even as he sat still. Fortunately, he wasn't shaking anymore, however he still looked weak. Our cover story should anyone inquire was that Grayson was seeking treatment from a doctor in Australia that specialized in medicine for a specific form of cancer with which Grayson had been diagnosed. Henry somehow, with the help from Kap, had official doctor's papers forged stating his condition. We didn't want to get stopped and quarantined by any security personnel that were concerned that Grayson may be traveling with an infectious disease. By having official documentation that stated he was undergoing a regiment of chemotherapy accounted for the sweating..

Robert barely made eye contact with me in the car. This continued as we made our way through the airport, checked our luggage, and found our gate. Yet, as we sat, waiting to board the plane, his eyes found mine. Though no words were said, his warning remained the same. In his eyes, I was as much of a threat to him as the werewolves were.

It wasn't long before we were able to board the plane. Henry had taken the liberty of booking us into first-class seating. This meant less people asking questions about Grayson's condition and a bit more freedom to discuss necessary plans and not about having more space for our feet or better food.

Grayson sat in the window seat. Robert started to sit in the seat next to him. "No." Grayson was shaking his head. "I want Ada to sit next to me. She and I have a lot to discuss."

"You've got to be kidding me, right?"

"Afraid not. Trust me when I say that she is not going to do anything to me at ten thousand meters in the air."

Grudgingly, Robert took the seat across the aisle and Codie took the one next to him on the other side. Nothing more was said before take-off. Only common talk, in fact nothing in depth was discussed during the first thirteen hours of the flight. We stopped in Singapore. There we switched planes and readied ourselves for another eleven hours to Sydney, Australia. I figured that Grayson had another reason for warding off his father other than talking to me about specific things. On the first leg of the flight, he had only reaffirmed with me that should things go south that I would be the one to finish him off citing that his father and brother wouldn't have the moxie to follow through and that many people could be harmed if I didn't. *Perhaps it had something to do with me being a valuable member of the team, I thought. If Robert continues to deem me as a threat to his son, my life is in danger. Sitting next to him on the flight might send a different message.*

The plane was dimly lit and time on the digital display was now 5:30 a.m. Singapore time, meaning it was 11:30 p.m. London time. Both Robert and Codie had drifted off to sleep across the aisle. Grayson had done the same, but was restless, twitching while he slept. Sweat dripped down his face. REM sleep. *Violence and horrors of hell probably consume his dreams, I thought.*

Grayson shifted forward and awoke with a gasp! His breathing was heavy, and his eyes were wide with fright. He looked around the plane, confused at first by where he was, but slowly started to regain himself. Grayson glanced at me then shook his head. Above him was the flight attendant button glowing bright against the shadowy cabin. "I need a damp towel," he said to me as he pressed the button.

"Bad dreams?" I asked.

"Yes. Horrible. I feel as though hell calls to me in my dreams." The flight attendant interrupted him. He glanced at her and lied, "Can I have a damp towel? My cancer treatment has been a bit rough."

"Certainly Sir." The woman left for a moment and returned with a warm, damp towel. Empathy was written across her face.

"Thank you." She nodded before returning to her cabin duties. Grayson wiped his face and the front of his neck with the damp towel. He draped it over his nape and looked across the aisle at Codie and Robert. "How long have they been out?"

"For a bit." I stared at Grayson waiting for him to continue his thoughts.

"What do you know about this?"

"About what?"

"This! Being bitten. I mean is there a way to come back from this? Or is this it for me?"

"I don't know. My people hunt the beasts, not study them. I know what I know through the Grimoire and things that people like Gerda have told me over the years."

"These dreams…they're terrible. I see things from my past, my sister." Grayson breathed heavy. His voice was strained. "I can hear her screaming. I see the green-eyed beast and the ones with red eyes. Things that I have read in the dairy of Dr. Bishop come to life and play out. Other things too… I'm in the church again staring down at Rex's body, only in the dream I'm the one who did it. I killed him. Tore his neck out completely. I can still hear his voice in my head, same with Laryn. I had bad dreams before the bite, but Rex and my sister sound like they are screaming from the depths of hell. Their voices come from everywhere and nowhere at the same time."

"What things play from the diary? What you mean?" His dreams were nothing I had seen someone experience in a person who had been bitten. Most we killed, then their bodies burnt, yet I felt that he was revealing aspects of this that were of great consideration.

"Dr. Bishop spoke about how she too was plagued with dreams. I feel that the memories of these readings have manifested into visions from her descriptions. I walk through the fields she described. I stare at the moon, time lapsed as it moves across the black sky. Then I'm surprised by the beast. Violence, blood is everywhere. I can't tell who it's coming from, but I can smell it. I can taste it upon my lips. A deep yearning for more."

"Perhaps this Marcus person can help."

"Perhaps." Grayson paused, wiped his face again with the damp towel before letting it rest again on his nape. "That's what I wanted to talk to you about but couldn't in front of my brother and father. Marcus isn't going to greet us kindly. My father tortured him to gain information that could help us track Dr. Bishop. I had to intervene forcefully to get him to stop.

We've been at odds ever since. He feels that Marcus was directly responsible for my sister's death and that I have betrayed him. You and I know differently that it was the darkness and nothing beyond that. Dr. Bishop was desperate from what I gathered in her diary and Marcus's journal. She solicited Marcus for help because he was an animal specialist. He recorded everything he could about Dr. Bishop in human form. After persuading her to let him study her in full werewolf form, they sought solace in the deep forests of Northern England. That's where we encountered the beast for the first time and Laryn was killed."

"Why are you telling me this?"

"Because Codie wasn't a part of the torture before and as you know my father is too wrapped up in his own rage to think and act clearly. I certainly cannot be trusted at this point, given my dreams and what I know I'll become. You're the only one who can remain objective and hear what Marcus may suggest. I will help you any way that I can, but ultimately Ada it's going to be you that persuades Marcus. There is a slim chance that he would help me if we were going alone, but considering how he gave in to Dr. Bishop, seeing someone like you, in need, may provoke his empathy again and drown out his own feelings of resentment."

"You want me to act weak and beg?"

"Not at all, the opposite…show him your strength. Prove to him that you are capable, but in need of knowledge. Play to his expertise."

"I'm not sure I follow."

"He is probably as tormented as we are having been exposed to the darkness. Yet, he had noted several times in his journal entries about not knowing the source of the evil. According to what Gerda spoke of that day she read from the Grimoire; she has a better idea about the source. In combination with what he already knows your information may prove revealing in some fashion."

"All right. I will keep my head about me. Can I ask you something?"

"Yeah, go ahead."

"How come you didn't shoot the werewolf that bit you?"

Grayson took a deep breath and released it. "I shouldn't be alive."

"Meaning?"

"Dr. Bishop had the chance to kill me two years ago but didn't. She was fully changed into a werewolf and we came face-to-face. I was powerless, but I wasn't her target. It showed me that there was more to these beasts than just the raging monster."

"Again, I don't follow."

"Moments before the beast had me, the eyes appeared green and I thought that the werewolf was Dr. Bishop. It was the green light, the fire. It caused me to flashback to that night and I hesitated." Grayson hung his head. "I understand what some of my fallen comrades must've felt during combat. Shell shocked, traumatized." Grayson looked directly in my eyes. "A near miss does something to the brain."

The conversation ended there. I had no response. What Grayson spoke added a whole new dimension to this evil. I understood what I had to do and what Grayson was encouraging me to do. Dealing with the darkness for the longest time was simple, I was trained, programmed to hunt and kill, destroy it any way possible. However, the darkness inside of humans was far more complex and complicated to navigate. One wrong step could build a lifetime of resentment, vengeance more fearsome than the werewolves.

We landed in Sydney, Australia right on schedule. The time on the cabin's digital clock read 6:30 p.m. but immediately switched to 8:30 p.m. Sydney time. Our first plane left London on Monday morning but given the time difference it was already late on Tuesday evening in Australia. I felt better knowing that we were able to get through customs and claim our luggage without any repercussions for bringing firearms into the country. Fortunately, if we were stopped and our luggage searched we brought the 9mm handguns which were suitable for target shooting at specific clubs. We didn't bother with trying to secure a hotel room. The thought was that we weren't going to be spending that much time in Sydney, a day at best. If we needed to stay longer there were plenty of hotels such as the Stamford Plaza, the Ibis Hotel or even the Holiday Inn near the airport. We did, however, rent a car so that we could travel with our sidearms and not have to worry about carrying them onto public transportation.

The address that Robert had was in Haberfield, the apparent Inner West suburb of Sydney. It was just a name to me. I had never been out of Germany. Once we had our rental car, the drive was relatively short, just over twenty minutes, and the GPS in the car brought us directly in front of a red brick three gabled home on Bland Street, with two chimney stacks and a short red brick wall lining the property. Inside the airport I had read a temperature gauge that indicated twenty degrees Celsius. There was no need for our coats, so I replaced mine with a zip up hoodie to conceal the sidearm that Codie gave to me as we got out of the car in front of the house. It was dark out and not a lot of people were stirring. The air was balmy, but quite a bit different from London. It was refreshing after the long flight and it helped ease the tension that I was feeling along with the responsibilities bestowed upon me by Grayson.

The yard looked trim, but no flowers were planted in the beds around the base of the house. A single lamp was lit in the window of the minute home. Cautiously, Codie and I approached the door. I could tell that the home had a security system installed by the small sign implanted in the ground next to the walkway, but I could also see the magnetic window mechanisms behind the glass on the front windows. If disturbed, the mechanism would surely set off an alarm, so breaking into this place was not a good idea.

Neither Codie nor I knew this person, so there was a good chance that he would open the door without much of a fit. We knocked twice, no answer. Robert and Grayson remained by the car. Codie turned to them and held up his arms as if to ask, *what now?*

I tapped Codie. "Listen." I could hear someone walking inside. It sounded stifled, as though it was an odd step, something unnatural. I reached inside my hoodie and fingered the handle of my sidearm. "Be ready," I whispered.

I gently knocked again with my free hand. The odd footsteps came close to the door. "It's a bit late for visitors. Can I ask you to come back tomorrow at a better hour?" His voice was muted but sounded a bit nasal.

"Mr. Holland. My name is Codie and I'm in need of your assistance." I looked at Codie with a disgruntled expression. He glanced back at me. "What else was I supposed to say?" he whispered.

"I'm sorry mate, but I'm afraid I'm not going to be much help to you. If it's an emergency I suggest you call the authorities."

"Mr. Holland, you don't understand, we –" I backhanded Codie. "I mean…I really need your assistance. It pertains to a subject you know a lot about."

"Crikey mate, I already told you I can't help you tonight. If you're from the university, you'll need to contact my research assistant, Zoey Harper. Now piss off before *I* call the authorities for you!"

I banged on the door one last time. "Mr. Holland…Marcus! I know why you were helping Dr. Mya Bishop and we need to talk to you about her!" Silence. No words. No footsteps. Nothing. I continued. "Do you have nightmares like we do? Does it haunt you even when you are awake?"

I heard several locking mechanisms unlatched, bolts being shot back and the gritty metallic slide of a chain lock being undone. The door opened enough for me to see his face. Dark skin, silvery wild hair and dressed in denim jeans with an untucked button-up tan shirt. "Who are you?"

"Someone who has been touched by the darkness and needs your help." I stared into his eyes and understood a little more about what Grayson was telling me on the plane. They were stern, but cautionary, inquisitive. His eyes suggested more than just a mere look; they were calculating, searching for meaning and purpose.

"How do you know these things?" His voice was still nasal, but more clear, direct.

"Because we told her!" the ominous, gruff voice of Robert stated as both he and Grayson walked up the pathway to the front porch.

Marcus's eyes went from searching to found with an angry yet fearful panic. "You!" The door to his home swung open wide as he held a cane aloft in front him like a swordsman. "I wondered if I would ever see your foul face again. You bastard!" He swung his cane through the air, hitting no one, but caused us all to jump backwards. "Piss off! I want nothing to do with any of you!"

He swung his cane again only this time he lost his balance and tumbled to the floor of his porch. I withdrew my sidearm as did Codie. Both of us pointed our guns at him. "Stop! We don't want to harm you." I held my left hand up in a stopping gesture while continuing to hold the gun on him with my right.

"Pleee-ase. It's better than the crippled state that mongrel left me in." Marcus wasn't even looking at me, but instead was addressing Robert. "Three surgeries to fix my leg and I still have to walk with a *fucking* cane!"

"Well at least your face has healed." Venom dripped mockingly from Robert's words.

"You Fuck wit! Two surgeries there as well from your hired dogs!"

Robert knelt close to him. "I was merely stating that it was a marked improvement." Marcus spat in his face. Robert recoiled in disgust wiping the saliva from his cheek. He charged at Marcus, but Codie held him back. "I should've killed you!" Robert yelled.

"I wish you would've!" Marcus hissed back. From inside the house a younger looking girl, dark skinned, but not like Marcus. Middle Eastern.

"What's going on out here? Who are you people?" she said as she looked over the situation.

"Zoey go back inside."

"No!" The girl named Zoey crouched beside Marcus, using herself as a human shield.

Marcus attempted to shove her back as he continued to address Robert. "Every day I'm in pain! I can't leave the house for fear of what's out here. I can't sleep well and when I do the nightmares are horrible! HORRIBLE! Do you have dreams Robert? Green eyes every night! And You! I dream of you! The worst ones are of YOU! I don't know what beast was worse, you or the werewolf that killed your daughter!"

Rage erupted from Robert as he freed himself from Codie and charged again at Marcus. I leapt back as Codie tried to keep hold of Robert. Zoey screamed out in fright and leaned over Marcus to shield him further. Grayson stepped between them and grabbed Robert by the throat. He lifted him nearly six inches off the ground with one arm and slammed him against the side wall of the front porch area. "I've tolerated YOUR misplaced rage long enough!" Fighting against the grip of his son, Robert's eyes began to roll back into his head.

"Grayson STOP!" Marcus yelled from the ground.

Grayson released him and Robert fell to his knees gasping for air. Codie moved to assist his father and I turned my gun towards Grayson half expecting him to change into a werewolf. On the plane, eleven hours earlier, he was still showing signs of weariness. That had since past and was replaced with a sinister strength characteristic of evil. He turned and faced Marcus, cold and serious, barely breathing hard. "*I need your help Marcus.*"

Aghast, Marcus stared back at Grayson. He blinked several times and tried to steady his breathing. "Crikey…You've been bitten."

~ 271 ~

Chapter 21

Bad Reunion
Grayson
Tuesday, February 28, 2012
9:55 p.m.

All of us sat on the living room furniture of Marcus's home. The furnishings were plain but practical. Nothing was lavish or showed any great wealth, but still contemporary with dark colors of brown and black that offset with white curtains. Despite being small it was well cared for, clean. Both Ada and I recounted everything we had learned from the Grimoire to the events that had transcended over the past couple of weeks. Zoey, Marcus's assistant, sat next to him on a chair she pulled from the kitchen area. She shook her head in utter disbelief about the history of Johan Stich and how groups were formed to combat this evil throughout history. Codie specifically sat close to my father making sure that he kept his rage under control, acting as the peacekeeper. Both were as far away from Marcus as they could be to prevent another outburst. He refused to speak. Instead, my father looked at the floor, perplexed rather than rational, sad rather than angered. Slowly, he rubbed the front of his neck alternating to his nape.

"March 8th is the next full moon. You don't have much time," Marcus said.

"No, I don't," I responded.

"You mean to tell me that everything they said is true?" Zoey crossed her arms and leaned back against the wooden chair she was sitting on. She stared at Marcus waiting for an answer, an explanation, something to quell the disillusionment from a lack of scientific reason.

He ambled to his feet, paying no attention to Zoey's plight. He walked with his cane across the room to a small antique desk and opened the drawer to withdraw a familiar looking set of books. Mya's diary and his journal of the events that he witnessed while trying to help her. He gave them to Zoey. "Here, read these they'll help you understand. As for you Grayson, I don't know how much help I can be. I mean just look at me, I'm a cripple. I've been suffering from acute anxiety disorder, posttraumatic stress disorder, bouts of agoraphobia, night terrors, you name it. It doesn't get any better and won't get any better even though I've been to two separate therapists. I can't tell them what's really wrong with me, what *we* really saw; otherwise, they'll think me mental. For a while I kept a journal of my dreams, the anxieties that I felt…it just made it worse. I was forcing myself to think about something I desperately wanted to forget. It wasn't like I went through a bad break-up where meeting someone new would help alleviate the ill-feelings. Or even a situation where having a positive mental attitude would balance out some of the negative thinking I was experiencing. You know as well as I do that there was no turning back, no cure, no mental rehabilitation for evil." Marcus sighed as he sat back down in his cushioned chair. "I'm not fit for the field anymore and have been reduced down to a data analyst for my research team and I teach a couple online classes for the university. I have my food and personal supplies delivered. I do my research and lab analysis in my cellar which I had converted into a laboratory. In simpler terms, I don't go outside anymore. Besides Zoey, you are the only ones who have stepped foot inside of my home in the last year and you are also the very people I was hoping to never see again. No offense, mate."

"None taken, I understand. What we did to you was terrible." I paused and glanced at my father. He still didn't look up despite the relevance of the conversation. I didn't feel bad for him. My father had behaved poorly and instead of recruiting Marcus as an ally two years prior, he turned him into an enemy. "Based on what we've told you there has to be something that you can do to help us. You're the only person to have studied these creatures as close as you did. I read in your journals, your notes. At least bring us up to speed on what you and Mya had discovered. You have to understand that my motives now are certainly different than what they were before and as you keenly pointed out; I don't have a lot of time."

Marcus sat pondering the proposal, fingers steepled. Zoey thumbed through the books that he gave her, peering up every so often to check the status of the conversation, but remained clearly enthralled with the writings. Codie looked on but stayed silent like my father. "The red eyes, what do you make of that?" Ada leaned forward from the couch and let her elbows come to rest on her knees. Her stare was piercing and firm, resolute in seeking answers to questions that plagued all of us.

"I don't know. Mya, thankfully, was the only werewolf I have ever encountered, no red eyes." Marcus turned back to me. "Insofar as bringing you up to speed…thermodynamics."

"I'm sorry?" I asked.

"Thermodynamics, the study of the relations between heat and other forms of energy. I don't say that to be condescending or arrogant, that's essentially what we discovered in Mya. Thermodynamics is what's taking place inside a human when they're changing into a werewolf, energy and, by extension, the relationship it has between all other forms of energy. We believed it to be chemical based."

"I don't understand. Chemistry causes a person to change into a werewolf?" Zoey asked more objectively though still with a level of *strong* disbelief.

"Yes. We all have chemicals in our bodies. Hormones like Epinephrine, Adrenaline are released when frightened and even when we're angry. More importantly they increase our energy output, increasing the energy output we believed increased the likelihood of changing into a werewolf because it would take *so* much energy to do so. Either the person making that kind of change would draw the energy from around them, or the energy must be contained within. When the moon rises, it obviously excites the behavior, much like any opportunistic predator, thus releasing more chemicals, thus increasing energy output. This is why silver bullets are so effective. Silver is the best heat conductor there is. This is also why I shouted for you to stop when you grabbed your father."

My father finally looked up and oscillated his glances back and forth from Marcus to myself. I looked back at Marcus. "Are you saying I could have changed into a werewolf by simply being angry?"

"Yes. The moment you grabbed him reminded me of the strength that only one other creature ever exhibited in front of me, Dr. Bishop. I don't know, call it flashback or something, a conditioned response, but I immediately thought that if you had gotten any more pissed off than what you were, we could've had one very large, upset dingo that wouldn't be too friendly to any of us." He glanced back at my father as if suggesting a point of view that had been missed.

I stared at my hands. They felt stronger, tighter, more enhanced. I glanced back at my father. He too had a new understanding. I could see it in his face. "Marcus I could control it though. I have been mad for a long time –"

Marcus held up his hand and shook his head *no* to cut me off. "You feel like you have control now, you feel stronger, but when the full moon rises you won't have any control. You would attack whatever you felt was more opportunistic."

"You know that Dr. Bishop could've killed me but didn't. Are you sure?"

"Yes. Regrettably, the night that I acquired certainty of this was the same night your sister died. Your sister was more opportunistic than the bait I had set out for Mya to attack. For that I am truly sorry." Marcus's apology was genuine, sincere. "Mya has since turned into the werewolf without the moon according to the details of your story within the church. She may have more control, but we don't know at what cost."

From across the room, I could see tears welling up in my father's eyes. He covered them with one hand and continued to disengage from the conversation holding back his emotions.

"Marcus." Zoey pointed to a notation in his journal. "Why do you have the word, *pheromones* underlined in your book?"

"It was a thought I had a few weeks after I had returned from England and was still recovering. When I first met Mya, I remembered distinctly feeling nervous as though something fearsome was stalking me or watching from a distance. I later deduced that it was Mya herself watching me from inside her manor and dismissed the notion entirely once I found out what she was. However, I asked myself why she was making me nervous and the only conclusion I could draw upon was that she was giving off some kind of pheromone which made me nervous. This sort of thing happens a lot in the animal kingdom. Prey are always a bit more wary, leery of approaching predators. If the prey catches the scent, sight, or sound of something they deem as a threat they will run. It's instinct. Humans, with all our arrogance behind our abilities of metacognition are still *not* above our instincts, whether we admit that or not. That aside, energy cannot be destroyed merely transferred, so if there is a higher amount of energy inside one person versus another they are going to have an effect on a person or creature with the lower amount of energy. Also, more energy means more pheromones. Our senses pick up on this kind of effect and it makes us feel *nervous*."

"So, what does that mean?" Ada asked still poised with seriousness.

"Nothing except that someone who is a werewolf may give off a strange vibe so to speak. Unfortunately, that doesn't help answer your earlier question about the red eyes. It was merely a theory that I never had the chance to fully test and after I wrote the word in my journal, I dismissed it as something I would never again get the chance to study. Trust me when I say, I was *okay* with that. The red-eyed monsters you described could be linked to the supernatural elements that we have yet to discover about the curse, beyond science. Both Mya and I believed it. The red eyes are merely support for that theory."

"Curse?" Ada asked.

Marcus nodded. "No one can deny that Mya's affliction was and still is a curse. The source was something that we had decided may be able to account for the elements, supernatural, that we were missing. The source was the piece to the puzzle that vexed us both. Before we parted ways the night she went looking for Corbin Paige, she had mentioned following this lead before going into hiding again. I can only assume that she thought Corbin may have some answers behind the curse, answers to possibly the *source* of the curse. All the legends and folklore suggest that getting rid of the source of the curse eliminates the curse entirely. The problem that emerges is that the source of any given curse is often elusive, something that is unexpected, not directly addressed or thought of. This is why they often last a long time. A true curse usually comes from someone who maliciously attempts to bestow ill tidings upon those that are innocent and the evil they wished upon the innocent backfires in a way. The curse may end there destroying the individual, but from what we have learned this curse is enduring, from the devil even, so the source won't be easy to find, if it even exists."

"Werewolves? The devil? Marcus there has to be some kind of science behind this. The devil is no more than a man-made entity to account for medieval hysteria." Zoey's brow was slightly furrowed, and she pursed her lips in disapproval. Such talk challenged her thinking and understanding of the world. "Let's consider for a moment that Lycanthropy *is* a recognized clinical mental illness. Second, adrenaline and other hormones, pheromones; you are simply describing a physical condition known as hysterical strength brought on by the adrenal gland malfunctioning. This perfectly explains Grayson's freakish strength when he grabbed Robert."

"I thought similar things too when I first met Mya, after she changed into a werewolf in front of me…that line of reasoning ended poorly."

"How is it that this Mya person has been able to go into hiding?" Ada broke into the conversation before Zoey could say anything further. She redirected the conversation back to more relevant speculation, rather than wasting time with Zoey's struggle to comprehend what we already knew was supernatural fact.

"Your guess is as good as mine. During the months after she was first bitten, she would retreat to secluded areas, forests, and the like, all-over Europe. I suspect she did it again."

"Germany?" Ada asked.

"Possibly. Germany certainly has its share of forests and secluded areas. Why Germany specifically?"

"We were tracking a werewolf across Germany when we were ambushed."

A momentary hush fell over Marcus. Mouth slightly agape. "How – were you tracking the werewolf?" Marcus leaned forward in his chair. The conversation had turned to familiar territory and he was suddenly more engaged. I could smell a change in his demeanor. His heartbeat echoed in my ears. I took a deep breath and released it slowly. He was excited but kept it to himself.

"Livestock were slaughtered in Hanover, then dogs near Ölpersee Lake and finally children in Königslutter. We felt the beast had probably traveled into Magdeburg, but we stayed in Glindenberg to resupply and investigate reports of the wildlife, Fallow Deer being attacked on the outskirts of town."

"That doesn't make any sense," Marcus asserted and shifted further to sit on the edge of his chair.

"What doesn't?" I looked at Marcus not following where he was heading with that statement.

He ignored me and stared at Ada. "You said that these werewolves, the ones your groups have been hunting in Germany and various parts of Europe for centuries wanted to stay secret, hidden from society at all costs…So why would they slaughter livestock, pet dogs, children…knowing full well that in modern times the media would be all over it? I mean come on, as evidenced by what you said about the tunnels under the club, they're willing to go to great lengths to keep themselves concealed."

"You don't think –" I started.

"Yes. I do. Mya," Marcus interrupted. We stared at each other for a moment. "Crikey, she said to me once that a person can only go as a ghost for so long before it starts to weigh heavily on the conscious. If it was her, I wouldn't doubt that she was trying to draw attention. Animal attacks certainly sound like her, children I can't account for." He looked at Ada again. "Perhaps the missing children were from your red eyed beasts. You said it yourself, your group thought they were tracking only one werewolf. Since Mya has the ability to change without the moon too and was so broken up by the death of Laryn, that I would wager the attacks on animals were her doings and she was probably trying to flush out other werewolves. If the world knew about these beasts, groups, like your group, would hunt and kill them much more efficiently than what has been done in the past. She might have been trying to flush your group out too."

Ada leaned back in silent contemplation of what Marcus had suggested. For Ada, it had always been about hunting and killing in secret. The realization that she may have been a pawn or even bait for other werewolves was not sitting well with her, yet she remained controlled. Anger inside her was as easy to sense as were the feelings of everyone else in the room. "Mya spoke in her diary of having enhanced abilities and senses. I can feel it happening to me as we speak. Is this – normal?"

"Crikey mate. Nothing you're experiencing is normal by the world's standards. And I don't have much to compare it to either except Mya's dairy. Being bitten by a werewolf certainly causes some scientific changes, but this kind of science challenges everything that we know as fact. I'm afraid that there is nothing more I can do for you."

"Rubbish." The voice was low and gruff, gravelly. I turned to look at my father, as did everyone else in the room. He stood from his chair. Codie stood with him making sure he didn't charge Marcus. A confident anger spread across his face and filled his body as he strolled from across the room to where we were all sitting. He looked directly at Marcus. "Rubbish. You were able to study Mya. You were able to collect data on Mya. You were able to track her whereabouts. Saying that there is nothing more you can do is a rancid pile of horse shit!"

My father loomed over Marcus from a standing position. Codie remained next to him making sure he didn't advance any further. Marcus, with the same venomous glare, looked my father in the eyes. "Maybe so, but why should I help you anyways. Perhaps I should just let nature run its course."

"I want you to insert the same device into Grayson that you did Mya. I know you have another device like that one."

"Get stuffed! I've got dozens of them, but that doesn't mean I'm going to help you." Marcus wasn't backing down. He stood the best he could to square off with my father. "Besides even if I did insert the device into him, someone still has to know how to use it. You can try to bully me all you want, but as I've explained, you left me in a state that prevents me from going anywhere or doing much of anything."

Both Ada and I moved to secure my father as Zoey stepped in front of Marcus. "I'll do it," she said softly.

"You'll do what?" Marcus turned to face Zoey.

"I'll monitor the device."

Everyone came to a standstill. "Zoey, you can't," Marcus insisted.

"I'm fully capable of inserting and monitoring the device. I've done it plenty of times on subjects in the bush."

"No...I mean this is more than just publishing a paper or name recognition, there's no turning back once you go down this path." Anger inside of Marcus turned to genuine concern. Zoey was important to Marcus. Academic in most of their relationship manifestations, but their closeness through friendship was also very apparent, almost parental.

"As strange as this may be, hearing all of you talk is also the most fascinating thing I have ever heard of and I'm taking into account that if they were willing to fly all the way from London just to talk to us about it then I'm willing to suspend my beliefs for this level of truth." Her voice was softer, though her scientific ambition had taken over. I wasn't going to complain. If Zoey was willing to take on the challenge in the name of science, I certainly wasn't going to stop her, knowing full well at first sight of any one of these beasts the truth would be revealed and she would have a new understanding of things beyond the realm of just science.

"Plee-ase Zoey, don't." Marcus was defeated, not by my father but by the concern he felt towards Zoey.

"Marcus. My entire family was killed by these beasts. I had to shoot my own brother after he was bitten because we had no one to help us. By helping Zoey, you will also be helping me. Helping me to avenge the fate of my family."

Marcus sighed heavy. "Fine…Fine…Damn it!" Frustration overflowed from him as he grabbed his journal and pulled from it a small envelope. Inside was a gold chain. Attached was a gold charm of the Archangel Michael. He closed his eyes and held the charm close to his chest. He made the sign of the cross before draping the chain around his neck. "Grayson, we need to go into the cellar. We'll insert the device and do an initial reading. All of them have been used on some form of animal or another, but that's not going to matter much for you. We'll be able to monitor you on the tablet which I'll have to remote into our company's server. The data will be transmitted and stored there too, but we'll be able to track you from anywhere. We'll be able to buy some time before my company starts asking questions about the subject we're following. Initially, your data will be catalogued as the previous subject, but once you start showing drastic changes the system will identify you as something different. Useful for studying the migration and feeding patterns of the dingoes and other things in the outback. Once we've completed the initial reading, I would suggest we go."

"Go where?" I asked.

"Germany," Ada said looking at Marcus, sensing that was his implication.

Marcus nodded. "Based on what Ada stated about Johan Stich, red-eyed werewolves, the attacks on animals…my thought is that Mya is there searching for the source. According to the legend, Johan had offspring, a daughter. Mya may be looking for that bloodline."

"We need to go back to England first. All that's left of my family is there," Ada implored.

"Fine. Just remember we don't have a lot of time before the full moon."

"I plan on killing Mya when we find her." My father's voice was still full of anger, resentment but less directed at Marcus though his comment was intended to provoke Marcus.

"I won't stop you," Marcus replied. He rubbed the charm between his forefinger and thumb that now hung around his neck. "…but you'll have to live with your choice."

Chapter #22

Retaliation
Robert
Thursday, March 1, 2012
10:55 p.m.

It took a day for us to ready the equipment, book the flights, and examine Grayson. Marcus and Zoey set up the device and made sure that everything was recording accurately. Marcus spent time establishing the remote link-up and that it was also working properly so we could track Grayson if necessary. His initial readings were odd for a human. Temperature was forty degrees Celsius, nearly five degrees higher than normal, which would cause most humans to sweat and shiver, but Grayson looked fit. Normal, better than normal. My mind was still coming to terms with the notion, the idea that he was bound to become a beast, a werewolf. It saddened me. Yet, it taunted me at the same time.

In some regards, I was like Zoey. Believing that there was some reality, science, even fact to the situation, but in complete denial that it was happening. Zoey hardly left Marcus's side, like a sponge, she soaked up everything she could with a childlike zeal. When she did leave his side she only really talked to Ada, again immersed in the quest for knowledge and understanding.

I hated Marcus, if for no other reason than I could not catch the thing that killed my daughter and attacked Grayson. His involvement was to blame. I hated his apparent lack of sympathy towards our, our loss. Yet, when Grayson grabbed me by the throat and bizarrely lifted me from the ground it terrified me. It was something that I lacked in understanding, but Marcus knew about, and I hated that. I hated him for his knowledge, and I hated him for viewing the acquisition of such knowledge as higher, more important than the loss of my daughter. For this reason, I sat alone, alienated the entire plane ride home to London.

It was late in the evening on Thursday before we made it to Heathrow Airport, London time. It was still busy. People from all walks of life scurried about from gate-to-gate. Others were enjoying downtime at the restaurants and pubs along the main corridors before their flights. Customs didn't take long to get through. Neither did our baggage claim. We had contacted Henry at the manor prior to leaving, to make arrangements for him to pick us up from Heathrow.

"Have you been able to reach Henry to see if he is here?" I asked Codie as we pulled the last of our luggage from the baggage claim carousel.

"No, it just rings before it goes into voicemail. I've left him several messages, but he hasn't called back yet.

Odd, to say the least, I thought. *Henry wouldn't blatantly ignore our calls.* "We'll try him again once we are outside. He might also be parked in a dead zone that's blocking the cell phone signals."

Codie nodded as he secured the strap of his own carry-on bag over his shoulder. Ada also secured her bag and made sure that the bomber coat was zipped tight. Outside the temperature was very different from Australia. There it was balmy, warm, whereas England was experiencing colder than normal temperatures. No snow or even a wintery mix, but cold winds that cut through those not prepared. Zoey and Marcus certainly felt the bite of the cold air, but I felt Marcus had a different kind of chilling bite. Not from the outdoor elements, but more from the dark unknown that he was being forced to contend with again. Being away from the security of his home was having a drastic effect upon him. Several times he had to steady himself on Zoey's shoulder to stave off a dizzy spell until he regained his balance. Though jet lagged, I felt comfortable being back in England. My nerves were shot from the plane ride, but more so by how the events had escalated, and Grayson just being near him made me anxious. The familiarity of being back in London, I felt gave me an edge and seeing Marcus flounder with his surroundings awarded me a strange sense of satisfaction. I was no better. My hand trembled and didn't subside as easily anymore.

The air outside was something I had grown quite accustomed to and longed for when I had to go without it for an extended period of time. I took it all in as we stepped into the briskness of the late evening, hoping to quell my nervousness. Perhaps it was the busyness of the city that I enjoyed. Knowing that millions of people called this country home; the rich history that encompassed both irrefutable accomplishments but also bore tragic mishaps. England always learned from the mishaps. I breathed out slowly. My heart still beat fast. *I wonder if England will become aware of the more sinister under dwellers of the land. The things that hide in plain sight that only a privileged few or I should say cursed few know about,* I thought.

I looked around outside half-expecting to see Henry parked along the road in front of the pick-up location. He wasn't there. No van. No car. No Henry.

"Do you see Henry anywhere?" I asked Codie.

He didn't pause to answer. He swiped his phone to unlock it and dialed Henry's number. Codie continued to scan the area in hopes of spotting him parked in one of the side lots. Codie tapped the screen on his phone. "Nothing, just went to voicemail again."

"What do you mean just went to voicemail?" I asked.

"Exactly that. It rang several times and then switched to his voicemail." Codie tried calling again.

"What's the matter?" Grayson was standing behind me with Ada to his right. Zoey and Marcus stood further away to the left. All were curious.

"We can't get a hold of Henry." Grayson pulled his phone from his bag and started to dial. "Who are you calling?"

"Kap." Grayson stood nervous, fidgety. "Shit!" He put his phone back into his bag and started towards one of the cabbies waiting nearby.

"What? What's wrong?" Grayson's reaction heightened the anxiety and any attempt to reduce it now was futile. Ada followed Grayson along with Marcus and Zoey. Codie shoved his phone into his pocket and urged me to do the same.

"Kap didn't pick up either!" Grayson stated over his shoulder

"What is wrong?"

"Kap always picks up. We've gotta get to the manor and fast!"

All of us weren't able to fit in one cabby. Codie and I rode in one while the others piled into another. My heart continued to pound. The worst thoughts imaginable were beginning to manifest in my mind and dance around in all sorts of directions. I didn't even try to keep myself calm as we rode in the cabby behind the other one. Adrenaline caused my hand to shake which had moved to my leg. Codie was also feeling the same way, for he too was fidgety; biting his nails while he stared out at the busyness of the city.

A half-hour seemed like a year before we finally pulled up to the manor. We unloaded the cabbies quickly, paid the drivers handsomely so they could leave, and we readied ourselves. My manor sat quite a bit back from the main road, private and secluded. As soon as the cabbies were no longer in sight and the only light outside we could see was the half-moon shining brightly above us, we withdrew our sidearms from the luggage. Zoey and Marcus stayed side-by-side, nervous and aware. Ada approached the door first, followed by Codie who unlocked it and stood off to the side. I stayed beside Zoey. My head turned on a swivel scanning the area for anything that might be lurking in the shadows outside. Grayson held his nose to the air as if to take in a scent that was too indistinct for the rest of us to pick up. He took several deep breathes through his nose. Without warning he charged towards the front entrance passed Codie and Ada into the house.

We all followed staying close upon his heels. Inside the air was stale and pungent with an odd, yet familiar odor. My study light was on to the left of the foyer, as were a couple of lights from the kitchen area down the corridor. Broken glass littered the floor amongst overturned lamps and decorative cabinets. Midst the glass and fragments of furniture was lots of blood and viscera. Bullet holes were interspersed along the walls. Images of Laryn's death immediately assaulted my mind. I could hear her screaming from a distant, disembodied place. I could see her dismembered body and the blood, so much blood.

"Kap!" Grayson whispered into the darkness. There was no reply.

Splatters of blood lined the walls ascending the staircase. It was still new and some dripped from the banister. "Gerda. Marlie!" Ada blurted out.

She pushed passed Grayson in the foyer and charged her way up the stairs taking the steps two at a time.

"Ada, Wait!" Codie shouted after then followed. We all did the same.

At the top of the stairs, we found Ada standing over a man at the end of the hall. Her arms by her side, staring at a body that lay in a pool of blood by the door to her quarters. Bullet holes again were scattered along the walls and ceiling, intermixed with a splattering of blood. Codie, Grayson, and I rushed to where Ada was standing. Zoey covered her mouth in shock and remained at the top of the stairs with Marcus.

"Oh my God. Is he dead? Is *he* dead?" Zoey's eyes were wide open, and the corners of her mouth were pointed downward as she breathed heavy. She turned away from the body but continued to turn back to verify what she was seeing was in fact real. Marcus stood silent, lips pressed tightly together, nostrils flared, and his eyes slightly squinted in a controlled anger. It was a feeling I knew all-to-well; a violation where nothing remained that could be held accountable; unhinged, shocking.

"KAP!" Grayson shouted as he quickly approached the blood-soaked body. He dropped to his knees, placing his sidearm on the floor next to Kap who lay motionless with head resting against the back wall. He still gripped his HK with his right arm. Several empty casings were strewn on floor next to him. Large gashes extended from his forehead along the length of his face. Flesh hung from muscle fibers in his cheek. The bone was exposed, and his right eye was missing. Deep cuts and lacerations were also visible on his arms and across his chest. His entrails protruded from his lower abdomen, kept in place only by his left arm. "Kap! Kap!"

Grayson and Codie feverishly evaluated Kap, continuing to call his name. Kap's breathing was shallow and he had a slight pulse. Blood continued to seep out of the wound on his face over the already dried blood. Slowly, Kap's left eye opened a little. A single tear dropped from the edge of the lid and rolled down his cheek. "I – I tried –"

"We're going to get you out of here. We need to go to hospital! Now!" Codie's voice was panicked. He and Kap had become close, just as Kap and Grayson had. But being a seasoned army Lieutenant, Grayson knew it was too late; as did Ada. Both of them had been around death enough to recognize its baleful presence. Kap shook his head slightly from side-to-side to inform Codie what the rest of us already knew.

"T-Too late. I – tried." Kap released his gun and let it slide to the floor. Blood trickled from his mouth as he spoke. "There – were too many of them. They – they came."

More tears flowed from Kap's remaining eye. "Codie, get water." Codie listened to Grayson, entered the lavatory next to us and filled a small glass full of water. He handed it to Grayson who brought it to Kap's lips. He sipped it before he choked up some more blood. "When? When did they come Kap?" Grayson asked in an obvious attempt to pinpoint the timeframe to assess the amount of danger we were still in.

"Early this – this evening. Henry –"

"Where is he? Where's Henry?" I asked. My heart was in my throat.

"Gone – just gone."

Breath trapped in my lungs escaped passed my lips with a push. "No. No, not Henry too. NOOOOOOOOO! YOU FUCKING BASTARDS!" Rage poured from me and echoed down the hallway and most certainly into the nighttime air outside. I fell to my knees, gripping my hair with both hands as tears poured freely down my face.

"Gerda, Marlie?" Ada knelt beside the dying man. "Are they still alive?"

"Gerda is gone. They – they killed her in front of me. They took –" Kap coughed again. More blood. "They took the bodies. They took - the bodies of our dead and theirs."

"Marlie? Where is she? Did they - take her?" Ada pleaded as she placed her hand upon his arm.

Kap shook his head again. "There." He motioned with his head to the closed door to his left. "I protected – her. I told her – to hide. I tried."

Grayson held the hand of Kap. "Easy brother, easy. It's over now. You did well." Kap said nothing more as his left eye closed and the last bits of air left his body. He was dead. Ada immediately stood, stepped over Kap's body and thrust her shoulder into the door. It was locked. She thrust again and again. "Stop," Grayson said.

"She's inside! I have to get to her!"

Grayson stood, lowered his shoulder and with one strong blow crashed through the door, removing it from the hinges that held it secure. I also stood and rushed in closely behind Ada.

"Marlie," Ada whispered. "Marlie. *Wo bist du?*"

Neither of us knew where she was. Ada lowered herself down to check under the bed. Marlie wasn't there. Both of us moved towards the closet, fearing what we might encounter. Abruptly, she swung open the door and knelt down. Ada shifted some boxes and clothing out of the way onto the floor of the room. I helped. Underneath was a scared little girl with wide eyes of fright. She was shaking. "Ada! Ada I hid like you said to!"

Marlie wrapped her arms around Ada as she lifted her from the closet. Grayson stood in the doorway and Codie just outside.

She carried Marlie, Ada stopped for a moment to look around the cushioned chair in the room. "What are you doing?" I asked.

"Gerda's satchel. It's not here!"

"Who cares?"

"The Grimoire! They took the Grimoire! Gerda must've had it on her when they killed her!" Marlie continued to cling to Ada.

"Didn't you make a copy of it?"

Sadness mixed with anger on her face. "Yes, but it was more than that. The letters they are gone too."

"That doesn't matter now, we have to go!" Grayson insisted from the doorway.

All three of us followed Grayson out of the room and past Kap's body. Ada covered Marlie's eyes so she wouldn't have to see the incredible violence that was bestowed upon Kap. I paused for a moment staring down at the lifeless body. Grayson had already grabbed his gun and sidearm. Ada stopped with Marlie still in her arms to see what I was doing. "You did your duty. I'm sorry it has to come to this," I whispered to him.

"Robert." I looked at Ada. "There will be time to mourn his death later. Grayson is right. We have to go."

Tears rolled down my face again as I looked upon Kap one last time. "What are we supposed to do now?"

"Burn it." I glanced back at Ada. She handed Marlie to Codie who continued to stand at the top of the steps. She paused for a moment to remove a picture from the wall that hung sideways with cracked glass. She handed me the portrait of Codie, Grayson, me and Laryn. "Burn everything."

I nodded as I made my last acknowledgement towards Kap who had willingly sacrificed his own life to protect Marlie. Regardless of where he had come from, what past sins he had committed while in the IRA or even as a mercenary, any ill-feelings that I may have still harbored were washed away by a wave of respect and admiration for him.

I joined the rest of the group that were waiting along the stairwell. Once downstairs, Grayson made his way to the safe that Kap had placed the other HK MP5's in and the extra magazines for the sidearms. Everything was still intact. Blood also trailed into my study. Inside the desk was stationary, still sideways from where I had tipped it over. Dark crimson soaked the floorboards and I couldn't help but wonder if this was where Henry met his demise or if this is where Gerda came to her end. Ada was correct when she said there would be time to mourn their deaths later. I had no more sadness left, only a loathing, a deep, dark abhorrence towards these abominations of the devil.

Ada placed Marlie in the care of Zoey and Marcus and helped Codie splash lighter fluid, rubbing alcohol, and anything that was likely to burn, including spirits that were above an eighty proof all over the manor. The wood floors and trim around every doorway in the home would burn well once ignited, as would the curtains and various other fabrics found throughout my home. Ada paid special attention to pouring a large amount of alcohol around the electrical sockets and natural gas lines.

Grayson and Marcus quickly loaded all our things into the van that was parked in the back, fortunately unscathed. The werewolves had come in through the backdoor as evidenced by the door crushed inward. *They came from the woods*, I thought as I waltzed through the back corridor over the broken glass and debris.

Everyone was securely in the van as Ada and I stood next to each other. I nodded.

"May the demons of the devil perish to ashes." She lit a Molotov cocktail and threw it against the stone walkway that led into the home through the back. Flames ignited and engulfed the doorway and spread throughout the rest of the home quickly. Codie drove as I watched my home, my possessions, everything I had aggressively pursued in my career and life go up in flames. I clung to the portrait that Ada pulled from the wall. Inside, I also burned. An unrelenting flame of fury and hatred.

PART 4

Chapter #23

A New Hunt
Ada
Friday, March 2, 2012
6:15 a.m.

"AHHHH! NO! NO!" Marlie awoke in a fit, more severe than the other times throughout the night. I sat up from the 'L' shaped workspace that was built into the wall that I was laying atop. I moved to the bed and wrapped my arms around Marlie. She and I rocked back and forth as I was replaying the events of the night before in my mind. I imagined what she actually saw and how her young mind interpreted it. There was little that any of us could do to help her. My hope was that she would drift back to sleep.

Fortunately, The White Horse Hotel on the outskirts of Hertford had a couple rooms available and we were able to secure one. We had checked in close to 2:00 a.m. and had stayed there for the remainder of the night. The hotel staff didn't notice that there were seven of us. No one wanted to be separate from the group. It was cramped having all of us in one room with only two beds, but we weren't planning on staying for any duration, a day or two tops. Marcus was urging us to go to Germany, away from Hertford. He had suggested that we leave as soon as we were fit to do so. Nothing much was said for the rest of the night. The shock of seeing Kap's ravaged body before he died, along with the knowledge that Henry and my beloved *Oma*, Gerda, were gone had everyone at a loss for words. I shed a tear for *Oma* and for those we lost, but only one. I suppressed the feelings of loss and loathing deep inside me. My anger gave me strength when I needed it, but I knew that it clouded my judgement and right now I needed all my wits.

No one slept. Sleep was elusive for everyone during the night except Marlie. Zoey lay on her side on the other bed across from Marlie. She stared at an open closet nook, awake and expressionless. Marcus lay next to her with his hands behind his head looking up at the ceiling, lost in thought. Codie sat on the red carpeted floor along the wall that led to the doorway. His elbows rested upon his knees with his head pressed against the plaster. Grayson and Robert both sat on the cushioned chairs with a small table separating them. Robert alternated between staring at the family portrait I had given him and his phone. At best, we took turns dozing in our designated spots.

Grayson was the only one that looked rested. Clarity filled his eyes despite having been up all night long. Overall, he looked fearsome in his alertness. I could tell that he was aware of things that were too quiet or indistinguishable for any of us to notice. His head would snap to attention or he would catch a scent of something in the hallway. This was the darkness. Sinister, relentlessly menacing and overall disturbing to those unfamiliar with it. Still holding Marlie in my arms, I looked at Marcus. "How do you think we can get to Germany?"

Marcus sat up on the bed and looked back at me. "Well, I wouldn't suggest flying. If we're going to Germany to hunt these things, we're going to need our weapons. Going to the airport with HKs isn't something we can just put in our carry-on bags and we can't take the chance of the airport losing or seizing our baggage. I would suggest taking the ferry then go by train."

"We're going to run into the same kind of security on the ferries as we would at the airport," Robert added. He laid his phone down and looked up. "In fact, the port security may be worse."

"Yeah well, I don't know what else to say then." Marcus looked at me. "Ada how did get your sidearms over to England without anyone noticing?"

"Sidearm and I disassembled it. And I got lucky."

"We're not going to be able to do that with the HKs," Grayson declared.

"Can we have them shipped to a location in Germany?" Codie asked.

"We might as well fly if we were going to do that. Plus, Kap had made adjustments to the weapons. The .40 caliber HKs always had problems. That's why they're not being manufactured as much as the 9mm versions, disassembling could make the problems worse and we don't have time to make the necessary repairs, at least not without Kap." Codie looked somewhat defeated with Grayson's explanation.

"Maybe we don't need the HKs," I stated. Everyone had the same confused expression. "I say we leave them behind and take only the handguns. They can be disassembled and hidden easier than the HKs."

"Based on what has happened at the club and what happened last night, I would recommend finding some other way to get the weapons to Germany. I mean…each time we've gone up against these things we haven't been able to overcome them and you're suggesting we face them again with *less* weapons? Are you mad?" Robert didn't hide his confusion or contempt for my suggestion.

"Parts of a gun are less noticeable than a fully intact one. Also, there was a safe house that I was supposed to take Gerda and Marlie too the night we were ambushed. We never made it."

"What's at the safe house?" Marcus asked.

"Two rifles and several other handguns, all with silver rounds. However, it was safe because it was secret. And we lost the Grimoire."

"Why does that matter?" Codie asked. "I thought the Grimoire was just a history of sorts."

"It had the locations of every safe house we had established and what to expect inside. If it has not been compromised, then we already have weapons in Germany. If so, then at least we have our handguns, no?"

"I don't like this at all." Robert stood from his chair and paced around the hotel room. "It sounds like a bloody suicide mission."

"We don't have much choice. He…" I pointed to Grayson. "…doesn't have much time."

"All right we move." Grayson also stood. "Dad, work on booking us ferry tickets. Portsmouth will be the best one to leave from. Then get us some trains tickets too. Make sure each ticket is separate, that way we can disassemble the handguns as Ada suggested.

"Wait, wait. Where are we going in Germany?" Robert asked.

"Safe house, right?" Grayson understood what I was thinking.

"Ja."

"Glindenberg or Magdeburg?" he asked.

"Edge of Magdeburg, but we also have to go to Glindenberg."

"Why?"

"I want to talk with the shop owner that warned us about the strange activities on the edge of town. I want to know how he knew about the animals being killed," I added.

"Are you sure that's not just a waste of time Ada?" Robert's voice was tense, impatient.

"That is the only starting point, I can think of." Robert didn't challenge my suggestion. Instead, he expressed disapproval with a hand gesture of whatever and shook his head before he sat back down to use his phone and start getting us transportation to Germany

"Someone will have to go for supplies. First aid stuff, rations, things like that." Grayson redirected the conversation back to the situation at hand.

"I'll go." Codie stood from his floor seat.

"Brilliant. Take Zoey with you to help carry things. Also, gets some luggage bags." Codie nodded in agreement.

Zoey sat up from her bed. "I - I don't know if I can do this."

Marcus turned to her. "I'm afraid there's no turning back love. You're going to have to see this one through."

"Marcus, I – I –" Zoey stopped before she could finish.

"I understand," Marcus consoled her. "The first time I saw the beast I was much the same way. I wrestled with my own senses and sanity. In your case, accepting that these things are real is the only option you have."

"I expected in some capacity that they were real. Science is what I was after, but that man back at the manor is dead. Dead, Marcus!"

"I'm sorry to say that there may be more of that before it's all over," Marcus imparted as he looked away from Zoey. Tears formed again in her eyes, not because of Kap's death. It was more so that she was still in shock over the trauma. It was written all over her face. Though she was a few years older than I was and with certainly more book knowledge, it was obvious that she had never come face-to-face with her own mortality. I envied her in a way. Despite the horrors she had witnessed the night before, she was still normal. I had become more programmed, less empathetic…callus, hardened against the darkness, desensitized towards fear. When I felt it, it turned to anger within me. I questioned whether or not I had the capacity to feel fear any more like a normal person. Or had I pushed so much of my own sorrow so deep inside that the very act of fear had been poisoned, unable to function for its intended purpose? *Is there any coming back for me once this is over? I thought. What will my anger turn in to? What will I turn in to?* Marcus again rubbed the charm around his neck between his thumb and forefinger.

"What is that charm?" I asked Marcus trying to refocus the situation on something other than the devastation caused by the deaths of the previous evening. If I dwelled too long, I may succumb to a debilitating sadness.

"It was given to me," he replied.

"Given to you by her, by Mya, right?" Grayson asked. Codie glanced at Grayson then at Marcus. Robert looked up from his smartphone, brow furrowed, and the corners of his mouth pointed down. I watched closely as Marcus oscillated his glances around the hotel room.

"Yes...it was. It's what had kept me sane over the past couple of years." Robert huffed short, acute shaking his head from his chair, suggesting that such trinkets should not be given reverence. Marcus looked at Robert. "Say what you will, think what you want. Crikey, considering all that we know as real, I'm surprised you scoff at these things now."

"I'm not scoffing at the charm or its meaning, I scoff at you. You could've gotten that charm from any jewelry store, the fact that you kept hers makes me believe that you think she's going to survive or that you are secretly hoping she'll survive."

Marcus sighed, "No more or less than you Robert."

CHAPTER 24

Glindenberg
Ada
Tuesday, March 6, 2012
3:15 p.m.

We were forced to stay in The White Horse Hotel through Sunday and into Monday. Robert managed to get us tickets on the high-speed ferry leaving Portsmouth, England to Le Havre, France, but the ferry didn't leave until Monday morning at 7:00 a.m. The ferry ride lasted just over four and half hours, putting us in France by 11:45 a.m. From there we caught the train to Paris St. Lazare where we were transferred to a new train that took us into Germany to the Karlsruhe station. We caught our last train to Magdeburg Central Station. Darkness covered all of us as we traveled throughout the night. Getting the disassembled sidearms through the port station in England and even through the various train stations proved to be easy. No one questioned the luggage or the various parts within each of our bags.

Once we were through the train station, Marlie and I wasted no time securing a VW Touran Van at the SIXT car rental. One-by-one our group sauntered out of the station, again to reduce the amount of attention we *could* draw. All seven of us were able to fit comfortably inside. I drove the van while the others took great care to reassemble the handguns we smuggled into the country. *At least we have these sidearms. If the safe house is compromised then I don't know what else we could use,* I thought.

The station wasn't far from the safe house. Garon had established the house by the Schleuse Rothensee channel locks on the edge of Magdeburg. It was nothing more than a storage house used by the ship lift operators to store heavy lift parts and mechanisms. Each of these massive parts were stacked in such a way that reinforced the metal walls and offered a clear line of fire for any would-be beasts that happened to show up. Our intention the night we were ambushed was for Marlie, Gerda and I to stay there until we heard from the remaining group. We had stored the weapons in various parts of the machine pieces and around the storage area. My aim was to get in, grab the weapons, if they were still there and leave. People were active around the locks, but the shift would end soon, and the cover of darkness would provide us with some concealment. We sat across the channel watching how frequently people walked in and out and around the storage space.

"How are we going to get inside?" Robert asked. "And might I remind you that time is *not* on our side."

"We can't just waltz up there and claim what's inside." My comment to Robert was direct, yet calm. I didn't want him to have an outburst.

I didn't like waiting either. We seemed to complete our journey unscathed. However, the full moon was two days away, looming ominous in the back of all our minds. Marcus suggested that this could certainly account for the strangeness in Grayson, his erratic behavior. It matched up with the entries in Mya's diary and notations in his journal. Grayson, himself, was more of a concern than anything else.

Though we all ate our share of food on the trains, Grayson's appetite was ferocious. His meat cravings were way above normal, so was his awareness of everything else. His head was snappy, clearly feeling things that he had never felt before. Sleep for him was rough and sporadic. This drew attention to him. No one said anything to us or him directly, fortunately. Anyone that noticed took a polite route of tolerance rather than being put out by his antics. *Lucky. Delays from people asking questions could've been costly*, I thought. We were running out of time.

Slowly, the day faded to twilight and nightfall surrounded us. The time was a little past 7:00 p.m. I could see a small sliver on the left side of the moon that was still dark. An early rise. It hung low on the tree line horizon undisturbed by the clear sky around it. Grayson was fully in its grips; staring directly at it, taking in deep breaths of the cold air as we got out of the van. The bite mark on his arm resembled an old scar as though it was acquired several years prior. Marcus called it his *mark of darkness* and that it would always be there even after he changed. Yet, any other injuries sustained as a human would simply disappear after the change. I didn't fully understand everything he was explaining, but most of it made sense. He also suggested the same would occur if he were to be injured as a werewolf and turned back into a human, they would not carry through unless the silver was still stuck inside.

We all held tight to our handguns as we approached the safe house two at a time, careful to stay concealed. From the outside it looked intact. No change from a nearly a month prior. The front had a metal garage door that slid up along the tracks. It was locked tight with a massive padlock. Yet, just to the right was a normal storm door with a dead bolt lock. Originally, when we stashed the weapons inside, only the lock on the door handle was being used. It was easy to pick. I had determined that if the dead bolt was locked, I would be able to drill into the latching mechanism to manipulate the mechanics inside. However, those tools were left in the truck that was abandoned the night we were attacked.

"*Scheiße!* Locked tight!" I whispered.

Grayson again lowered his shoulder and made as though he was going to crash through it. "Don't!" Robert said.

"How else are we going to get inside?"

"Break this lock instead." Robert pointed to the garage door.

Grayson looked around cautiously but obeyed his father and tugged hard on the garage door padlock. The lock itself stayed intact; the same could not be stated for the bolted latch that held the lock. Grayson had stripped the bolts from their sockets, twisting and contorting the metal. We opened the door partially and rolled underneath. Inside was dark. No windows meant no light. I made my way through the piles of over-sized parts the best I could without stumbling too much. I felt around the spaces that I remembered Garon had stored the weapons. Nothing. My heart raced. I scrambled, checking every possible space in which the guns could be. Again, nothing. I stood with my hands upon my hips, heavy with breath. My head sagged in defeat.

"What's wrong? Where are the weapons?" Robert asked as he noticed my pause.

"They're not here."

"What?" Robert's voice was strong, though carried panic. "What do you mean there not here?"

"Gone. Taken. Removed. However, you would like to say it."

Robert moved closer to me. "We left the other weapons behind because *you* said there would be more. Now you're telling me there are none?"

"I don't know what to say." I looked at Robert. "You knew this was going to be a gamble, I didn't hide that." I was ready to take the onslaught of venomous words and accusations.

"Are you sure this is the correct place? Maybe we took a wrong turn or something." Codie's words were innocent, but inaccurate.

I looked at Codie, "No this was the right place. Workers at the channel locks may have found the guns and reported them to the authorities. Or the safe house may be compromised either way, they are *not* here."

"So, what are we going to do now?" Robert's voice was louder more irritated than before.

I glanced back at him. Through the shadows cast by the moonlight under the door, I could see Robert's condemning stare. It was more so that I knew his expression rather than saw it. His aura emanated loathing, malcontent for everything we were experiencing. "Crack on, as one would say. Right now…we have to leave and use the handguns we brought with us!"

"Bollocks! This plan is a damp squib! I can't believe we came all this way –"

"Did you have a fucking better idea? I didn't hear you tossing out suggestions in London!" I didn't try to hide my frustration.

"Save it!" Grayson elicited immediate compliance from both of us. "Complaining about a cocked-up plan isn't going to fix it." He intimidated all of us at his present state, but his father was most affected. The incident in Australia hadn't been wiped clean just because of the subsequent events over the past couple of days. "We listen to what she says. We have six sidearms total. That's two for you, Codie, and Ada. I'm obviously not going to need one. But for now, we go."

No one said anything further. We quickly made our way under the garage door the same way we entered. Two-by-two back to the van. "Where are we going now?" Marcus asked from the back. Zoey said nothing. Marlie sat between them.

"Glindenberg. We can talk with the local merchants and stay there tonight."

"But what about more weapons? Two handguns each is a load of tosh," Robert inquired still testing his newly formed boundaries with Grayson.

"Let's hope we can find the source. It doesn't matter how many guns we have; we only need one silver bullet." At Grayson's last word I started the van and made towards Glindenberg.

The ride was short, roughly fifteen minutes from the safe house. The tutor structures with the red tiled roofs were a familiar sight that carried a dreadful memory. As we drove into the town's center circle, I gripped the steering wheel of the van tightly to hold back the sadness and anger making their way to the surface. Images of Garon flashed into my head. He looked happy at first but was immediately replaced by the tortured image of his death. It was the same for the other members of my group. Ramond, his jovial banter, annoying at times, replaced by his torso being torn in two. The screams, Olis, Kyland, Monika, the blood. I looked at Marlie in the rearview mirror; the Vogals, Manny and Nadine, just gone. Audrick and Alika Huber, all gone. *Oma*, I didn't want to think about the horrors she must've experienced. I touched her rosary that I still wore around my neck. A tear fell from my left eye, but I rubbed it away before anyone could see it. Except Grayson. I could see his eyes in the rearview mirror. He knew my sadness, my rage. He could sense it; he could smell it.

There were a few open parking spots at the Glindenberger Hof lot. I longed to stay at this location, for a sense normalcy, but not under these circumstances. I imagined staying at the hotel, eating my fill of *Filetpfännchen* with pork especially, wild mushrooms, and onions in a cream sauce. Or *Kaßlerwaldpilzpfanne* like *Oma* used to make. I twisted my head from side-to-side to crack and stabilize the vertebrae. I took a deep breath releasing it long and slow. From where I was standing, I could see the edge of the tree line where our alcove was located, where we were consumed by death. I turned to face my new group.

"We need a room. We also need to talk to the market owner two blocks down." I pointed down the street as I glanced back and forth between the group members. No one was real keen on dividing the group.

"Zoey and I will get the room with Marlie. We need to test a few devices anyways." I felt my heart pound heavy inside my chest at the thought of leaving Marlie behind. I handed Marcus a sidearm. He was hesitant. I could tell, but he didn't challenge his own line of thinking. He glanced at it once and then took it without a word. It was clear that Marcus also wanted a few moments away from Robert. I couldn't blame him. Robert glared at Marcus. No words, nonetheless, his eyes, mistrustful, were a warning. A clear cautionary decree that suggested their unfinished business would resume should he fail. Robert was everything that Grayson had told me on the plane. Like me, his pain was his poison, but it made him irrational, unhinged, boorish.

We didn't waste any more time. Before parting ways, Grayson made sure that Codie, Robert, and I had all the remaining sidearms securely holstered under our coats. It was already dark, and we were exposed.

Grayson followed close behind the three of us. His gaze never left the moon that was continuing to climb higher into the sky. Lights from the local businesses along Wolmirstedter Street were lit which provided a soft glow onto the walkway. Food aromas from local restaurants filled our nostrils. We stopped outside the storefront where Garon had acquired information about the strange happenings in the area. A small bell chimed as we entered.

The store owner looked up from the debris he was sweeping into a small pile. The man was bald across the top of his head leaving only short stubble along the sides. Glasses, that he wore down on the bridge of his nose. Casually dressed. *"Wir werden bald schließen. Fünfzehn Minuten."*

I glanced at the clock on the wall and the time was now 7:15 p.m. *"Englisch?"* I asked, hoping that I wouldn't have to translate again for the others to save a few moments.

"Ja"

"We are not here to buy anything." The store owner's face grew grim. "We are not here to cause trouble either. We would like to talk to you about some things that happened in the area over the past couple of months."

The store owner's face remained static with anxiety. "Are you talking about the shootings a month ago? I heard gunfire and that is all."

"No. I know all about that. The news is very informative," I lied to him. I wanted to make him feel at ease as much as possible despite the fact that Grayson's presence was probably enough to elicit such nervousness. "I want to know about the animals being attacked." I pointed over my shoulder. "In the tree line."

"Are you scientists or hunters?" he asked.

"*Ja.* Why do you ask?" I didn't want to reveal too much, but I also wanted to know his line of thinking.

"All the reports suggest that a predator has been pushed out of one area and has moved into this area, looking for a food source. I figured that you were here hunting the animal that has been doing these things. It's got everyone in town spooked."

"*Ja.* We are researchers studying the migration habits of dangerous animals. Possible wolves moving back into the area or even a bear. Brown bear maybe, even though bears haven't been reported in the area since the 1840's. When did you first notice the wildlife being attacked?" I asked playing up my usual role of a researcher.

"I didn't. It was one of my employees that reported them to me."

"Can we speak with him?" Robert asked.

"Ah, a British man. *Her* actually, British, like you and no she no longer works here."

"What do you mean?" I noticed that Grayson was exchanging looks between his father and Codie.

"She quit a month ago, just before the gunfire in the woods. She told me about the wildlife attacks, and I said it was too dangerous for her to ride home to Magdeburg at night in the dark. Smart, church girl, loved to talk about it. I suspect the fräulein may have been timid. I never had a problem, but I was nervous for her. After all, she was petite. But like I said the rest of the town was spooked so I didn't blame her for leaving."

"What was her name?" Grayson asked serious-minded, bent on identifying the woman who had obviously taken on a familiar description.

"Shannon. Shannon Murphy. Is she in trouble?" The store owner was still nervous, more so now that Grayson was directly speaking to him.

"No, she isn't. We would just like to know when and how she came across the dead animals. Do you have way of getting ahold of her?"

"I had a number to call, but when I called it the day after she quit in an attempt to offer her better hours during the day, the number was no longer in service."

"Do you know where she lived in Magdeburg?" Robert was equally intent on finding this woman.

"No, I don't sir. And even if I did, I wouldn't be able to tell you that kind of information. I'm sorry that I cannot be of any further assistance. If you don't mind, I would like to lock up on time. *Guten Abend.*"

Grayson tapped his father on the shoulder and motioned for him to follow. Codie and I both did the same. Outside, the evening had grown quiet. A few people walked about, but mainly to get into their cars or were also closing their businesses. The wind was fierce again and reminded me of the night we were ambushed. We walked halfway down the block towards the hotel before Grayson stopped. "Codie call Marcus."

Codie didn't question him. He took out his phone and started to dial.

"Stop! They can track the phones!"

"There are too many in the area to differentiate us. If they are bold enough to attack in the middle of a town, then we'll take them on. More than likely –" Grayson began.

"More than likely nothing! This is how my family died!"

"With all due respect to your family, it's possible that they could've tracked your cell phone signal, but highly unlikely. In the club was different, it was isolated, signals could be tracked easily, not here. I suspect there was something else at work here."

"Do you think it's her?" Robert asked Grayson. Codie continued to dial.

"I do. It fits everything we know."

A sudden rush of relief washed over me at the thought that I may not have caused my family's death but mixed with anger at the notion of how the ambush came to be. "Are you referring to this Mya person?"

"Yes." His response was quick because Codie was able to get through to Marcus. Grayson reached for the phone. "Let me talk to him. Marcus, I need to know what names Mya used in the past to stay hidden."

"Crikey, give me a second to look." Several moments past before Marcus came back on the line. Grayson put it on speaker phone for all of us to hear. *"She's gone by Dr. Bishop, Dr. Cassandra Bishop, Shanna Murphy, and Maia Murphy. Originally she was named Shannon Maia Bishop."*

"Marcus, what was that last one you said?"

"Shannon Maia Bishop."

"Do you think that she would use the name Shannon Murphy?"

"I don't see why not."

"Right. We think she may be in Magdeburg. We have no address, but the shop owner stated that she was a church girl and loved to talk about it. I am going to need a list of churches in the area."

"Catholic. Remember Grayson, she's Catholic and she would probably gravitate towards the older ones. Old structures were the only thing that she allowed herself to take pleasure in."

"Magdeburg Cathedral," I chimed in. "It's Lutheran, not Catholic, but it's one of the oldest churches around."

"Marcus can you pull up that church?" Grayson asked.

"Got it, but I'm afraid we've missed the services if that was what you were thinking."

"Bollocks!" Grayson paused as he looked around at everyone in the group before stopping to look at me. "We're going to have a go at it."

I nodded at Grayson. I would've suggested better planning, but as Robert had pointed out on several occasions already, we didn't have the luxury of time.

"Before you click off. I have the remote tracking device running. I've a strong signal from the transmitter inside your arm along with all your vitals. The main system has already ready flagged you as a species requiring further study. Ironically the system is recognizing you as a dingo with the possibility of rabies."

Grayson's expression was incredulous. "What are you getting at Marcus?"

"Nothing except that the device and transmitter are working properly."

Within a few minutes, all four of us were loaded into the van and headed towards Magdeburg. The drive was short, approximately fifteen minutes. Soon the gothic steeples of the church extended high into the night's sky. Light from the moon shown down and cast ghostly shadows around us, while other lights shown upwards on the towers illuminating the old grey stone. Streetlamps and fixed lighting surrounded the base structures of the cathedral and glowed an orange yellow allowing the interspersing walkways between the buildings to be visible.

There were a few people walking around the ornate church. Some were heading towards the Bralo House restaurant down the street on the left from where we parked. Most were probably deterred by the falling temperatures that accompanied the chilling wind that bit at our cheeks.

"We should not stay long." My words seemed to fall upon deaf ears. No one even acknowledged the statement. Instead, Grayson, Codie and Robert meandered around the front entrance of this magnificent church. Grayson walked to the right side of the church to a corner snow-covered knoll that was lined with leafless trees. Codie wasn't too far behind him. Both were visible from where Robert and I were standing. "Why are we here?"

Robert didn't look at me but instead kept his eyes locked on Grayson and Codie. "In addition to being a religious person, Mya was also a very routine person. Grayson told me that she would attend church for confession before every full moon. If it was her that was in Glindenberg and if the source is here then there is a very good chance that *she* is still here."

"Do you still think that she was in London? That day we were taking pictures?"

"Maybe. It could've also been one of the other werewolves we encountered in the club."

"You want to kill her, *ja*?" Robert nodded. "If we find her here what are you going to do?"

"Again, I don't know. That fool Marcus seems to think that she could benefit us in some way. And given the circumstances Grayson has also bought into this rubbish. I will let things play out but killing Dr. Mya Bishop hasn't changed."

From a distance, I could see Grayson lower himself to the ground to take one knee. His head was turning from side-to-side on a swivel. He stopped and tilted his head to one side, as if listening. Without warning, Grayson took off in a full sprint down the right side of the cathedral.

"COME ON!" Codie yelled as he started his pursuit.

Both Robert and I withdrew a sidearm each and held them low and inconspicuous as we ran after Codie who was in hot pursuit of Grayson. We ran all the way to Fürstenwall Street before turning left around the cathedral. Codie was running along the brick wall past the Hoflieferant restaurant gun also in hand. Patches of ground were visible where the snow had melted but turned back to ice with the falling temperatures. Running along the wall was slippery and difficult to maintain traction.

Codie stopped a little ways from us and held his gun with both hands low, off to the side. In front of him was Grayson, standing by a cobblestone tower that overlooked Schleinufer Road and the River Elbe.

"Grayson! Are you all right?" I heard Codie ask as we approached them both. Just like Codie, we held our guns low and to the side.

"Can you hear it?" Grayson asked as we approached.

"Hear what?"

"The heartbeat. I can hear it. It's fast and strong like mine. You can't hear it, can you?" Grayson looked at me and I shook my head no. "Stuff like this started on the train, but the people were close. This was close at first, but then became distant as if it was running. I can still hear it. Whatever it is, it's still close."

"Grayson, we should go." A strange awareness of my surroundings filled my being. Grayson was right. Something was close, watching, waiting. Both Robert and Codie felt it too. It was the same as the day we took pictures, the same as the night I was ambushed. "We are vulnerable and this could be a trap."

"I don't think it is. I only hear one."

"I still don't want to take that chance." Thoughts of Marlie poured into my head. I could see her small frame crouched in my trailer with her arms around her knees. Then another thought of her in the closet at Robert's manor. I placed my hand upon Grayson's shoulder. "We need to go. We plan tonight and start here tomorrow."

Chapter 25

Green-Eyed Monster
Grayson
Wednesday, March 7, 2012
3:15 p.m.

Thump, Thump…Thump, Thump…Thump, Thump. Breathing heavy…Fog and leafless trees…time elapsed…day rolled into night…chasing through the fog… Thump, Thump…Thump, Thump…Thump, Thump. Laryn screaming… Rex eyes open quickly…Holding a gun… "Give me a reason!" distant…chasing…Kap on the floor… "I tried Grayson…I tried." I see it…black silhouette in front of the cobblestone tower… "They're coming Grayson." Green eyes flash from the silhouette. "GRAYSON!"

Startled, I sat straight up in the hotel bed. My shirt was wet, breathing heavy I could still hear my name being called as it faded into the distance. "Sorry," Codie said as he stood over me. Nervous, he had his sidearm in hand. "I didn't mean to scare you, but it's almost time to go."

I swung my legs over the edge of the bed. "What time's the service?"

"4:00 p.m. You've been asleep all day."

"It doesn't feel like it." Codie re-holstered his sidearm under his coat. Looking around the room, it was only he and I. "Where is everyone?"

"Marcus and Zoey are in the room down the hall. No offense, but you were acting very strange last night, and we all were a little spooked. We allowed you to take this room, just in case." He sighed, "I believe Marlie is with them. And last I checked Dad and Ada were down by the van."

I rubbed my hands over my face and twisted my head from side-to-side. "Water. Can you get me some water?"

"Sure." Codie turned from me and walked into the hotel's lavatory. I took the opportunity to put my boots back on. A deep throbbing hunger consumed my thoughts. I held my eyes tightly closed hoping the sensation would pass. It didn't. The hunger was relentless….empty, ravenousness, painful. Codie returned with a small glass of water. "I would ask if you're all right, but I know that you're not. Do you need anything else?"

"Food. I'm hungry."

"We don't have much except for the rations we purchased. I wouldn't recommend eating at the hotel. Don't want to draw attention to you, plus if we don't go soon we'll miss the service."

"The rations are fine." Codie brought one of the black luggage bags to me. Inside were several food bars and bags of assorted nuts. I ate them all, greedily. The food took the edge off, but in no way filled the empty void in my stomach. There was a yearning for something more. Fear also played a significant function in how my body and mind worked. The full moon was less than twenty-four hours away and though I felt we were getting closer to the unknown, it was still the unknown. "Come on, let's go."

I put on my coat as we exited the room. Down the hall, Ada was on one knee talking with Marlie. Marcus stood at the doorway. All three looked with cautionary expressions as Codie and I approached. Ada hugged Marlie one last time before she stood. Fearful, Marlie ducked back into the room.

"Your father is waiting by the van. We all have ear buds so we can communicate."

"You're no longer worried about being tracked?" I asked.

Ada took a deep breath. "No. If they track us then we will kill them. You were right. The likelihood of them tracking us is small."

"Grayson, the signal from your transmitter is strong and working properly. But I insisted that we can communicate back and forth with each other," Marcus interjected. "Zoey, Marlie and me will be staying behind to monitor the situation and provide tracking support. I'm no good in the field, but I can still shoot; one entrance that I can defend." Marcus turned his body so that I could see the Sig .40 mm sidearm lying on the desk in his room. Two additional magazines lay next to it.

"Two magazines enough?" I asked.

"It'll have to be mate. We only have two extra for each handgun. Zoey will be talking to you through the ear bud and the one tracking you."

"Right then, off you go."

Marcus grabbed my arm as I started to turn from him. He was rubbing the charm around his neck. "Remember, when you turn, you won't be able to control it and you won't have control over yourself. Your readings are higher than they were yesterday. If you feel it coming, run from everyone. Get as far away as you can so you don't go after your own family."

"How will I know it's coming?"

"Crikey, I don't know. I believe it will be somewhat of a situation that when it starts, you'll know. All I can tell you is that it's going to hurt."

I didn't like how candid he was about me changing into a beast, but there was no point in glossing it up. The likelihood of the moon rising before we found the source was very high. I could see the same level of concern that he had towards me when I gave him back the diary when he was in the hospital. Eyebrows raised in the center mouth slightly agape. I looked past him. Zoey sat on the edge of the bed with a similar worried expression. Marlie was next to her, clearly frightened. "I'm sorry you've been pulled into this situation."

"We both played a part, but this might be a chance for me to *right* some wrongs."

I stuck out my hand. He grasped it firmly and shook it. We had an unspoken understanding. Nothing more was said between us. I turned from him and followed Codie and Ada out to the van.

The streets were busier than the night before. Restaurants were full and people were buzzing around the church entrance despite the ever-present cold and gusting winds. All the sounds around me were amplified. Cars rushing by were thunderous, yet the drips of water into the storm sewer were just as augmented, but clear. Perfumes and colognes from people all around assaulted my nostrils yet remained distinct enough that I could still smell the individual bath salts and cleansing products that they had used earlier in the day. Everything was sharp, well-defined in sight. I closed my eyes and breathed slow and deep to allow my brain to adjust to the enhanced senses that were unfamiliar and dizzying.

Much like the catholic churches that I had attended, incense hung heavy, dense inside the cathedral. Bright light poured from the tall-paneled windows. It caused the monumental marble columns and archways along with gothic statuesque sculptures to glow a radiant white. Additional elongated, paneled windows shown bright illuminating the golden crucifix at the end of the center aisle. People had filled in the rows of chairs that permeated the center congregational space all facing the pulpit and center altar. Imbedded high above into the wall behind the congregation was a gleaming, chrome pipe organ that was illustrious and grand with its presence. As the crowd amassed, there was standing room only, in which people filled the vast open side bays beneath the adjacent windows. We preferred this because it gave us the liberty to move about during the ceremony if we needed to.

The service began in song as everyone stood. Codie took his spot close to the pulpit at the far-right side of the congregational space whereas Ada moved along the left side. My father and I remained towards the rear center. I listened, desperate for the heartbeat again, desperate for anything that stood out against the harmonious hymns that reached high into the massively vaulted ceiling.

My father touched his ear bud. "Okay we're all in position. Stay alert."

"Copy that," Codie stated.

"I'm in position," Ada Confirmed.

"Can you hear us ok Zoey?" my father asked.

"You're breaking up a little because of the songs, but I'm still gett'n ya."

I remained in the rear center and my father moved to the left, closer to Ada. The reverend that stood before the congregation started with the apostolic greeting followed immediately by the Kyrie. "Lord, have mercy..." The reverend spoke out, but his words trailed off.

Something was wrong. His words seemed disjointed, slurred, interfered with. Whispers within the congregation were overpowering and more indistinguishable than before. They overlapped with each other, impossible to tell apart. Heartbeats intermixed with breathing. Every sound seemed to beset my hearing so much so that clarity was gone. As the reverend spoke the salutation, his mouth uttered words that I couldn't decipher, as though he was muted and everyone else was amplified. He motioned for the congregation to bow their heads in the prayer of the day. All went silent.

"Grayson..." A long whisper echoed into my ears goading me to look up and around the congregation for its source. It was too distant to be anyone trying to talk through the ear buds. *"Grayson..."*

No one appeared to notice the whisper. Both Codie and Ada remained alert with heads on a swivel, but not attending solely to me. My father stared straight ahead as though the biblical lessons were more enthralling than he had anticipated.

*Thump, thump...thump, thump...thump, thump...*started low, but grew louder, closer. Incense that hung heavy in the air dissipated, replaced with a unique scent that was strangely alluring, akin to the night before, only stronger. I caught the side profile of someone moving against the crowd along the right side. I pressed the ear bud. "We may have something."

I started to walk towards the mysterious person. *"Grayson wait, I've lost sight of you in the crowd."* My father seemed panicked.

"I've got him." I heard Ada say, but she was on the opposite side of the cathedral.

"Zoey, are you still tracking me?"

"Yes, your signal is strong."

"Codie, I'm by the right corridor that leads out of the main hall."

"I'm making my way there."

My hope was to get Codie to follow me since he was the closest, reassured that even though my father had lost sight of me Ada still had eyes on me and my transmitter was still sending a strong enough signal for Zoey to track me.

"Grayson." This time the whisper was shorter, less drawn out but closer. So was the heartbeat. *"Grayson!"*

I turned to see a petite woman standing several meters down the corridor. As soon as I saw her she turned to run down another smaller corridor to the right that connected to the larger one. *No*, I thought. Without hesitation, I ran down the corridor fearing that this was my only opportunity, the only moment I may get to circumvent the ill-fated pathway that lay before me. I turned the corner only to stop at the understanding that the petite woman who stood before me was holding a gun. Casually dressed, black leather coat, denim with knee high boots. Her hair was short, spiky on top and buzzed on the sides. Fiery green eyes cut through me and were the same that filled my nightmares.

There was disbelief, shock at who was standing before me. "Mya." I swallowed hard as I uttered her name. A name that had brought so much terror and consumed so much of the passing days since the church in Cambridge. Scarcely anyone was in the corridor with us, but she still held the gun low making it difficult for anyone else to see. Her eyes were iridescent within the dim corridor. Bits of light touched them from the nearby windows and caused them to glow like that of a dog at night. Cold, fierce. "I didn't think it would come to this. You, killing me in a church."

"If I wanted to kill you in a church, Grayson, I would've done it two years ago."

"The rest of my team is only moments behind. I suggest –"

"Then I suggest you listen closely," Mya interrupted. "If you value the lives of your team, then you'll come with me. I know you've been bitten, and you don't have as much time as you think you do. We have to go, *now!*"

"And if I don't?"

I could hear Codie and my father speaking through the earbud trying to locate my position. They were closing in on us. "Then you'll most certainly put your team into a situation that will result in their deaths."

Laryn, Kap, Henry, Gerda and all the others. Too many, I thought. I nodded towards Mya. "Lead on."

"Leave the earbud," she stated. I removed the earbud and dropped it to the floor of the cathedral. Without a second consideration she turned and sprinted away from me down the corridor towards the exit. I followed. I kept stride behind her as she rounded the corner and through the exit. "This way!"

Cold immediately hit my face as we passed through the ornate doors. It was more of a refresher than a hindrance. Inside my coat was warm, almost too warm. We ran around the right side of the cathedral, the same as I had done the night before. The sun was low in the sky. *Another hour or two and the light will fade into darkness,* I thought. I stopped running at the cobblestone tower. It was more silhouetted with shades of grey rather than illuminated stone like the evening before. Mya continued down a stairway which led onto a walkway along Schleinufer Road. "Wait!" I shouted.

"There's no time!" Mya shouted back over her shoulder.

I unzipped my coat before I resumed my chase. Mya turned right at the foot of the stairway, slowing her pace to a brisk walk. I was able to catch up with her. "Where are we going? How can I trust you?"

"Trust? I don't ever expect you to trust me." She held out a remote starter. A grey Volkswagen GTI parked along the road flashed once before starting. "Get in! As for any other questions, I'll answer them once we're on our way."

"Damn it!" I stopped in front of the car and glared at her over the roof. Anger flowed from me. "You tore my sister apart! You hold me a gun point! And I have every right to leave you dead and rotting along the road. The least you can do is tell me where we're going!"

Her expression matched mine. Cold, stern with furrowed eyebrows over fierce green eyes, piercing. Her jaw clenched as her upper lip lifted in a bit of a snarl. "As you will soon find out the beast inside of you will consume you. Just like it did me the night Laryn died! Let me ask you Grayson; Are you hungry? I was before my first change too. Hungry like no other time. It's what fuels our change." Anger towards her shifted as I listened. "The moon is scheduled to be full tomorrow night, but the full moon only occurs for a split second, too fast for our eyes to see. But it will be full enough in a few hours to cause you to change. I want to get you as far away from this town as possible. Now get in the goddamn car!"

Not for a moment taking my eyes off Mya, I lifted the door handle and sat in the front seat. She shifted the gear from neutral to first and pulled out onto the road. "What did you mean that in a few hours I'm going to change?" My voice was still laced with anger, but alarm suppressed the emotion.

"The full moon is mostly an optical illusion, but this illusion still elicits the same excitement in us, same response. So, the moon creates at least two nights where the light shining down appears to be full. Our eyes can't tell the difference. I'm afraid that if you stayed with your team, you would've changed into a werewolf not knowing the change was coming. When you change, you'll be unhinged, and you'll attack *anything* in your way. People would've died. It's said that God works in mysterious ways, but so does the devil. A curse is not something that plays by the rules."

I couldn't believe what I was hearing. Emotionally, I had met an impassable barrier. *I came within hours of slaughtering my own family and she stopped it,* I thought. *But she was the one who killed Laryn. She could've killed me, twice, but didn't.* "If change is inevitable, then I have to tell you. My team is tracking me."

There was a long pause, a deepened contemplation that had struck Mya silent. Heavily she sighed, "Marcus." Her voice was short, curt, not devoid of anger, but fused with a discontent towards the thought that Marcus was involved. "After you were bitten did you seek him out?"

"Yes."

"Same device?"

"Yes." I showed her the small mark that was on my forearm just above the wrist from where he had inserted the transmitter. "It won't take them long to find me."

We merged onto a larger highway, 189 north, before merging onto B71 heading west. "Damn. We're going to have to work fast."

"Work fast? You still haven't told me where we are going or what we're doing."

"The source." Mya's voice was very matter of fact. Marcus's involvement bothered her greatly. I could sense a change in her, but she was holding something back.

"I'm sorry, what?"

"You and I are going to the source. The source of the curse." Mya glanced at me without really changing her expression.

"How, I mean who? What? I thought you said you were taking me far away?"

"I am taking you away from the town." Mya's response was coy, evasive and didn't sit well with me. She was perfectly okay with keeping her agenda secret. "Bursting into a werewolf in the middle of the capital city of the state of Saxony-Anhalt, Germany is certainly *not* a good idea. Harming someone in werewolf form is a burden you don't want or need to carry."

"That's a safe answer. What are you hiding?"

She pursed her lips. "You're not the only ones hunting me. But you've openly chosen this so I'm not responsible."

"Please explain!"

Mya continued to drive, passing cars as we got close to them. She let a few moments slip past in a defiant silence. My stare was equally fierce, relentless, and urged her to explain. Reluctantly she started. "After the night at St. Teresa's, I fled, keeping mostly to the wooded areas and regions without much civilization. I scavenged for food, slept in hostels, but I had also discovered that when I changed into a werewolf that night, I had more control, and it reaffirmed that I could control when I changed. The moon, for now, still has its sway over me…" she looked at me. "…us…and maybe always will, but if I focus my emotions, my anger, hard enough –"

"You change," I interrupted.

"Yes. Marcus told you, did he?" I nodded yes and let her continue. "Though I have more control, the thirst to kill is also stronger, it's a hunger. What's left of my humanity is quickly dying. Letting the darkness in the night at St. Teresa's came at an awful price." She glanced at me again before returning her eyes to the road. "A month had past of hiding throughout England, mainly wandering. I found myself staring across the River Thames at the London Eye ready to give up when an uneasy awareness washed over me. It was an awareness of darkness…evil. I could sense it, feel it with my entire being. This evil was all around me…all at once, as if the London Eye had zeroed in on me directly. The sensation was so strong that I found myself backpedaling wanting to run…but I had no idea as to where. At that moment I knew I had no choice but to continue, continue to find the answers behind this dreadful curse. I fled England to Berlin, Germany seeking answers to questions I had about Johan Stich. Corbin told me that there were others like us. He too knew about the legend of Johan Stich, but laughed as I mentioned it to him, claiming that it was a tale of weakness. I considered Johan to be the source at the time, but I remembered he had a daughter and that she may be the source. It seemed more probable. However, every search I did online, everywhere I looked, every book I read ran into the same dead end. His daughter was killed. Some stories suggest that she was butchered because of her father's curse; others suggest that her father did the butchering. Either way all church records of the time indicated she was gone."

The time was now 5:00 p.m. and even less light was in the sky than before. "I don't see how this is relevant."

She glared at me but continued without fielding my objection. "I remembered what Marcus and I had discussed about curses. Curses always have a source, but the source may not know they have a curse until it's too late. One of the pamphlets that I was able to pull up at Cambridge library showed a holy man, clergy holding a cross over a depiction of Johan. I also read that the priest had damned his entire bloodline before his execution. Priests are supposed to be the holy men that offer God's redemption, not function as judge and condemner. I began to seek out priests of the day that could've been associated with Johan. Again, all my searches produced nothing, even while I was living here in Berlin, no records. I knew the legend well, I knew that it supposedly took place in the far east of Germany, but what I had always assumed was that the holy men of the day were Catholic. They were Lutheran. I feel the source is a Lutheran Priest, not Catholic."

"Why does it matter?"

"From a research standpoint, all of my searches were geared towards Catholicism. More importantly, Lutheranism was more prominent in the region after Martin Luther in 1517 published the *95 Theses* in Wittenberg, Germany. Lutherans have priests too. Many scholars believed this was the start of the Protestant reformation. Magdeburg became a leader in this reformation. Lots of turmoil. During the Thirty Years' War, Magdeburg was raided and much of the artwork was destroyed or looted which carried key records of supernatural events. Lutherans and Catholics were at arms with each other in this time period; blame was and is certainly shared.

I decided to spend my time in this area searching for the others, searching for the priest that caused it. But it didn't really matter who or what caused it. What's more important is that this evil was allowed to endure. Mankind's judgement and petty squabbling over how to worship or what practices should and should not be performed has been and probably will remain a distraction from evil. True evil is faceless and isn't confined to one facet of faith.

What I found was that this evil was more evil than you and I. Just as I could sense your presence and you mine, so can darker forces, especially around the full moon. They had followed me from England. I could feel them the same as I did on the river that day in front of The Eye. Perhaps they followed me for what I had done to Corbin or maybe because I was close to finding another entrance into the catacombs. I didn't have to search them out, they found me."

"The red eyed werewolves?" I asked.

"Perhaps. I've only seen one, when I was bitten, but I have felt them. Evil, like Corbin, but worse, darker, more demonic."

"Where do you think this second entrance into the catacombs is?" I asked knowing that access through the club was not going to be feasible any longer.

"I believe it to be just north of the New Scotland Yard building. Storm sewers empty into the river just below the main walkway. Not easy to access and probably not used as an official entrance, but the sewers may connect into the catacombs."

"Are you sure about this?" I asked in a need to know more information.

"Grayson, I'm not sure about anything, but I have learned to trust these disturbing emotions." Mya's voice was controlled and serious. For now, I was just going to have to trust her knowledge.

I paused for a few moments before I changed my line of questions. "Is the name of the priest you have been searching for Father Amsel?" I asked thinking back to Ada's account from the Grimoire.

"I don't know. All I do know is that they were close to acquiring me, but I fled again, back to England. I knew that if I had located the source alone, I risked becoming worse than what I am now or dead. It needed to be destroyed. While in England, I stopped at the church in Cambridge where I was almost killed in the hopes of uncovering something. A year had passed since our altercation. The church was repaired, and the event was nearly forgotten. No access to anything. Pain washed over me like a wave in the ocean, sadness, a lament for release, a need to be rebuilt like the church. That wasn't going to happen as long as I knew evil was enduring. I returned that night to my estate, but quickly realized that I needed to stay on the move, or they would catch up with me. Only one other time did I return to my home."

"Why?"

"Facts. Facts always uncover what is hidden if they are used properly. I needed to know how to kill the beasts, the true darkness. Like I said, all curses have a source. But I couldn't take them on all by myself. I needed people who could hunt them and have been hunting them for centuries. Corbin had also mentioned that there were groups that hunted our kind and if they were known then they would become the hunted. I used what I knew, the facts about how agents of the devil were destroyed, by burning and when this sort of ritualistic execution stopped. Any thereafter would stand out."

"King Charles II abolished the practice in 1676."

"In England, but not all over Europe. Germany was not under his reign. Besides, just because a *King* puts down a decree does not mean it's upheld, especially if those who are breaking the law of the land are hunting werewolves. That aside, I wasn't able to complete my research at my estate. I heard people that night and so I quickly left. Escaped into the garden behind my estate and watched. It was just the authorities posting something to the door."

"Auction notice."

"Yes. I read it. I hadn't paid any taxes on the estate for some time. I knew it was going up for auction and that this would be the last time I went to my home." Mya took in a deep breath and released it. There was pain inside of her that was deeper than I had felt, even with the loss of Laryn, Kap and Henry. "What I did know was that Corbin was ordered to burn, but he was in England and the hunters had very little sway over his execution. The first order that was written up and stated clearly that he was sentenced to death by means of burning. Yet, the church and the King's decree were being upheld. It delayed the process only to be denied. There was a petition formed by the hunters and formal evidence submitted that would allow his burning. Again, it was rejected. In an attempt to do God's work, the hunters exposed themselves and they were slaughtered, and Corbin escaped."

"I think Corbin was part of their group. We found out that Club Red was an outpost and he was their guard dog. That's where I was bitten, they all had red eyes."

Several more moments slipped by and Mya merged onto L41 north. "I don't know what constitutes the red eyes. I just know that it's far more evil, and I feel it's closer to the actual source."

Mya looked straight ahead, focused on the road. She seemed impenetrable by my comments, but I could still sense that my words had an impact. There was a deep resentment that mixed with sadness and anger which was unattributed to anything that I could identify.

"For two hundred years, I tried to remain in the shadows, but my best ally I have learned was exposure. In the digital media world, nothing can stay secret. Because of my ability to control the change, I have a need to kill, but God doesn't condemn for the slaughtering of cattle or dogs. I am hunted by this evil, but I am also being hunted by mankind. By killing the livestock and other animals I brought my sins to light, made myself known. My hope was that if the group of hunters still existed that they would emerge to track these killings. They would follow me, and the two groups would come together and in their fight the source could be identified... and destroyed."

"Bloody hell! Do you know what you've done?" Fury seethed and escaped with my words. I could feel my heart pounding and my breathing became short and acute. "The group of hunters that you drew out was ambushed because of you! Slaughtered, torn to pieces like my sister! They were Ada's family!"

"I don't know Ada and I don't care!"

"Don't care? You goddamn hussy!"

Mya slammed on the brakes and brought the car to a screeching halt along the side of the road. Before I could react, she had reached across and pinned my left arm with her own. She drew her gun again and placed it to the side of my head. "Listen to me you *fucking* muppet!" Her hand shook. She held back a tremendous amount of emotion. A tear dripped from her right eye. An image of Kap's mangled body flashed into my head. "I – am – sorry I hurt you! I am sorry for the loss of your sister! I'm sorry for the loss of the others! While other people have enjoyed their lives, mine was cursed! I wanted love, a family, children, I didn't choose to be this!" she yelled. "I – was – bitten! Ada's family *chose* to be hunters and if they died, then they died as such! She should be thankful they didn't become agents of evil, because there isn't a day that's gone by that I don't wish that beast would've killed me. Curses, demons, and the devil are real Grayson, but so is God! That is the *ONLY* thing I have left to cling to! No one has cried for me Grayson! Those who would've are dead. I don't want to shoot you, but I will. To me it'll be one less werewolf."

I controlled my breathing and stared into her eyes as more tears flowed. "What do you want Mya? Are you trying to be a heroine? What are you protecting?"

"My – soul." She pulled the gun away from my head. "I've prayed to God so much, hoping that He would rid me of this curse. I've abided by His law, without His guidance or blessing. For so long I thought He had abandoned me, damned me. But if you and I are real, then so is God and maybe His blessings will come after my death. Perhaps this dark gift was His workings, to combat a greater evil."

Daylight was fading from the sky as the sun lowered itself behind the tree line. I stared at Mya. She was tormented. "There's not going to be a happy ending. Werewolf or not, my father wants to kill you."

"I know." She lowered the gun. "And there have been days where I thought of letting him do it. But the darkness would endure. Help me destroy the source and I will accept whatever fate may come my way."

Our eyes remained locked. Another tear dripped down her face. "Where are we headed?"

"Walbeck. A sleepy German town, surrounded by trees. I went there before the full moon knowing that there was a seemingly endless forest that I could hide in after I changed. But I have sensed more evil there lately than any other place. Perfect to hide for centuries if you needed."

"And you're sure the source, this priest is there?"

"No, I'm not. After the attack in the forest of Glindenberg, they stalked me. I've felt them. They followed me back to London and kept me on the move. They didn't want exposure, so I hid in plain sight. I stayed in the public places and spent my time in libraries. What I discovered was several ruined areas littered throughout Germany that could've been the place where it all started."

"Wait, you were in London again?" I interrupted. "It *was* you that day at the club, wasn't it? You followed us?"

"Yes."

"My father also spoke of the day outside of his office, it was you then too?"

"Yes."

"Why? Why follow us?"

"The same reason as before. I can't kill them alone. You were so apt at tracking me before that I thought if I exposed myself, you might hunt me again…and you did. But, just like that the feeling was gone."

"Bait, you used us as bait!" I held back my anger. Anger over being used, but also over the loss of family and friends. "People - are - dying!"

"And more people will follow if we don't succeed! But life and death doesn't matter very much when you think of one's soul and eternity. The balance has shifted. They can't stay hidden anymore. That's why they're hunting me and they would've eventually come for you."

I considered everything that she was saying. "How did you find me?"

"I returned to Magdeburg to explore the areas I mentioned. I ventured north. Nothing. I ventured further south. Again, nothing. Yet, a week ago I ventured west, to Walbeck. There I felt it again only stronger. They had let me alone in Magdeburg, but they didn't go far. The feeling was awful. Dread filled me. It was as though the devil himself had taken up residence. I retreated back to Magdeburg to research the area. A ruined abbey sits atop the hill, perfect…for a priest. That's when I felt you and I thought you were them, so I ran again." Mya laid the handgun between the center console and her seat. "Yet, the feeling wasn't the same. I watched from a distance last night. When I saw you, I immediately recognized you and I followed you to your hotel. When you came back to the church, I knew that you had been bitten. I could smell it, feel it, and when I saw people around you unconsciously moving away from you during the prayer, I was certain."

"Then you called to me?"

"Yes. Though the innocent that have fallen are in God's grace, guilt for what I have done to your family filled me and I knew the best thing to do was to get you away from more innocent lives."

I was right about her. She wasn't just a mindless beast. She was still human, but a human that was trapped and tormented by a great evil that now had its wicked claws around *my* soul. My anxiety remained but empathy filled my heart. I sighed heavily. "And if we can't find the source, then what?"

"At least you won't be in the center of the town and we can retreat to the forest. More importantly you won't be around your team, or your father."

"How far is it from here?"

"It's another twenty minutes." Mya gestured towards the road in front of us.

"Alright. I'll help you. How long until the moon raises?"

"Last night it rose early. Fully visible at 7:00 p.m." Mya looked around. Trees lined one side of the road. The other side was still a relatively flat pasture, with a few rolling foothills. "I would say the moon will rise around 6:45 p.m., but it won't be fully visible above the tree line until 7:15 p.m. or so."

The time was 5:45 p.m. "Well, isn't this just bloody brilliant. Shit!" Nerves raced through my body. A genuine fear filled my mind and body of what was coming.

Mya shifted the gear and sped away from the side of the road. "Though the abbey is surrounded by thickets of trees, the deep forest is just under a kilometer away from the town. If we haven't found anything by 7:00 p.m. we'll make our way there. Like I said, I've done it before. Endless forest."

Mya was a few minutes off with her timeframe. We parked on the edge of town at 6:08p.m. She grabbed a small LED flashlight and her gun. A roughly paved road led up to the town which was lined with trees. The remaining bits of light cast a twilight glow of oranges and reds that streaked from below the leafless trees and reflected off the clouds that rolled in above. It was a long walk in the dark. Time was against us. Wind rubbed the bare branches together. Snow remained on either side of the road. There was something else. Something drew the hairs to stand on the back of my neck. A feeling, a presence, a watchful eye from the trees perhaps. It started more as nervousness, a light tingle of the stomach that mixed with a deep sadness, then a fuming rage. I could feel the anger in the air with no particular thing to ascribe it too. Mya looked at me but said nothing, she only nodded in acknowledgement of the feeling. It grew worse as we climbed the hill to the ruined abbey, almost sickening. From our vantage point we could see the roof tops of the traditional tutor homesteads. Lights could be seen from within each one. No one was outside.

Grand as it was in its day, the abbey stood in ruin. Most of its roof had long since collapsed and been removed. We walked through the main portico and into what was formally the main hall. The structure was purely a skeleton of its former self. Nooks and alcoves led off through shadowy archways. Debris littered the stone flooring and was now dusted with snow. Stone pillars towered over us, standing in defiance of time and weathering. Mya lowered herself closer to the ground, closed her eyes and took a deep breath through her nose. She then pointed to footprints in the light snow that led across the ground to one of the darkened openings. "Someone has been here recently."

"This is a tourist site, right?"

"Yes, but I mean someone else. These prints wouldn't last long with the wind blowing as hard as it is."

I listened closely for a heartbeat different than Mya's, nothing. Wind whipped through the archways, howling like a banshee. I leaned closer to the ground and also took a deep breath. No smell either. "There's no scent I can pick up on. I don't hear anything abnormal either, but I can feel something's wrong."

"Me too."

"The prints lead through there." I pointed to one of the alcoves. "This could be a trap, Mya."

"I know." She didn't seem to care one way or the other. Time was slipping by quickly. The alcove led into a darkened portion that was still roofed. Mya clicked on her small flashlight. Inside was empty but led down a dark corridor into a sublevel of the abbey. Snow had blown inside and down the steps into the impenetrable blackness. Any rays of light were all nearly consumed by the new nighttime sky. My senses were sharp and everything in my body warned me not to descend into the bowels of the structure. Yet, with time waning and stripped of any daunted considerations Mya continued to follow the footprints.

The stone stairwell curved slightly as it descended. No more snow along with no more footprints. There was a chamber at the foot of the stairs that extended deep under the main level. Our only light came from Mya's flashlight, but it was enough to navigate the room. "What are we looking for?" I asked.

"I don't know exactly." Mya scanned the enclosure with her light.

"Something draws closer, I can feel it. We need to work fast."

Mya didn't respond to my assertion, instead she fixated on an object at the far end of the room. A book of sorts lay on the stone flooring. There were no markings or insignia that I recognized. Mya knelt and examined the book closely. I held her flashlight as she opened it gently and thumbed through some of the pages. The script was handwritten and from what I could tell nothing I could read. "It's in German," Mya uttered. "And written a long time ago."

"Can you translate it?"

"Yes, but it may take some time, time we don't have."

Thump, thump… thump, thump…thump, thump.

Deep and more distinct than I had heard it before, more than hers, more than mine, the heartbeat returned.

"We're not alone," I whispered.

"Right…let's go!" Mya quickly shut the book and handed it to me. As she turned to walk back the same way we came, Mya froze. A cigarette lit and illuminated the darkness. Before us stood a silhouette of a man. He took a drag and for a moment, his eyes glowed red. The feeling of angst and anger was incredibly strong. Mya pulled her handgun out and pointed it at the black silhouette along with her flashlight.

"I vouldn't do zat if I were you." The voice of the silhouette was deep and strong, masculine, but with the maturity of an older gentleman. Heavy German accent. He stood far enough away that we couldn't see the features of his face. The man walked further into the room and took another drag. He exhaled slowly as he spoke, "You are a very hard voman to track down Dr. Bishop, but you have grown predictable. In the woods around us are my family." He flicked his cigarette to the floor. "They vould be most unhappy should you pull zat trigger. Please lower your weapon…let us talk."

"Who are you?" Mya asked. She kept him at gun point as I held the flashlight on him, "Are you him, the priest Father Amsel, the source of all this darkness?"

"Come now Mya, you speak so negatively. Yes, I am the *priest*. Father Amsel. But let's be positive, I come offering you a gift and opportunity. The book…is our history, take it, learn ze truth."

"What do you want from us?" I asked. The wind howled down the stone corridor and caught the flaps of the man's overcoat.

Father Amsel's sinister eyes glared at me in the glow of Mya's light. "Grayson, one of our newest family members. You have questions…ve have answers. More importantly, I vant a truce. So gallant. So strong, a varrior. Too much death has occurred between us even though this is the first-time ve have met." A growing sense of dread was forming inside my stomach, getting stronger with each passing moment.

"How did it start?" Mya was adamant, forceful even. "The curse? Did it start with Johan?"

He glanced back at Mya. "Ah yes Johan. A foolish man. Vicked and misdirected. Ve dealt vith him properly and burned him." His voice was controlled and venomous.

"How did the curse transfer to you?" Mya asked.

"There are things zat you have not yet learned Dr. Mya Bishop, but I told you it is all in ze book." Father Amsel pressed a button to illuminate his watch, then looked back at us. "Time is fading from us and this is your only opportunity. In less zan twenty minutes the glorious moon vill be visible."

"What's stopping me from pulling the trigger and ending all of this right here, right now?"

"Mya, you should know by now zat zee pebble zat causes the avalanche is meaningless once the larger stones have already begun to fall. I am merely the pebble." Mya studied the man as she lowered her gun. She still held it tightly in her hand. Father Amsel held out his hand. "Both of you, come vith me now. All of your questions vill be answered, and ve could stop this pointless violence."

I looked at Mya. She stared deep into my eyes, contemplative for a second. She took a deep breath and exhaled through her mouth slowly. "No," she said still staring at me. With a quick motion she raised the gun back up and fired!

BOOM!

Father Amsel's head whipped backwards as his body fell to the floor. Mya moved closer, stood over top of him with the gun still pointed at him and squeezed off three more rounds.

BOOM! BOOM! BOOM!

The blood looked black as it coated the stone surface. "Holy shit!" I said still staring in awe of Mya.

"This man is just a pawn!" She grabbed her flashlight and held it over the dead man's body and pointed to his hand. "Look there at his wrist and forearm. The scarring. It's a bite mark. His mark of darkness. I saw the edge of it first when he lit the cigarette. Then again when he touched his watch. He was bitten just like us. He's not the source. Besides the feeling inside of me is only getting worse. There's still something out there, beyond this place."

"Are you sure?" I asked.

"Do you feel any different?" she asked.

"No. I don't."

Mya grabbed the hand of the dead man and illuminated his watch again. "Damn it! It's 7:02 p.m. Grayson, we've got to go! There's hardly any time to get to the tree line! We have to go."

I merely nodded in agreement. Both of us quickly ascended the steps. We passed through the small alcove leading back into the main area. Howls in the distance combined with the blowing wind. Looking out onto the horizon was a soft glow of the light. It was only minutes before the moon crested the jagged tops and shown down upon the town. "This was a trap!" I said as dread thoroughly gripped me knowing I was going to change, but that there was also something much more evil closing in on us, fast.

"We're going have to make a run for it! We can't take them on by ourselves! If we change before we make it, I shall do my best to keep you away from the homes. Remember you won't be able to control it!"

"GRAYSON!" a gruff voice yelled from in front of us. My horror was complete as we looked forward. Ada, Codie, and my father stood in the portico of the main hall; weapons drawn. It only took a few seconds for my father to realize who I was standing with. Despite the darkness, I could see the maddened rage on his face as he raised his gun. The moments that followed seemed to progress in slow motion. Knowing his intention and what lay just beyond the walls of the abbey, I shoved Mya out of the way as my father fired.

CHAPTER 26

Werewolves
Ada
Wednesday, March 7, 2012
7:10 p.m.

The bullet missed Mya and punched a hole right through Grayson's chest. He crumpled and rolled to his back. Blood poured from the wound.

"NOOOOO!" Robert yelled still holding the gun. He aimed again at Mya as she ran. "YOU FUCK'N BITCH!"

BOOM! BOOM! BOOM!

The rounds missed. Mya continued to run through one of the darkened alcoves. Robert started to chase after her before Codie stopped him. "Dad! Grayson's been shot!"

Robert dropped his weapon to the ground in realization of what he had done, while Codie and I rushed to Grayson's aide. Robert hit his knees, his eyes wide. He let out whimpered cries as he crawled towards Grayson's wounded body wriggling in pain. In the darkness we tried to apply pressure to his wound. He coughed several times expelling blood from his mouth. "Roll him to his side!" I said to Codie.

There was an exit wound behind his right shoulder. "What can we do?" Codie was frantic. Robert was still in shock from what he had done. He knelt near us with his hands plastered to his forehead, continuing to let out horror-stricken weeps.

"The bullet passed right through him, but it probably punctured his lung. He's going to die unless we get him some help."

Grayson coughed out more blood but shook his head *no*. "Ru – Run!"

"Run, why?" Codie asked. "Grayson, we have to help you!" Codie pressed his ear bud. "Zoey! Grayson's been shot. He's in real trouble! We need the nearest hospital!"

"I hear ya Codie, but everything on my end showing his vital signs increasing. He's getting stronger."

"The moon –" Grayson coughed again. "The moon – is rising. Full. Run!"

"Full moon? I thought it was tomorrow?" Codie asked.

Grayson shook his head no again. "Now! Book - take it!"

Tears spilled from Robert's eyes. His head hung low with his arms draped on either side in defeat. Codie stayed by Grayson's side as I ran to the edge of the Abbey. Just over the tree line I could see the moon rising. I pressed my earbud. "Zoey it's Ada! Grayson said the moon is going to be full tonight!"

I heard some shuffling through the earbud. *"Ada it's Marcus. All of his vitals are increasing, he may be right!"*

"He is going to die if we don't get him help!"

"No, he's not! He's changing! Get away from him! His wound will heal during the change! Run! Now!"

The moon crested the tree line and poured its light across the small rolling pasture and over the town. It was full. Grayson's body shook as the rays of light teemed through the spaces between the pillared ruins. I turned to face Codie "CODIE! GET AWAY FROM HIM!" I yelled.

I ran towards Codie and grabbed his arm pulling him backwards. "What are you doing? He's dying!" Codie protested and yanked himself free.

I grabbed him again. "He's changing! Come on!" I continued to pull him away from Grayson's body towards where Robert had been kneeling. An understanding of what I had said set in on Codie. He abandoned his heroics to help his brother and grabbed the older-looking book that was lying on the ground.

"What do you mean he's changing? I thought the full moon wasn't until tomorrow?" Robert stood and recoiled in fear.

"It's full enough!" I yelled as I grabbed his gun from the ground and handed it back to Robert. "Here! Come on!"

Codie held one of his guns in his hand and clutched the book in his other. I held my gun with both hands as Grayson let out an agonizing wail. His chest pushed towards the sky and his scream morphed into a grizzly, snarling howl. In the light of the moonlight, I watched as the hole in his chest that gaped and gushed blood, close. He rolled from his back to his knees. The coat he was wearing split and peeled from his torso as it grew. A snout pushed forward from his mouth and oversized canine teeth extended on either side. Grayson held one arm up towards the full moon as his skin burst forth into black fur. His arm and leg muscles grew and the rest of his clothing ripped from his body. Grayson's face was no longer recognizable as a human, replaced instead by an oversized fearsome wolf. Pointy ears projected out from atop his head and his eyes glowed white in the moonlight.

Grayson was no longer, a werewolf stood on its hind legs and towered over us. It shook from side-to-side. The beast was immense. I took aim, but Robert blocked my arms before I could fire. "No! Don't! That's still my son!" Tears still dripped from his eyes.

"We gave him every possible chance! I have to! I promised him I would!"

The monster's head snapped forward setting its eyes upon us and let out another growling roar. It lowered itself, snarled and lunged. Massive claws were extended. I pushed Robert backwards as the werewolf collided with me and we tumbled. Our momentum rolled us over each other several times and I dropped my gun. Its claws dug into the heavy bomber coat I was wearing, tearing through the leather, piercing the skin across my chest before we broke free from one another.

It slid on the frozen ground, scraping against the snow and ice as it righted itself for another advance. I knelt and blood trickled down the front of me from the wounds. They weren't deep enough to be debilitating, but still caused a struggle when I stood. Our eyes locked as we squared off with each other. The werewolf blocked the portico forcing me to back up into the open space of the abbey's main hall. With vicious snarls, it held its arms out to either side. A second howl of hell erupted to the left of me as a brown werewolf leapt to the top of the crumbling wall. It momentarily distracted the black werewolf. Its green eyes were piercing.

BOOM! BOOM!

The frozen dirt burst forth in front of the black werewolf. Codie stood next to me firing into the ground. The beast leapt to the right to avoid the shots as the other werewolf bounded from the ruined wall into the open space. I drew my second gun to take aim again as Codie grabbed me in a bear hug preventing me from raising my arms. Pain seared across my chest "Ada, Stop! That's Grayson if you shoot, he's dead!"

Garon's death flashed into my mind. *Oma's* too. I swallowed hard. Robert appeared next to us; gun drawn ready to fire. In the dimness of the abbey, the two brutes both looked black. There was no way of telling them apart except for their eyes; one set white, one set green, both sets cutting through the shadows. They swiped at each other and had seemingly forgotten about us for a moment. Beyond the walls, several more howls emerged all around us. Our hunt was over, our escape had begun.

"Come on!" Codie yelled as he pointed to the back archway. A few steps into our stride, we stopped as a third beast, red eyes of fury blocked our escape. The moon shone bright on its back. Before I could even raise my gun, shots rang out beside me.

BOOM! BOOM! BOOM!

The .40 caliber rounds punctured the werewolf. It reared up, howling in pain before it fell to the ground. Robert continued to advance on the beast with a stern fury.

BOOM! BOOM!

Its red eyes went dark as blood coated the ground. Robert's face was fierce, unyielding, contorted into an angered desperation in the moonlight. He stood over the beast for a moment ensuring it was dead. I glanced back into the abbey, two red-eyed werewolves bounded over the wall, into the main hall and attacked the fighting beasts. The white-eyed werewolf sprang through a darkened alcove to escape. The green-eyed werewolf lunged towards the nearest red-eyed beast and sunk its teeth into its neck. It ripped and thrashed at the monster yanking a huge chunk of furry flesh from its upper torso. In that moment everything I knew about werewolves was shaken to its core. *I can't believe it! Grayson was right,* I thought.

OWOOOOAH!

The howl was immediately followed by several others, the same as it had happened in Glindenberg. They overlapped with each other which made it impossible to pinpoint their exact location. *This is another trap.*

Illuminated by the bright moon, all of us tore across the clearing just beyond the abbey towards the crest of the hill. It sloped down through a thicket of trees. Just beyond the trees was the main road that led to our van. Adrenaline raced through my body. Sounds were muffled from the heavy thumping of my heart that echoed in my ears. Vision acute. I breathed heavy and fast, aware of all my surroundings. Focused. Beasts emerged from within the surrounding woods. "Stand your ground!" I yelled.

BOOM! BOOM!

I shot one of the lunging beasts in the head. Blood spray silhouetted against the bright moonlight and its body crumbled before us. Codie, Robert, and I pressed our backs against a large tree within the thicket. Robert had both of his guns drawn. Codie dropped the book between us and drew his second handgun. "How will we know if we're shooting at Grayson?" Codie asked.

"Shoot the red-eyed ones in the head and body, wound any others!"

"To the left!" Robert yelled. A black fiend came crashing through the brush, red eyes angry and violent.

BOOM! BOOM!

The beast yelped but didn't fall. Codie turned and fired three more times at the brute.

BOOM! BOOM! BOOM!

The werewolf tumbled and fell to the ground dead.

"In front of you!" I screamed as another red-eyed werewolf lunged. Codie ducked and rolled. It crashed into the tree we were using to shoot around. I stuck my gun at its head and fired!

BOOM! BOOM!

Its blood covered the tree and sprayed back onto Robert. More howls could be heard around us. "We have to get to the van! We aren't going to last long out here!"

"Right! It's just up ahead!" Codie shouted. He holstered one of his guns and grabbed the book that lay next to the tree. It was coated in blood.

Codie led as I covered our right and Robert covered the left. The red-eyed devils were relentless. Howling was louder and closer. Brush and small branches broke as the beasts closed in on us through the trees. All of us were at a full sprint. Simultaneously two werewolves advanced on us. One leapt at me to head me off as I ran. I slid on the snowy slope and fired into the belly of the beast.

BOOM! BOOM! BOOM!

It lost its traction in front of me and crashed into the underbrush. Blood sprayed and the beast yelped but didn't die. Codie took aim, rushed towards the beast, and fired!

BOOM!

Blood sprayed from its head onto the forest floor. Both Codie and I turned to witness the second beast attack Robert, swiping at his leg. The massive claws dug into the front of his thigh and tore the large muscle open. Robert spun, wailing in pain as he dropped his gun and fell to the ground tumbling further down the forest hillside. The beast steadied itself and stood on his hind legs. Its eyes were as white as the moon. Blood dripped from its claws, Robert's blood.

Robert wriggled in pain desperately trying to hold his leg together. Rushing towards him, I took aim and fired my remaining two rounds at the monster.

BOOM! BOOM!

The werewolf avoided the shots amongst a thicket and continued its advance. The giant beast stood but a few feet from Robert when a shot rang out! *BOOM!*

It yelped as blood sprayed from the beast's right shoulder. *BOOM!*

A second shot rang out and pierced the leg of the beast coating the forest floor with more blood. It was enough, enough to cause the beast to lose its traction and roll further down the hillside.

Codie rushed towards us. Blood was pouring from Robert's leg, in squirts. "Ahhhhh! FUCK! Ahhhh!" he yelled as he clutched his leg.

Even amongst the shadows of the trees, we could tell the muscle was shredded. "Fuck'n A! The muscle is torn apart and it must've hit an artery!" Codie applied direct pressure the best he could, but the blood was still pulsing out in spurts.

"Your belt! Take it off! Tourniquet!" Codie quickly removed his belt and wrapped it around the upper leg of his father. He pulled it as tight as he could and jammed the latch through the leather to form a new hole.

"AHHH!" Robert yelled again. The blood still leaked in several rivulets from the massive wound but was no longer coming out in spurts.

"Grab his gun! We have to get him up! The van is not far!"

Codie grabbed Robert's gun that lay a few meters away. "What about Grayson?" Codie asked.

"We will have to track him if he lives!"

Codie clutched the arm of his father and lifted him up so that he could drape it over his shoulder. I grabbed the book Codie was carrying and took the other side of Robert for stability. We could still hear howls from behind us as we approached the van along the main road. I opened the sliding door dropped the book inside and helped Codie lay Robert on the floor. Codie entered with him to tend to his father as I leapt into the driver's seat. I turned the key to start the van as a beast crashed into the side of my door. The intensity caved in the door forcing me to duck to the right. Glass from my window shattered throwing shards onto my lap and across the van. To avoid the monster's thrashing, I stayed crouched to my right. One of its eyes was dark as if it had been burned from the socket, the other was red.

"PUNCH IT ADA!" Codie yelled from behind my seat. He took aim at the monster and fired.

BOOM!

The sound was deafening and caused all our ears to ring. The bullet passed through the beast's midsection but did little to stop its advance. I reached for the shifter and forced it into drive. With my hand, I pressed on the gas pedal. The van spun along the frozen ground before it gripped the road and surged forward. It was enough to free us from the werewolf's thrashing. I sat up in the seat and pressed the gas pedal as hard as I could, but not before the monster hit the sliding door, denting and damaging it severely. The van gripped the road and sped off. In the rearview mirror, I could see the one red eye of the monster still staring at us. The creature stood on its hind legs and howled, sinister and with a deep malice. Ringing from Codie's shot was heavy in my ears, yet I could still hear the beast's howl echoing from among the trees as we rounded the bend and headed away from the abbey.

Chapter #27

The Wound
Ada
Wednesday, March 7, 2012
8:10 p.m.

"Drive faster!" Codie yelled from the back of the van.

"I can't go any faster, the van is too damaged." I looked in the rearview mirror and saw Codie trying everything he could to get Robert's leg more stabilized. Every bump we hit Robert screamed out in agony. Blood pooled on the floor of the van so much that it had run under my seat and made the vehicle's pedals slippery.

"I can see his femur and he's losing a lot of blood Ada! We have to find a hospital, fast!"

I didn't respond. I knew we needed to get to a hospital, but I had no idea where the nearest one was. Even though I was from Germany, the abbey was in a remote region, further out from the Magdeburg. I needed Marcus's help. Somewhere amidst the mêlée my earbud had fallen out. Keeping control of the van the best I could, I dug into my inside pocket and pulled out my cell phone. There were several missed calls from Marcus. Without a hesitation, I tapped the screen to call him back.

"AAAAAAAAAHHHHHHH!" Robert let out as Codie tried to compress the wound. Startled, I dropped the phone to the floor of the van. It rang twice before I heard Marcus pick up. His voice was muffled from the floor of the van and he was going to be zero help if I didn't get the phone. With a quick thrust, I shoved a free arm to the floor of the van and felt for the phone. All I could feel was thick, sticky blood. The van veered a bit before I could correct it, but that was enough. Enough that Codie fell to one side and released the compression he had placed on Robert. Robert screamed.

"What are you doing Ada? Keep the fuck'n van steady!" Codie yelled.

"I need to get the cell so Marcus can direct me to hospital!" I made several sweeping motions with my hand until, finally, my fingertips hit the edge of the phone. "Got it!"

I quickly placed the call on speaker and secured the phone in the dash. *"Ada…Codie…"*

"Marcus…this is Ada…find us the nearest hospital! Robert is hurt really bad!"

"I'm on it…I'm tracking your phones, so I'll talk you through where to go."

"GRAYSON!" Robert yelled. "That…was Grayson…" his voice trailed off.

Codie reapplied the compression to Robert's leg. I could see Codie in the mirror. His expression was rattled, but there was still a sobering factor that we all seemed to know. "Grayson wasn't himself…we both know that…"

Codie looked up at me in the rearview mirror as Robert slipped into unconsciousness.

CHAPTER 28

The Book
Ada
Friday, March 9, 2012
4:00 p.m.

We were fortunate to have escaped on Wednesday and were able to get Robert to the hospital. He was immediately rushed into surgery. I claimed to be his niece so that I was able to discuss his condition with the physicians. The surgery lasted until the early hours of the morning to save what was left of Robert's leg. The muscle nearly torn completely from the bone and the femur directly above the knee was too badly damaged to save. Amputation just above the knee was the only option. There was simply too much blood loss and tissue damage to save the lower half of his leg. According to the doctor, if we would've arrived any later than we did, Robert may have died.

The van was horrendously damaged on one side, so it was easy for us to claim a car accident to ascribe the damage. Hit and run. Since both Robert and I had injuries, it was the most fitting answer. We were certain that the likelihood of someone checking into the facts behind our story were slim. Yet, we were also more than willing to pay additional fees to the car rental company for any extra damages the vehicle had to keep the real story unknown.

The cuts across my chest required stitches, but nothing serious. When the doctor asked about my old wound, I simply resorted back to the story of being an animal researcher who sometimes has to deal with dangerous species. The storyline was weak, but I knew that there was nothing else that could be proven.

I sat in the hospital room in Magdeburg with Marlie as we kept watch over Robert while he slept. The room was drab. White walls, sterile smelling, a lavatory by the entrance, nothing exemplary. Marlie mostly slept too, which gave me a chance to review the book that Codie had picked up from the abbey. I had taken the liberty of cleaning the blood from the book and in doing so revealed a strange insignia of a poorly etched eye encompassed within a circle on the cover.

"How's he doing?" Marcus asked as he limped into the hospital room with his cane. I could tell that he had little pity for Robert and that he merely asked about his well-being to keep up appearances.

"He will live. He suffered tremendous amount of nerve damage and the doctors explained that he may not have a lot of feeling in the remaining portion of his leg for some time, if ever again. They had to amputate. The amount of nerve damage is going to be a constant source of pain."

Marcus stood at the foot of Robert's bed, staring at him with contempt. He shook his head before sitting in the chair diagonal from the love seat Marlie and I were sitting on. "How are you doing?"

"A few cuts, a few stitches, bruises, but nothing I can't handle. You? Grayson?"

"Me? I'm doing better. As it turns out facing your fears *is* the best therapy one could have for bouts of agoraphobia, PTSD and the like." Marcus did seem better; not quite as weak or dizzy. "Grayson's whereabouts, unknown...the tracking device states that he is somewhere in the middle of the forest just beyond Braunlage in the Lower Saxony region. With whom is also unknown." I was nervous. My face showed it. "We'll go after him when we're better prepared. They will probably never discover the fact he has a tracking device inside of him, but my company will deactivate it in time, so it won't really matter anyways."

Marcus tried to sound reassuring, however there was no way that could happen after what we had experienced. And he was right we were in no state to combat these beasts. "Codie and Zoey?" I asked.

"Codie went back to the hotel to check on Zoey. They both will be back within the hour." Marcus had secured another rental car considering the van was destroyed and we needed to return it immediately to stay congruent with our story. Marcus sighed softly as he was deep in thought. We both stared at Robert while he slept. A few moments past and he glanced down at Marlie as she lay in the fetal position on a love seat with her head resting on my lap. He looked back at me again. "She's all right too, you know?"

"I know. *Danke*…for taking care of her." I closed the book and brushed the hair from her face.

"Have you been able to learn anything?" Marcus nodded towards the book.

"Yes, some. It is an older dialect, but I have been able to translate a little. A lot is still sketchy."

"What did you find out?"

"Well…from what I can tell, it's sort of a history. This book outlines how a priest, Father Heidrich, while condemning Johan Stich, placed a cross upon his forehead and Johan attempted to bite him on the hand. Instead, Johan bit his son-in-law, Manfrit. In a skirmish, the priest was burned by one of the hot irons used to remove Johan's skin. This Lutheran priest was Father Amsel, which was a part of my ancestors' group who later changed his name to Father Heidrich."

"So, the priest *is* the source."

I opened the book again. "No. The later entries were written by someone else that claimed to have killed Father Amsel."

"Then I'm not sure I follow."

"It starts with entries from Father Amsel and clearly stated why he changed his name to Heidrich, to hide. He speaks about how he sought out the daughter of Johan Stich, Lena, and attacked and killed her. She was set with child and her husband, Manfrit, was later blamed since he was bitten on the hand previously by Johan. Her husband was burned to death. It was my ancestors, again, who did this, the burning. Father

Amsel went missing after that. But the entries state that he retreated Southwest to the Black Forest. They tell how he spent his years deep within the forest. There he would change into the werewolf, secret and secluded. We suspected that the skin of Johan had survived, but never knew how. However…" I flipped through the pages to a portion of the book where the entries became different. I pointed to the page. "…look here. This entry is twenty years later, a different handwriting and is different all around."

"How so?" Marcus was inquisitive. I could tell his scientific mind was starting to come out.

"It boldly states…" I pointed to an entry line in the book as I translated for Marcus.

"…He's dead. The beast that killed my mother, blamed my father, and left me to die in the womb of my mother is no more. I sought him out, in the trees, through the darkness and consumed his heart in the hopes that this monstrous fury may be laid to rest. I was mistaken. A devil I still am. Of God's creation, I walk in darkness, though I bear no marks upon my skin as told from the legends of old, though I sought no vengeance towards anything my entire life, though I have only known love. Yet, the devil in me slaughtered my sisters of the cloth upon the full moon of my maturity. The baby that they removed from the belly of my mother, miraculous, God's miracle, but born of darkness and should've been left in the shadows. For now, I live with darkness. I am darkness, damned to live."

I looked at Marcus. "It was thought that the baby was killed, but this entry claims that a group of nuns found the body of Johan Stich's daughter, Lena, and miraculously the baby showed signs of being alive inside and they removed her."

"More than likely the bite to the mother, though dead, transferred to the baby still in the womb. No bite marks, the perfect source to lay dormant until maturity." Marcus leaned back in the hospital chair. A new understanding was apparent. This was a missing piece of a puzzle that had vexed him for some time. "Is there a name or anything?" he asked.

"No, but I'm sure it was a girl. A boy orphan would've been turned over to the priests, given more choices. Yet, an orphaned girl would have been raised by the nuns to become a nun, especially since there was no father to set the girl as a wife of a man. The book goes on to talk about growing up in convent raised by nuns and being groomed to become a nun. That her being alive was God's miracle and that she was destined to do God's work."

"How then was the slaughtering of the nuns not known in history as a werewolf attack?"

"Because of the turmoil throughout Germany between the Lutheran and Catholic faiths. My ancestors burned the convent. The years that followed were laced with war and much of the records were seized or burned by raiders on both sides. It was written off as an attack on Catholicism from Lutheran raiders. Truth of such events were lost or limited only to the Grimoires. Over the years, truth became mere legend. Scarier is what actually survived, it states here…" I pointed to the text again.

> "…I have come to learn that my survival as a child not yet born was of the flesh. Flesh of my mother, though dead, made me stronger than those who have just been bitten by the darkness. It is the moonlight and the flesh of another of our kind draped over the bitten in the beginning that makes us strong, that unites us as a family."

"Are you suggesting that this entry states that if the skin of another werewolf is draped over one who has been bitten, during their first change, will make them into a stronger werewolf, like the ones with red eyes?" Marcus was cautious.

"I wonder if the same thing occurs to a person who already is a werewolf…meaning, has already changed once …or more?"

"I don't know…I hope that we can learn more in the days ahead."

"Are you sure the skin of another beast is the source of the red-eyed werewolves?" Marcus asked.

"Yes, but not just from any werewolf…I'm convinced that it must be the skin from another red-eyed fiend. If it was the skin and flesh that created the source, to keep it going must be the same. When we were in the catacombs there was a space. A space where the moonlight could shine between the buildings into the darkness below. Stone chairs all around, built into the walls. This is what Corbin was guarding. This is what we infiltrated. This is why they all were red-eyed fiends. That is why they attacked the home of Robert. Gerda…" a tear fell, but I wiped it away quick. "This is where the red-eyed werewolves are made."

We stopped talking as one of the nurses entered the room. She completed the vitals check on Robert, checked his bandaged stump of a leg, and nothing more, but it was enough to wake him. We both moved to his bedside. Marlie moaned a bit as I stood but remained asleep. Sweat had formed across Robert's forehead. He winced from the pain as he waited for the nurse to get another dose of pain medicine. He looked at me. "Thank you – for saving me." He winced again. "Thank you – for…for not killing my son." I nodded in acknowledgement. "Grayson?"

"We have an idea as to where he is, but we're not prepared to go after him," I spoke softly.

Tears dripped from his eyes as he clasped his hands together holding them towards the ceiling of the room. "Oh God." Robert turned his attention to Marcus. "Marcus. I – I am heartily sorry for what I did to you." More tears flowed from his eyes. Marcus's face softened slightly as his eyebrows peaked a little in the center. Less contempt. "I too now know why you were helping Mya and I have to ask you to please, find Grayson, help him, and my family. Please. Please oh God help my son."

Marcus rubbed his forehead and briefly glanced at the ceiling. He didn't confirm that he was going to continue helping us. "Where do we go from here Robert? Your manor was torched along with all of your belongings."

"Before we took the ferry. I – I had spoken with Ashland Simmons, my financial partner." Robert cut off as the nurse returned with his pain medicine. She injected it into his IV before making sure that he didn't need anything further. Robert shook his head no and the nurse left. He turned back to Marcus and me. "My insurance policy on the manor will cover the cost of the home…but no new build…I informed him that I wanted to buy an estate in Cambridge."

Marcus held his mouth open in disbelief over what Robert had just stated. "Crikey. You mean to tell me that you are purchasing Mya's estate? How?"

Robert nodded. "Taxes, unpaid." Robert's eyes blinked several times. His pain medicine was a heavy dose which was causing him to fall asleep. "By paying the back owed taxes, we staked a claim to the estate, just after Grayson was bitten – Grayson, Grayson could…"

His sentence failed as his eyes closed and he drifted off to sleep again. "What was he trying to say?"

"Mya's estate has a lower level in which she had constructed a large cage built into the far wall. When we find Grayson, he could easily stay in the cage during the times of the full moon, just as Mya had done in the past to stay secret and without hurting anyone."

"Wouldn't that make us an easy target?"

"I suspect so, but right now, I don't know of a better place than there."

"So, you are going to stay with us? Help us?" I asked. I didn't want to beg him, but we needed his help.

"I told Grayson that once you look into the darkness there's no going back. I can't speak for Zoey, but I must stay. My company already knows that something is completely skewed with the transmitter and I'll either have to explain it in full to them, which isn't going to happen, or I lie, telling them the transmitter is faulty, which will result in them deactivating it. We're going to have to find Grayson *fast*."

"How? I mean if your company deactivates the transmitter…Grayson could be taken anywhere. There will be no chance of us finding him after that."

"I can help…I'll be able to find him," a soft, solemn voice said from the doorway. A wash of nervous energy filled the room and caused my heart to race. Robert and Marlie were fortunate to remain asleep, but fear gripped both Marcus and me. A petite woman wearing a hooded Cloakman jacket stood at the door staring at the floor. As she lifted her head and removed the hood, her bright green eyes were irrefutable.

Neither of us could say anything, until Marcus broke the silence and uttered the name we both knew, "Mya…"

CHAPTER 29

Psychosis
James Lawrence
Monday, April 2, 2012
9:00 a.m.

Acute Stress Disorder brought on by trauma; that's what the doctors said initially. They agreed that when the charges of homicide, two counts, were dropped that my symptoms should start to subside: lack of sufficient evidence. They didn't. Post-Traumatic Stress Disorder was then considered. I was placed into group sessions so that I could talk about my troubled feelings. This just made it worse. My so-called symptoms intensified, the nightmares were more vivid, even when I was awake. Richard's agonizing screams were a constant echo. I could see the red eyes in everything. Reflections, in other people's eyes, all around. The doctors began suspecting me of adult-onset Schizophrenia, paranoid type. They refused to acknowledge any part of my story. Hundreds of stitches because of the slash marks were seemingly dismissed as a result of broken glass. Their lack of analytical prowess was irritating.

They kept me in my group therapy. I was told that it would help with the realization that the things in my head weren't real, a manifestation of chemical imbalances or some other rubbish. Our meeting room was a dull cream; no wild colors or anything to look at, as to not provoke any unwanted outbursts of rage or hostility from the other psychotics. We would sit in a circle and share what was happening inside our heads, then the psychiatrist would attempt to explain away the visions, voices, nightmares or whatever else was plaguing an individual. The doctors also told me that I'm improving with the antipsychotic medication. Risperdal is what I started with to treat the atypical symptoms; to restore chemical balance in my brain. I didn't feel it. No restoration. The medicine gave me the runs after several hours of a mind numbing, drooling haze. *There's no pill for what I saw*, I thought. Despite group therapy, there was no way I was going to continue this line of conversation. *I have to play the game until I'm released.*

I had it in my mind that I was going to start playing the game with this round of group therapy. It would begin with my turn in the circle. I would tell them what they wanted to hear. Yet, as our group session was about to start, one of the psychiatric technicians interrupted. His booming voice echoed in the meeting room. "Excuse me, Doctor Wilkinson, Mr. Lawrence has a visitor."

"We're about to start our group session now and visiting hours aren't until 4:00 p.m." The doc's voice was stern, with a touch of irritation. I watched from my chair as the two continued their short verbal volley.

"I understand Doctor, but I was told to tell you that this will be brief, and that Mr. Lawrence will be able to return to his session immediately following."

Doctor Wilkinson sighed, "You know this goes against treatment regulations and practices." He didn't wait for the technician to respond. Instead, he looked at me. "Mr. Lawrence are you okay with taking your turn when you get back?"

"Yeah doc, that's fine." I didn't want to participate in group anyways, other than to start the process of getting out of here. With the wave of his hand, the technician and I exited the meeting room. We walked down one of the corridors before entering a smaller, more private room.

Inside, were two round tables with a few plastic and metal chairs. The walls were just as dull as the group therapy room. At least the walls had color; brown, nothing special. I sat at one of the round tables. My morning medication was really starting to take effect. Dizziness and the churning in my stomach at times made me nauseous and forced me to close my eyes until it subsided a little. I could feel the bubbling inside and the onset of anxiety. *Just breathe James, just breathe*, I thought as I took deep breathes through my nose and exhaled out through my mouth.

I heard the door to the room open, but I still kept my eyes closed to fend off the nauseating anxiety that seemed to be increasing by the second. Heels tapped on the tiled flooring, which was followed by the slow grinding slide of the metal chair legs. I continued to breathe.

"James." The voice was familiar but was lined with disdain.

I blinked my eyes open. Before me was not a person I had expected to see. Iris sat across from me poised, upright with her fingers interlocked and her elbows resting on the surface of the table. As usual she was formally dressed with her hair pulled back and rolled into a bun.

"Iris. What happened? What are you doing here?" She wore a black patch over her right eye and I could tell from the furrowed brow that she wasn't here to discuss our personal well-beings.

"I'm here for you, James."

My nerves were jumping. I stared at her; mouth agape unsure of what was transpiring. I couldn't tell if the medicine was causing the feeling I had or if Iris was. "What do you want from me?"

She leaned forward a bit more onto the table. "I'm here to ensure that you stay here, permanently."

"I don't understand." My breathing increased alongside my heart rate. "Why? This place is dreadful."

"I told you, James, to get off it. I told you it was a closed case. Instead, your stubbornness led you down pathways you shouldn't have gone. Cambridge, Scotland, and the abandoned club. You cost me my family!" Her words were more venomous than I had ever heard her speak before.

"How? What – I mean…I don't understand."

"Your digging. Your persistence. Your exposure opened the doorway for them to hunt us. *You* are to blame."

I slid my chair back, away from the table. "It was you." My heart raced. "You're the beast!"

"Yes."

"You killed Richard. Bloody hell, you tore his face off in front of me!" My words spilled out unchecked in a whimper. "And Lydia. You killed her too!"

"Richard, yes. The ambitious little twit was happy to double cross you. Spy on you. Let me know everything that you were doing, where you were going, and for what, the promise to him that he would take over your team. But his services were no longer needed. Lydia, on the other hand, is quite valuable and I'm going to take good care of her."

"You lied to me! The case never went cold. You locked the files on Dr. Bishop, didn't you?"

"Yes. With all the footage that came from the club that night, I knew you would track her down eventually, if you stayed on the case. I used Sabastian's credentials, as the tech guy of your team, it made sense. I knew that if you confronted him, it would end poorly. When Sabastian had requested to leave your team, it just made the scenario all the easier. Those files are gone now. And your new Scottish friend, Duncan Sheehy, will also be dealt with soon enough."

"Why? Why Dr. Bishop?"

"She doesn't know it yet, but she's my sister in darkness. Without a choice, lost, alone, hunted, but stronger than the others, smarter. When she did not accept the offer Corbin gave her, I expected her to fall weakly. She didn't, she survived, she continued searching. I knew she would find me sooner or later and those files contained photos of her throughout the years. They revealed her to any who was looking. If she was found, then I would be found too."

"Corbin Paige?" Iris simply nodded. It made no sense, but it made all the sense at the same time. Everything was clear, too clear. Dizzying. "Robert Osborne, the death of his daughter can be laid at her feet! And Richard's at yours."

"Robert told me he learned long ago that sometimes you have to take the challenges people bring to your doorstep head-on. I gave him every opportunity to stop, just like I gave to you. I told him that he would not hear from us again unless he came to us. He did come to us and I had to protect my family," Iris asserted.

"You lied to him too!"

"Oh, that was a *partial* lie. The Osbornes are a meddling bunch; Robert was driven by bloodlust from the incident with Dr. Bishop. He hunted Mya and stumbled upon us. He took the challenge head-on, so did I and I brought it back to his doorstep after he came to mine. He killed some of my family, so I killed some of his. His son Grayson now belongs to me." Her demeanor was controlling, sinister and menacing.

The churning in my stomach was too much. I leaned my head forward between my legs and expelled everything that was inside my stomach onto the floor. I looked back at Iris. "You're a monster! You and Mya both deserve to be hunted!"

"I accept what God has made me." She stood from her chair and straightened her suit coat, adjusted her eye patch. Her face remained contorted with a furrowed brow.

"Why tell me this stuff? You'll just be hunted more!"

"I now have the locations of all the safe houses used by those who will try to hunt me. They failed to acquire their weapons in Germany, and they have nowhere to go to get more." Her head shifted to the right as if to look at me better with her left eye. "More importantly, I want you to be tormented by your own thoughts."

"I'm just going to expose you." Anger mixed with my anxiety.

Iris smirked. She leaned forward placing her hands on the table's surface. Darkness surrounded her. "James, I'm counting on that. But who will listen to your story in here? You already accused Sabastian of occult activity, landed yourself here by claiming you saw a werewolf, and then further confirmed the psychotic diagnosis by accusing Robert and Grayson of being involved in the whole werewolf scheme. I'm afraid that if you continue this storyline by adding these *new* details, they'll never let you out. You'll remain here medicated, drooling on yourself, barely able to function. Yet, you're too smart for your own good. If you play the game right, bide your time, say what they want to hear, you *will* get out. And when you do, we'll be waiting for you, to finish what I started in the club. There's no one to help you now, James."

Iris turned from me and walked to the door of the small room. "NOOOOOO! You're a werewolf," I yelled at the top of my lungs. "Stop her! She's a — were — "

Two of the technicians rushed past Iris into the room. The two men grabbed me by the arms and forced me out of the chair and onto the floor. I struggled against their grips to get free. Several other technicians and nurses rushed into the room to assist in holding me down. I felt a needle prick on my right arm. My breathing began to slow as the sedative raced through my veins. Around me, the room grew hazy. Iris remained at the doorway watching. I don't know if it was the sedative, but with my last look at Iris, her one eye glowed red as the room was consumed in darkness.

THE END OF BOOK #2

Acknowledgements

Thank you to my friends and family for always encouraging me to chase after my dream of writing and for being patient as I worked through this exciting sequel.

Many thanks to the amazing publishing team at Reader2writer Press for helping to make this sequel a reality. Thank you to my awesome editor, Kayla Hardin, for your wonderful insights and enthusiasm, and to my illustrator, Brendon Miller; your style is uniquely suited for this set of books.

This list would not be complete if I did not include the creative writing department at Northern Kentucky University. This journey started there and has set me on a life path of creativity, wonder, and inspiration.

Thank you all.

About the Author

After 16 years of experience (...and counting) teaching Middle School English and Language Arts & Creative Writing in urban districts, two master's degrees, and a massive amount of black coffee, Brian came to realize the dire need for creativity and imagination in a classroom setting. Taught at The Ohio State University in his graduate program to design lessons and curriculum from scratch, yielded very minimal opportunities to indulge his profound love of writing. Ultimately this led him to Northern Kentucky University, where he acquired his second master's degree in English/Creative Writing. Since then, he has produced multiple lesson plans, materials, short stories for adolescents, and several other manuscripts for both adolescents and adults.

Also By

Book #1: "Forgotten Sin", There is more than darkness that lurks in the shadows!

"Dark Steps", A demonic tale of torment, torture, and retribution!

Watch your step...

"Life Like", Some say a picture is worth a 1,000 words but in this story two girls learn they are worth a *lot* more.